# NOBODY WATCHING

# NOBODY WATCHING

*By*

*Maurice Collis*

Copyright © 2011, Maurice Collis

ISBN 978-1-257-96325-6

*For my wife Lidia who encouraged me to start and finish this book*

*To my friends Roger and Kathy Sarkis, Peter and Jenny Alexander and John Grant who after reading "The Truth Unfolds" asked for another*

*Thanks to Diala Issa for the cover and the drawings.*

# Contents

| | | |
|---|---|---|
| Foreword | | xi |
| Prologue | | xv |
| Chapter 1 | August 1962 | 1 |
| Chapter 2 | September 1962 | 13 |
| Chapter 3 | October 1962 | 29 |
| Chapter 4 | November 1962 | 37 |
| Chapter 5 | December 1962 | 49 |
| Chapter 6 | January 1963 | 67 |
| Chapter 7 | February 1963 | 83 |
| Chapter 8 | March 1963 | 97 |
| Chapter 9 | April 1963 | 113 |
| Chapter 10 | May 1963 | 143 |
| Chapter 11 | June 1963 | 179 |
| Chapter 12 | July 1963 | 195 |
| Chapter 13 | August 1963 | 221 |
| Chapter 14 | September 1963 | 251 |

## *Author's Note*

This book is centred around the suburb of Llandaff North, where I grew up, in the 1960's. The geography may not be exact but is as I remembered it as a boy. Regrettably, the Old Oak tree is not there any more although I have left it in for fictional purposes. Povey's field also is not as it was. However, much of Hailey Park remains unchanged. The historical references are broadly accurate. The actions and characters are completely fictionalized.

For a young boy growing up Llandaff North was a wonderful place as are most childhood places viewed through the telescope of time.

I live and work in the Middle East and I am a full time HR Director. I write in spare time when I can. Nobody Watching is the second in the series "The Seven Lives of Gareth Adams". The first in the series is "The Truth Unfolds".

# Nobody Watching
## Foreword – 30 September 2009

*I'd like to keep this precise. You will see that you don't really want to hear anything from me but rather you might wish to hear the voice of the young boy writing in his journal.*

*To set it into context. My name is John Peters and I moved into a house in Hazelhurst Road Llandaff North in April 2009. I live there alone. In moving in I did what most people do when they move into an old house, which is check the house from top to bottom. You never know what "skeletons" you might find or little surprises tucked away at the back of cupboards and behind drawers.*

*I found nothing in the main part of the house and decided to check the loft. The loft itself was clear also. At some stage it had been lined with fresh insulation and it looked surprisingly clean and fresh. Looking at this you would think nothing was there. Indeed, this is what I thought. Anyone laying the insulation would have come across anything unusual and taken it. But in my experience those who hide things in a serious way are never so obvious. If something is to be hidden then generally the hider will take care to ensure that it is indeed well hidden.*

*So having abandoned the possibility of something lurking under the insulation I also abandoned the idea of something taped to the exterior of the beams. This too is very obvious and practiced searchers will find these very easily and to be honest such "treasure" is usually hardly worth the effort. More often than not these items are not meant to be hidden as such but kept out of the way of prying eyes and easily retrieved by the person who has concealed them. I'm sure your imagination may well allow you to guess any manner of items hidden away like this. A quick scan determined that there were no such surface items available.*

*Maybe another time I would have left off the search but this house felt as if it had something. I could not let it go.*

*When these houses were first built the lofts were open all across the terracing. You could go in at the first house up into the loft and come out at the house at the end of the terrace giving the owners quite a surprise I'm sure. Over time the quest for privacy led to these areas being bricked up either side with a double skin to maintain a privacy. It also allowed a storeage area for the occupants who would no longer be concerned about casual pilfering with the wall in place.*

*It was to these walls that I applied some scrutiny. I searched for some time but finally my diligence and patience was rewarded. My find was not at the edge of the brick structure as you may have thought but several bricks in. I found a loose brick in the second row and six bricks from the back of the house on the left hand side. At first of course I thought it was just that: a loose brick. I eased it away from the others, the grating noise sounding large within the loft space. The hider was clever. When you put your hand through the gap and felt around – always a nervous moment of course - there was nothing. Initially, I felt my instincts had misled me but something urged me to check further. I went back downstairs to find a small chisel and a hammer. On returning I lightly tapped away at the brick above the gap loosening the mortar. I did not want my neighbours thinking that I was bursting through to join them. The mortar was old and well worn and crumbled away with each gentle tap. Before long I was able to prise it away. I now had a sufficient gap in which to place my hand and arm. First I explored with my right arm finding nothing but dust and cobwebs and wondering not for the first time how spiders managed to do that in what seemed to be a sealed interior. And where were they going to get the damned flies!! This search revealed nothing.*

*Then I placed my left arm in to explore in the other direction and in but a moment as our Greek friend articulated, "Eureka", I found it. It was closer than I expected. Usually people leave these things at the reach of their grasp. So when I felt it I intuited that either this was the work of a short person or a child. Reach, as you know, is very much related to body size.*

*Ah, that initial touch was good, I must admit. The culmination of thought and persistence. I grasped the package and brought it out into the open air. What did I find? I found this package wrapped in thick plastic with strong cord binding it all around. Could it be money, I thought. I knew from the weight that it was not gold but also there was a chance that it was photographs or some old documents. I took my Swiss Army knife from my pocket and opened a sharp blade and cut through the cord. A paper fluttered to the floor as the plastic wrapping was removed revealing an old exercise book. I did not mind. Some times these things are more interesting than money. I reached to the floor and picked up the paper.*

*I held it up to the fluorescent light on the beam and read it. It said:*
*"Well done! You have found it. Enjoy the journey if you can."*

*Somehow I was startled. The writing was childlike but the sentiment felt more than that — more adult like. However, I felt a connection with the writer immediately. It was as if an equal were speaking to me and not a child. I revised my thinking. Maybe this journal was the work of an adult with immature handwriting.*

*I delayed the satisfaction of knowing until I left the loft closing the aperture and descending to the rooms below. I decided to read the pages of this exercise book in my bedroom and lay on my bed holding the book wanting but not wanting to know more. The book looked and felt old but was not frail or at risk of damage. It had been well protected. I opened the book and began the journey.*

# *Prologue*

See it says Prologue. Big word, huh. I like reading and I saw it at the start of this old adventure book before the book really starts. So I thought let's start with a prologue before we get in to the chapters.

You see I love reading but there was not one book in our house until I reached the age of six and discovered the library. Someone told me that they let you borrow five books at a time. Five! I couldn't believe it. That was five years ago. I must have read a lot of books in that time. I got no idea why my dad doesn't look at too many books at least not when I'm around. He's a clever bloke even though if you saw him you wouldn't think so.

I'm getting ahead of myself. You don't know anything about me yet. Let me tell you some things and if you feel like reading on afterwards go ahead. If you don't, I'm not going to know anyway. But look don't kill me if I get mixed up with tenses and things and spelling. I'll get better when I get older. Anyway that's what Dad says.

My name is Gareth Adams and I live in Llandaff North which is in Cardiff, Glamorgan, South Wales. Our terraced house backs on to Hailey Park and over the years I've spent a lot of time playing on or around it. I've sketched a map below so you can get an idea of my world.

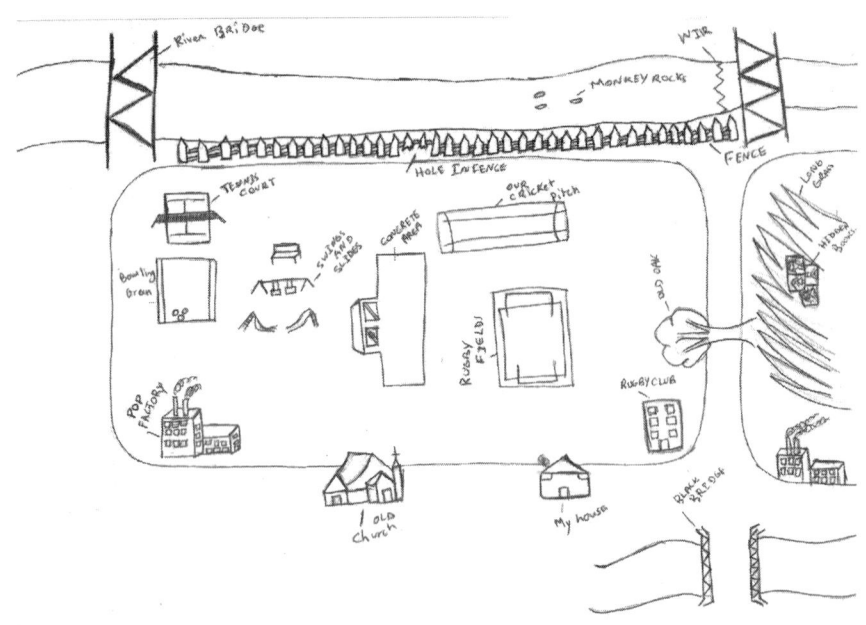

*Include map of Hailey Park and Llandaff North*

I sometimes try to think back about earliest memories. I think I can remember my mother holding me when I was little and I remember Dad moving us from Solihull to Cardiff. I remember standing outside our house eating an apple and smiling at some bigger boys on bikes watching me and suddenly bird muck dropping from the sky to cover my apple and I remember the tears that came from me and the laughter from the boys. I remember my first day at infants school and not liking it so just getting up and walking home with no-one stopping me. I remember feeling sick in infants and scratching everywhere and then to be home in bed with chicken pox. I remember Dad getting me a three wheeler bike and the big boy across the road pushing me round the block many times. I remember seeing a big boy with a yo-yo and swopping my bike for it and dad getting mad and going to find the boy to get it back. Funny thing is as I'm getting older I'm beginning to forget them, especially the picture of Mum.

I have a father and a brother. My brother is called David. We don't have a mother but you might have guessed that from what I said. She was German and my Dad says she was very beautiful. She died after giving birth to David. We're not supposed to know this as

Dad has kept it a secret but my best friend Tom says there's no secrets where we live. Everybody knows everything that's going on.

Tom is in our gang and he is really the leader of the gang even though we say we don't have one. Everyone listens to Tom and so they should. He's a good pal and a friend to everyone. So in the gang is Tom, me, Alun West, Nigel Carter, Dafydd Wilkins, Geoffrey Peters and Phil Thomas. We've always been together and in the same class since infants. We have arguments from time to time and storm off just like any other kids but Alun is the worst of us for that but it always blows over in a couple of days.

So you worked it out that there's seven of us so no cracks about the Secret Seven. We're not that stupid. You know, the seven of us boys were together from infants but when we got to standard 3 last year Tom said we should make it a proper gang with a name and a ceremony to join. So we decided that the ceremony would be by the Old Oak in Hailey Park. To be part of the gang you had to nick you right thumb with Tom's sheath knife and drop seven spots of blood on to an oak leaf on the branch. Tom knows about keeping safe and things like that so he would always clean the knife in soapy water, wipe it in a clean white handkerchief and heat the blade with the lighter he borrowed from his Dad. We all did it on the last day before going back to school after the summer holidays. We all did OK but Alun who went last nearly took the top of his thumb off. Mind you he had plenty of blood to splash on the oak leaf but Tom had to wrap his thumb up with the handkerchief and Alun had to go home and tell his mother he cut it on a piece of glass when he fell over. We got away with that one but if it had been Nigel's mother we'd have been in the shit for sure.

We been meaning to write the rules and punishments ever since but we haven't got round to it yet. Maybe just before we get back to school.

See I'm beginning to write a lot in this book already. It's a thick lined exercise book with blue covers. The covers are hard too, not paper. I've stuck a label on the front which says "Gareth's Writing" and underneath "If found please return to me at Hazelhurst Road, Llandaff North, Cardiff Glamorgan, South Wales, The World, The Universe". Today is 31 July and I've just started to write on the first page. I'm writing this cos somehow I know things are going to change and I feel some funny workings in my stomach. From

September I'll be going back to Hawthorn Road Junior School for the last time and will start working for the 11 plus exam. We'll take the exam in March and they'll tell us the results in May. If I pass I'll probably go to the Grammar School at Canton High in Fairwater. If I fail I'll go to Glantaf Secondary Modern, Whatever happens me and my pals will be split up with some of us going to Canton, some to other grammar schools and some to Glantaf. I've worked with my dad for hours during this summer to make sure I don't have to go to Glantaf.

Some of the boys who were 13 or so and who go to Glantaf used to meet us in the park and tell us they were waiting for us. We stick your head down the toilet on the first day and pull the flush, they used to tell us. This terrified me and so I really don't want to fail that 11 plus. It's going to be fear that will get me to pass.

My Dad works as a plumber. Tom, my friend, says that he didn't do this first of all after the war. He told me that Dad moved us from the Midlands when I was two years old and when David was a baby. In the Midlands Dad had run a few clothing stores and was getting successful but when Mum died he sold the stores and came back home. He took a course in plumbing and worked with another tradesman for a while before going out on his own. He was always busy and always had work but he was never late home. He was always with us by 5.30 so we could have tea together and on Saturday he only worked until 1pm and then he would go straight to the Rugby Club at the end of our Road to drink beer and eat meat pies.

Dad looks after us really well and the house isn't too bad. "Aunty" Nancy, Janet's mother, comes on a Wednesday when Dad's in work and we're at school. She cleans the place up and does the washing. Then she comes on Saturday morning as well to do the same. Sometimes she leaves us Welsh cakes or a rice pudding. Her cooking is great but Dad makes the best tomato soup going and great bacon sandwiches.

Anyway, tomorrow is 1 August and I decided to write about some of the big things that are happening each month from now until I go to Canton or Glantaf. I'll write about my Dad too and my brother David and my friends. Maybe I'll even tell you a bit about Susan who is the best and prettiest girl in our class and who is going to be my girlfriend one day. All I got to do is be able to speak when

I'm with her on my own. Once I can do that I'm sure it'll work but when we're on our own together my face goes really red and this seems to stop me knowing what to say. Does this happen to you? How can I stop it?

I'm going keep this book too. It's 1962 and in thirty eight years it will be the year 2000 and I will be forty-nine. I'm going to take it out and read it then if I still can. I'll be an old man then sitting in a chair and reading the paper. I don't want to think about. It sounds terrible.

So let's see what happens from tomorrow.

# CHAPTER 1
## *August 1962*

In the long summer holidays me and my pals we had many things we could do. We played cricket until we got fed up, walked along the river bank of the Taff to the monkey rocks and raced with small sticks, walked along the Long Woods and sometimes as far as Radyr. Sometimes too we just hid in the long grass in Povey's field next to Hailey park just past the Old Oak. We even played bowls sometimes. The old granddads taught us one quiet afternoon. It looks like an old man's game but it's deadly. The bowling green is at the top of Hailey Park close to the play ground. You can see it all on the map I drew for you.

There was only so much you could do in the summer holidays and towards the end of the long holidays we would get bored but not bored enough to want to go back to school.

During the last week before we went back to school me and the boys were playing cricket in Hailey park up by the playground. It was a good rolled surface. Alun's dad had bought him a good set of stumps for both ends and a great bat. He wasn't much good at batting but he did have the best bat, that's for sure. Mine wasn't too bad but I wished I could have a bat like Alun's.

It was a late august sunny day with no wind in the air. The ground was dry as it hadn't rained for a while. The sky was blue and the sun was getting to make us feel warm. It was a perfect day for cricket. One day I am going to play for Glamorgan as opening bat. I can hit the ball really well on both sides and really love to slog it in the air. So it is easy to catch me out if people are in the right place. It just doesn't seem right to hit it into the ground and let it fizzle through the grass. The ball is meant to be whacked high and as far as you can send it. And when you hit it just right and that ball sails, well it is such a feeling. I knew that once I opened for Glamorgan and got an average of around 78.2 it wouldn't be long before the England selectors picked me. That would be fun, a Welsh boy opening the batting for England.

We had a nice knock around that morning for a while. The first session we play always gives everyone a good chance to bat and bowl. We work out who bats first by seeing who can roll the ball closes to the stumps and the one who is next bowls and then we've got our turns for batting and bowling. In this first round you can only face four overs so that's 24 balls. Doesn't sound a lot but you can get a good few slogs done in that time and it doesn't matter if you get caught out or bowled, you get your full 24.

After everyone has bowled 24 balls and batted for 24 balls then the first one goes back in again and stays in until someone gets him out. This is where the fights can start!!

I was closest to the stumps that day. I really wanted to bat first anyway and was in the mood for hitting the ball. I was angry with my brother for running off with my Hotspur and Eagle comics before I had chance to read them. He'd pay it for later when I got my hands on him.

And that morning I was hitting the ball high and long. Where we set up our pitch is a fair way from the concreted area just before the playground. Sometimes the ball rolls onto the concrete but it's never really a danger to anyone. But during that first session Alun sent a ball down to me that was perfect for driving back over long on. That's to the right of him at about 10 or 11 o' clock and longggg!!. And did it go high and long. It was the best shot I ever made in my life. The swing of the bat met the ball as it was rising and I knew as soon as I heard that sound of ball on bat that it was a good 'un.

I watched it soar but what I hadn't seen was Old Ma Brown, one of our dinner ladies at school, walking across the concrete patch to go through the playground on a shortcut home. From where I was stood the direction of the ball and the top of her head were going to come into collision very soon. We all froze as the ball dropped towards her. She was a small, fat lady who wore her overcoat in winter and summer. You could set a clock by her because she also walked across that concrete path around quarter past eleven after going to the shop to buy groceries. So there she was waddling along with two shopping bags and this ball whizzing towards her nut and I couldn't help thinking of the double helping of mashed potato she always gave me when I gave her a smile. Please don't hit, please don't hit.

She should have felt it touch her hair and then heard the whack on the concrete but she walked on not noticing a thing. I fell to the ground pounding the grass and thanking God that nothing happened. The others piled on me laughing like anything now that we were out of trouble. I decided I don't like being scared but it seems to happen a lot around here.

"Just missed her then, Gary, you lucky little bugger," we all suddenly heard. I didn't look up. I knew who it was. It was Ceri Borthwick. He is the only person I know that calls me Gary and I muttered Gareth under my breath not loud enough for him to hear.

Ceri is two years older than us and he failed the eleven plus and went to Glantaf. He's one of those boys you don't argue with. He doesn't seem to have a lot of friends from Glantaf and if he can find us he likes to hang around with us. He bullies us and pushes us around but he thinks it's just a bit of harmless fun.

We all get up and Ma Brown, who'd sent shivers of panic through all of us as the ball was sailing towards her nut, is quickly forgotten. We've got past that worry and now we've got to deal with Ceri until he gets fed up and walks off.

He stood there, lobbing the ball from one hand to another and trying to put spin on it. If he dropped it as he usually does then it'll take all our effort not to burst out laughing. Ceri thinks he's a good bowler and an even better batsman but he's useless. However, out here on Hailey park on the cricket pitch he is the king and we are his slaves. If we laugh we'll get a thumping, an armlock, a Chinese burn or a headlock.

"OK," Ceri said throwing the ball at Alun, and I mean at Alun. Ceri never throws the ball to you, he throws it at you and with force. He laughed when Alun knocked the ball downwards to avoid a thump in the chest. "It's my turn to bat and Alun's bowling."

Well, you can imagine the picture. I've told you about Ceri and it was just as usual for about half an hour. It was always best to send him easy balls so he could try to hit them as far as possible. He liked to run between the wickets and we cheered him when he did hoping he would wear himself out fast. After a while he got fed up with Alun's bowling and put Geoff on. Geoff is a spinner and can be a bit sneaky but like the rest of us he always pitches them up nicely so that Ceri can get a good swing at it. Afterwards he said he didn't do it on purpose because normally he has a go at off spin. He did bowl a couple of off spinners but then he went for a leg break. He said he was thinking about Richie Benaud at the time. I can understand it. He's an Aussie Richie Benaud but a great bowler. So anyway these leg breaks are hard to do but Geoff had been practising and he flipped one down which Ceri didn't see coming. Well look with Ceri you're lucky if he sees anything coming and of course this one slipped inside the bat and caught him high on the inside of the thigh. It might have caught part of his knob too because when he fell down he was giving it a good rubbing.

I have to tell you something, I don't really like Geoff. I don't think he's really one of us. He came from Newport and joined us in Standard 1. I don't like his dad too much either. He sells second hand cars or something like that. Geoff puts brylcreem in his hair and he swings his arms as he's walking in a swanky way. He smiles a lot and thinks he's a big hit with the girls in our class. His skin tans easy in the sunshine and he laughs at the way my skins burns red. When we get back to school he will captain Glyndwr (the red team) and I will captain Caradog (the blue team). I'm going to make sure we beat him by the time we finish even though he can sprint just a little faster than me. I'm going to work on it.

Tom knows I don't like Geoff and he laughed about it. He said it's because I think he's got his eye on Susan. He told me I'm stupid because Geoff likes Janet and she likes him too. I was surprised when he said that and felt a little sad that Janet liked him. But I liked it when Tom said Geoff wasn't after Susan.

Anyway, I just wanted you to know that I don't like him. But seeing Ceri on the floor rubbing his willy and Geoff looking sick because he knew what was coming I couldn't resist a smile. It would be nice to see Ceri give Geoff a good whack. I felt guilty thinking that but I couldn't help it. Geoff knew what was coming too and as Ceri scrambled to his feet he looked at Geoff and growled, "Wait till I get my hands on you, you little bugger."

Well, Geoff wasn't stupid. He turned and ran and with his speed he could outpace Ceri easily. Even Ceri knew that. He took two steps and stopped and let Geoff race away. But Ceri had some pain to hand over to someone. "What are you grinning at Adams", and before I could copy Geoff and leg it he had me in a headlock. This was the worst, a Chinese burn would have been better. In close to Ceri's armpits was no joke. There was no point in trying to fight it. The only way to satisfy him was to shout, "Gerroff! Lemme go!" a few times and to whimper a bit. The thing we know with Ceri is that he is a soft bully. If he feels he's hurting you too much he backs off.

He threw me down when I whimpered. "You shouldn't have grinned, you pillock. It was Geoff I wanted to get. Tell him I won't forget."

He put his hands in his pocket and walked off and there was no knowing when he would turn up again. That was Ceri for you. Phil pulled me to my feet and brushed me down. "You can stop the bawling now, Gareth" he punched me softly in the belly, "Ceri's too far away now."

"Anyone see Geoff hiding anywhere?" I asked wanting to give him a thump myself.

"You know the rules, Gareth", Tom said picking up the ball and going to the bowler end. "He'll have run past the tennis courts and gone through the hole in the fence by the bridge and cut back down the river path. He'll be heading for home. Come on in Phil, you're in to bat."

We all got fed up just after 1 o'clock and went off home arranging to meet up later that afternoon by the Old Oak Tree. My brother was in the house sat in one of the big chairs by the fireplace. He had a plate of fish paste sandwiches in his lap and was muching on one of them. He'd also got my envelope of Marilyn Monroe pictures which I kept in our bedroom wardrobe so Aunt Nancy won't see them. I liked that one where she was stood holding her dress down when the wind from a train was blowing it upwards. All my pals like to look at pictures of her.

"I told you to keep away from those," I told him and went for him. I was planning to get revenge for him running off with my comics and to give him a headlock just like the one Ceri had given me. "Lemmee alone or I won't tell you," he shouted out before I could grab the little so and so.

I stopped. "Tell me what," I asked. My brother was only a kid but he seemed to get news and know things very quickly.

"She's dead," he said pointing at the pictures of Marilyn. Now this news wasn't as bad as him telling me he'd seen Geoff kissing Susan but it came a close second. I felt butterflies in my stomach.

"You're lying, "I gave him a push to let him know I didn't believe it.

"It's true," I heard some men talking about it outside the Post Office. I could see he was telling the truth and later that night when Dad came home he told us too. She looked so nice. To be honest I'd always hoped that she would come from America to visit Cardiff and see my Dad in Queen Street. He wasn't bad looking my Dad and maybe she'd see him from the motor parade and their eyes would meet and that would be it. It would be great to have Marilyn Monroe as a mother. I used to think about it. It would really annoy Geoff and his swanky Dad. Anyway, no point in dreaming about that one now but I think Dad was unhappy about it too. I'm sure he had ideas about it himself even though he kept saying there was no woman who could be as wonderful as Greta. That was our mother's name. She was German, did I tell you. Anyway he said even if he did marry Marilyn Monroe it would only make Elizabeth Taylor jealous.

We didn't play cricket for a few days after Marilyn Monroe died. Mostly me and the boys went for walks along the river bank or through the long woods. We all brought with us our pictures of Marilyn Monroe cut from newspapers and magazines. It didn't seem right to play cricket.

Nigel said we should make an agreement never to play cricket again in memory of Marilyn. Well, Nigel wasn't that good at cricket so this was an easy one for him. I could see the boys didn't like this one too much either looking around at each other to see who would say something. Tom did the trick though. He said we shouldn't give up cricket as Marilyn wouldn't want that but we should always start with a minute's silence in her memory before the game. Well, that brought the cheers on from the boys. Nigel gave in too when he got shouted down. So we wrote it up on a piece of paper and we all signed it. Alun wanted us to sign it in blood but I went back to the house and got a red biro which is just as good as blood when you come to think of it.

This is what we wrote:

"The boys of Llandaff North who go to Hawthorn Road Junior School do hereby swear that before every cricket game there will be a minute's silence in honour of Marilyn Monroe. The boys who sign this below will do this for the rest of their lives, so help me God. And if they don't may they suffer plague and pestilence and locusts on their house."

Nigel wanted this last bit. He remembers a lot more of the Bible than the rest of us do. Most of us are choirboys at All Saints but it's easy not to listen when Father Tebbit is speaking.

So we signed the paper and Nigel agreed to look after it and bring it before every game to read. We all placed our hands on the paper and swore never to forget the beautiful Marilyn.

We set up for cricket a couple of days later. We waited for Nigel to take out the paper and read it but he didn't have it. He'd left it in the pocket of his shorts and his mother had washed them. Nigel goes really red when he's embarrassed and he was then. Tom said it didn't matter. We should have the minute's silence and we did. It felt good too and it felt good to getting back to cricket.

Most of the time our territory in Llandaff North is safe. Most kids from other parts of Cardiff keep to their own area but you're always on the lookout for strangers just in case. Of course they come through sometimes and mostly nothing happens. Sometimes they'll talk with you to get directions or to see if you know kids that they do. But now and again you get tough, older boys coming through who just want to pick on smaller kids.

Tom was batting while Geoff was bowling and Phil was behind the wicket. I was at slip and Alun, Nigel and Dafydd were in the outfield because Tom could hit the ball well. So it was only me and Phil who saw them coming. There were three of them and I didn't recognize them.

"Phil, give the signal," I called to him without moving my head and trying not to move my lips. Phil had seen them too. He raised his gloved hands above his head and tapped them twice at the finger tips then brought them down in a wide circle and squatted to wait for Geoff to bowl.

The signal was enough to make the boys know someone might be coming. I watched the three as they got closer. They were not looking at us and were noisy. They were going to pass by very close to Dafydd and about twenty five yards from the wicket. Geoff was starting his run up to bowl and so Dafydd moved closer in to the wicket. He wanted to put distance between himself and the bigger boys and I didn't blame him.

Geoff made his delivery and Tom made a great hit. I don't mean that he hit it for four. He played it about 10 yards to the side of Dafydd so that Dafydd needed to run away from the boys to pick it up.

The three boys stopped walking and stood to watch us play for a minute or so. The biggest of the three called out to us and they all walked towards Dafydd, He moved closer to the wicket towards me, Nigel and Tom.

"Hey, boys we're looking for Mervyn Pratt," he said. We have two heroes in Llandaff North. One was Aubrey Williams who was just great at baseball and the other was Mervyn. Mervyn Pratt was the most popular man in Llandaff North. He was great at Rugby and baseball and all the girls liked him. He was about eighteen, I think, and we only ever saw him in the early evenings sometimes or at the weekends. Sometimes he was with a group of friends walking in Hailey Park and other times he was walking alone with his huge Alsatian dog, Odin. Although this dog was huge it was gentle as a kitten and often little kids rode on the dog's back. It crossed my mind that the dog was like Mervyn. He always spoke to us, asked questions about us and laughed with us. He was our kind hero.

"You won't find him till later," I said to them. I swallowed a bit. They made me feel nervous. "He helps his Dad in the daytime but he'll be out in the evening."

The boy didn't reply but looked around at us. "OK, well we'll play you at cricket – you boys against us."

"You're much bigger than us," I said to him. "It's not a fair game."

"Hey, kid" he said poking me in the chest and pushing me backwards. "There's twice as many on your side so it evens it out. Anyway, we're batting and you are bowling. If you get us out you guys are in and we'll field. Fair enough."

He just wanted an excuse for a fight, this kid and we were smaller and easier to deal with. We had no choice but to go along with things until they got fed up and moved on. "Sure, sounds like a good idea," Tom replied to him bringing the bat forward. "We'll have fun. Geoff, throw the ball over and we'll all get out to field."

Tom was the strongest and toughest of us in our gang. None of us would try to fight him and we never had reason to anyway. He'd get funny like we all did from time to time and get angry but he was OK. We all knew he was telling us now to go along with this so we did. The big kid went into bat and one of his pals took the bowling. The other kid sat behind the wicket chewing on a piece of long grass. This kid was a slogger, just trying to hit the ball as high and as far as he could. We spread out along the edge off his range with Phil behind the wicket and Geoff at mid on.

For ten minutes or so he had a few slogs and ran between the wickets. The kid behind the wicket cheered sarcastically when the big one hit the ball. Well, a mistake had to come and it did. He mishit one ball and it flew up but dropped short of Geoff. He scooped it up fast. The kid ran forward out of the crease but stopped to see where the ball had gone. Phil ran forward to the stumps to collect the fast thrown ball from Geoff and whipped the bails off.

"Owzee" Geoff shrieked, "Owzee. We gotcha. Our turn. You're out." Geoff was jumping up and down with glee at getting this kid out.

Of course, this was not part of the deal. This kid wanted us to stand around for a long while just returning the ball to the bowler. Younger kids getting him out was not the way he wanted it.

He turned to Phil first. "I'll deal with you in a minute, you black bastard." The big kid growled. I was shocked. I'd never heard anyone speak to Phil this way before. In our gang it's true our skin was white and his black but we never thought about it. Phil was Phil, one of our friends and part of the gang. Phil was shocked and I could see his eyes bulge not believing what he heard. Tears sprang to his eyes.

"It's you I want, "the big kid shouted throwing the bat down and running for Geoff. This time Geoff was too slow and the kid pushed him to the floor and fell on him. He pinned his arms down with one hand and started to smack Geoffrey across the face softly at first and then getting harder. All of us ran forward to help Geoff but the other kids had come either side of Geoff to push us away and we couldn't help. Geoff started to cry.

"Let him go," It was a voice I never thought I'd be pleased to hear. "If anyone's going to whack this little bugger it's going to be me. He's got a thumping coming to him from me."

The big kid got to his feet to look at Ceri and to size him up. In his face you could see that he realized that Ceri was older than us but not as old or as big as him. The big kid told Geoff not to move.

"Who's telling me to leave him alone," the big kid sneered looking around at his two mates and smiling. He was confident that Ceri would back off

Ceri walked towards him and folded his arms in front of the big kid. "I am. They are my friends." he said and smiled in the big kid's face. To be honest I didn't think Ceri stood a chance against three of them but guessed he was counting on us to pitch in.

The big kid laughed and poked Ceri in the chest with a finger, "Yeah, you and whose army".

The next second the big kid was on the floor with blood spurting from his nose. He cried out "get him" to his two pals but he stayed down himself. Ceri walked towards the two other boys clenching his fist. "Which one of you wants the broken nose first," he hissed through his teeth. They turned and ran away.

The big kid was getting to his feet. "Just you and me then," Ceri said getting into a boxing position. "You ready for another scrap. I'm a bit tougher than these little kids but closer to your size."

The big kid was wiping the blood from his nose with his sleeve. When he got to his feet he squared up to Ceri but then changed his mind and ran off following his friends. We cheered and laughed to see them running off. We knew that Ceri was tough and he bullied us a little but right at that moment he was the best person in the world. We were dancing around him and slapping his back, crazy with relief that those kids had gone.

I think Ceri was enjoying the moment. He looked at Geoffrey whose eyes were still a bit red and he was shaky for sure. "You ready for your turn, Geoff. I'm still getting pains in the todger and rubbing a lot of cream it in every night, you so and so."

Geoff's face went from relief to shock. Ceri laughed, "I think you've 'ad enough for one day. I'll save you for another time." He clipped Geoff across the top of his head to show he was pulling his leg.

"Come on then lads. What you waiting for. Tom, give me the bat and Alun you're bowling. I don't trust Geoff today."

Well, we made sure Ceri had the time of his life and never in the days that followed did we feel our hearts sink when Ceri arrived on the scene. Funny, how what you think about a person can change so quickly.

Later that night I spoke to my Dad after David, my brother, was asleep. I didn't tell him the whole story but I told him that these strange boys had called Phil "black". I said I knew that Phil was black but didn't see why they said it. They didn't call Geoff "shorty" or me "lanky".

I could see from my Dad's face that he was upset. He held my shoulder. "Son, this is a difficult one for me to explain. Most people in this country look beyond what they see with their eyes and look at what someone is like. There are some who cannot do this and just see that they are white and others are black and for some reason this difference scares them. Thank God that here where we live in Landaff North most people treat people for who they are and not what they look like."

He asked if I understood and I told him I thought I did. But I knew I would be thinking about it for a long time.

See I told you my dad was clever even though he doesn't read too many books. He thinks a lot though my dad. Yeah, he thinks a lot.

\* \* \* \* \* \* \*

Tom says that the tradition of a picnic in Hailey Park on the last Saturday afternoon in August used to happen when his mum was a little girl too. This year it was busy and a lot of families came about 2 o' clock or so. Always the mums and the kids first. The Dads usually have a couple at the Rugby Club before coming over to be with us. Because Dad was at the rugby club me and David we sat with Tom's family. Last year we sat with Aunt Nancy. Aunty Margaret and Aunty Nancy both make good sandwiches and stuff so me and David we don't mind. Although I like being with Tom and his family most of all.

While we were waiting for our Dads we were trying to play Jacks on top of a folded over newspaper. It was a laugh. It's great fun and we were eating a lot and drinking a lot of Tizer while playing. There's always one Dad who's going to come over obviously having too many to drink. This year it was Geoffrey's Dad. My Dad was walking alongside him and pretending to have his arm around him like they were big mates but really he was helping him so that he wouldn't stumble. He took Geoff's dad to his family and he sat down with a thump on the grass, lay back and fell asleep. Geoff's mum stood up and spoke to Dad, thanking him I think. She squeezed his arm and smiled with thanks. I looked at Geoffrey. His face was bright red as he watched his dad beginning to snore. I felt a bit sad for Geoff.

Dad came over and I could smell the beer on his breath as he knelt down to check on me and David. He then sat next to Uncle Charles. He was jolly like happens when the grown ups drink beer.

Later we played cricket. Dads against sons. This was so good although Dad will never play for England. Geoff's dad was still sleeping so he didn't join in.

And as I talked about cricket let me tell you it's been a great summer for England. See I don't mind supporting England at cricket because England also includes Welsh players – when they choose to pick them that is!!

This summer we slaughtered Pakistan with four wins and a draw. Add when I say slaughtered, I mean it – two wins by an innings and two by 10 wickets and nine wickets. You ever seen John Edrich, Ted Dexter, Colin Cowdrey and Ken Barrington bat. They are great! My favourite is John Edrich.

At bowling you've got Freddie Trueman and Brian Statham as well as Brian Close and Fred Titmus. I love to watch Freddie Trueman but I'd like to bowl more like Richi Benaud. To be honest my favourite is Richie Benaud and I'd like to bowl like him, even though he's an Aussie. I just think there's something more tricky about slower bowling.

England are going to Australia for the winter. I'm going to listen under the bedclothes with the radio on and hope Dad doesn't catch me.

*JP's Note: Kids outside playing on their own without any adult supervision. Imagine that, now. And yes we share a common lament in the untimely passing of Marilyn Monroe.*

*I read about the England batsmen and bowlers in the 60's. Was it more fun then, I wonder?*

# Chapter 2
## *September 1962*

Back to school in a few days so Me and Tom and Nigel we decided to watch the last cricket fixture between Radyr and Taffs Well. Tom's Dad is a spin bowler for the 1st team and he's always encouraging us to watch and wants us to join the club as youth members. They play on a Saturday from 1 o'clock in the afternoon so we start our walk through Hailey Park about 12. Well, there's lots to see and do on the way. Straight after Hailey Park you get to the Old Black Bridge. You can't resist scrambling up the side of the bank if you hear a slow goods train coming. It's great to put small pebbles or a penny on the line when a train goes over. The pebble is dust when you go back to look and the penny gets squashed paper thin. The only thing is you got to be a bit careful that the driver and guard don't see your face. So you have to put the stuff down quick and the scramble back down the bank and lay flat till it's gone by. The buggers are always on the look out for kids like us. We're not that stupid to get in the way of a moving train but you try telling that to an angry driver or guard. The worst thing is if they see you they call out your name – oh yeah, they know us all – and say they'll be around in the night to see your father. You'd think they'd forget about it but they don't. In the evening he'll turn up at the house and talk to your Dad. Crazy, aren't they. On this last day before school we were lucky we got a slow goods train and no-one saw us.

As we scrabbled back down the bank afterwards towards the pavement Tom caught hold of the bridge. There's a ledge to the black bridge that you can easily put your foot on. It runs all the way across to the other side of the road. Before I could stop him Tom was on to the ledge and moved quickly sidestepping face in to the bridge all the way across to the other side. I couldn't move I was so scared he was going fall.

Do you want to do it, he called out to me and Nigel. I thought about it and put my foot on the edge. I really wanted to do this and took four steps until I felt myself going away from the bank. I took a look down and held the bridge tight. I'm going tell you I started shaking. I kept thinking what would happen If I fell, so I eased myself slowly back to the edge again. I'm angry with myself for this. I've seen my brother David scamper across this edge a dozen times without any fear. But then I'm sure he must have been a monkey at one time.

Nigel just slid to the pavement not wanting to try. Fair enough to Tom he never said a word. Other kids would be calling out "chicken" for weeks. I think I like to stay safe and not be in danger. I wonder sometimes if I'm a coward and might not have any guts. My Dad told me once that you only know if you have guts when danger comes. Is that true? It sounds true doesn't it. I only hope I do the right thing when real danger comes. Have you had this happen to you? What did you do?

So anyway after that bit of fun we walk along the old canal bank and past the Melin Griffiths work and Forest Farm and then get close to Radyr weir which is also a great bit of fun. You can skip stones along the surface right into the waterfall and see how many skips you can get. Dafydd seems to be the best at this. He has the knack. There's no knowing what you're going to find under the small stones there near the water too and sometimes elvers (hey big word, that's baby eels if you don't know) are in their thousands trying to slip their way up the side of the weir. Once I saw this big kid walk across the edge of the weir to the other side. We all know the water's not that deep up there but Tom reckons if you fall that you'll go under the waterfall and it'd be hard to get out. Just gives you the shudders, doesn't it. But I wish I had the guts to give it a go. Just like one day I'd like to get across that Black Bridge.

Up from the weir there's a foot bridge across to Radyr. You know when you pass over this you feel you are leaving safe territory and going into foreign land. You can see it on the map I did for you but you notice that Radyr is outside our boundary. That means danger but with Tom's Dad around and other Llandaff North blokes we're OK.

We didn't watch much of the game as we spent too much time playing in the nets at the side but Radyr Cricket Club has got a nice feeling about it. As it's the last game of the season there's a few people about and you can hear the sound of applause when someone gets a wicket or hits a boundary. There's the sound of tin too as the bloke who's changing the score moves the tin numbers for everyone to see.

The best bit is tea time. The wives of the cricketers make loads of sandwiches in the pavilion tea room. My favourites are these Shippams paste and the egg sandwiches mixed with some creamy tasty stuff. Course we have to wait till the cricketers have had their scoff but there's always loads left over when they get back on the pitch and this day we were lucky there were loads and a few glasses with a couple of inches of beer. Don't really understand why the blokes like it but the funny thing is you've always got to try it if it's hanging around.

Radyr won that day so Tom's Dad was really happy and stayed with his mates for a few beers in the pavilion after the game. Me, Tom and Nigel made our way back across the foot bridge for home. It was starting to get dusky in the sky. So soon our summer is over and school coming back to us. I felt a stab of pain or fear in my guts as I thought about it. Or was it those creamy egg sandwiches cos a few seconds later I let off a good one which had Tom and Nigel thumping me all across the bridge. We picked up a bit of speed to get home. The dark was coming fast. We'd seen a tramp in the woods during the summer and if he was living there we didn't want to run into him. We started to jog as the sun was going our eyes looking all around for danger, especially that tramp. It's funny how ordinary things in daylight give off shadows in the dark that scare you.

Finally, we reached the edge of Hailey Park and the street lights showed and we slowed. We were safe now. Almost home. Me, Tom and Nigel walked along Hazelhurst Road to Hawthorn Road. Here they both left me to walk up Hawthorn Road and for home. We said goodbyes and I watched them walk off. Tomorrow we would be back to school. I watched them walking slowly away thinking would we be walking together next year or would it all be over. I thought too would I have the guts to talk with Susan and ask her to be my girlfriend. I sighed as I lifted the door knocker to let Dad and David know I'd come home. Life is getting too tough.

\* \* \* \* \* \*

Where we live is right in the middle of Hazelhurst Road in Llandaff North. From our front door we can see down Hawthorn Road West and from our door it's about two hundred yards to the school.

I think the school must be very old. Loads of the Mums and Dads went to it when they were kids. Old Pop Rees who teaches in Standard 3 will sometimes say to one of the kids that they are so like their Mum or Dad. Hawthorn Road Junior School is great but it doesn't have any grass like we used to have at the infants. Let me draw you a picture of how it looks.

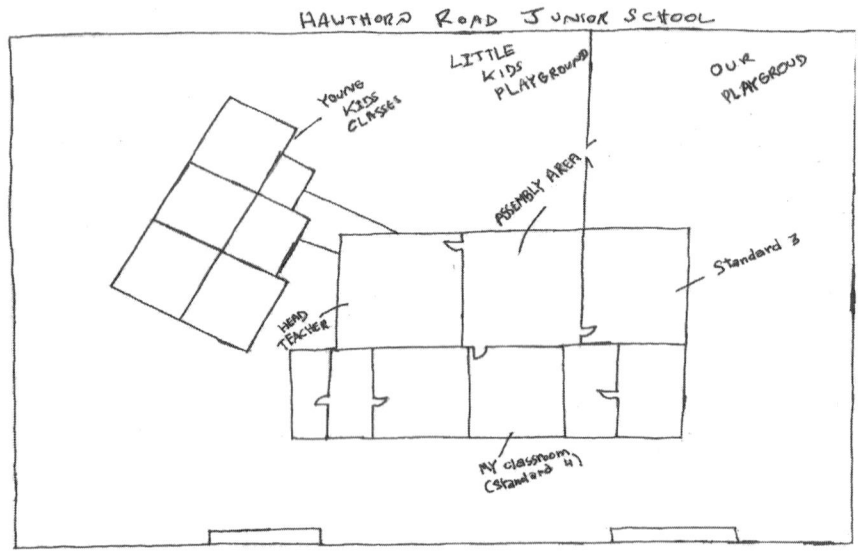

*Map of Hawthorn Road Junior School*

So we have two separate playgrounds – one for Standards 1 and 2 and one for Standards 3 and 4. This is a good idea from the teachers. See they do have good ideas. It can get really rough in our playground with football and running. Sometimes even the girls choose to go to the little kids playground but the boys are not allowed.

Well, September is well under way and we've been back at School for a couple of weeks now. The summer holidays and all we did are forgotten. I was nervous going back to school. It would be our last year at this school before going to a Grarmmar School or to the dreaded Glantaf. In late February we'll take the 11 plus and Dad has already stocked up with more practice books in English and Arithmetic now that the ones we worked on in the summer are full. David, my brother, finds it funny. He hates books and hates school but I've never seen any other boy work so hard in putting an Airfix Lancaster bomber together. He's got them over his bed where Dad has attached threads to them to hang them from the ceiling. It looks good, but give me a book any day of the week.

Let me tell you a bit about my brother, David. He's about 18 months younger than me. Mothers adore him. He looks like a little angel, or so I hear them say and he knows how to use it. He's not that good at school and he does not like books. Put him with a box of soldiers or a set of meccano and he's very happy.

He's not too bad as a brother but I don't like him hanging around with me and my pals when I'm out. I'll do anything to stop that happening. Our house backs on to Hailey Park as you can see from the map I did for you. I have the key to the back door but like all families here the key to the front door is on a piece of string which hangs from the inside of the letter box. Just put your hand inside the letter box, take the key and open the door. You must think we're mad right. Anyone can walk in, yeah? It's true, they could. But nobody does and nobody would. Dad says it's mostly because there's nothing to nick but also there's always people walking around and in the street and no stranger could get into a house anywhere.

You couldn't do the key on a string on the back door though. Why? Because there's no letter box, of course. So I had the key. If I wanted to lose my brother in the holidays I just picked my time to dart out of the house through the back door, lock it and be off. By the time he'd got through the front door and ran to the lane and on to Hailey Park he wouldn't know where I'd gone. Sounds bad doesn't it. But if you are reading this and you are an older brother or sister of my age and you have a younger that wants to tag along, I know you'll understand.

But if we are at home together we play a lot and chat a lot. We have a good laugh and we play a lot of jokes on each other. He hates it if I crack my knuckles. I don't know why but the knuckles on my little fingers love to be cracked. When my brother hears this he goes stiff with rage. I feel he's going to jump on me. Once on a Saturday lunchtime just after I'd cracked them Dad placed tomato soup for us on the table. I leaned over mine to smell it. It was beautiful and the little sod pushed my face in it. He got in big trouble with Dad for that one.

He also loves subbuteo and I like it too. Do you know this football game? It's got little football figures on circular bases and you flick the base with your finger to hit the ball. I'm pretty good at keeping hold of the ball with these flicks and passing but my brother is ace at shooting. So of course I try not to let him get into a good shooting position and I win most of the time. We played this game once where he was leading 1-0 with five minutes to go. In the last five minutes I scored 9 goals.

When you're playing he doesn't like it if you grin or smile when you score. You have to look serious. But I ask you, could you look serious when you just scored 9 goals in five minutes. I wasn't just smiling I was rolling on the floor laughing.

He went really nuts. He smashed my figures with his fist and this made me laugh even more. I knew it wouldn't be long before he came after so I jumped up grabbed my book and raced to the toilet, locking the door behind me. He was banging and kicking on it for half an hour before he got fed up. It didn't bother me. I'd picked up "Black Bartlemy's Treasure". This is a book written by Jeffery Farnol years ago. It's got a lot of "he quoth" and old language like this but it's a great story. Once I was in this book it would take a nuclear bomb to make me hear anything.

It's these crazy moments from my brother and his not liking books that gets him into trouble at school. He's getting better at the junior school but in the infants he was always in trouble. The headmistress used to wait at the entrance to catch sight of me so I could take a letter home to Dad about his behavior. I got fed up with it. If I saw her at the entrance I ducked down amongst the other kids and got out without her seeing me. It only delayed it though because she used to give me the letter in the classroom next day.

But like I said he's not so bad in the junior school. You know, I think younger brothers must always want to beat their older brothers at anything. He can't beat me at chess but he's getting good. With board games like monopoly and cluedo it's a lot of luck but all the time he wants to beat me. And it's anything. Who can throw a ball the furthest, who can skim a stone the most times across the river, who can kill the most flies with an elastic band. You know there was this one time last September when Dad took us to Southerndown or was it Ogmore on a Sunday. Anyway the waves were really big and crashing on the shore. It was a bit cold too. So we made up this game which is like chicken. When the tides goes out you walk to the place where the wave crashed last time and then when it comes in again run away at the last second to escape a soaking. Dad was watching us and enjoying the game too but then said he'd walk up and get some ice cream for us. He pointed to the ice cream van and told us to come up to it in five minutes. Well David is getting a beating in this game he chickens out too early every time and I'm winning by a mile.

Then I saw this really big wave coming and I turned and ran calling my brother to move fast but he was so happy that I ran first that he moved too late and the wave went right over him. I ran back and could see him being pulled in by the sea. I was really scared and ran in to try to get him. This grown up pushed me back and waded in to pull David out. I was so relieved when he got him. David was crying and shivering and I held him tight. We were both a bit cold and I'd read somewhere that if you hug each other you get warmer. He didn't like that and pushed me away, telling me to get off. Well, he's not so bad I thought and hugged him again, relieved he was safe.

The grown up man told us off for being stupid messing about when the waves were so high. So we said sorry and ran off towards the ice cream van. We looked a sight and everyone was staring at us. We were both soaked through and our hair was dripping wet. I told David not to tell Dad what happened. Just to say we got soaked by the spray from the waves.

Dad handed us a "99" each and stood back to look at us. He said he hoped we'd learned our lesson and told us to walk to the car with him to get some towels. He rarely got mad with us you know. He looked more ....disappointed.....yeah, disappointed if we did something wrong.

My brother! He's a pain but he's my brother. That's enough isn't it.

If Dad is out somewhere in the evening, David, he likes us to watch TV together. The house can be a bit scary at nighttime if Dad is out so David sets up the two big easy chairs and puts a blanket over the top of it. He likes us to get inside to pretend we're in a tent or a caravan. We like a lot of programmes but David gets scared if we are watching Outer Limits on our own if Dad is out. Sometimes, it does make you feel scared to walk upstairs to bed afterwards and it's worse if Dad forgot to top up the meter with shillings. If he's a bit late and the light goes off it's pitch black. David gets really scared and I don't like it too much either. When we look out of the lounge down the hall to the front door there's a window above the door. When the lights go out a shadow comes on the glass and I swear to you it looks like a goblin's head. Now I know goblins are only in books but David is not sure and when I see the shape I'm not so sure either. I know they are not real but if you looked at this shadow you'd think there was a goblin on the roof across the road from us looking down through the window. In the dark everything which looks ordinary in the light seems to scare you. I know when the light on is on that ghosts and goblins are in books but when it's dark and things look different you start to think that maybe they do. Have you ever been in the house when it's so dark that you can't see properly and when you stare into the dark you can see different shades of dark so some look like white spots. When you look harder you can start to see a shape in the dark and it's never a nice shape. Never.

So even though me and David we might want to go to bed we hide in the lounge until Dad gets back and brings the light on again. When he comes we love it but we also shout at him for leaving us in the dark. He doesn't seem to think it's a big problem for a little while and always tells us we have a torch and the change is upstairs on the bedside table. Yeah, but going upstairs with a torch in the dark is not easy. You just don't know what's up there. I'm going to tell him to leave a couple of shillings on the mantle piece so we can get the light back next time. Better still, I'll put some there myself!!

Me and David we share the same bedroom and a lot of nights we talk to each other before sleeping. Dad shouts up the stairs sometimes to tell us to sleep so we try to keep it to a whisper. In the dark I can see his shape lying in his bed across from mine. He doesn't like the dark too much my brother but Dad says that only babies have the landing light on at night and that we are not babies. When we first came to this house a couple of years ago there was no inside bathroom. It had to be put in and for a while we used a toilet outside the house. David would only use this in the day time but if he was desperate in the nighttime he pleaded for me to go with him and stand guard. It was at these times he could be really nice to me. He took a candle inside and I'd be waiting outside by the door with a torch. Once our cat, Timmy, went inside to sleep. It scared the pants off him when she growled in surprise.

But in the dark in the bedroom where nobody can see he likes to talk about Mum. What it would be like if she was alive and looking after us with Dad instead of just Dad on his own. Sometimes I convince myself I can remember her but I was only little when she died. The photographs are around us in the house and there is a big album of photos which David loves to look through. I don't like to. I don't know why. I guess that you cannot get back what is gone. David loves to talk about what we would all do together if she was alive and what it would be like to go for walks with Mum and to sit with her at breakfast and for her to make us tea when we come home from school. He talks and talks until I can hear the tremble in his voice and then I know he's crying. He stops talking and is asleep quickly. He never knows that the tears are trickling on my face long after he's slept.

What it would be to have a mother.

\* \* \* \* \* \* \*

He has a good idea, I think, that I like Susan. He walks with me every morning from the house to go to school. Once we get inside the gate he can see that I'm looking around for her. I've liked her ever since we started school. She has a pretty face and straight blonde hair parted in the middle. What can I tell you about her. She's not noisy and loud but a little shy, but not as shy as me when it comes to her. Her friends are mainly Janet, Catherine and Lesley. I see she helps them with work, gives them little gifts, hugs them when they are upset. She seems so kind to everyone that it makes me feel good too. She knows that I like her I can tell. She looks across at me sometimes and smiles and I know that she means for me to talk to her. I can if it's about something like schoolwork but if it's what I really want to talk to her about I can't. I guess this is a load of rubbish to you but I suppose when someone likes someone else it always seem stupid to somebody watching. Is that right, do you think??

This last year of school we both captain Caradog. I'm captain for the boys and Susan for the girls. Did I tell you how this works? When you come into the school in Standard 1 you are put into a team. These are Caradog (blue), Glyndwr (red), Llewellyn (Green) and Hywel (Yellow). When I was in Standard 1 I really wanted to be in Llewelyn because of the story of Gelert but I got to like being in Caradog. He was a King in the olden times who resisted the Roman invasion. The Romans called him Caractacus. They captured him in the end and took him to Rome and made him stand inside of the Parliament to be judged. He shouted at them and said he had a right to fight back for his country. Amazing people the Romans, because you know what, they let him off. He must have been really brave, can you imagine standing in front of all those people and telling them they were wrong. I wish I could be like that some day. It must be great to be brave and fear nothing.

Well, anyway these teams we are in compete through the year to get points. The main events are at Christmas, St David's Day, Easter and Sports Day. Glyndwr have been winning for the last few years with Caradog in second, Llewelyn third and Hywel last.

This last year of my school days in Hawthorn Road I want me and Susan to help Caradog win the Shield. I have some ideas on how we can beat Glyndwr and wipe the smile off Geoffrey's face. He's the captain of Glyndwr. I know he thinks that he's going to beat us but I've got other ideas. Some time during this school year I'm going to ask Susan to come with me to the Plaza or the Tivoli. I dream of holding her hands when no-one's looking and maybe in the dark of the cinema I'll kiss her. Well, that's what I'd like to happen and I know Martin Conisby, Caractacus or James Bond would not have the nerves that I got. They'd just do it. I will one day too, you wait and see.

You can see I get side tracked when thinking about Susan. It just happens. I was going to share my secret with you on how I plan for Caradog to win and beat Glyndwr. Well to be honest to beat Geoffrey. I have a lot of friends in Glyndwr but as I have told you before and I will tell you many times I can't stand Geoffrey. He thinks he's going to beat us but he's not!.

Do you want to know how me and Susan are going to do it. Ok, she doesn't know the plan yet either but she's going to love it when I tell her. It is so simple. You see it's true that Glyndwr in Standard 4 is a strong team, maybe even stronger than Caradog. Yeah, hard to believe with me in the team and team captain, I know. But sometimes we have to face the facts.

See, what usually happens is that Standard 4 – where all the captains are – just look after themselves. What I mean is they only pay attention to what's going in on in their teams in Standard 4. They pay no attention to what's going on in Standard 1, 2 and 3, and that's where me and Susan are going to be different. We are going to work with the younger team captains in all the Standards below us to check what's going on and to help them. You get judged on various competitions at Christmas, St David's Day Easter and so on like I told you before but now we're going to work with the younger kids to get the best results. Nobody's done that before because nobody's cared about the younger kids. Not a bad idea is it?

I'm going to give Susan the full idea next month because we'll have to start thinking about the Christmas competition. Geoffrey's going to get a big shock. I like that. He's not going to get it all his own way.

\* \* \* \* \* \* \*

There were two other things that were starting to worry me. When we got back to school Mr Cox, our teacher, straight away reminded us that this was the school year we would take the 11 plus. I looked around at all my friends in the class at the time he was saying this. Most of us had been together since infants and we knew each other very well. It would all change next year. Some would go to Cardiff High, Some to Cathays, some to Canton High and some girls to Howells. And then some of us would go to the dreaded Glantaf. But this was the last year we would all be together as one. It would all be different next year.

But another big worry is the selection for the football team. Old Pop Willis does this. It's always boys from Standard 4 in the team unless there's some kid from Standard 3 who's really good. It's not that difficult to get in the team. There's 32 of us in the class, 15 boys and 17 girls so the chances of getting a place in the team are pretty good but there's a lot of shame if you are picked as a reserve. I'm not that good with the ball like Tom and Geoffrey but I can run with the ball pretty fast and kick it long. But everyone knows that Pop Willis likes people who can dribble with the ball and get past people. I can't do that too well.

I'm scared about the selection because I really don't want to be a reserve. I thought my chances were going to be OK but there's this kid in Standard 3 called Patrick Murphy who is really good. He's better than most of us. Old Pop Willis has been running a few practice games using some of the kids from Standard 3 and Patrick plays better than Tom.

I should be in because Jack is too fat to get in and Simon, well Simon has no chance but with Patrick doing so good it means more kids are going to be reserves.

I tried to get something out of Pop Willis yesterday on the walk back from Hailey Park to school but he wouldn't say anything. I can see he doesn't really care if he ruins my life by making me a reserve. I tried to tell him that it was important that the Captain of Caradog in Standard 4 should be in the football team but I could see that his nodding meant nothing. It didn't help too that I was having to run a bit to keep up with his fast walking. In the end he told me I'd have to wait to know like everyone else and he would pin the team selection up on the board tomorrow.

\* \* \* \* \* \* \*

Well of course all last night I was not sleeping right. I was dreaming about football and seeing the list on the notice board. We were all gathered round it and that git Pop Willis had put me as a reserve. Geoffrey was laughing and pointing at me and Tom had his arm round me saying it wasn't that important. But it was, I was lumped in with Jack and Simon. How could he do this to me. Worse still I could see that Susan was watching us and she turned and walked away when she saw them laughing at me. It was awful.

Do you ever wake up after a nightmare and thank God that it was only a nightmare. Sometimes dreams seem so real you're sure it's happened. So when I woke up all sweaty and with a headache I felt great that it was only a dream but then wondered if it was a dream that would come true. I couldn't stand it if they were all going to laugh at me.

Well, all the boys were nervous at school this morning but trying not so show it. Maybe not everyone was nervous. Jack would die if he saw his name on the team list and Simon couldn't care less but the rest of us would die of shame if we were not in the team. I know I would.

We tried not look too interested but looked on the notice board when we got to school but it wasn't there. He put it up after we were in class and before morning break. It wasn't like a cattle stampede at break time but close. Geoffrey got there first and cheered. I dragged my feet getting to the notice Board really scared of bad news, This is what I saw when I looked at the Board.

*Nobody Watching*

### Goal Keeper
Clive

**Right Back**             **Left Back**
Alun                       Gethin

**Right Half**    **Centre Half**    **Left Half**
Nigel             Phil               Keith


**Right Wing**  **Inside Right**  **Centre Forward**  **Inside Right**  **Left Wing**
Gareth          Patrick           Tom                 Geoffrey          Michael

**Reserves:** Dafydd, Paul

But first of all I couldn't see my name and panicked. I looked at the reserves first and saw that my name was not there. This made me panic even more. What if I hadn't even made the reserves. Then I saw it. He'd put me as right wing when I'd expected him to put me as Right Half. I phewed in relief blowing the air out slowly. I wouldn't have to worry about what the others would say to me and I could still look at Susan without feeling ashamed. Do you ever get into this situation where you panic worrying you're not going to be picked for something? Is it always like this? All the way through being grown up or does it get easier? Or maybe you get to the point where it doesn't matter one way or the other.

Dafydd's in that situation right now. You know when I saw his name on the reserve list first I didn't really take it in cos I couldn't find my name. But after when I was safe my eyes went back to his name on the list. Dafydd's not bad at football but he doesn't care too much about it. He came alongside me to look at the Board. "Looks like I don't need a new pair of boots, then" he said giving me a nudge on the shoulder. I turned to get a good look at his face. Where was the terror at not being picked.

"You don't care" I asked him.

""Why should I?" he threw back at me. ""If Pop Willis had picked me I'd have played. He didn't so I won't. I'm not bothered either way."

I wish I could be like that you know, not caring about what people think. It must be great. Funny, I just got a picture of myself

26

like one of those birds or a lizard with a head that can twist almost all the way round and eyes always moving. You know the sort I mean always twitching to see what's around and to check there's no danger even when eating something. How do you get to be like Dafydd. That's what I'd like to know.

*******

When me and my brother got home after school one day Dad had got back early. We always loved this. He was chatting to Aunty Nancy. They were talking about John F Kennedy. He's the President of the United States of America. He is a hero to all of us at school. I'm not sure why but the teachers and grown ups seem to like him. Dad and Aunt Nancy were talking about Russia. From what we hear this is a bad place and they don't like us here in Europe or America. There is a big wall all the way across Russia so no-one can get in or out. Dad says no-one tries to get in but there's plenty who get shot trying to get out. Must be a bad place if so many people want to escape. Anyway, Dad and Aunt Nancy were saying that Russia is getting friendly with Cuba. I don't know where Cuba is. After Aunt Nancy left I asked Dad where Cuba was. He got an Atlas and showed me on the map and drew a line with his finger all the way from Cuba to Moscow. That's the capital of Russia. He said that Russia and Cuba are friends and that Russia gives weapons to Cuba. He showed how close Cuba was to America and said that President Kennedy would not be happy about that. He said I shouldn't worry but I could see from his face that something was worrying him.

*JP's Note: The days of kids without computer games. Incredible!! Gareth provides us with first hand evidence that at that time there was a serious worry of a nuclear war. People were afraid and thought the world was going to end.*

*Brothers don't change. My older brother acted in a similar way, always wanting to leave me out of things!!*

# CHAPTER 3
## *October 1962*

You can start to see it getting tough in school now. Mr Cox still goes through the usual things with us like Reading, Writing, Arithmetic, Geography, History and Scripture but he's now started to spend about half the time on preparing us for the 11 plus. We are going to get exams in Verbal comprehension and spelling, non verbal reasoning, arithmetic and an essay. I like the English stuff best so I have to do extra work with Dad on the ones I don't like.

Jack Sims was not going to find any of it hard. He is a real "brainbox". While the rest of us are getting nervous and anxious about the exams next year you can see it's not even on Jack's mind. He beats me at most stuff except sport of course and Welsh. He's not so good at Welsh.

Miss Rees gives us Welsh on Friday afternoons too did I tell you that. She says that we are Welsh boys and girls and should learn the language of our country. "Cariad" means "sweetheart". I like that one. "Ysgol" is school, "ffenestr" is window. I overheard her mutter "twp" one time and looked it up in the dictionary. It means "dopey" or "stupid". I wish I could be better at Welsh but Dad doesn't speak it and I think you need a lot of practice. There is a school not far from us which kids go to who are taught in Welsh. I wish I could learn it like them. It's like a secret language which you can use and others don't know what you're talking about.

I think we were all glad when the weekend came. School made us feel that things would be changing and would never be the same again. I've been in the same class with Susan as long as I can remember but if we pass the eleven plus we will be separated. Even if we both went to Canton High, she would be in the girls' school and I would be in the boys' school. We would be separated by a tall fence but we would still be able to walk to school together and come home together. I had to keep reminding myself of this.

During dinner hour on Friday I told her my idea for getting Caradog to beat Glyndwr in our year. She liked the idea and gave me a hug. I think I went bright red. I hope you think it's a good idea too so if you find this book and are reading it please keep this a secret. And don't tell Geoffrey. We're going to work out how to help the younger ones at the Christmas concert. You get points for singing carols, reading, the best model of the nativity scene and the best made Christmas card for parents. We decided that Susan would help with the card and the nativity scene and I'd help them on reading and singing. I like to be picked by Mr Evans, our Headmaster, to read the passage from the Bible at the morning assembly. And I don't mind if the reading is in English or Welsh. I'm not a bad singer also. My Dad says that one day I might be lucky enough to sing with Shirley Bassey. Dad winks at David when he says that and they both have a good laugh. They are going to get a shock one day, that's for sure.

But like I was telling you at school now we longed for the weekend. There are around thirty boys and girls in our class and groups of five or six who mess around together in school and outside. I already told you about the gang I'm with. The girls have their own gangs too but we never mix with them at the weekend. We see them of course but they're not interested in what we do and the same goes for us. Well maybe sometimes we play Statues with them but not very often.

On Friday evenings after school it is cubs night. Most of the boys in our class are cubs but I didn't join for a while. It wasn't the boys who made me join in the end it was the fact that the Brownies started to meet in another room in the church hall. And guess who is in the Brownies.

Because I started late I had to do all the entrance stuff with younger kids, learn the scout promise and the scout law and all the funny stuff that you do in cubs. I don't really like putting on uniforms and things like that but I was willing to put up with it for a chance to meet up with Susan.

I mean some of the things you do seem very funny to me. Hey, I hope you're not in the cubs or scouts or anything. I didn't have any problem learning the scout law and the scout promise but every time we go to cubs we start off with this ceremony. Everybody seems to take it seriously but it makes me want to laugh.

We're all in a circle and we squat down and balance ourselves with two fingers from each hand. Then we all shout:

*Ah-kay-la, weeeeeee'll do our best!*

Then we all jump to our feet and put up two fingered salutes which is supposed to be like the ears of the wolf cub

Akela then goes:

*Dyb, Dyb, Dyb.* This means do your best and then it's left hand down and the right hand spreads into the two fingered salute.

Then we all shout out, *"Weell, Dob, Dob, Dob"*

This means, we'll do our best. Well, have you ever watched this? It looks stupid. Sometimes in the summer we start off in Hailey Park and do this. I can't stand it if there's people around. The boys in our gang seem ok with it and it's only me that's laughing inside.

I think Akela has known about this over the last couple of years since I've been in it. I've got more badges than most in the pack but I'm only a second not a sixer. What that means is that I'm not in charge of a six but I take charge if our sixer is not there.

When I first started the Akela was pretty good. She was younger than most of the mothers who came to see some of the things we did. Something happened though and suddenly Nigel Carter's mother became Akela. I knew this would be trouble. She's very strict and doesn't like me too much. Hey and guess what, Nigel became a sixer. Fancy that, eh? My Dad always says it's not what you know but who you know. Dead right, if you ask me.

Next year we will leave cubs and move up to scouts but I'm not sure I'll bother. I said to Dad I wasn't too keen on all the dyb, dyb things we did at cubs. He told me I shouldn't be a mason then. I asked him what he was talking about. He knew I wanted to be a journalist and didn't want to go anywhere near stone. This really made Dad laugh. Grown ups, I realise, only like to tell you part of the story. They think it's clever to keep you in the dark. Even Vince does this. Let me tell you about Vince.

Saturday and Sunday mornings I get up early and meet Vince, the milkman who drives his electric truck. Vince is not a tall man and he's not as old as my dad but he is big, not fat. Just big. He has thick black hair and big, big hands. He doesn't talk too much but I notice he watches everything especially pretty girls.

I meet him where Hazelhurst Road meets Belle Vue Crescent where he starts his Llandaff North deliveries. I've been helping him for a couple of years. I stopped him one day outside our house and just asked him if I could help. Vince did the job running constantly with a load of bottles held by his big fingers. It was great to watch but I couldn't copy that. I put the milks in a carrier and took them to the house porches. If they were well off they had gold top. You could see the thick yellow cream at the top three inches of the bottle. Others took red top which was not so creamy and the ordinary milk was with a silver top. The glass bottles were cold and wet. The first couple of times I broke a bottle or two. Vince put his hands on his hips and told me if I was an effin butterfingers he'd have to give me the sack. I couldn't find effin in the dictionary. I found elfin but I'm sure he didn't mean that.

He didn't talk too much on the delivery. There was no time. We were always running. He would say that we had to get the job done and slope off home. Half way down Hazelhurst road on Saturday he always told me to have a half hour break and go have some toast at home. He said he was going for his cocoa. When I got back after half an hour and I was never late Vince would come quickly. He always looked happy after his cocoa and said that cocoa was one of the finest pleasures in life. I hated the stuff myself but Vince said he couldn't get enough of it. He said I'd be the same when I got older but I can't see it myself.

I only asked Vince if I could help because I liked the job. I liked the idea of it being a game to see how quickly we could finish Llandaff North with no breakages with a stop for Vince's cocoa. Over time we got into a really good rhythm and eventually we were looking to see if we could break the time of the week before. Vince would look at his watch and say not bad, five seconds quicker than last week or something like that.

After the first month of helping him he told me my trial period was over and now I got paid. On Sundays he would give me a shiny sixpence and a big bottle of Kia-Ora orange. He knew I hated milk. And with the sixpence I felt very rich and I don't spend them. I keep them hidden in a little tin in the house and I have a plan for them when there is enough. I think Vince knows that I've got a plan. He always tells me to keep it safe.

After the delivery on Sunday I rush home to get my cassock and surplice and go off to All Saints Church to sing at morning service. All my pals are in the choir except Geoffrey. He and his family don't go to church. Most other families in Llandaff north do and the church is full on Sunday morning for Holy Communion. You have to be confirmed to take the bread and wine and next April we all will be. Can't wait for that.

Now I know I told you that I was a really great singer but the rest of the choir are way better than me. When we are at choir practice I try to keep in tune and bluff Mr Preece, our choirmaster. He's blind but I tell you he is not deaf. He's always picking me up. Anyway, I'd like to be the best singer in the world but I'm not and hope I don't get chucked out because I do love singing the hymns and I like the four shillings we get if we have to sing at a wedding. I can also get a great view of Susan and her family from my place in the pew. She comes with her older sister, Jackie, and her mum and dad.

You know those sixpences I'm collecting every week from Vince. Have you guessed what I'm going to do with them. I bet you have.

The service is not so bad. Father Tebbitt is a big, round man with a round face and a deep voice. I listen to everything he says except the sermon because I don't understand it. But he is kind and friendly just like Mr Evans, our headmaster. I like them both a lot.

In the service we have hymns and readings, the money collection, communion, sermon and announcements then another hymn and everyone is off home. During the sermon to make it go faster I take out a piece of candle wax you can always find around the place. It passes the time to carefully wax a piece of paper on both sides to make it slippery and soft. Before you know it Father Tebbit is on to the announcements. Only once was the silence disturbed in the choir stalls when Dafydd let one off. It could only be heard in the choir stalls but it went on for about five seconds. Father Tebbit turned while he was giving the sermon to see why we were making those noises you do when you're stopping a laugh. The tenor behind me leaned forward and spoke in Dafydd's ear. He said he was going to bring a cork next week.

Now don't laugh at me but I really like going to church. Do you believe in God, I wonder? I do. We couldn't have got on this world by accident, could we? Once we had a bloke as our Sunday school teacher who filled in for a few weeks. He said he was a student from some University or other. He told us something that stuck in my mind. He said to remember it if ever we doubted there was a God. He said imagine you were walking along a beach in Australia and as you walked along you saw something shiny in the sand and picked it up. He told us to picture holding in our hands a watch like the ones that fits into a grandad's waistcoat pocket on a chain. He said that when you looked at it and opened up the back and saw all the cogs and wheels moving it would be obvious that someone had made it. Then he told us to close our eyes and imagine ourselves floating above our planet earth and further and further out. We would see all the planets circling and moving gracefully, he said. Gracefully, that's a really nice word don't you think. And with my eyes closed I could see it all like a great big machine. Those planets whizzing through space and being held by something so that they didn't fly off and crash into each other. All of them moving gracefully like the parts of a machine. I could see this bloke was right. When you look at all those planets and suns and the way they move it's just obvious that God made it all.

I know He watches over me too and I'm sure He's got me out of a few scrapes in the past and how He watches over so many of us I just don't know. I just know He is there and I feel safe.

Geoffrey doesn't believe in God, you know. Once he told us that his dad had said that believing in God was like believing in Father Christmas. It was just for kids. He said that there was no such thing as Adam and Eve at all and that human beings had come from apes and just become smarter over loads of years. He said a bloke called Darwing had worked it all out. Well Jack normally keeps himself to himself but he pipes up when Geoffrey is going on about this. He says to Geoffrey, OK so where did the apes come from and what if God was practicing with the apes before he came to making man. That shut old Geoffers up. He didn't know what to say. It was obvious he was just spouting what his dad had said and he hadn't thought about it one bit.

Well anyway talking of Geoffrey I saw him on the way home. He was circling on his bike in Hazelhurst Road. He was the lucky one. Although my Dad was one of the few people in Llandaff North to have a car and we had a telly, Geoffrey had a bike. It had always been a rule that you only got your first two wheeler bike when you passed the eleven plus. Obviously, Geoffrey's parents did not like sticking to the rules.

"Lemme, see you in your choir boy outfit," he says to me bringing his bike to a screeching stop and pointing at my bag.

"Piss off, Geoff" I says to him. "I'm going home for dinner."

I walked past him and crossed the road for our house. You think you're gonna beat me. Caradog beat Glyndwr. Huh, we're going to smash you. I didn't answer and just walked on but I was boiling inside. I'd tell Susan what a git he was.

Dad and David were home before me. Dad makes a great Sunday roast and I was looking forward to it. I knew we would have rice pudding afterwards as well. When I got in I could see he was worried listening to the radio. They were talking about missiles in Cuba that came from Russia. I asked Dad what it was all about. He shushed me and went on listening to the radio. Me and David knew it was best to let Dad listen. He'd tell us in time. Later when we were sat together tucking in to roast beef, Yorkshire pudding and piles of vegetables and mash Dad told us not to worry. He said Russia had put missiles into Cuba but President Kennedy would not let a World War start. I had pictures in my head of big missiles flying across continents to hit cities. I wondered if they would think of Cardiff. It made me shudder. Dad still told us not to worry.

In school next day I asked Susan what she thought. She said her Dad had said that President Kennedy would stop any war happening. I hoped so too but things seemed different with teachers and grown ups and me and Susan noticed it. On the telly and the radio they played the sound of the sirens if there was a three minute warning. This meant the missiles were coming. It made me shiver for a while.

We only talked for a bit about this because everyone was singing Love me Do by a new group called the Beatles. They've got long hair but their music is really great. Susan loves them too just like I do. Geoffrey won't join in because he says Elvis is still the best.

But even though a war might be coming, President Kennedy, missiles and the Beatles music all took second place to getting the bogey and the guy ready for Guy Fawkes day. Tom's older brother, Jack, helped us with this. He's great at putting bogeys together. Do you know what a bogey is? I'm guessing you do. It has two larger wheels and a seat at the back. Then a narrow plank of wood runs from the seat to a smaller plank and its bolted together in the middle but in a way which allows the smaller plank to move. It has two smaller wheels either side of the plank. From the seat you can reach the smaller plank with your feet and steer it with your feet. There is also a rope which is attached to either side of the smaller plank and is long enough for you to hold in your hand. So if you want you can steer with the rope too.

We get Jack to make them for us in the summer holidays so we can race them down the slope at the edge of Hailey Park when we get bored. It's easy to fall off so you can imagine the scrapes and cuts we get but we never seem to notice till we get home.

Once we're back at school they get put away until, at the end of October, we pull them out of Tom's shed in the garden and start to make our guy. It doesn't take too long to make the guy. We get some old clothes and stuff them with paper and straw for the body, arms and legs and Tom's mum sews it all together and makes the head for us. The hard part is always trying to find someone to give us a wide hat but we always manage it in the end. There are three pitches which are really good for collections. One is the bus stop on Station Road at coming home time and the other two are the Railway pub on any evening and the Rugby club on Saturdays. We say "Penny for the guy" but if we smile and are polite we usually get a lot more than that. We take it in turns and pool the cash to get fireworks. Well, we don't exactly get the fireworks. We have to give the cash to our Dads to do it for us and they have all the fun setting fire to the guy and letting the fireworks off in Hailey Park. But it's a great night and loads of kids and parents come out to enjoy the party. There's lots of hot dogs, onions and fun. Only a few more days and we can enjoy the party.

*JP's Note: The fear of war is still there. Funny how there was a Beatles/Elvis divide back then. I'm not sure if kids know either of them now.*

*And what about this bonfire? Imagine the licences and regulations needed for that these days?*

*I hope Gareth joins the scouts. He will enjoy it. I know I did.*

# Chapter 4
## *November 1962*

Sometimes Tom's mum invites me over to his house and we eat loads of beans on toast. One day I will burst. He has an older brother and sister like I told you so Tom is the youngest. They don't bother us too much, maybe tease us from time to time but they're really nice – well most of the time.

Tom is the best friend I will ever have. I've never known a time when we have not been together right from infants school. There's not many weekends that have passed without us doing something together whether it was with our gang or just me and him. He never seems to get angry or anything especially not the way Alun does. He's great at cricket, football and he practices rugby with his brother, Jack. Jack says he's going to be really good at this later when he's bigger. He's pretty quick at running too but I can just about keep up with him.

My Dad says he's sensible. What this means of course is that he doesn't get into any trouble, throw stones in the wrong places, be cheeky to grown ups and is very polite. Dad likes it that we are friends and always likes it when Tom comes to visit. It's true that Tom does not get into trouble too much but the thing is that mums and dads only see a little. They don't see what we get up to when we are out on our own. The only way they know is if another grown up sees us and tells our parents. Where Tom is good is in spotting when grown ups are around who know us. Come on, we are boys and boys get into trouble one way or another.

David likes Tom too and as you know David would love to be part of our gang but he's too young and that's it. Specially he likes it when Tom's mum invites the two of us over for tea after school. Tom's parents are just like him – really kind. His Dad drives a big lorry for some company and sometimes it's parked outside their house. It's so big it stops the light in the front of the house. He's a quiet man, a bit like my Dad and we don't see him around too often as he gets back late from work.

Tom's mum does not work but is always doing something like cooking, cleaning, sewing, knitting or ironing clothes. Tom's house is a busy house as he has Jack and Carol as an older brother and sister who always have friends inside the house. Sometimes it seems as busy and as noisy as Cardiff centre but I noticed that when Tom's Dad comes home his mother makes sure that he gets peace and quiet.

David likes Tom's father but he loves his mother. He calls her" Aunty" Margaret and when we were little and used to sit on the sofa for "Listen with Mother" he used to snuggle up to her just before it went "ding de dong, ding de dong, ding, ding" and then the woman says "Are you sitting comfortably, then I'll begin". He loved it especially if the Grand Old Duke of York was on. But it wasn't just the programme but also being close to a mum. You could see he was so happy being close to her. Sometimes he fell asleep and "Aunty" Margaret just could not move in case she woke him up. She made a habit of keeping the sewing or knitting nearby in case it happened.

Why do I always get off track when I want to tell you something. Anyway, on this day I can see that Tom has something on his mind. So after we finished the toast and bean mountain I asked him what was wrong. Tom always comes out with it straight off. He said we'd always been a good gang of pals but he'd noticed that Geoff and me were not getting on well at all. He's like that Tom, always looking to be peacemaker if there's a bust up.

Well, I couldn't lie. I said to Tom that he knew there'd always been arguments between me and Geoff. But he knew that I was going to put in a big fight for Glyndwr to beaten by my team, Caradog.

You know Tom surprised me. He laughed. He said who cares who wins. It's only fun for everyone and keeps the younger kids happy. Tom's in Hywel so I know he doesn't believe they stand much of a chance. I told him he must be crazy. I said that the competition between Caradog and Glyndwr is like the Oxford and Cambridge boat race or Wales against England in Rugby or England v Australia in cricket. And we, Caradog, had to win and Geoffrey had to lose. Of course Tom is just falling about laughing at all this.

He likes Janet, he told me when he stopped laughing and falling all over the place. Just came right out with it. She likes him too, Tom said to me. It's funny but you can feel disappointed and happy at the same time. I like Janet and I can't see how she could like Geoffrey.

He's not so bad, Tom said to me. He's been part of our gang for a long time. We all have our fights but I can see it's getting worse between you and him. Now you know he's not interested in Susan you should be OK.

Who said I'm interested in Susan, I asked Tom trying to look baffled. He laughed and laughed again and didn't answer. We moved on to other things then.

We don't have a leader of our gang but also we do. It's Tom. We all look to see what he thinks and says. He's a 10 year old like the rest of us but he seems to know more. I think it's because he has an older brother and sister. Nothing seems to bother him too much either. You know, I'm scared of everything like failing at school, gangs of boys outside Llandaff North, falling in the river, Dad dying and me leaving our junior school. There I said it but it's true. If you look on my map you'll see the area I live in and don't go beyond, well not unless there is a gang of us or Dad is with me or I'm feeling crazy. Past the top end of Hailey Park beyond the tennis courts is the river bridge that takes you to Llandaff and then on to Cardiff City Centre. But it also takes you to Canton High School. It's in Fairwater I've never been there and I've never seen the school. In a story book I was reading in the library once it showed a map of an imaginary land. At one end of the map was an arrow which pointed to land not yet explored. By the arrow it said "Here be dragons". That's how I feel, if you understand me. The dragons scare the life out of me.

But you know later that week in school Tom showed how much he knows about us all. Susan and me we got together at lunch break with the kids from Standards 1 to 3 who were captains of Caradog and working on their projects for Christmas. We gave some help and showed some of the things we were working on. They were doing great. I got my fingers crossed. You know these little kids they look up to us. It's a good feeling.

After we'd finished we walked back to the playground but Susan stopped me on the way. This is for you, she said holding out a package. I looked at her surprised wondering what it was all about.

I didn't want to give it to you while everyone's around but it's for your birthday, she said while my face was beginning to burn red and my heart was doing things it never had before.

I blurted out, but my birthday's tomorrow.

I know that silly, she said laughing, but I wanted to give it to you today on your own. But you mustn't open it until tomorrow.

Who are you, the person who is reading this. Are you a ten year old like me or older. If you're older maybe you think it's all strange but I was thinking that maybe you've been through it too. If you are the same age as me then you'll know. You see I could tell that when she gave me this package it was a very important moment. I wanted to give her a kiss on the cheek to say thank you but something inside was telling me not to, that she wouldn't like it, that she'd laugh at me. All these things were in my mind. But for the first time I didn't listen. I took the package from her and leaned forward with my burning face and kissed her on the cheek.

She gave such a big smile that it made my heart turn over. And you know she reached out and held my hand and let it stay there until we both heard Mr Evans door open in the corridor. We smiled at each other and raced to the playground.

Later that night I thought about things and something came to me. Now I don't know if I'm explaining this so well but give me a chance. I think that as we grow up we find there's barriers like learning to read and write, climb a tree, go right to the edge of the monkey rocks, swing out on the rope over the river and things like this. But also it's with friends and strangers too. It's like a choice comes up, do something or do nothing. For the first time with Susan I did something. I kissed her even though I was scared what might happen. But I didn't need to be scared you see. It all turned out OK. It's like you should always do it even though you're scared because there's half a chance you're going to be happy. If you do nothing you're just left wondering and feeling sad.

I talked to Dad about it a bit. I knew how he had come to meet Mum but I didn't know what happened. David was watching telly so I got Dad in the kitchen while he was making a sandwich. I asked him if it was easy to get Mum to marry him. Just like that I said it. I thought he might tell me to bugger off but he finished making the sandwich and sat down.

He didn't eat the sandwich but looked at it. He said he didn't think it would happen. He said that she was the most lovely lady in the world and he was patient in seeing her until she saw him as he saw her. When I felt she liked me, Dad said, I asked her to marry me and she said yes. It was a feeling I'll never forget. He looked down at his sandwich then, picked it up and started eating and I could see that he would say no more. I went and sat with David to watch telly.

It was "Treasure Island" she bought me. It was a really great copy and a book I love to read so much. Inside she'd written a message to me and given me a funny birthday card. It makes it easier to bring my own plan together now!! Dad bought me "Swallows and Amazons" and you know David surprised me. He bought me, well I guess dad bought me, "Seven White Gates" by Malcolm Saville. I'd just finished the first in the Lone Pine series, "Mystery at Witchend" and I loved it. I was so pleased I gave David a hug. He pushed me away, of course.

It was so different in school. I didn't feel bad about things with Susan or anyone else and when I had the chance I thanked her for the book and the card. Before I felt like jigsaw pieces in a box but now I feel like I'm all put together. When I got Susan on her own in a corner of the playground I told her I was so happy with the present and although I could feel myself going red I got on with it. I told her that ever since I'd been a little boy in infants I'd liked her so much but never had the guts to tell her that I liked her. She just listened and was smiling at me. I said that I'd always wanted her to be my girlfriend and that I had wanted this for so long. She just said to me, I know. I've been waiting for you to ask. She laughed and held my hand and said, well we are girlfriend and boyfriend now. And that was it. I'd done it. I can't really explain this big feeling I felt swelling in my chest and I don't think I ever felt so happy in my life.

I bet you think I'm crazy or something. Hey, but you know the big thing, I don't feel so jealous – Ok I said it – jealous of Geoffrey. But I'm still not going to let his Glyndwr beat my Caradog. Ha! Some things will not change.

\* \* \* \* \* \* \*

By the way I forgot to tell you about Guy Fawkes Day a week or so back. We had a great time. Me and Alun were on the last collection run together after school. We started at the bus stop on Station Road but then slowly pulled the bogey with Guy Fawkes down to the newsagents and the Post Office. We crossed the road and walked past the Railway pub as it wasn't open till later. We walked past the fish and chip shop and crossed the road again to look for spare change outside Percy Evans sweet shop. We couldn't be bothered to cut through as far as the Candy Bar. Well Alun couldn't be bothered to go as far as the Candy Bar. To be honest we'd made a good collection on the last day which was a bit surprising because Alun hasn't really got the knack of smiling sweetly and asking for money.

He's dead clever but doesn't really care about it. He has old parents and a brother and sister who are at work. I've never been into his house. His mum and dad, brother and sister act like we are invisible. It's weird. When you knock the door to see if Alun is in they look at you, turn away and call him. That's it. I'm going to tell you that sometimes when I'm on the way home from somewhere on my own and I pass his house I do a rat-a-tat ginger on their door just for the fun of it.

Have you played rat-a-tat ginger. It's a bit mean and a bit scary if you get caught but although it's naughty it is fun. It's especially fun if you do it to people you don't like. It's better with a few people as you laugh more. You just go up to a door in the street and ring the bell or bang the door knocker and then run and hide. It's great if you can find a place where you can see them open the door but they can't see you. As soon as they've closed the door you race back and do it again. It's all down to timing 'cos sooner or later they get wise and close the door only to throw it open fast and give you a good telling off. "Wait till I tell your mothers about this".

Anyway, Alun's got a bit of their weirdness too. He can get into a fight with any one of us over nothing and then maybe you won't see him for a few days. If you call round his house he won't come to the door even when his Mum or Dad say you're outside.

He might have an older sister but I think they must all keep their clothes on all the time. Now I only have a brother and no sisters but I found out more about girls and their bodies than Alun. OK, so you know I like books and going to the library. Well they got this section on old paintings and you can see the difference between girls and boys. Girls get bigger chests but they don't get a willy like we do. You can see the space. It's their bad luck they don't have a willy. It's really funny having a pissing contest over the dubs wall at school. Philip is the best and can get it over the highest. I'm not so bad but there's a lot who can't even reach the top. But anyway, me and Alun are walking along one day and you can see something is bothering him. Suddenly he goes to me, You know when we have PE and the girls are in their knickers and we're in our shorts? Yeah, I go and he goes, but their willies must be smaller than ours because you can't see any lump. I looked at him to see if he was trying to be funny but he wasn't. They don't have a willy, I said. You know he laughed and told me to stop joking. I dragged him straight to the library and pulled out one of the old painting picture books and opened it up for him. He looked at it for ages and went really pale. But why don't they have a willy like us, he kept saying. I told him I didn't know but there must be a good reason. Girls and boys had to be different, didn't they. In the end I had to close the book and push him outside. Then he went right into deep thinking.

That's Alan, he has his own way of doing this. He spends a lot of time thinking and many times you need to shove him to get a reply. This only happens with me if I'm reading. Hey, I'm reading Billy Bunter at the moment. He is so funny. Maybe my Dad will be rich enough to send me to private school one day. I'd like to play cricket in the school grounds, have food parties in the dorm at night and be a decent chap like Harry Wharton or Bob Cherry. I mentioned it to Vince when we were delivering milk one Sunday. He laughed and told me my Dad would never let me go even if he was a millionaire and if he was crazy enough to let me go I should make sure the cord on my pajama bottoms was knotted so tight it wouldn't open. When I told Dad about it he said I shouldn't listen to all of Vince's stories. Anyway, I've started to practise knotting the pajama cord really tight. When I thought about I realized it's to stop your stomach grumbling in the night just like the cowboys used to tighten their belt when they were riding across the plains searching for food.

So anyway, if you have forgotten me and Alun were doing the final turn collecting Guy Fawkes money around Station Road and outside Percy Evans sweet shop when we saw Mervyn Pratt and a couple of his friends. They were talking to these big girls. You could see they liked Mervyn a lot. They kept smiling at him and giggling a lot. Girls can look really silly sometimes when Mervyn is around. He was with one of his friends I don't really like. His name is Peter Stephens. When Mervyn is not around he is nasty and shoves us or tells us to piss off but he won't act like that in front of Mervyn. He gives us a look that says yeah you go and tell him and watch out what happens when he's not around. One day Mervyn will catch him and then that will be the smile off his face.

Like usual we hung about at a distance watching what was going on. Mervyn had his dog, Odin, with him. Odin was the biggest Alsatian I've seen in my life. You'd think he couldn't wait to sink his teeth into your arse, but not Odin. Odin is as harmless as a fly and loves to play with kids. So anyway Mervyn is paying more attention to Odin than these girls but Peter Stephens he thinks it's his chance to show off and impress these girls.

Me and Alun we're pretending to fix the guy before moving on but we're watching. He's asking these girls if they know the facts of life. Me and Alun look at each other. He whispers to me, "The facts of life. What are they." I shrug my shoulders and give that look which says I don't have a clue. But anyway, I'm watching these girls and I can see they don't really know either but they don't want to look as if they're stupid. So they're giggling back, of course we do, of course we do. Mervyn's not paying much attention but suddenly stops playing with Odin and says goodbye to everyone and turns away. He sees us then and comes over to talk for a bit and gives us some money for the guy. As he walks away we follow him. It's not safe to be left alone with Peter Stephens around. Anyway as we look back blowing raspberries at Peter we can see that the girls are losing interest too. Our laughing and acting like baboons out of the zoo doesn't make him look too happy either. We stay with Mervyn until it's safe to make our way home.

It was good at the bonfire night on the ground by the rugby club. As usual it was mostly families and teenagers. It was noisy and good fun with a big smell of cooking food and firework powder. All my pals were there and so was Susan. I saw Geoffrey there too and he was holding hands with Janet in front of his Mum and Dad. I looked at Susan and wished I could hold her hand. If only I'd known that a week later I would!!

I told you the open land was right by the Rugby Club and so pints of beer were coming out all the time and disappearing fast. When it was towards the end and the guys were burning and the big rockets were going off one big bang scared David and he clutched at me but let go quick when he realized what he'd done.

Geoff's Dad had a few beers that night and was going round cracking a joke to everyone. He kept saying if Russia wanted us to go out with a bang then we might as well go out with our own bang. Everyone laughed a bit and you know, if a bomb did go off in Cardiff while our fireworks were going we wouldn't have heard a thing.

Later when we were walking down Hazelhurst Road towards home I asked Dad if he could tell me what the Facts of Life are. I asked him if it was a list like the Ten Commandments or something like that. It must have been the beer I think because he laughed out loud. He asked me where I'd heard about that and I told him about Peter Stephens and what he'd said to the girls. Dad said there was no need to think about it until I was older. He said there was plenty of time for me before I needed to know about the birds and the bees and once I was a few years older he said I'd be thinking about it a lot of the time. He said too I shouldn't mention it at school as the teachers might not like it. You know he wouldn't say any more after that even though I brought a laugh from him when I said it was the Facts of Life I wanted to see not the Birds and the Bees. Anyway as we got to our door we bumped into Dudley Potts and his father. Dudley is a great rugby player for Llandaff North. His Dad was holding him up a bit so he must have been tired after work or something. I like Dudley. Once he gave me a huge collection of Eagle comics and old cigarette cards showing footballers. He was always giving treats to me and David.

Anyway, I didn't mention the Facts of Life to Dad or anyone else afterwards but I decided to go to the library to see what I could find. I went off on my own the next Saturday afternoon after football. I started with a dictionary and then began to look at books on nature and animals, human beings and stuff like that. I got it in the end. If you look long enough you can usually find what you want.

I went straight round to Alun's house. It was one of those good days when the door was answered, Alun called and he came to the door. I said to him, do you want to know why boys have a willy and girls don't? Funny thing, he looked back into the house before closing the door quickly and coming with me. When we got to the library I set out the books for him so that he could discover it just the way I had done. When we came to the final book and he understood Alun's face was shocked. "Why did you show me this?, he asked me quietly but he wasn't looking at me. Because it's the Facts of Life, I said to him. That's how we get born. Not brought by the stork or found under the gooseberry bush like the grown ups said but like this.

I wish I didn't know he said and got up and walked away on his own. I knew what he was feeling. It was like finding out a secret that you might wish had stayed a secret. But you know there's something that I think might be true which is that the more secrets you know perhaps the easier things can be. What do you think? Maybe you know the answer to this already. Do you know a lot of secrets or only a few?

For Alun it was a secret he did not want to know and as I expected I did not see him other than in school for more days than usual. It made me feel a bit guilty.

\* \* \* \* \* \* \*

Guess what? Dad took us to Cardiff town centre to give us a treat. We went on Saturday morning so that first we could look around the indoor market. Dad likes to buy cheese and polony and me and David we like to go to the upstairs part to see the pets for sale. When you go into this market it has so many smells. I like to stop and close my eyes first and then breathe in. You get the fish as the strongest but then you can pick up cheese and then leather from belts and shoes and then the sawdust smell from where the pets are kept. And there is so much noise as the stall owners call out to the customers walking by. It's not like Llandaff North at all. It's the same out on the streets. They are packed and all the way along Queen Street past the Castle to the river it's full of people, some cars, trams and buses. There is noise from people, traffic and the smell of fumes from cars and buses. We both stay close to Dad. These people are like a forest. And ever since one time David got lost in British Home Stores Dad does not let us stray too far from him. There is no Dad like my Dad.

When we've finished walking about the market and the streets he takes us to this place in an arcade where they have a Sasparilla shop. Dad has a big one in a pint glass and we have two smaller glasses. It's great in winter because the sasparilla is hot and tasty.

Afterwards, he likes to take us to the Sandringham Hotel when we go to town. Me and David like this. Dad loves their fish and chips and we do too but first we like to have lots of toasted teacakes with butter. We eat so much that we are struggling to eat all the fish and chips, but we manage. Dad has a beer and we have Tizer pop. It's great.

Dad was really relaxed and having fun. I asked him why he was so happy and he told us everyone was. He said that it looked as if a World War might start over the missiles in Cuba which I told you about before. Dad said it was all over now and the missiles were being taken away from Cuba. In my mind I could see thousands and thousands of these big missiles rising out of the ground in Russia and America pointing at cities over the World. It made me shiver. I'd seen pictures in a book in the library of what happened when the Americans dropped nuclear bombs on Hiroshima in Japan. It was horrible. I imagined what it would be like if one dropped on Cardiff. You see you can run away from boys like Peter Stephens and strangers who might be bullies but you can't really run away from a bomb, can you. Not when it's a big nuclear bomb. I didn't say anything to Dad or David about what I was thinking. Anyway, it would give David nightmares. But as Dad said, Thank God, it's over.

Hey, I was just about to mark a new entry for December when I saw something on the news. France and Britain are going to build an aeroplane together and it's going to be called Concorde. Dad laughed at this. He said there's been an "ontaunt cordial" for fifty years and it's never been bloody cordial with the French.

I saw the pictures of what it will look like on telly. It looks great. It will fly to America in half the time. Maybe one day I will get to be a passenger. Maybe if I get rich and earn a thousand pounds a year when I grow up, I will be able to afford it. That would be something.

*JP's note: Cars have changed things. Back then Llandaff North was Gareth's world. London would have seemed a far off place like a foreign land. And the innocence of first love? Is it still like that now.*

# CHAPTER 5
## *December 1962*

For as far back as I can remember David has dreamed of Christmas. Usually he starts thinking about it in June. When we get to bed at night and talk for a little before sleeping, at some point he will ask me the number of days to Christmas. Well in June this is around 180 of course but he's never put off. Week after week he'll keep asking me to do a recount and when we get to December his excitement gets more and more.

From November the iciness in the house gets worse. There are only two places that are warm in the house and that's the kitchen and the sitting room where we have the telly. The kitchen is warm because in the evening Dad has usually got the gas oven going or burners on the top and in the sitting room we have a coal fire. From the beginning of December to the end of January this fire never goes out. Before he goes to bed Dad dampens an old newspaper and places it over the fire and then piles up powdered small coal over the top of it. He then covers the fire with a guard and during the night the coal burns away keeping the sitting room a little warm.

Me and David dread going up to bed in winter time. It's freezing up there. OK, so Dad goes up first to put hot water bottles in our beds so that helps but we undress downstairs first and get into our pyjamas. Next we stand in front of the fire to really warm up and once we are ready we race upstairs and dive into our beds quickly and grab the hot water bottle. We pull the blankets over our heads to keep the freezing cold air out. Even with this you can't help yourself shivering for a few minutes until the bed has warmed up. It's best to stay still then if you can. If you move your leg too far you get into cold territory. Dad comes upstairs a few minutes after we've gone up to put our bedroom light off but he leaves the landing light on.

## Nobody Watching

During the night when the hot water bottle goes cold I push it with my feet to the end of the bed. It's another cold spot to avoid then. When sleep comes it's great so you can forget the cold. In the morning I wake to the sound of Dad poking the fire to get it flaming up. Before Dad converted the upstairs back room to a bathroom twice a week on Wednesday and Sunday he'd fill the bath in front of the fire so me and David can get clean. We were never too happy about this in Winter and always hoped he was going to forget. But once the bathroom was finished me and David dreaded it even more because there's no heat in there. Dad says he's going to put in an electric wall heater. Me and David keep telling him to do it.

When you wake up in Hazelhurst Road in Llandaff North in Winter to test how cold it is you do three things. First you pinch your nose to see how cold the inside of your nose is and then make an O with your mouth and blow out air. If clouds come out you know it's cold. The third thing you do is check the window. If the condensation on the inside has frozen then you know you are in for it.

Dad will kill us if we try to go downstairs without washing face, hands and cleaning teeth. So me and David do that quickly and then shoot downstairs with our clothes to dress in front of the fire. It might be freezing in the bedroom and bathroom but once you get into the sitting room it's warm as toast. You don't notice till you get there that you've been holding your muscles tight to stop the shivering and trembling but once you get through that door you can relax. The fire in the grate warms you right through so much you don't want to be more than two feet away from it if you can help it.

Dad's quieter than usual in the morning. He always seems half asleep as he makes breakfast in the kitchen. We don't have too much, just milky tea, toast and hot porridge with sugar over the top. Dad let's us read comics while we eat breakfast. I told you before he's a great Dad.

Just before school time Dad wakes up a lot and makes sure we get out the door in time for school. Me and David we're not too keen on this idea in December specially when it's raining and windy.

If it's dry we'll play in the school yard before the school secretary comes out with the bell in her hand to ring for assembly. On this day I'm looking forward to school because me and Susan we have everything completed for the school concert. It's coming up soon before we have Christmas holidays. Many of the Mums and a few of the Dads will come to our Assembly and hear us sing and look around at our work. It's an exciting day because it's one of the last days before we break up and everyone is looking forward to Christmas.

At break time I sat with Susan to talk about our plans. I haven't told you much about her have I? Well, you know she has straight blonde hair that's parted in the middle. It's not long but it's not short either. It seems to curl under the sides of her face. She's a little bit shy like me I suppose but has the best smile you've ever seen. Maybe a couple of the girls in the class are prettier but I think Susan is nicer. I've seen the way she looks after the younger kids and cares for her friends when they are upset about something.

She is clever but you'll never see Susan with her hand straight up saying "Me, me" when Mr Cox asks a question. But if he asks her she'll probably know the answer.

What I'm telling you is that I like the way she looks and also I like the way she is with others. Last year I so much wanted to hold her hand and this year it's happened. I guess it sounds stupid to you, right. But I don't care because it means the world to me.

Of course Geoffrey saw us talking at break time and came over with that swanky walk of his. I remembered what Tom had said and tried to keep myself calm. He wanted to know what we were doing as you can guess. What are you up to with your *girlfriend*, he said to me. You know you can hear that sarky sound in his voice. Is crummy Caradog trying to think of a way to beat us? We just smiled and waited for him to go but like I said to you Geoffrey may well be smarmy and a real git (Tom wouldn't like this) but he's not stupid. He'll think of something if we're not careful.

Do you think he knows what we're doing, Susan asked me. I said he probably did but thinks we are wasting our time. We are going to win for a change and that's final.

Something funny happened at the end of school one Friday. Now to be honest I don't get into fights. I'm tall anyway and most people don't want to bother. And I'm not stupid enough to upset some of the hard boys who can easily kick the shit out of you like Philip Bell and Kevin Redbrick. They are ok but hard and it's not a good idea to upset them.

So anyway we were outside school just talking before splitting up and going home when Nigel gives me a shove that almost knocks me over. I looked at him surprised, wondering what was going on and then he pushed me again. If Tom had been around he would have stopped it but he wasn't. If it had been raining that day we wouldn't have hung around outside school but it wasn't. It was cold but dry.

Normally, Nigel doesn't say boo to a goose. I don't think I ever saw him fight before. He can be noisy and laughs a lot and his closest friend in our gang is Alun. His mother is the Akela of Cubs if you remember me telling you. She's strict his mother but Nigel is Ok. He and Alun invent these complicated board games which nobody is interested in playing but themselves unless it's their version of battleships. He's not that special at football or running or any sport but he has a go but as he was shoving me I couldn't see the Nigel I usually see. He was so mad with me over something.

But you know I didn't want to fight him. I kept pushing him back and telling him to stop it and perhaps I should have walked away. Have you ever been around a school fight? It's not really that nice. The two kids who have got themselves into it don't really want to fight and there's a lot of pushing and shoving. But it can be different if one is a bully or much bigger and he knows he can beat the other kid. But most of the time it's not like that. Two kids have had a silly argument and they get angry with each other and their friends push them into a fight. They can't get out of it.

I should have walked away and let the kids who had gathered laugh at me but I couldn't. Nigel was pushing me and pushing me and kids from younger years had turned up to watch. We'd now moved away from the school into Belle Vue Crescent out of the view of school teachers who might be leaving.

I don't think I had a choice or that's what I thought afterwards. He pushed me one time too hard and I fell on my back. The other kids cheered so I got to my feet and I knew the look on my face had changed. Nigel was not my friend any more. He was a kid who had made me look silly in front of my friends and other kids. I don't like fighting and will do a lot to get out of it but he'd pushed me too far.

Watching him I remembered a fight I'd seen in the summer just gone in Hailey Park. It was between two boys who were best friends from our school and just leaving to go to Canton High School. The boys names are Keith Reeves and Stephen Green. They were always together and were at the top of Standard Four when we were in Standard 3. They were great at school work and both brilliant footballers in attack. They scored so many goals for our school team that last year. But for some reason their friendship turned bad and an incident in Hailey Park led to a fight. It was Alf Tupper versus Roy of the Rovers or Georgeous Gus. Steve is a bit on the scruffy side and Keith always looks like a prince. They were an odd couple but they really liked each other and no-one ever found out why they fell out that day.

I watched the fight. Steve was hunched over like a boxer and shuffling towards Keith to try to hit him. Keith was on his toes skipping from one side to the other to dodge Steve's heavy swings. After each swing Keith darted in and did something I'd never seen in a fight before. With his curled fist he rapped Stephen on top of the head. It wasn't a punch to the face or the body, just a very hard rap. I can hear the sound of the crack now. For a while Steve was able to ignore these raps stomping his foot down to move closer to Keith but after fifteen or more of these raps he stopped to clutch his head with both hands. It made me shiver. Then he charged at Keith with fists flying but Keith stepped aside and threw out a fist that rapped Steve again on the side of the head. He fell to the grass holding his head with both hand and rolling from side to side.

It was obvious that the fight was over and Keith walked away. Normally people cheered after a fight but this time they didn't. A couple of Steve's friends stayed with him and everybody else walked away too.

Some time later that summer I saw Keith walking along Station Road and spoke to him. I reminded him about the fight. He didn't look too happy at the memory of it but I asked why he'd rapped Steve on the head the way he did. He shrugged and said it was easier than punching someone in the face. He'd never been able to hit someone in the face properly but the rap was easier. I didn't ask about Steve. Some of the boys said that they'd made friends afterwards but it wasn't the same as before.

It's hard in Llandaff North to stay bad friends with someone. You see them every day and you can't hide away or ignore people for ever. Sooner or late you make it up and get along as best as you can. It always changes things after an argument or a fight. It's like you've taken a chip out of a good cup. Somehow your lip always finds the rough edge and it's like that after you've had a row with a friend. You always feel the rough edge.

So, I now forgot that Nigel was my friend. I forgot there would be a rough edge between us afterwards. Most of all I needed to show him that I would not be pushed around. You know, the awful thing is I knew that I would beat him and that the best thing was to walk away but I could not stand the thought of them chanting "yellow, yellow," if I did so. I feel ashamed.

This time when Nigel charged me I pushed him back hard and he fell back. I told him to stay down and not get up but he wouldn't listen. He charged me again so using my memory of Keith's fight with Steve I rapped him and rapped him and rapped him. I did this until he grabbed his head just like Steve did before. I don't want to go into all of it. In the end Nigel held his head in his hands and did not want to get up.

And you know what I saw out of the corner of my eye. It was Geoffrey bringing Janet and Susan to see what I was doing. I saw a look of pure joy in his face but I didn't see that in Susan's face. She looked hurt. I felt so bad I pretended I didn't see her and walked off home. I didn't even notice that David was trailing me until we go to our house door. He seemed happy. He was copying the way I hit Nigel.

When Dad came home I told him what had happened. A frown came over his face but he patted me on the shoulder. Although he doesn't say too much about it I think Dad was a scrapper when he was a boy. When he'd been to the rugby club one afternoon and came back happy he was thinking about school when he was a boy. He told me and David that he got six of the best on his hand a few times for fighting. He said the best way to take the sting out was to hang onto the cold railings on the school wall.

He said to me, well boys get into fights. Nothing to be done about it but it's not your fight with Nigel that bothers me but the fight I will have with his mother. She'll be around later. But Tom arrived first. News had spread fast about my fight with Nigel and he came to talk to me about it. We went into the front room away from David and Dad. It was freezing in there as it doesn't get heated unless we have visitors. Tom wanted to know how it started. Like me Tom thought it was odd that Nigel would start a fight. He asked me if there was anything I had done to annoy Nigel. You know, I couldn't think of a thing. I wanted to say that I thought Geoffrey had something to do with it but I couldn't. Tom left telling me he'd ask around and see what he could find out.

I had to face the music for sure when Mrs West came to the house. She was so angry. She had called the Doctor for Nigel who had developed a bad migraine because of me. I tried to say sorry and wanted to tell her that Nigel was pushing me but she wouldn't let me. Dad held his hand up for me to stay quiet and he spoke to Mrs West. He said that boys will get into fights as they both knew but he stood up for me saying that he had never known me to cause a fight but only to fight back if somebody went for me. She then shocked me and Dad too. She said that maybe Nigel would not have got so angry if I hadn't said such bad things about her.

They both turned to look at me then. You know I didn't have an idea what they were talking about. It's true I'm no favourite of Mrs West and I'm not too fond of the way she runs cubs but I've never said a word about her to anyone. You know, I went bright red which made me look guilty but I looked her right into the eyes and said I promise I never said anything about you, Mrs West.

I think she wanted to call me a liar as I saw her mouth open and close. If Dad wasn't there I think she would have done. Dad asked if it was possible there was a misunderstanding about all this. She shrugged her shoulders and huffed a bit and then said she'd better go and sit with Nigel. The guilt came all over me again then and I said sorry again and again.

Dad told me not to worry. He said if it was the truth I was telling and he'd always known me to tell the truth then everything would be OK. It still didn't stop me spending the next twenty minutes in the toilet with guilty pains in my stomach forcing me to go. To be honest with you I felt a little bit scared about all this. Nigel thought badly of me, his mother did and by the look on Susan's face she had gone off me too. I sat there on the toilet straining at nothing. I really wondered if it was easier or harder in life as you got older. There are so many things that can go wrong. At Sunday School we had often heard stories of monks who lived in monasteries in silence and lived behind closed walls and saw nobody other than monks. They read books, prayed and worked in their garden. Sometimes to me this seemed like a good thing to do. If you didn't speak you couldn't hurt anybody or get into trouble, could you?

On Saturday morning I still felt awful. Tom came around to the house and said that Nigel was to stay in bed for a couple of days. He didn't stay that long and I knew he could tell that I didn't feel like going out. He told me he wanted to check on a few things. Usually, I would have gone out if the weather was ok and we didn't have a soccer match but I just wanted to sit around the house and read. Even David liked it if I did this. He tries to get me to mess around with Meccano but I can't be bothered. Sometimes he will persuade me into a game of Totopoly or Diplomacy but this day I just wanted to read and keep what had happened out of my head. When I'm like this I'll read "Shadow the Sheepdog". It's a book by Enid Blyton. This dog is just great and makes you wish you had one just like it.

Dad came home around 12 o' clock and he was putting on his "I'm going to cheer you up" face. He'd got the ham I like and cheddar cheese and a steak and kidney pie. He was really trying to get me out of it. I told you, he's the best my Dad.

While he was in the kitchen Aunty Nancy came to the house. You remember, she is Janet's mum who helps us out around the house. She came through the back gate and to the kitchen door so I only knew she was there because I heard her talking to Dad. When I went to the kitchen to see what was going on Dad sent me away and closed the door. I felt that funny feeling in my stomach again and went to the toilet.

I told you Tom is the best of best of friends anyone can have. If it wasn't for him I'd be feeling lousy for weeks. You know what he did when he left me. He went round to Janet's house and got talking to her. In the end she coughed up the truth. It was Geoffrey. He didn't like how pally me and Susan were getting with the younger kids in Caradog, so do you know what the bleeding git did? He got one of the younger kids that he knows to tell Nigel that I thought his mother was a cow and that she was a useless Akela. He wanted to split me and Susan. Janet didn't know about it while were fighting but when Geoffrey saw how upset Susan was about it he thought he'd won. He couldn't stop himself telling Janet.

So you can understand why Nigel went off his rocker.

Now I already told you that she's not on the top of my favourites list but in our village you learn it's not a good idea to say anything bad about anyone. You might think it but keep it in your head. Also, I like Nigel. He's one of my friends and I would never want us to fight. Hah! Never want us to fight. But we did and all because of that bleeder, Geoffrey.

So Janet confesses to Tom and Aunty Nancy gets involved. She goes straight to Nigel's mother to tell her what happened and then my Dad went to Geoffrey's house. Geoffrey's father called him into the room with my Dad and my Dad – so he told me afterwards – asked him straight if he'd got a kid to tell lies about me. Dad said Geoffrey wriggled and that the little kid must have got mixed up about what he meant but Dad said you could see he was trying to get out of it. In the end Geoffrey's father apologized to Dad and told Geoffrey he'd speak to him later. Dad then went to see Nigel's mother and explained things to her. He said no more but he told me to put it all behind me and forget about it. It was a misunderstanding

Most of all I wanted someone to tell Susan that I was innocent. I didn't like the disappointed look on her face. That Saturday afternoon and evening I didn't know what to do until Tom came around. I am eleven years old but if I get to be as old as fifty I hope that Tom is still my friend. He told me he'd gone to see Susan to tell her what really happened. She told him that she was still angry with me for fighting Nigel and he told her what it's like to be a boy who is challenged by another. You want to walk away but you can't. He reminded her that I'd never really been in a fight before only some pushing and shoving. He said that she saw it in the end and was OK now and that I should go visit her on Sunday.

I nodded but I knew there was something else I had to do first. I went to find Dad after Tom left and told him I needed to go out. He looked at me and smiled with that Dad smile that says I know what you're going to do and I like it. Because of course I was going to see Nigel.

Mrs West was different when I knocked the door. She smiled as best she could and let me in and fussed my hair. She said I could go up. Nigel's head was bandaged and I thought I could smell vinegar in the room. I wondered if people really did put vingegar and brown paper on the head after a bang just like in the little kid's nursery rhyme.

You know what? He said sorry before me. Yeah. I told him not to be stupid and said I was the one who was sorry. I should have held on to you until you told me why you wanted to fight me, that's what I said to him. I should never have done what I did. I felt guilty all over again.

He just wanted to forget about it and get back to normal. He switched to talking about Subbuteo and said he wanted to start a league. I smiled and said count me in and David too. David's nuts on

Subbuteo but I knew that none of the other boys would join. They preferred to be out rather than messing about with tiny plastic figures. But joining Nigel's Subbuteo league I hope will make up for my hurting him.

It was all over now. It wouldn't be spoken about again. That was the way it worked in our village. Even back at school it wasn't mentioned. Geoffrey looked away when I stared at him on Monday. He had a face like a smacked arse so I'm sure his Dad had given him what for. He deserved it, the git. His plan did not work and although Susan had a disappointed look on her face for a couple of days, it passed. It made me more determined than ever to beat the bugger.

Parents came to our school on Friday 21$^{st}$ December for the carol service and to look at the stuff we'd done. All the hard work me and Susan put in to help the younger kids really paid off. Course all the judging is done before the carol service but Mr Evans reads the results all through the carol service so you don't know which team has won right until the end.

Hey I'm getting good at doing tables now after all this work with Dad so let me show you the results that came out at the carol service. I put 1st, 2$^{nd}$, 3$^{rd}$ and 4th for each year and show the points and then the overall winners. Not bad, ay??

It's four ponts for 1$^{st}$, 3 for 2$^{nd}$, two for 3$^{rd}$ and 1 for 4$^{th}$. So here's the table and see what you think:

|  | Standard 1 | Standard 2 | Standard 3 | Standard 4 |
|---|---|---|---|---|
| Carols | Caradog Glyndwr Llewellyn Hywel | Llewellyn Cradog Glyndwr Hywel | Caradog Hywel Glyndwr Llewellyn | Glyndwr Caradog Llewellyn Hywel |
| Reading | Caradog Llewellyn Glyndwr Hywel | Caradog Glyndwr Llewellyn Hywel | Glyndwr Caradog Hywel Llewellyn | Caradog Glyndwr Llewellyn Hywel |
| Nativity | Hywel Caradog | Llewellyn Caradog | Caradog Llewellyn | Glyndwr Llewellyn |

|  | Glyndwr | Glyndwr | Glyndwr | Caradog |
|--|---------|---------|---------|---------|
|  | Llewellyn | Hywel | Hywel | Hywel |
| Christmas Card | Caradog | Caradog | Caradog | Glyndwr |
|  | Llewellyn | Glyndwr | Hywel | Hywel |
|  | Hywel | Hywel | Llewellyn | Caradog |
|  | Glyndwr | Llewellyn | Glyndwr | Llewellyn |

Final Scores:

Caradog     55
Glyndwr     42
Llewellyn   35
Hywel       28

See, the plan worked, we won but I know you're dying to check my arithmetic so go on. See if you can find a mistake!!

At the end of the Carol service Mr Evans announced the final result and called me and Susan up to take the trophy. It had our blue ribbons on it. It would stay in the school hall now with the blue ribbons on until March. I hope they stay blue after the St David's Day competition. The Caradog captains in the younger classes came rushing up to me and Susan at the end. They were so pleased and so were me and Susan. I didn't dare look at Geoffrey's face though cos I guessed he would not be happy. I couldn't trust myself to look in case I smiled with too much victory. Round 1 to us.

Dad was at the concert and he looked really pleased too. He came to find me while I was holding the trophy with Susan and feeling proud of the blue ribbons. Susan's mum and dad came up too. I felt a bit shy at this as I didn't really know Susan's parents and it's stupid I know but I felt guilty being Susan's boy friend. Maybe her mum and dad wouldn't like it. I felt a bit scared to be honest and must have been looking nervous. But I shouldn't have worried. Susan's mother just simply asked Dad if it would be ok for me to go their place to have tea now that me and Susan were closer friends. You know, I think she smiled and winked at Dad when she said closer friends so I realized it was all ok. Great! So after all the talking was done me and Susan left with her mum and

## Nobody Watching

Dad. When we got through the school gates Susan held my hand. I didn't know what to do. It was great to hold hands but I was really scared her mum and dad would turn around and see us. But they didn't look back and thank God it's only a short walk from the school to their place in Station Road. It was so good to be there. David would have liked it too because of a mum being around. After a while Susan's sister, Jackie, got back from Canton High School. Jackie is a couple of years older and in Form 2 at Canton High School. She teased us a bit when she saw us together but I could see that Jackie is as nice as her sister.

She told us she hoped we would come to Canton High School too. I wished she hadn't opened this one up. It reminded me of the 11 plus and Glantaf and everything changing. I liked it sat here with Susan and her family eating jam sandwiches and watching Blue Peter and being together and you know, keeping things as they are. But you can't can you. You just can't.

At 7 o'clock I said goodbyes and left. Susan walked down the stairs with me to her front door. We kissed on the lips for the first time. It was quick and we both giggled afterwards but it felt good. I ran all the way home in the cold but I didn't feel it and I was looking forward to seeing my Dad and David too. In fact I would have been happy to see anyone.

But let me tell you something funny that happened when I kissed Susan. I had this funny but nice feeling that came ….now you're not going to laugh at this are you….it came from my around my willy and my willy seemed to grow a bit. OK sometimes I wake up in the morning and it's stiff and when I'm on a bus it goes stiff too. What's it mean. I bet you know. It's this Facts of Life thing isn't it. There's something more to it than I saw in those books, isn't there? There's something I'm missing but how do you find it out. Is there something you can read to tell you or have you just got to find it out on your own. You know, don't you. How did you find out? Everything's a secret, isn't it, like I said.

Last day of Autumn term before Christmas was, brhhh!!! Freezing!! Did I tell you it was cold in December? It was so cold that we stopped playing football over at Hailey Park. The ground was getting too frozen and then on the night of 22 December it got really cold. Me and David are complaining to Dad that we need a heater in the bedroom. You want to see the ice on our window. And it's inside and thick. You know I think he might do it. I think he's finding it colder than usual too.

You think I've forgotten to tell you, don't you. Well I been keeping it a secret of course. Even from Dad, David and Tom but I saved all the money I got from Vince and pocket money that Dad gave me and yes I got a locket for Susan and a Christmas card. On Christmas Eve I walked over to her house and knocked the door. I had my hands behind my back of course and when she came to the door I smiled, said Happy Christmas and gave her the wrapped up package. Of course I wished I'd done a better job on the packing but it didn't look too bad. Susan hugged me which was great and ran back upstairs and down again quickly with a package for me. We both promised not to open until Christmas Day. We kissed quickly hearing Jackie coming to the top of the stairs and I ran home full of happiness again.

\* \* \* \* \* \* \*

I'm writing this now on 27 December 1962. It's been bloody cold over Christmas. Dad bought two paraffin heaters, one for our bedroom and another for the landing. He told us to be very careful. It's made a big difference.

Christmas. Well ours is not like others I think. It's just me, Dad and David. Aunty Nancy always invites us to be with them but Dad never wants to. He says he just wants to be with his boys. And you know he's really good and gets the party going. He cooks a great Christmas dinner. We have Turkey with sage and onion stuffing, bacon wrapped round little sausages, roast potatoes, mash potatoes, swede, carrots, peas, all of it. And Aunty Nancy gives us one of her special Christmas puddings which has a few silver sixpences in it. Me and David fight over those of course. We are really stuffed afterwards.

But I'm rushing this too much. Let me tell you what happens. For us Christmas starts on Christmas Eve and Dad doesn't work this day. For David Christmas has started long before. I've already told you he counts the days from June but around the beginning of December he starts his search for where Dad has hidden our gifts. He started doing this when he realised that they came from Dad and not Santa. I don't know why he does this. In the beginning Dad didn't expect him to search and so he left them in easy places but once he noticed that David was picking the sellotape to have a peek inside he got craftier where he hid it. But this year he didn't bring them home until 23rd December and it drove David nuts searching everywhere. Good old Dad. He had a good joke on us.

Christmas Eve morning Dad took us into town when I got back from seeing Susan. It's really good with the Christmas decorations up in Queen Street and on the Castle. They are everywhere. Everyone in the street is happy and smiling and calling out Merry Christmas. Dad says the pubs will be full at lunch time and in the afternoon they'll be singing and dancing in the streets and a lot more. But we do the usual which is go to the market and then to the Sandringham. It's great being with Dad on Christmas Eve.

I'd like to be in town when people are coming out of the pubs. I've seen some of the blokes coming out of the rugby club and the Railway. I like the way they sing but Dad made us come home well before that.

In the afternoon we went to Aunt Nancy's house. We've done this for the last couple of Christmases and it's nice. Dad chats to Aunty Nancy and Uncle Ron and us kids play games. This year was a bit different and maybe you guessed it. Yeah Geoffrey was there. I still just don't understand why Janet has hooked up with him. Anyway, I acted as if nothing had happened and so did everyone else. And I didn't even mention that we smashed Glyndwr at the Christmas concert. I thought David was going to say something but I gave him a kick and he kept quiet.

When we left with Dad around 6 o'clock I glanced back just in time to catch the crafty git giving me a sneer. He knew I'd seen him but I just looked at Janet and wished her Merry Christmas. I'll get him. I'll get him.

At 9 o clock we went over to Aunty Margaret and Uncle Charles house so we could stay and watch telly with Tom and his brother and sister. Of course Dad is going down the pub with Uncle Charles and a few of the other blokes. We watched some carol services on telly that night. It was good and of course Dad and Uncle Charles came back about 11 o clock singing Christmas Carols. But they weren't quite as good as the choirs on the telly. Why are Dads always so funny when they go to the pub together, and they usually give you money afterwards too.

It was bloody cold on the way back to the house. Thank God Dad had put the heaters on upstairs. Even though David was trying to talk to me I was asleep in seconds. I'm not as keen as him to wake so early now. A couple of years ago David would be awake every ten minutes to check if Dad (Santa Claus) had put the sacks at the bottom of the bed. Once he got me up at quarter to two. I think the sherry he'd sneaked off Aunty Margaret might have been helpful because he didn't wake me till four o' clock. Four o' clock. And even though I was dying to go on sleeping I got up with him and we took the sacks down stairs. It wasn't so bad once I'd poked the fire and got it going.

David is always half way through his stuff before I even get going. There is a pile of Christmas wrapping paper around but he does put the games and boxes of soldiers in a neat pile.

I just hope mine is mostly books and annuals like the Eagle, Hotspur, Hornet, Beano. If there's any soldiers amongst the parcels it's straight over to David. But suddenly he produces this long really good looking plastic sword, like a rapier. I say gissalook and he tosses it over to me.

During the week we'd watched some film or other where there were a lot of musketeers or cavaliers and one dressed all in black with flowing blonde hair and a golden beard. Before he killed them all he took out this rapier and bent it right over and let it twang back and then got into the fighting. So I sprang to my feet and called out, avast you varlets and bent it in two. Of course I then realized that metal bends better than plastic and the bloody thing snapped in half at the centre. I thought David was going to murder me with the broken end and it took two chocolate oranges and a box of soldiers to calm him down.

Pity I broke that sword I muttered half to David and half to myself. I could have challenged Geoffrey to a duel and skewered the bugger. David didn't hear me because he was distracted by meccano so I put the sword to one side, piled up the books for reading and went to the kitchen to make me, Dad and David cups of tea. I gave David a hug as I went past mostly to knock him off while he was doing a tricky bit on the meccano. It was Christmas day so he didn't get up to fight me, not really sure if I did it on purpose anyway.

Dad doesn't get up with us On Christmas Day. He likes to lie in until about 9 but I still take him a cup of tea with a few biscuits. He likes McVities digestives. He really likes to have this brought to him and a refill as well after half an hour. Me and David we pretend we haven't got him anything for a while but Dad knows the game and plays along. This year we bought him a big bottle of Old Spice after shave. It was David's idea. I think he wants Dad to wear a lot of it so he smells good. I wonder why? Can you guess?

So anyway, we had Christmas with Dad to look forward to. Loads of good telly from 9 o clock and stacks of food. It was a great day. Sometimes I wish we had Christmas holidays going on much longer so Dad is with us and there's no school and we watch telly and eat turkey for days. It's always too short and Dad has to go back to work and we have to go back to school.

But this year I don't mind. I still got my duel with Geoffrey and time with Susan.

You know it's true there's things I don't mind but also there's things I worry about. As I keep telling you in a while we take the 11 plus. This scares me. Last night I was walking in my sleep. I didn't know anything about it. Dad found me at 2 o' clock in the morning downstairs in the kitchen in the dark with progress papers on arithmetic in front of me. I was working on it in the dark. He told me about it in the morning. I don't remember it at all.

But you know why I'm scared don't you. I'm scared I will fail it and all the others will pass. I don't want to be on my own in Glantaf. I don't want to be in Glantaf at all. I'm scared that Susan and Tom will be in other schools and I will lose my friends. I don't want to lose my friends.

Wow, we woke up today on 29 December and you should see the snow. There'll be no going out today. It's a blizzard out there. Dad kept listening to the radio and later the telly and he told us that the snow was 20 feet deep in places. Some trains had stopped running and many roads you couldn't use. It looks so white from the window and deserted. When the snow stops me and David will go out with all the boys and make snowballs and build snowmen. I'm going to take a sneak look at the river as you never know it might be frozen, but I'd be in deep trouble if I tried to walk on the ice, and stupid too.

I just wish we had leather gloves to play in the snow. We got those woollen ones. It's OK to start with because you're busy grabbing the snow and throwing snow balls and making the snowman. While you're doing this the woollen gloves are getting wet but cos you're busy it doesn't matter. But then you stop and the melted snow starts to freeze on your gloves. You have to throw your gloves off fast, put your hands together like you're going do an owl hoot and blow air from your mouth through them. They're still going to ache like hell but it's worse if you don't. OK, so you can buy me those fancy leather gloves for Christmas. Good idea but all my pals will laugh at me!!

After Christmas Day and Boxing Day is over, I don't know why but you feel a bit down. I guess it's all the thinking of the presents you're going to get and all the excitement for just one day then it's over.

Me and Susan we got invited to Aunt Nancy's House on New Year's Eve in the day time. She invited David too and of course Janet was there with Geoffrey. I wasn't looking forward to it too much because I'm finding it very difficult with Geoffrey. I been thinking about it a lot. I know we're very different. He likes Elvis, I like the Beatles. He puts Brylcreem in his hair and I don't. He looks in windows to see if he's looking OK and I don't. But you know I still can't really understand why he's causing a problem for me. There must be something I've done but really I don't know what. Like I said before I thought it was because of Susan but that's not it. So what is it?

To be honest all through the day at Aunt Nancy's it was OK. It was like a truce was on. We played loads of monopoly, cluedo, snakes and ladders and ludo and for a laugh we put on Listen with Mother. You know dum ti dum, dum ti dum. Are you sitting comfortably, then I'll begin. Aunt Nancy kept us going with plenty of food. Her mince pies are just great.

Geoff was smiling and laughing and having fun with us and he wasn't so swanky. You know we had a good time. You see, I don't really like to be bad friends with someone. I don't like it if someone doesn't like me. I want everyone to like me. So with Geoffrey being good fun and not nasty I liked him a lot more. I even smacked him on the back when we left about 6. Susan was really happy that we had such a good time. I think the argument between me and Geoffrey was causing problems between her and Janet. So when we left she was smiling and so happy as I walked her home. I let David come with us too and didn't even mind his snigger which he turned into a cough when me and Susan held hands. Course when we got to her door I just had to say goodbye. I wasn't going to kiss Susan in front of my brother.

When we walked back home and we did it quickly because it was freezing, David said something interesting. See the thing with David is that he can stay quiet for long periods playing on his own. He brought a whole load of soldiers and meccano with him to Aunt Nancy's and so sometimes he played monopoly and sometimes he didn't. He played on his own. So he said to me on the way home, he still doesn't like you, you know. So I said how do you know? He said, because I see how he looks at you when he thinks no-one is looking.

We stay home with Dad on New Year's Eve. OK he does slip out for a couple of beers with Uncle Charles for an hour or so but he's always back at the house by 11. Funny thing is the telly's not so good on New Year's Eve. For the last couple of hours it switches to some Scottish hog and hay show. It's all men in kilts and women in tartan stuff dancing and singing. Anyway we get the Auld Lang Syne at midnight which is not so bad. After that we open the front door even though it's still bloody cold but we do put our coats and gloves on. Everyone is in the street dancing, singing and calling out Happy New Year. Dad always takes a few pieces of coal from the bucket by the fire, The other Dads do it as well and you can see them crossing the street and bringing a piece of coal to a neighbour's house. Dad calls it first footing and says it brings luck for the year to a neighbour's home.

Anyway, whatever it is it's a laugh to see everyone in the street full of snow having fun, singing and dancing and crazy Dads taking coal to houses. Me and David went out into the street to join in. Jack was there, Alun, Janet and a few others. We messed around with snow. One caught me hard on the side of the face when I wasn't looking. It was snow on the outside but there was a hard piece of ice on the inside. I turned quickly and did I see Geoffrey skip behind a few people. Yes, I think I did.

As we got back inside Dad hugged both me and David. Happy New Year, he said. We said it back. Happy New Year. I would do all my best to make sure it was just that.

\* \* \* \* \* \* \*

*JP's Note: Boys will always fight. That hasn't changed – but central heating has made sure the house is warm everywhere. That big freeze of 62-63 was terrible and with no central heating? I would have died. They were made of tougher stuff then.*

# CHAPTER 6
## *January 1963*

We went back to School on Monday 7 January. Me and David ran all the way from the house to school. It was freezing. Big clouds of steam came from our mouths while we were running and we had to be careful we didn't slip. David wanted to stop to break ice patches but I wouldn't let him. I just wanted to get close as possible to those big hot radiators in the school, so hot they burn to the touch. Lovely!!

Mind you, even though it's freezing cold somehow they managed to clear off the snow at Cardiff Arms Park for Wales and get the ground soft so that Wales could play England at Rugby. I wish they hadn't. We Welsh don't like getting beat by the Saesneg at rugby. We don't mind so much if it's Scottish or Irish but when it's the English it's painful. We lost 6-13. I watched some of it on the telly on Saturday afternoon but when I saw we were losing I went to the kitchen and made toast. This always cheers you up. Well, there's always next year, right?

When we got back you know you could feel something was different at school straight away. Mr Cox wasn't bothering with any of the usual stuff we used to do just keeping us working on things for the 11 plus exam.

I told you before didn't I what we had to work on. Remember it was mental arithmetic, an essay and general reasoning. Well we went over this stuff again and again and spelling test after spelling test.

I always got on with Mr Cox ok. He could be serious and doesn't laugh too much but he always lets us get a bit noisy at times until he decides to stop it. He wasn't as kind as Mr Rees who we had in Standard 3 but nobody was really scared of him either. Sometimes a teacher singles out one boy and one girl as their favourites. They thought they didn't let on but everyone could tell. They always get the nice jobs or involved with something special. You had to give it to old Coxy he didn't have any favourites at all. He could be a bit moody and quiet sometimes and even get angry a bit but he made you think about things and I like the things he taught us.

So I was really shocked and I'll be very honest with you I don't know how I stopped myself from crying this day. Mr Cox has his own way of putting you in desks. When we started we sat where we liked but after a week or so he worked out who needed most help or was a trouble maker. Then he rearranged us so that those he could keep an eye on were in the front. I was in the back row in the middle at a double desk sat next to Tom. There are three rows with six double desks. Either side of me and Tom are Geoffrey and Jack on the left and Gaynor and Catherine on the left. In front of me and Tom are Susan and Janet. Susan is on the left hand side so I get a good look at her pretty face when the lessons are easy to follow. I think she knows I'm looking. Can you feel someone looking at you, do you think. While I'm watching her I can see a smile begin to make its way on to her face and then she quickly turns to look at me. I'm never quick enough and I always blush and with me a blush is deep red.

But anyway I was telling you about Mr Cox. I've never really got into trouble with him. Ok a little while ago me and Tom got told off for larking about when we were on milk duty, sorting out the crates of milk for each class. He was really angry that we were hanging about instead of getting back to class but it was nothing serious.

So any way, old Coxy sets us a test. It's a spelling test and it's a tough one but not that tough for a boy who reads at least three books a week. We get down to number 17 out of 20 and so far I know I've got the previous 16 right. He comes out with auxiliary. Well you know this is a tough one. Even a grown up can leave out the second i because you can hardly hear it when it's said. In fairness to old Coxy he pronounces each letter like it never is when you say it. So he says aux – il – i – ary. But it can still catch a load of people out. I write it down and look around to see who's struggling. To my surprise Geoffrey is stabbing at the paper with his finger. He looks at me and points at the paper with his finger and nods for me to look. Well stupid me, I go and do it leaning over to see what he's up to.

"Gareth, put a line where that word is as you cannot copy from Geoffrey. You know that."

Old Coxy got me and so did Geoffrey. Suddenly, the whole class looked to see what was going on and did I look guilty. My face was burning red letting everybody see I must have done something wrong. Susan looked at me in disbelief. Tom just stared and Geoffrey looked like a surprised innocent lamb.

I'd been framed good and proper.

"Finish the test then come and see me," Old Coxy said and his face looked angry.

I can't remember what the next three words were but I knew I got them right. It was the first time in a spelling test that I'd not got 20 out of 20 for as long as I could remember. At the end of it Old Coxy gathered the papers and then gave essay work so we could start thinking about writing for the 11 plus exam. Once he'd done it he called me to his desk. I stood right in front of the desk and not at the side. If I stood at the side all the kids would see my face and I knew it was going to go very red. I just wanted to hide that.

Now I remember it happening like this:

"Why did you cheat, Gareth. It's not like you."
"I didn't. It must have looked like it but I didn't."
"You were leaning over to look at his paper"

I shrugged my shoulders. I could see what it looked like. I'd never felt this experience before when you tell the truth but nobody believes you. Has it happened to you? You know people can look at it in a bad way but they could also look at it in the way it happened, but they will just not believe you.

Then I remembered.

"Why would I want to cheat, Mr Cox? You gave this word in a test about six weeks ago and I got it right. Please look in my spelling book."

It was very quiet behind me. I can't believe any of them were writing, but just listening to what was going on between me and Old Coxy. I have to give it to old Coxy he did reach for my spelling book and flick backwards through the pages till he found the test with auxiliary in it. He stared at the book for a bit and I could see he was thinking.

"You forgot how to spell it then and copied from Geoffrey."

My mouth opened wide and I just looked at him. My face got redder and redder. I couldn't really speak properly. When I did it was like a whisper and I was swallowing a lot and getting the words out slowly.

"I didn't…… Mr Cox you know………I never get………a word wrong…….once I know it….I never forget…..I never…….cheated"

"But I saw you looking"

"I…never…..cheated" I was getting redder and redder and feeling terrible. Always I had been believed before. I could be naughty but if I did something wrong I owned up to it. I expected Old Coxy to believe me when I told him something. I didn't expect him not to. And there was no way I could say Geoffrey tricked me into looking."

And then worst of all I felt my bottom lip start to tremble. I was going to cry in front of the whole class. This is the worst thing that could happen to anyone in Standard 4. What was the matter with me?

"Go, sit outside Mr Evan's office. We'll deal with you later. Go on, go."

I hung my head in shame and left the classroom turning my head away from everyone so that they could not see that my face was quivering and moving all over the place to try and stop me from crying. I can't wait until I grow up so I won't cry any more. And as I left the classroom I felt I hated Old Coxy and that I hated Geoffrey even more. They had both done this to me. I'd never been shamed like this before. Never been a quivering wreck in front of the whole class. I'd seen it before of course with other kids and I always said it would never happen to me. But it did. It bloody…….well……did.

To be fair, afterwards Tom said that nobody could see what was going on but were really surprised that I was sent out. He said it was possible that Old Coxy sent me out so nobody would see me getting upset. I didn't want to believe this but I had to say it was possible.

I sat on the chair outside Mr Evan's office and tried to recover. I tried to put it all out of my mind and started reading the instructions on the red fire extinguisher on the wall outside his office. After twenty readings I reckoned I knew what to do and I was calming down. It was then that Mr Evans came out and saw me.

He was surprised I could see. He liked me I knew that. Mr Evans did have favourites and he liked to pick me to do readings like I told you before and if he came to our class he would ask me questions. He made you feel good inside. Do you know what I'm talking about?

"Have you brought a message for me, Gareth?"

I shook my head.

"Then what are you doing here, boy? You haven't done something wrong, have you?"

I thought the fire extinguisher had sorted me out but the bleeding thing had not. His soft, kind way of talking got my face doing the jumps again. But Mr Evans is a good bloke and he didn't want me blubbing in full view either.

He told me to sit in his office and wait for him. And you know what five minutes later he brought two cups of tea, one for me and one for him. He must have put about four sugars in mine. It was sweet and great. He didn't ask me anything until I'd finished most of it.

"So what happened, Gareth"

I told him and I explained that yes I'd looked over but it was not my plan to copy Geoffrey's work and I could see why Mr Cox would think so but I could spell auxiliary in my sleep and most of all I would never cheat because I like to get things right without help and everyone in the class knows this even Mr Cox and I can't understand why nobody will believe me because I don't cheat.

It all came out in a rush see just like that. I went on drinking my tea to get more of that sugar inside me.

"I believe you". This is what he said and I almost dropped the cup.

"You do. Why? Nobody else does."

"It's a misunderstanding, Gareth. These things happen. You'll see more of it when you get older. People see something and make an assumption."

Funny thing is as he said that word I saw Mr Cox in my mind saying ass –ump – shun. He'd given us that once the week before. I smiled to myself.

"See, you're feeling better already" Mr Evans said mistaking my smile for something else. I grinned back at him though because I was feeling better. He believed me. See what I mean about him making you feel good inside.

The bell rang for break. These days they gave us a choice. You could walk about in the school yard but no running because of the ice and snow or you could stay in the hall. I waited to see what Mr Evans wanted me to do.

"Get your coat and go outside for a while. It'll be fine when you come back."

When I got outside most of the boys were around the milk crate with coat and gloves on. Geoffrey looked up and saw me coming, glugged his milk and walked off. Ruddy git!! It was bloody cold. I can take milk in the winter from the crate because it's not warm. In the summer the sun warms it and it's disgusting. God knows why but there's always a fight over the bottle in the crate which has got sukie sunkap written on it. It was supposed to be for orange juice but sometimes they got it mixed up at the milk place. I took a bottle today but drank it as fast as I could and put a pear drop that had been hanging round in my pocket for about a week to get rid of the milky taste.

The boys were looking at my face of course to see if I had been crying. Well as I told you it was a close thing. Tom said that Old Coxy was very quiet after I left and kept looking at my spelling book and towards Geoffrey. He said that he knew I didn't cheat. Jack Sims was by the milk crate so I called out to him.

"Did you see what happened, Jack"

He shook his head. It was a long shot. With Jack's thick glasses he puts his head very close to his work. Anyway I guessed if he'd seen anything he'd probably want to keep out of it. I looked around and saw Geoffrey heading for the boys toilets. I said to Tom and Jack I needed a piss and headed straight for it. Geoffrey must have been desperate because nobody takes a crap at school unless they really have to and especially not in freezing cold winter. The doors won't lock, the paper is like grease proof paper and sometimes not even that is there. I took a piss and looked round to see which door was closed. Because most kids kicked the door open if it was closed so they could laugh at you taking a crap. No-one sat down. The trick was to hold your bum above the seat and lean forward and hold the door with one hand to stop the buggers kicking it open. You didn't want a long job in there for sure.

I pushed the door that was closed a little bit with one hand. Sure enough I felt it pushed back and Geoffrey called out "Bugger off or I'll kick your 'ead in when I get out."

"Why did you drop me in it, Geoff?" I called out to him.

He stayed quiet. I could hear him straining to get the shit over as quickly as possible. The thing is you can't shit and talk at the same time.

"I didn't." He grunted trying to both shit and talk. It didn't sound like he was having much luck.

"You know you did." I called out and moved back to get more room to kick the door. I lashed at it with my foot and the door sprang open pushing Geoff down on to the seat. I knew it would be freezing cold on that seat but once you're caught like that you don't stand up.

I laughed when I saw him. He was hunched over with one hand between his legs shielding his willy. His pants were round his ankles and he looked stupid.

I walked away calling out "Get your mother to wash your pants. Those skid marks look dangerous."

I felt better as I walked back to join Tom and the others. Tom looked at me, raised an eyebrow but without saying anything. He'd seen Geoff go to the boys bogs too. I just winked and smiled. Then the school secretary came out to ring the bell to get us back to class.

I felt different straight away. Leaving Geoff in the bogs with his pants down covering his willy had made me laugh but at the sound of that bell I got butterflies in my belly. You're grown up right? You know sometimes when I'm writing this I wish that you'd leave notes at the side for me to help me. Funny, uh? What I mean is you know all the answers, don't you. You're probably reading this and been through most of the stuff I've been through. Wouldn't it be great if you could leave me a note that I could read and know what to do. Are you shouting at the page saying do this son, or don't do that kid. Or maybe just nodding saying I wouldn't know what to do there either.

You see the thing is when you are a kid you are afraid. You know that? No, I mean you're more than afraid you are terrified. You know the way that I see it when I think about it sometimes? It's like as a kid you're in a canoe going along the early part of the river. It's shallow and there's rocks on the bottom and sandbars or whatever you call them and rocks sticking up out of the water and the water is taking the canoe very fast. You spend all you're time avoiding the dangers and your eyes are everywhere.

That's what it's like as a kid. You're small and without somebody to defend you a lot of the time. If you're out you panic if a strange gang of boys comes along, you're scared you won't understand stuff at school, you're scared something will happen to your Dad and you'll be on your own and you're scared you'll fail the 11 plus and go to Glantaf. You're scared of going to Canton High School if you do pass the eleven plus and you're scared of growing up in case you can't do what grown ups have to do. All these fears and worries and you know when you're in that canoe trying to make it through the rapids you can see the river way ahead wider and going slower. It looks so much easier up ahead but I think you just hope you can get there. Sometimes I think I'll be stuck in the rapids forever. Did you think like this? I guess you're taking it easy through that slow moving river right now. Hey! But what happens at the end. Maybe that's your big fear, uh, reaching the end of the river.

So maybe you got your fears too but they're different ones. I have to think about this.

Anyway, like I said the bell rang. Suddenly my guts got the wobblies like I told you and I dragged my feet to the class.

And nothing happened.

To be honest I was expecting Old Coxy to have a go at me but he acted like nothing had happened. I didn't want to look at him right in the face but I sneaked looks at him when he was busy at the blackboard and he seemed Ok. It's a funny thing sometimes you have a really big fear that things are going to get worse and then it all just disappears.

At lunch break Susan asked me what happened. I told her the truth and about what happened with Mr Evans when I got sent out. She squeezed my hand and said that she knew I hadn't done anything. She also said that she saw Mr Cox and Mr Evans talking at the milk break. She said that Old Coxy did not look happy at first but then started rubbing his chin and nodding to Mr Evans. She asked me why Geoffrey was being so nasty to me. Had I done anything to him recently. You know I can't think of a thing. Yeah, I know I told you many times I don't like him too much but I've not done anything other than yes....we beat him at Christmas. Would he do this just because we won? Yeah, I reckon he would. He's trying hard to get between me and Susan and me and the younger kids in Caradog. I told all this to Susan and I could see that it was making her think.

Sheesh, it will be good to be grown up and be with people who don't play silly games on other people and act like kids.

You know that afternoon Geoffrey was glancing at old Coxy and at me. I could see he didn't know what was going on. He couldn't understand why it had all blown over. I felt like shouting at him — Because some people can tell when the truth is being told pal, some people can tell.

And thank God I thought to myself.

You know next day Susan was a bit angry and she doesn't get angry too much. Janet didn't know what to believe and Susan had told her that Janet knew me better than anyone. She should know that I hadn't cheated. But Janet told Susan that Geoffrey said I'd got away with it because Pop Evans liked me too much. If not I would have been in big trouble.

You see Geoffrey is clever. It sounds possible, doesn't it. It could be what happened if you wanted to believe it. It seems more to me these days that truth is really just what you want to believe. You think so too?

I told Susan that we'd have it out with Geoffrey at cubs that night. We all meet up where Hazelhurst Road meets Station Road and the walk to All Saints Church together. Tom comes to me first and we meet Geoffrey and Alun on the way. We stopped outside my house.

Look, I said. I don't know what's got into Geoffrey but twice now he's tried to make me look bad. Tom nodded. OK, I'll talk to him when no-one's around. You and him wanna win this competition so much. It's crazy. We met Geoffrey half way down Hazelhurst road. He was cheery and joking and laughed with Tom. Me, I couldn't hardly raise a smile. We met Alun and the rest of the gang and went off to cubs.

There weren't too many of us at Cubs. It was cold and windy with lots of snow and ice on the ground. Half the kids didn't turn up. Akela got us practicing knots and kept us all close to the stove. Akela, Bagheera and Baloo were making loads of hot drinks for us. They brought hot roast chestnuts too. It was great and they didn't work us too hard but just let us have some fun. I used to like tying the reef knot over and over but now I enjoy doing tougher ones like the sheepshank, clove hitch, sheet bend and bowline. It's even better when I get a chance to try them on my brother!! Only joking, honest.

*Nobody Watching*

While I was working on the sheepshank I noticed Geoffrey get up to take a break outside. Tom got quickly to his feet and followed him. When they came back Geoffrey was redfaced and it's not often you see him like that. This is my special sport. He was rubbing his belly too.

There's nothing much that gets passed Akela and she was on it like a shot.

Are you ok, Geoffrey?

She looked between Tom and Geoffrey to see if something had happened. You could tell she could smell something was wrong. You're out of the gang if you snitch on anyone so we were all pretty sure that Nigel had kept his gob shut on many of the things we'd been doing.

Just feeling a bit sick, Miss, Geoffrey answered rubbing his belly more. Akela told him to sit to one aside and brought him a hot drink. While this was going on Tom knelt by me pretending to look at the knots I'd been working on.

I think it's over now, Gareth, he said to me.

Why, did you whack him one.

Tom just tapped the side of his nose with one finger, telling me to stay out of it. Later Geoffrey came over and tapped my shoulder. He was holding out his little finger on the right hand. I put mine out as well and we locked little fingers giving them a big shake together. This was supposed to mean the fight between us was over. I knew that Geoffrey had been forced by Tom to do this but I wasn't sure looking at Geoffrey's face if he really meant it. You could never tell with him.

But it's a funny thing, you know about kids. I look around our classroom at the boys and girls in it who I've known all my life. I know who I am better at in class and who is better than me. I know that I am a bit better than Tom in schoolwork and he often asks me questions on things he's not sure of. But......But Tom has something which I have not got. Remember I told you about Bob Cherry in the Billy Bunter books and Martin Conisby? Well Tom is like this. Kids in the class look up to him and most grown ups like him too. The kids do what he says and they smile when he tells them what to do. I know most of the kids like me and the ones in the younger classes certainly do but when Tom speaks to them their faces shine. He has no problem asking them to do anything.

I've known this about Tom for a long while and once I asked Dad about it. He knows I like Tom a lot and I already told you that Dad likes Tom. I found it hard to explain it to Dad but he got what I was talking about straight away. He smiled and said to me, so you've noticed this as well.

"Well," he said to me." I could use a lot of big words to explain it but you'll be using them yourself one day. Tom has got a power that's like charm mixed with authority. If those big business tycoons could make a pill which you took to get it, they'd make a fortune."

He laughed in a funny way. "I certainly don't have this charm which Tom has got but you might have it, son. It comes out at different times in different people. Tom has it now and he uses it in a good way. Not everybody does."

What Dad said made me think. He was right. As I looked around more and more at the kids in school and the teachers and other grown ups I could see that some had this thing, this charm and others just did not. Like in school Mr Evans has it for sure but Old Coxy does not even though he's not bad. I'm going to look out for it more and more because the kids who have it seem to have more friends and less fights with others. Maybe I'll learn something. What do you think??

Not long after the cubs night I was on milk duty with Philip Thomas at school. He's not a big talker Phil. Yeah, not like you I can hear you thinking. Ok, but I gotta tell you something I talk a lot more in my head than I do out loud. You got me.

Me and Phil on milk duty doesn't happen all that often as me and Tom usually team up but Old Coxy wanted Tom to do something else. I like Phil. He's not a big talker but he's a big laugher and a huge smiler. You tell a joke when Phil is around he really loves it and his laugh gets everyone else laughing too. He lives with his mum and dad and younger brother in Caldy Road so it's on the other side of Llandaff North from most of our gang. I've no idea how our gang formed. It seemed to happen when we were in the infants. Phil was in it then and he's in it now and he always will be. He's in the cubs, I told you that right? Well, there's always a battle between me and Phil during "bob a job" time. You know, no-one can beat him. I've tried. I thought I'd managed it last year. It didn't look as if Phil was being so busy on it at all but wham he came in with the biggest total. Phil's mum and Dad came from the West Indies and his Dad works as a bus driver. Phil talks like us with a "Caadiff" accent but his mum and dad talk this sing song like English, "you know marn". It's nice but sometimes the lingo is hard to understand.

Phil's in the choir of course and he's a really good singer. It's nice to watch his mum and dad in their Sunday best in the congregation. Sunday morning communion service is always full and Phil's mum and dad come early and sit three rows from the front. When we sing the hymns you can hear them over everybody and they look really happy while they're singing but they are the only ones who sway from side to side while singing. Everybody else is stood straight with a serious look on their face. Sometimes I look at them so happy while they are singing that it brings out a good feeling in me. You know they look like a bright dab of colour on a white sheet of paper. And they are the only family in our village who come from another country. Well Ok there's some who come from England or Ireland but that doesn't really count does it. There house is full of colour too and with lots of music and laughter but don't have the hot sauce on your meat sandwich. Wow, is it hot!!

But we could have done with that hot sauce on milk duty. It's still a bloody cold January so we're going as quick as we can to finish the job and Phil is having fun pushing the crates around the school yard for each class. When we're nearly finished he says,

So does it bother you that I am coloured.

I looked at him and my mouth dropped open.

I don't know what you mean, I said. Why would it bother me, Phil. You're my mate. I never even think about it. And what difference does it make anyway?

It makes a difference in America, he said looking down and kicking at a lump of ice that had fallen off one of the crates. Aren't you watching the news with your Dad?

When he mentioned it I remembered some things about it. But I don't know if it's he same with you but I don't really think about things going on in other countries. Sometimes on the news you see pictures of fighting, kids not getting enough food, big storms and floods but because it's not happening in Llandaff North I don't think about it. My worries are when will this bloody cold winter be over.? Will the big kids from Whitchurch come down looking for a fight? Will that git Geoffrey win the trophy for Glyndwr? Will Dad come home from work safe and sound? Will the mormons knock on the door and give me a sermon? Will I get stuck in the middle of Hailey park on my own when a loose dog comes chasing after me and most of all will I fail the eleven plus and get my head stuffed down the toilet at Glantaf? Now these are real worries, I can tell you!!

So anyway I said to Phil that I didn't really know much about it. Phil got a bit mad and if you know Phil you know he never ever gets mad. He's always laughing and smiling like I told you. He told me I should think about it because it's really important. He told me that when His mum and dad came to Britain his uncle went to New York in the United States of America. He's a taxi driver there. His uncle writes letters to them and says New York is OK but in the south of the United States of America the white people are separate from the black people. He told me that the white kids go to one school and the black kids to another. They have different buses and don't use the same swimming pools and all things like this. That's crazy isn't it? Why would they do that? I realized Phil was right. I had to think about all this a lot more.

When I got home I talked to Dad. Maybe you were working it out a bit now that I like my Dad. You can ask him things and he explains it easily. I hope when I grow up get to be a Dad like him. So anyway, I asked him about white people and black people in America and if it was different to us.

When dad gets a bit surprised at you he lowers his head a bit and stares at you as if he's looking at you for the first time. It's a look Old Coxy gives us when he peers over the top his glasses when he's surprised someone's given the right answer. But Dad does it without wearing glasses. It's funny to see him do it but it's also like he's a little bit proud of you. It gives me a good feeling when he does it.

So he says to me, Where's this come from all of a sudden. I can't recollect you giving one thought to the USA and you've never talked about coloured people before. So I told him about the talk I'd had with Phil. Dad nodded and told me to get the newspaper from the kitchen table. He opened it up to a few pages inside and showed me a picture of a man in a suit. You could see that he was giving a speech to a load of people. Underneath the picture it read like this

*"Segregation now, Segregation tomorrow,*
*Segregation forever"*

Who is that man Dad, I asked him and what does it mean. He told me the man was Governor George Wallace of Alabama. He said that this Governor wanted to keep black people and white people apart even though the laws in America said they should not. He said that now this Governor had made a stand it would cause big problems.

I asked him why and he said it's normal for everyone to be want to be free and to do the same as everyone else. He then took hold of my shoulders and looked me straight in the eyes. He said, I want you to listen to this, son, and always remember it:

"For every action there is an equal and opposite reaction"

I knew this. Hey Dad that's Newton's Law I said to him pretty much pleased with myself. He nodded again with that look on his face.

"Well son you're right but it applies to more than science. It applies to life too," he said to me raising his finger like he was a teacher making a point, "Now we'll see what happens throughout this year."

It's a funny thing you know I'd never really notices that Phil was black but now I did. I didn't see him as any different but I kept wondering why other people would. I thought about it a lot. Let me see if I can get over to you what I thought. I always think that the colour blue is blue and everyone will agree it blue. But what if you and me we say it's blue and someone else comes along and says it's indigo. No they don't say it, they shout it and they keep on shouting it. Well what does it do to you. Does it give you a doubt that they might be right even though you know it's blue. And you know, this is now what scares me and I mean scares me more than being stuck in Hailey Park with a loose angry Alsatian dog. What if a lot of people keeping shouting something which we know is wrong but they do it over and over again and louder and louder. In the end do we give in and agree that what they say is right. Or do we do what Dad says and be the "equal and opposite reaction." What will we do? Makes you think, yes?

I liked my days when blue was blue.

*******

I was hoping to write good news about cricket in Australia. By the way, I got myself this ear piece thing so Dad and especially not David can hear me listening to the cricket. I must admit though I do fall asleep half way through. Anyway, I thought it was going to be great as England won the second Test by 7 wickets after a draw in December. But Australia won the third by 8 wickets and the fourth was drawn. So we're all square and one to go. Come on England!! Like I said it's OK to say that because England means England and Wales in cricket!!.

*JP's Note: Gareth wanted someone to leave notes to help him. I wish I could tell him that what he writes is helping me! I know what he means about not being believed. What can you do?*

*He use the word "coloured" also which comes as a great surprise now to read it but it was a common expression in those earlier days.*

# CHAPTER 7
## *February 1963*

This is it, the last month of practising with old Coxy over and over and over and with my Dad too. At the end of the month before St Davids's Day on Thursday 28 February we will take the exam. It's all down to arithmetic an essay and verbal reasoning. I have to pass, I have to pass. I looked around in the class today and wondered where we would all be in September. Would I be with my friends and Susan??

I told you before didn't I that when you're a ten year old boy you really are afraid of everything and most of the time trying not show it. I look at the grown up people and see them having nothing to be afraid of. They are lucky.

When you are a kid like me you don't think you're going to die. It's too far away to think about. But when you get past about five years or so you start to think you're mum and dad will die. You want them around for ever because they are the ones who look after you. That's their job. If they die and there's no-one to look after you go to an orphanage. That scares you too.

But I been thinking about this a lot lately. Course you never think of your mum and dad as kids but once they were. They probably didn't want their mum and dad to die either but they did. My grandparents are all gone and I never saw them. Dad must have been like me not wanting them to go but they did. He grew up, married mum and then me and David were born. Somewhere Dad must have stopped worrying about his mum and dad passing away.

I was wondering about this. What happens to you so that you don't worry about them being around any more. I decided to watch kids with mums and dads who also had mums and dads. In Llandaff North grandparents live really close.

Then I got it. I got the answer.

Maybe you're going to think I'm nuts but look yourself and you'll see it's true. This blue is blue and only blue. Got it? Right, well you watch and you'll see that an age comes where the kids take care of their parents. See, think about it.

When you are born as a baby it has to be your mum and dad who look after you. Your mum and dad are strong and you are weak. You stay being weak and afraid until you grow up and get a job. Then you become strong. You stay strong for a long time but your parents get old and not so strong and now they become afraid. So now it's time for the kids to take care of their mum and dad and protect them. I've seen it many times in our village.

You know I never really bothered too much with these old people in Llandaff North but I see I've been very, very stupid. You know why? I guess you worked it out. It's because these old people are like us kids. I been watching them. You can see that when they're out in the street they're looking around to see if there's any danger. A lot of times they've got one of their own grown up kids with them or another grown up to look after them. I'm going to talk more to them. You know, I'll let you into a secret. A lot of times I've been afraid of them and I don't know why but that's not going to happen any more.

There's a very old man who sits on the same park bench in Hailey Park in the summer for a couple of hours every day. His name is Haydn Hughes. My Dad often talks to him and I've said hullo to him in the street but never really talked to him. I've heard some of the kids say that he was in the great war and had a bad time. When this freezing cold weather goes and we get back into the park I'll find him and sit with him for a while.

I talked to Tom and Susan about it later. They both have nannies and grampies so they see old people a lot. They said it was a good idea for me to talk to him. I don't know why but that made me feel happy.

It's still so very cold. It has been frosty every night since before Christmas and the snow has stayed. We rolled a great big snow ball in Hailey Park until we could push it no more. After Christmas we could dive in the snow when it was soft but it has gone hard now. There have been a few more snow storms since Christmas but the ice underneath makes it dangerous. On the weekends lots of us, even the mums and dads, built snowmen in the park. From our bedroom window me and Dave we can look out over the park at night especially when the moon is shining and see them. They were a bit spooky at night like an army of boogeymen waiting to walk towards the houses.

Out in the streets we had to be careful going to school. The ice was so slippery and the teachers and mums and dads will not let us throw snow balls any more after one boy was hit in the face with a lump of ice. A few days ago the snow came again for two days and it was a blizzard of snow. We couldn't go to school and dad couldn't go to work. It was like Christmas again. We had the hot coal fire in the living room, paraffin heaters upstairs of course and me and David were not looking forward to Sunday. Sunday is a day to be scared of these days. I don't mean going to church on Sunday morning or evensong. Nothing like that. But after Evensong Dad makes us have a bath even if we are not dirty. This is crazy if you ask me. Especially now when it's freezing!!

It wasn't so bad to be honest when we didn't have a proper bathroom upstairs and the bog was outside. Then we had a metal bath which Dad filled up with hot water in front of the really hot coal fire. This was OK. The room was warm. Now we have a bathroom upstairs it's awful. OK you can get a Gipsy's kiss and a Tom Tit without going to the outside bog but Dad won't let us put a paraffin heater in there. Like I told you, he promises to put in an electric bar heater on the wall. I hope he does so soon. It's OK in the bath but when you get out and start drying you shiver like hell. I wish he'd just let us wash ourselves down every night in front of the fire. That should do it. David does his best to get out of it every time, pretending to be sick and all sorts but Dad doesn't fall for any of it. I bet you got a bath with heating in the bathroom, don't you and a shower probably too. Dad says too much heat makes you soft but I bet you don't care, do you.

So I was telling you like this cold weather just goes on and on. Dad says it's the coldest weather for 200 years. Two hundred years!! That would be what in....1763. Was that when Shakespeare was writing? I'm not sure but the point is this – they didn't have coal then did they so it must have felt bloody colder. Also who went around writing the temperature down and how did they do it? I bet they never had thermometers or anything like that then. I reckon they're just guessing.

But now I was beginning to miss Saturday football. I told you before that I play on the wing. Like I said I'm not very good but can do enough to kick the ball over to Tom and Geoffrey who can really dribble the ball. Old Pop Willis is in charge of the football team and even though we say it's not so bad playing on snow, he won't let us. Thing is, I think we all need a good runabout. We've been cooped up like chickens between home and school. We've been waiting for Derek Tapscott to visit us. He play's for Cardiff City you know and Wales. Before that he used to play for Arsenal. We'd all like to play and score goals like him but for me I don't think this will happen ever. Tom, maybe because he's as good as some of the best players but I'm just in it for the fun of being with my pals and having a good kick around. So on sports afternoon we switched to going swimming at the Guildford Crescent baths. It was a crazy idea, I thought. Bloody freezing outside, boiling inside and then when you got back out you freeze again. Most of us had a few days off school until Old Coxy told Old Pop Willis that it might be a good idea to think of something else.

Nigel was crazy about Subbuteo as you know so he suggests to Old Coxy and Pop Willis that kids bring their subutteo sets and we have a tournament in the school hall. Actually, it was a really good idea and we had a lot of fun. Mostly it was the boys playing but some of the girls had a go. Even the teachers enjoyed watching and were nearby if there were any arguments over cheating.

Now let me tell you something about gangs. You have a gang like ours but then it's a bit more than that some of the people in the gang have other friends who are not part of the gang. This usually happens because their mums and dads are friends and they visit together. So take Nigel he was mostly friends with Alan but also he was friends with this boy Gethin. Now Gethin was only interested in rugby and not much else. You'd often see him at Hailey Park kicking the rugby ball around and taking practice kicks at the posts. Mostly he played on his own but sometimes we joined in. I don't know why but the school wouldn't let us play rugby even though we have a great rugby club in Llandaff North. If we want we can join the rugby club boys team when we are 11.

But Gethin was only a rugby boy. When we played soccer at school they put him at full back because that's where he says he likes to play in rugby. And you know what he plays his soccer like he would if he's playing rugby. I don't mean that he tackles the other side with his arms but when the ball comes his way he kicks it high and straight up field. None of us can kick that far. You'd laugh at the number of times he's caught out the other sides we play cos he's good at getting the ball right to Tom or Geoffrey then they got a good chance to score. He can't do anything else with it like dribble or stuff like that. He just traps it with his foot, pushes it to the side if there's an attacker coming and whack. Then he just stops and walks around at his end of the pitch watching. He doesn't do a lot but it doesn't matter. His kicking is always worth a goal but the thing is he doesn't care. I can tell you I never seen this Gethin smile or laugh. All you'll get out of him is a "Hah" if the kick goes spot on where he wanted it to go.

He's the same in class too, never puts his hand up and never speaks unless he's asked. Some kids used to think he was weak or shy but they soon found out he wasn't. Gethin is one of those boys who doesn't need to speak unless he has to but the thing that does get me most is that nothing, absolutely nothing seems to make him laugh or smile. Like I said the best is a "hah" or a grunt or twisted lips. Even if we are laughing like crazy in the classroom when Old Coxy is in a good mood and joins in the fun you won't see Gethin put his head back and have a good laugh. He just looks around at us with his twisted lip expression. Me, I'll laugh at anything and let me tell you something when my pals find out I'm ticklish I am dead. David found this out a while back but he knows not so say anything because if he does I told him I'll get Tom's older brother Jack to put him in the small cupboard in their back bedroom. He did it to me once when I was a little boy and it scared the shit out of me it was so dark. David was there at the time and when they let me out he was white faced and shaking. He was only about six at the time. On the way home he begged me not to let them do that to him. He hates the dark, David, hates it.

Gethin's Dad works for the GPO and he's something to do with putting up telephone poles and lines. There's only about three people in Llandaff North who have a telephone in their house. It doesn't make sense to me to have one unless there's people you know living miles away but if all your family and friends live in walking distance what's the point of a phone. I can see that if you are running a business you need it to call customers and other businesses and stuff like that but honestly don't you think it's better to talk to your friend when he's right in front of you. Can you imagine what it would be like if we were all stuck in different rooms with a phone to our ears and no-one going out to see people. It'd be a crazy world. It's the same with the telly.

## Nobody Watching

David can't get away from it and if it was on all day and all night I'm sure he'd be there. But you know some of the programmes are good but they stop you from getting outside and having fun.

But there is some good stuff on the telly. Let me tell you what there is. I like:

The Beverly Hillbillies – and so does David. Do you know the song – "And up from the ground comes a bubbling crude – oil that is". The show is so funny especially with this dumb bloke Jethro who says he's going to be a brain surgeon.

Z Cars – I like it but David doesn't

Candid Camera – we both have a laugh at this

The Good Old Days – we watch this with Dad. It's funny.

Zoo Quest – we both like this

Dixon of Dock Green – this is great and we all watch it. Dad as well.

Gunsmoke and Wagon Train - both Westerns and Wagon Train is really great. Flint Mcollough is brilliant and Charlie Wooster who does the cooking is so funny

Rawhide – we all love this but have our favourites. I like the trail boss Gil Favor who always says "Head em up, move em out" at the start. David likes Rowdy Yates, the ramrod and Dad loves Wishbone, the cook. Everyone likes this one. You can hear people humming and singing the tune in the street sometimes. Do you know the tune? The best bit goes like this:

*Keep them doggies moving, Rawhide. Don't try to understand em, just rope 'n roll 'n brand em, soon we'll be living high and wide"* It's great.

Bonanza – David and Dad like this but it's not as good as Rawhide, I think

Opportunity Knocks – Dad and David like this. It's with this little smile all the time Hughie Green and all kinds of people come on to do acts.

The Flintstones are brilliant and we all have a laugh at this.

Juke Box Jury – I'm the only one that watches this. I like it

Mister Ed – David likes this. It's one about a talking horse. Stupid!

The Twilight Zone – I love it and it scares the pants off David. He's usually hiding behind the chair watching this.

Grandstand – we all like this. It's great for rugby and wrestling. Kent Walton who commentates on the game really believes that they are fighting for real. It's all a fake but David says it's not. So maybe he's right? What do you think? Writing this reminded me that me and David watched Wales play Scotland at Murrayfield on the telly. Murrayfield is the rugby ground In Edinburgh where they play. It was great and you know although we're freezing here there's hardly any snow in Scotland. We got their share too. So because it's not so cold it was easy to get the game going and guess what? We beat 'em 6-0. Still, I wish it was the English we had beaten.

Well anyway I was telling you about Gethin's Dad and him working for the GPO. Dad went over to see him once to talk about it and me and David went with him. Dad was thinking of us having a phone so people could call him for plumbing jobs. I don't know why because they always come to the house and ask him. I told him it would be a waste of money and it would be better to spend it on an electric wall heater in the bathroom. He burst out laughing at this.

While Dad was talking and having a cup of tea with Gethin's mum and Dad me and David went to the front room to play. Gethin had invented his own kind of subbuteo but for rugby so he showed me this while David and Gethin's brother, Dennis, messed about with soldiers and meccano.

Dennis and David got on OK. David is in standard 2 and Dennis in standard 1 so they know more about each other. Dennis is as different to Gethin as David is from me. Dennis laughs and jokes and is noisy and so different from his brother. He came up to me while I was talking to Gethin and said, "Hey, I'm in Caradog too. I want to help us win". I liked this and said we'd see what he was good at so we could get him to win some points for us. He told me he was a fast runner and he was going to win the 60 yards race for us on sports day. I gave his hair a ruffle just like I do for David except Dennis liked it

And I could see too that Gethin likes his brother a lot and while were messing around with the toy rugby players he was glancing over - do you know what -to half smile not big smile at his brother playing with David. I caught him in the first near smile I ever seen from him. Well, yeah, I suppose David's not so bad too when he's playing with someone else. Hay,hay!!

Gethin's mum brought us in some pop and some fruit cake too. David loves it when a mum comes in the room. I try not to think about it as much as him but when you visit someone else's home you can feel the difference from ours. You can't explain it really. It smells different and feels different and when we go back to our house you feel it straight away.

Anyway, let's not think about this. So Dad had a good talk to Gethin's Dad about the phone and you know I think he's going to get one. It'll take him time though. I know Dad. It'll be just like the electric heater for the bathroom.

Dennis came to find me in school a few days later to talk about helping Caradog. He made me smile cos he was so different from his brother, such a smiling chatterbox and so keen that Caradog would win. He wanted me to watch him run in the playground to see how fast he was and although I wanted to catch up with Susan I had to go with him and I'm glad I did. He was so fast for such a little boy. I clapped him on the back after his run and said I was proud of him. He could run almost as fast as the wind. He really liked this.

He wanted me to go with him too to his classroom so he could show me the paintings he had done for St David's Day. I could see he really wanted me to go but I saw Susan passing on the other side of the playground and I needed to talk to her. I made him an excuse and I saw the hurt look on his face just before I ran off to catch up with Susan.

That was the last time I saw him. When you read this do you get the feeling that I like my life. I know we're not rich and we have a small house with no electric heater in the bathroom and there's things to be afraid of. I told you all about them many times now but we have fun in all the things we do. We have a great Dad me and David and the school is a kind place and Llandaff North is like a big home. And I have Susan as my girlfriend now so I couldn't be happier. Sometimes when I sit alone I try to think about the way things will work out for me. I'm a bit nervous but I think I will pass the eleven plus. I'm scared that I will not be as clever as many of the boys in Canton High School but I will study hard and there are so many good books that I haven't read. I don't want to work in a factory or be a plumber or electrician or put up telephone lines. I haven't told Dad this but I think he guesses. I have written down what I want to do in order.

Number 1, I want to write stories for children like Hans Christian Anderson and the brothers Grimm.

Number 2, because I will need money to live I would like to be a teacher and writes stories at night and at weekends

Number 3, I would like to work in an office and write stories at night and at weekends

Number 4, I would like to play cricket for Glamorgan and write stories at night and at weekends

Number 5, I would like to be in the army and write stories at night and at weekends

Number 6, I haven't got a number six yet.

So when I think like this I think of different Gareth Adams doing the different things. I see me but I see a different me each time. You getting me?

And I see myself marrying Susan and we have children and a lovely house and live together till we're very, very old.

I don't think I'm going to die. Well I'm only ten years old. This doesn't happen to little boys, does it? They are supposed to grow up and have lives. That's why they get born. But Dennis will not. No he will not. Dennis lives across the main road in Hilton Place but he does not live there any more. That night, on the same day after he showed me how fast he could run, a car showed how fast it could run and beat him. The grown ups don't say much but as far as I can tell Dennis left his house to go to Percy Evans shop to buy some sweets. It was dark but he must have crossed Station Road hundreds of times. Maybe the driver didn't see him or he was going too fast because Dennis was using the crossing. When you're on the crossing you always know the car will stop, don't you.

Dad took me and David over to Gethin's house to pay respects. It was terrible. There was so much crying in that house and Gethin's mum and dad looked so different. I've never been in a house before where someone has died. It's like all the happiness leaves the place and all the light. I could only see black and shadows and tears. And Dennis is only a little boy, he's younger than me, younger than David. It makes you wonder why God didn't save him, make him run faster that day or for the car driver to see him and slow down. Then he would be alive and their house would be smiling and laughing and full of light instead of coloured black with long shadows.

Dad took me and David over to where Gethin's mum and Dad were sitting. He was holding my hand and holding David's hand as he led us to them. He said something, I can't remember what, in a low voice to them. I don't know why but I suddenly said, "I'm sorry I didn't look at his paintings. I should have. I meant to. I'm sorry."

Gethin's mum looked at Dad to say thank you and then looked at me and David. I never heard a cry come like this from anyone before. It was a cry of pain that made me feel pain too and Gethin's mum turned and grabbed on to Gethin's dad. He held her in his arms.

"Why did we let him go out," she cried. "Why did we let him go out."

I never felt such sadness. I wanted to get out of this house and get away from the pain. I wanted to run. I could tell that David did too. He was pulling on Dad's hand and burying his face into Dad's side. He was scared and so was I. Dad nodded to Gethin's dad and said something again. Gethin's dad screwed up his lips and nodded back but said nothing. He was still holding Gethin's mum. I could see her shoulders shaking as she cried quietly. Dad turned us away and we left the house. It was a cold dark evening but you know to me it felt brighter and warmer than Gethin's house. I hadn't seen Gethin but when I looked back at the house I saw him in an upstairs window. He was standing still and looking out but I could tell that he did not see us. He was staring into nothing.

Gethin wasn't at school for a couple of days and the funeral was on Saturday. The church was packed and there was quiet all round, with just the noise of feet moving and sometimes a muffled cough. When Gethin's mum and Dad and family came in everyone stood up and there was a complete hush. I don't remember much about the service or what was said. I just remembered Dennis asking me to look at his pictures – and I didn't. I prayed over and over again, Please God forgive me, Please God forgive me and I felt my face wet. Tears were leaking out of my eyes and down my cheeks and there was nothing I could do to stop it. Dad gave me a big white handkerchief and while I was dabbing my eyes I saw Geoffrey sneering at me with glee. He caught me looking and quickly got back to a sad looking face. I told you there's a sneaky, nasty awful thing about him.

I asked Dad if I could walk back with Susan to her house and stay there for a while. He nodded and took David by the hand and walked homewards. We didn't talk too much at Susan's house. I went over with her again and again how I should have looked at his paintings. In the end Susan put her arms around me and told me I was forgetting something. She reminded me that I'd stayed with Dennis and watched him run and said nice things to him. This was the thing to remember, she told me.

This did make me feel so much better.

But for not going to see his paintings please God, forgive me. But please God help me understand too why you were not watching out for Dennis that night?

\* \* \* \* \* \* \*

So today was the day, 28 february 1963. The day of our 11 plus. In a way it was like Christmas Day but opposite do you know what I mean. What I mean is with Christmas Day you feel excited waiting for it and then it's over. With the 11 plus we have been in fear of it since the start of the school year and now it's been and gone and there was nothing to it.

If you ask me to go over the day I'm not sure I can. I remember Dad giving me the biggest hug ever at breakfast time and telling me to do my best. David too was helpful but after that it's all a blur. It was quiet in the playground and none of Standard 4 was running around. We just stood in groups quiet like we were waiting in a queue for the dentist. We were all afraid.

Old Coxy was quiet and understanding that day as he laid out all the papers on our desks to take the exam. I told you before the test was in parts with mental arithmetic, an essay and general problem solving. I just got on with it once Old Coxy gave us the instruction to turn our papers over and begin. I don't remember finding it too hard. I remembered what Old Coxy and Dad had said, if you find one is too hard go on to the next and finish and then go back over the ones that seemed hard. This was a good plan and I think I did most. All I remember really is a little a bit I wrote about a train journey where I fall asleep to dream an extraordinary dream.

After it was all over I just remember thinking I have done my best. Looking around at my friends it was like a scene from the films after a bomb has dropped. Some on the edge of the destruction seemed fine and like usual, some seemed sleepy and puzzled and some seemed out cold. I looked around at my close friends and I could see in their faces what they thought. Jack Sims wasn't a close friend but I spent a lot of time around at his house as you know. You know he looked like he'd sat and drank a bottle of milk. Me although I felt I did OK, I felt like I'd been put through a wringer. I was exhausted. But as I looked around I felt my heart sink looking at the faces of Susan and Tom. They had a scared look in their faces.

I closed my eyes for a second just to make a quick prayer to God. I needed both my friends with me wherever I went. The look on their faces told me they were worried. Have you been around after an exam? I bet you been around loads. This is my first and when we all gathered in the playground afterwards there were some like Geoffrey who smirked and said it was easy. The ones like Geoffrey were confident they'd passed. I don't know how they can say this. Then there's ones like me who say I don't know, I'm not sure. I think I did Ok but I can't tell. Then there's others who say I didn't understand it. I failed for sure but you feel they may not be saying really what they feel. Then there's others who say nothing, who just screw up their face when you ask and shrug their shoulders. Susan and Tom did this and a few others.

Inside I think I passed but I'm not saying, but you know I think I'd rather fail than not be with Susan and Tom. I'd even be willing to face my head dunked in the toilet. How could I be alone in Canton without these two. How could I?

We stayed talking for a while and after the bell rang went back to school. Old Coxy was grinning. Because you worked so hard today, he said, Mr Evans has agreed you can go home early and get some rest.

Wow, that lifted the spirits and off we went. Nobody wanted to talk any more but just went home. As soon as I was in I raced upstairs to get Robinson Crusoe to read and lay on the bed. I started reading. I love this book and woke up when David came home calling me from the bottom of the stairs. I couldn't believe it. I slept in the afternoon before 5 o'clock!!. I never ever did that before.

But waking made me think of Susan and Tom. I sighed. David called again and I dragged myself off the bed to go down to make some toast with loads of butter for me and my brother who had this torture to come.

\* \* \* \* \* \* \*

Blast it!! The last one was drawn, so we didn't win the Ashes. Still we didn't lose the series. But the good news is we beat NZ by an innings. Well, they are not the best side in the world. There's two more in March and we shouldn't lose.

*JP's Note: There's so much here. Imagine a world now without immediate contact by phone and no daytime TV!!! And the school has competition between teams with winners and losers!! Bet there's not many schools do that now. And Gareth's description of death is touching. No-one that young and close to me has ever died. He's seen a lot this boy.*

# CHAPTER 8
## *March 1963*

St David is the patron saint of Wales. You know of course that for Scotland it's St Andrew, for Ireland St Patrick and England it's St George. But for us it's St David. St David is from Wales but none of the other British patron Saints came from their countries. He did a lot of miracles of course and was clever as a kid. God picked him out as a young boy and he set up a lot of monasteries around the country. He lived a very simple life, helping loads of people and you could always recognize him because he was followed by a white dove which is a mark from God if you are a good person. So guess what, you won't see one of those flying around Geoffrey!

How do they get picked I wonder to do God's work. I told you already I believe in God a lot and I really want to be a good person. I don't think I can be a monk or anything like that even though living alone in a cell and not upsetting people sounds good sometimes. But really, I know I want to grow up and be a Dad just like my Dad and they don't let monks get married. And it seems like they just live on bread and water. This is very hard. I could not get by one week without feasting on a pile of beans on toast. I keep asking God if there's other things you can do. He doesn't speak back to me of course, not in words. I guess he must speak to the Archbishop and the Pope and people like that but not to boys who don't want to be monks. But you know I think he does leave you messages but you got to look out for them. So like I said I been asking God what I can do when I pray in my head at night and you know I can't get this picture out of my head with one of these monks like St David working in the field with a plough and me sat at a wooden table at the side stuffing beans on toast into my gob.

So anyway in the couple of weeks running up to St David's Day the Welsh teacher she gives a talk on St David and gives us a free booklet the museum were giving away to schools. And you know I got the answer, well I think I got the answer. St David he said, "Be joyful and keep your faith. Do the little things you have seen me do and heard about."

This is the message I was waiting for. See, be happy and do good things. They don't have to be big things like miracles but little helpful things along the way. This is what I'm going to do from now on but I think there is this one problem that might hold me back with God and I'm sure it's why there's no dove near me. You see I know it says in the Bible "Vengeance is mine saith the Lord" but inside in my heart I know I like to take my own revenge on bad things done to me and those close to me. Alright Jesus says you have to "turn the other cheek" but bloody hell this is hard to do. I'm going to need a lot of help from someone to get near this.

On St David's day there is no school work. The girls come in Welsh dresses and Welsh hats and carry a daffodil. The boys wore waistcoats and black shoes and if you had one you wore a flat hat. When we were little boys we brought daffodils but no boy in Standard 4 would carry a daffodil or any other flower now. We take in a leek. In the classroom that morning the smell of leek was everywhere. Everyone all over the school is excited and you can hear the sound of voices and giggles coming from every classroom. We all know that at 10 o' clock mums and dads will come to the school to watch our concert. There will be readings from the Bible and about St David and Welsh songs and hymns. The hall is full of the paintings that we have done for St David's day but the difference is they now show the winners from all classes. I can't get a chance to work out what it all means and there's no point. At the end of the concert Mr Evans will put up the chart which shows everything.

But there was one thing that I noticed. I got to see Dennis's painting after all. There it was the winner for Standard 1 and for Caradog. I had put all this out of my mind, you know the thing that had happened but seeing this it made me sad and happy at the same time. I couldn't look at it for too long as I knew it would upset me a lot. I knew I had to put it out of my mind and think about it later.

All the classes were getting a chance to sing and read. It would be the same as usual we would sing Ar hyd y nos (all through the night), Calon Lan (pure heart), Sosban Fach (little saucepan) men of harlech in english and Cwm Rhondda to finish. Most people call it Bread of Heaven and all the parents join in with this one. You know the singing sounds really good and when you look out at all the parents you can see they love it.

The judging of the readings and singing and the painting has already been done but we don't get to know the results until St David's Day. The judging for best Welsh costume for each boy and girl in the class is the only one that happens on St David's Day.

The concert starts with an opening from Mr Evans and then usually we have the readings starting off with Standard 1 and then up to Standard 4. Mr Evans gets one person to read from each class and it's always the competition winners. I read last so you know what that means don't you? Yeah I won the Standard 4 reading contest and for Caradog and for Susan too and my dad and brother as well. I read the story of St David when a miracle took place to make the land rise up into a hill so that everyone could see and hear him. I asked Dad once why we don't see miracles any more. He laughed and said you have to look closely and you will find them. He said look in a hospital where a doctor saves lives, the telephone, the television and the motor car. He said these must all be miracles. He's got a good point when you think about it.

Then we have the songs which most people love best. We've got great Welsh songs you know. I wrote them down you for a couple of paragraphs ago. Like I said we finish with Bread of Heaven which really gets everyone going.

After all the singing is done Mr Evans announces the winning team from each class and by this time you have no idea where you are with the arithmetic or who's in the lead. And you know it seems he loves the excitement he's generating cos all the kids are waiting for the final board to be shown.

We all know this is going to come after he calls up the boy and girl from each class who won the Welsh dress competition. The teachers have been wandering from class to class all morning and then they get together to vote on the winners. And hey Janet wins it for Standard 4 girls but to be honest I thought Susan's outfit was better. I told her so too.

Then comes the moment we've all been waiting for. I can't say the parents have cos they don't care about this as much as we do.

Mr Evans uncovered the results. He'd done it on big pieces of paper and in big writing so we could all see. This is how it looked:

|  | Standard 1 | Standard 2 | Standard 3 | Standard 4 |
|---|---|---|---|---|
| Singing | Caradog<br>Glyndwr<br>Hywel<br>Llewellyn | Caradog<br>Glyndwr<br>Llewellyn<br>Hywel | Glyndwr<br>Hywel<br>Llewellyn<br>Caradog | Glyndwr<br>Caradog<br>Llewellyn<br>Hywel |
| Reading | Glyndwr<br>Hywel<br>Caradog<br>Llewellyn | Caradog<br>Glyndwr<br>Hywel<br>Llewellyn | Glyndwr<br>Hywel<br>Cardog<br>Llewellyn | Caradog<br>Llewellyn<br>Glyndwr<br>Hywel |
| Painting | Caradog<br>Glyndwr<br>Hywel<br>Llewellyn | Llewellyn<br>Hywel<br>Glyndwr<br>Caradog | Hywel<br>Glyndwr<br>Caradog<br>Llewellyn | Glyndwr<br>Llewellyn<br>Caradog<br>Hywel |
| Welsh Dress | Llewellyn<br>Glyndwr<br>Caradog<br>Hywel | Hywel<br>Glyndwr<br>Llewellyn<br>Caradog | Caradog<br>Llewellyn<br>Hywel<br>Glyndwr | Glyndwr<br>Caradog<br>Hywel<br>Llewellyn |

Final Scores:

Glyndwr     50
Caradog     43
Hywel       35
Llewellyn   32

Ok, so Glyndwr scraped past us on this one but overall we are still in the lead. I could see Geoffrey smiling all over his chops when the results went up and trying to get me to look his way but I didn't. This is what the overall score looks like now:

| | | |
|---|---|---|
| Caradog | 55 + 43= | 98 |
| Glyndwr | 42 + 50= | 92 |
| Llewellyn | 35 + 32= | 67 |
| Hywel | 28 + 35= | 63 |

So he can grin as much as he likes! Two events gone and we got a 6 point lead. Nice!!

All the kids were finding their parents now and walking around to look at the paintings. It's nice to see mums and dads do this. Our Dad never misses it and walks around with us to look at all the paintings the kids in the classes have done. On our way round we stop in front of Standard 1's to look at Dennis's painting. It's good and to be honest it's better than the stuff I do. While we are looking at it his mum and Dad come alongside to talk to Dad. Gethin is with him but he hangs at the back. He still doesn't want to talk. I stay quiet too and so does David. We just don't know what to say. His mum is better than then when we last saw her and she finishes talking to dad and looks at me.

"I know Dennis would have wanted you to have these, Gareth," she said to me handing a big folder of papers. I could see they were a lot of Dennis's drawings and paintings. "He talked a lot about how you and Susan came to work with them. Will you look after them for me? I might want them back some day but you keep them until then."

I took them without saying a word. Why? Cos I couldn't speak, that's why. Dad patted me on the shoulder and said some things to them but I can't remember what it was. Dad led me and David away and home. I was so numb I didn't even look round to find Susan. I just wanted to go home and watch something, anything on the telly.

*******

Well, the snow and the cold has been with us for so long I thought we would have a summer of winter but today on March 6$^{th}$ it decided it was time to leave us. Since late December we have had snow on the roofs and icicles hanging from our houses. Then today the thaw started. Me and David we woke up and knew something was different straight away. It was warmer. Outside we could hear a quiet tapping as all the icicles on all the houses in our street started to drip.

Going to school was funny. For so long the ice and snow had been very hard and now it was just beginning to turn so slush. It's funny it felt great that it was getting warmer but somehow too you wanted it to get colder again and maybe to have more snow. When I told Dad this he laughed. He said I wouldn't think that way when I grew up. Dads, sometimes they don't know a thing.

In school all day you could hear the sound of water running as the snow melted away. The teachers seemed a lot happier and were smiling a lot. Old Coxy is being a bit easier on us. There is just a few months to go before we leave Hawthorn Road Junior School forever but it looks like Old Coxy has decided to give us an easy ride anyway after the 11 plus exam.

Because the thaw had come they gave us a longer morning break. For a change we get together with some of the girls from our class and started singing. There's a new record out from this group with long hair called the Beatles. I told you about them before. This is what we were singing:

> *Last night I said these words to my girl*
> *I know you never even try, girl*
> *Come on, Come on, Come on, Come on*
> *Please please me, oh yeah, like I please you*

These are the only words we know at the moment but we're going to learn all of them. You can hear it all the time on the radio right now. Of course while we were singing it I looked at Susan and yeah you guessed it, I blushed red.

I've not really said much about Jack Sims yet, have I except little bits here and there but I want to write about something that happened to him. Jack was streets ahead of everybody. In our class that's Standard Four, like I told you I knew that I was not top of the class but in the first four. I never said I was scared about school work to anyone else. My friends thought I found it easy, but I didn't. The only one who found it easy was Jack. No-one could beat Jack Sims that was for sure. His name sounded tough but Jack really did look like the "brainbox" you think of when you imagine a school swot. He was overweight, wore thick glasses, hated sports and used words which most of us had never heard of. It was obvious he breezed through the 11 plus. He didn't even break out in a sweat like I told you.

Jack was the first to catch on to any new school work and most of the time it seemed like he knew it anyway. For most of us new work was terrifying. The teacher would go through this new stuff which sometime you picked up right away and sometimes you struggled to understand it. I hated this feeling. Even as a kid you know that there's so much that they're going to teach you and that a day will come when you don't get it and you'll never be able to get it. When you are struggling to understand, your eyes dart around the classroom looking to see if other kids feel the same as you. The last thing you want is to be the only one that doesn't get it.

When you are ten years old you think that each new day in school might be the day you don't get it. I can still remember feeling terrified at five years old when I forgot how to write the number 8. I'd got used to writing it all in one go, starting at the top with a curve to the left and then slashing down the right to form a loop which crossed back over, curved around to the right and joined up where I started.

But I couldn't remember how to do it!

I was close to tears and making desperate efforts to get this 8 right. Then Janet saw me about to cry and asked me what was wrong. When I told her she just picked up a pencil off the table and drew a circle on my page just like this 0. Then she drew another circle above it just like this: 8. You see, two circles one on top of another make an 8.

I can still remember now that it was amazing that there was another way to do the same thing but easier. I remember I felt the same way when accidentally I found a different route home from the next village. I didn't want to go down the usual road because I could see a gang of bigger boys and I was on my own. I took another road and walked till I came to the railway line and then followed it until it came to our village. I suppose you get comfortable with the same road over and over but after that I felt better about trying different roads and seeing where it led to.

I guess Janet made me see this. We've always been in the same class from infants until now. She has always been my friend. When we got into Standard 3 last year her friends dared her to kiss me when we were on milk break in the playground. I could see she was scared that I would push her away and I knew if I did her friends would laugh at her. I knew too that if she did kiss me her friends and my friends would laugh at me. I put up a struggle but let her kiss me. I owed her for those two circles.

And when she landed the kiss I looked for Susan. I couldn't speak to Susan the way I could to Janet but I loved Susan more than anything. At the time I thought it might spoil things for me with Susan but you know now that I did not need to worry. Afterwards, I spat on my hand and rubbed it into my face where Janet kissed me. My friends would have laughed more if I didn't.

By the way, I told my dad about the circles some time ago and how Janet helped me. He thought a bit about it and told me that there were two types of women in the world. He said there were those who could not let you struggle and would help you for nothing. He said the other type would watch you struggle and help you if they could get something better back from you. If they couldn't see this then they'd be happy to watch you drown. He told me that most men were stupid and always fell for the second type. He said I'd understand when I got older. I wondered why he said that. He wasn't thinking about Mum was he? He couldn't have because he never ever said anything about her unless it was good. I wondered if something had happened afterwards to make him think this. I'm still wondering about it.

But anyway I was telling you about Jack Sims, remember. I used to get invited to his house now and then. He lived a few door away from my house. In our village most of our friends were not that far away.

His dad is a mechanic and I think he looks like Clark Gable. He's got the same mustache and hair and he talks in a different way to my dad. He always seems interested to play games like chess, draughts, monopoly, snakes and ladders and anything. Jack's mother was always painting her nails or checking her make up or fiddling with her hair. When she walked past a heavy nice smell went with her. It smelt good and didn't make you sneeze too much. She wasn't pretty like Susan but she was kind and smiled but covered her mouth. Sometimes you could see that her teeth were not that straight.

There was always fun and laughter in their house and I liked it there. Sometimes I felt I never ever wanted to go home. It made me feel guilty, though. I was sorry when they moved after....well I'm coming to this. I miss them a lot.

After a while I did wonder if it was because of Simon that they left. You know I said that most of the time you feel free from grown ups except when at school. It's true. Dad works hard and spends some time with me and my brother at night when he gets home and sometimes on Sunday. But it isn't often he makes you feel scared or afraid. In school you can feel scared of a lot of things. The teachers are fine most of the time as you've seen me tell you but they can get angry and sometimes you don't really understand why.

Anyway, I just mentioned Simon so let me tell you about him. Simon is the exact opposite of Jack. He comes from a really poor family, wears plastic shoes all year round and old clothes. He is at the bottom of the class and finds it hard to learn anything. Simple Simon we call him but not in front of his face. Most of the time he is quiet and when you look at him his eyes seem far away. But sometimes he becomes very angry over nothing. It is like the tantrums you see in a two year old kid. In a few minutes it will be over and he cries like a baby and calls for his mother too. But Simon is like me. He doesn't have a mother but his mother didn't pass away like mine. The rumour in school is that she ran away. Sometimes you hear the grown ups talking about it but they shut up quickly when they see you are listening.

You can't really be a friend of Simon. He is strange and most of the time he laughs when we laughed and when we are talking he'll repeat the last thing someone has said. When we go for a walk he'll pull along behind him a yellow plastic duck on a piece of string. He'll kneel down and whisper to it. None of us dares to laugh.

The teachers banned Simon from trailing the duck in school but he hides it in his desk. He lifts the lid when Old Coxy isn't looking to check on it from time to time. Of course we laugh quietly at him but not that he can see. We all know what would happen if Simon got angry. He is big and if he lashes out he hurts you.

So in our class we have brainy Jack and not so brainy Simon. They were with our group but not really part of our group. It is funny that they both found friendship with Helen Patterson in Standard 2. Most people in Standard 4 would never talk too much or play with the younger kids. Yes, you had to look after them sometimes and be kind to them if they fell over and hurt themselves. Stuff like that. But you don't play with them. You stay with kids in your year. This was true even though me and Susan worked with the Caradog school captains in the younger years. We helped them but we didn't play with them or hang around with them.

But Helen is a little different from the rest of the younger kids. I could see that. She is taller and brainier than the kids in Standard 2 and didn't walk round with a dopey look on her face. She did look as if she belonged with us and as well as friendly she was a pretty girl. Maybe she had kindness and knew things better than we did. She seemed older in a way or that's what I thought when I started thinking about this and decided to write it all down.

Because she understood better I think this is why she became friends with Simon and Jack. So she was friends with the brainy one and the thick one. I'm blushing now as I write this and a guilty feeling is coming. Maybe, I'll think about this later.

Because they weren't in the same class they could only meet at break time and lunch time. But you'd never see the three together. That never happened and it looked like they took it in turns to be with her.

Yes, it's true we laughed about it but I never asked the others how they felt, but me, I felt …ashamed. That's it, I felt ashamed. I see it now that what we really did was push them outside. They were in our year but they were not really with us. They were our age but one seemed older and the other younger and they were different. They were different.

They …..were……different.

That made me think

\* \* \* \* \* \* \* \*

I put the dots in to let you know I stopped for a while to think. I needed to think about what I'd written. The teacher told us once that when you practice writing and thinking that you get *insights*. I never really understood what he meant by this until just now.

But back to the story. Helen, she seemed to care for the two of them like a mother. It was like she knew what each needed and gave it to them. You know what it was? She gave them what we didn't. She made them feel as if they belonged. See what I mean that Helen thought in a different way.

Helen doesn't live near us like most of the others. She lives across the main road. Most of us simply walked home after school but if you lived across the Main Road then usually a grown up came to get you especially after what happened to…to ….. Dennis. Usually Helen's mother used to meet her and if she couldn't come then one of the girls, Jenny Jones, from our class walked home with her.

But one day Jenny forgot. She ran off when the school bell rang leaving Helen behind. When we got to the gate Helen was waiting and asked about Jenny. She didn't seem to mind that Jenny had forgotten. Anyway, Helen wasn't like a little girl. She had more sense than most of us.

"I'll walk with you," Jack said surprising us all. As I told you before Jack lived close to me and Helen's house was not on his way home.

Helen said yes and asked him to take her as far as the edge of Corwen Crescent and then she said she would walk from there. She reached for his hand and off they went. I remember stopping to watch them go. There was the podgy, brainy boy with this tall clever but younger girl and I tell you, it looked like she was leading him. While I was watching my little brother came out and punched me in the stomach so I had to chase him all the way home.

The next morning was the worst day in my life in school. As soon as we got to morning assembly the teachers and Headmaster were at the front as usual. They were not looking at us and smiling like they always did. They looked like all people do when they are at a funeral.

We slid along the benches to our seats quickly. I felt a strange feeling in my tummy. I think everyone did. Nobody dared speak. Mr. Evans, the Headmaster, waited for everyone to get to their seats. Then he spoke quietly and seemed sad. He said that there would be no assembly service that morning. Instead he called for Simon and Jack to come to his room.

The rest of us were led away by our class teachers. Mr. Cox, our teacher, did not give us maths as usual or show any workings out on the blackboard. Instead he told us to take out our copy of Wind in the Willows and to read quietly.

We did and no-one dared speak. I'd never known anything like it in all my days in school. My eyes kept moving to the empty seats of Jack and Simon. What had they done? It was then I noticed that Jenny's seat was empty too.

At ten o' clock we always had milk break and slowly the class room clock ticked towards it. Just before ten o'clock Miss Preece, the school secretary, came in to our classroom and handed a note to Mr. Cox. She whispered in his ear too and then left. Mr. Cox opened the note, read it and sighed. Then he looked at us.

Milk break will be later, he said. We have a special school assembly first. School Assembly at this time of day. We never did this unless it was something special like St David's Day and we had some show to give to parents.

*Nobody Watching*

When we went to the hall Mr. Evans was already stood at the front holding tightly one of Simon's arms in one hand and holding a cane in the other. I looked at the clock behind his head and it was one minute past ten. Jack was on our class bench. I could see he had been crying. His head was looking downwards and he shook with sobs. He didn't look up when I called his name.

Take your seats quickly, Mr. Evans growled at us. He rarely sounded like this. We all watched as Simon squirmed and wriggled in his grasp and he was beginning to make a low whining sound like a scared dog. At a sign from Mr. Evans, Mr. Cox came forward and held Simon as Mr. Evans released him and stepped forward to the stand where the Bible was usually resting. It wasn't there. He put a book like a school register in its place and some other papers on top.

I've tried to remember most of what he said. I don't think I ever listened to anything so carefully before this. What he said was something like this:

"I've called everyone to the hall to tell you about an incident that happened yesterday after school. Helen Patterson's mother could not meet her yesterday to take her home. Kindly Jack Sims offered to walk with her and see her to her home and walked with across the Main Road and left her at Corwen Crescent. From this point to her home is around 100 yards and she persuaded Jack that he need go no further. He waved goodbye and turned homewards. He had taken her home safely, or so he thought. What Jack and Helen did not know was that Simon (and Mr Evans turned to stab a finger in his direction) was in hiding. When Jack was out of sight he called to Helen pretending that he was hurt and in pain. You all know that Helen is a good hearted and friendly girl who has been very kind to Simon. He repaid her kindness with wickedness.

As she approached he sprang forward and beat her about the legs with a thin branch, not much thicker than this cane."

He held the cane up for us to see and sliced it through the air. We all heard the sound that it made.

"She ran away in terror and he continued to beat her legs until she was close to her house. It's incredible that no-one was around to see or stop the beating. She ran to her garden and to her father's shed. She went in and hid there. When her mother came home she did not find Helen and worried, she went to search for her. She thought she may have gone to a friend's house and went in search until sick with worry she came home. A few minutes later Helen's father arrived and he decided to search all areas of the house and garden and found Helen hiding in his shed. So the facts of this incident came out.

I've no idea why this boy would choose to hurt a friend who has shown him nothing but kindness, but he did. You may not understand right now but he damaged more than just her legs."

He paused and I saw him swallow. His lower lip shuddered a bit.

"You see this book. He held it up for us to see. It's a book to record corporal punishment for pupils in this school."

He held up the pages for us to see and let them open. It was an empty book.

"You know, I know all of you and most of your fathers and mothers sat where you are now. You all look so much like them. This book was empty then and it's remained empty all those years. It was my hope that I would never have to open it. It's going to have one entry now and I pray that I never have to open it again."

With that he slammed the book shut. The noise echoed in the hall. I never felt so scared in my life and I don't think anyone else did. I didn't hear clearly what he said next. The sound of that book slamming shut seemed to do something inside me. I think I felt older. I realize I felt more scared of growing up than ever.

He said something about Simon getting six swipes of the cane on his hand. This woke me up. He turned and took a couple of steps towards Simon. Simon was still being held firmly by Mr. Cox. "Hold out your hand, Simon" Mr. Evans said in a loud and firm voice.

Simon wailed. I could see he was scared stiff about the pain to come. He held out his shaking hand and turned his head away. Mr. Evans raised the cane above his head and brought it down fast. The air fizzed with the sound of the cane but at the last moment Simon pulled his hand away and the cane hit nothing. Another time and I would have laughed out loud but I didn't dare. I put my two hands to my mouth to stop any sound coming out.

Mr. Evans said nothing but nodded at Mr. Cox. He held Simon firmly with one arm and stretched out Simon's arm with the other. There was no escape.

"I didn't mean it", Simon shrieked.

Fizz – thwack.

"Ahh! I did..I didn't mean it"
Fizz – thwack.
"Owww. Lemme go. Lemme go." He struggled to get away.
Fizz – thwack
"Mam, mam" his screams shook us all.
Fizz- thwack.
"She's my friend. Stop it"
Fizz – thwack
"It was Jack's fault"
Fizz – thwack
"It was Jack. It was Jack."

Six doesn't sound too much does it? Try counting from one to six. I did later and looked at the second hand on my watch. It takes no time at all.

This went on and on forever. I couldn't take my eyes off it all. When he called out Jack's name Jack shook like he was being beaten too. When it was over Mr. Evans was breathing deeply. I saw him put his hand, the one without the cane, to his chest. He took a step backwards and I'm sure I heard him say, God forgive me. Simon was slumped only held up by Mr. Cox and he was whimpering as he rubbed his two hands together to numb the pain. I looked at the clock it was four minutes past ten.

I watched Mr. Evans turn back to the book and unscrew his fountain pen. After that I just remember being in the playground but not how I got there.

Simon never came back to the school. He was sent somewhere else. Jack was away for a few days and when he came back just stayed quiet, not really wanting to join in with anything. A few weeks later he told me that his dad had a got a better job in Bridgend and they were leaving Llandaff North. They'd only really been waiting for Jack to take the 11 plus exam. Now that was done they could leave whenever they wanted.

Jenny was away for a few days too. She lost her smile for a while but over time it came back. Helen was away for a couple of weeks and I didn't know what to expect when she came back. The funny thing was she was exactly the same. I thought I would see some pain or sadness in her eyes but no, she was the same.

I saw her one day go towards Jack in the playground but he saw her coming and ran away. You can do that in school if you don't want to see someone in another year. One milk break I was sat reading the Faraway Tree in a corner and Helen came to sit by me.

"Jack doesn't want to talk to me any more," she said. I nodded.

She went on. "I feel sorry for Simon. He really didn't mean it. He just got upset." She smiled and paused for a while. "I hid in the shed from my parents you know."

"Yes, they told us," I replied.

"It wasn't what you think, Gareth." She made me put the book down and look at her. "I wanted the marks to go down. I hoped they wouldn't see them. I knew Simon would be in trouble.

I tried my best not to tell on him"

I think I dropped the book. "But Helen he hurt you"

But she wasn't listening to me now, she was thinking. Her eyes suddenly brightened like she'd realized something. "I didn't think properly. Why didn't I change from the dress to trews. I should have thought."

"Why would you do that," I said to her. "He beat you"

"He didn't mean it."

The school bell went off then sending us back to our classrooms. I was very confused about things. Later, I realized that Helen was different too but different in a way that I might never be.

\* \* \* \* \* \* \* \*

The thaw didn't help us at Rugby by the way. Wales should be the best Rugby team in Britain and Europe for sure but the warmer weather didn't help us. Look at these scores: Wales 6 Ireland 14 and France 5 Wales 3. It hurts, it really does.

But the England cricket scores cheer you up. We beat NZ twice in March by an Innings in the second Test and by seven wickets in the third.

You know I'd be happier if Wales won at rugby!!

*JP: Reading this the kids had more respect for their teachers than maybe they do now. The caning incident is horrific. Can you imagine that in a school these days?? Nothing's changed on the Rugby side for Wales either although Gareth would have seen the glory years in the 70's I guess.*

# CHAPTER 9
## *April 1963*

It's April Fool's Day today!! This means you can trick anyone up until 12 o'clock. I got David first thing in the morning. I'd put a toy mouse in his slipper and when he went to put his foot in I gave him a warning that I could see a mouse moving in it. He almost ran a mile when he saw it and I laughed for ages. Course he said he was going to get me later. I knew it was going to be one thing after another in school until 12 o'clock came and I guessed Geoffrey had something in store for me. But I had a surprise for him too. I'd been thinking about it for a while. The one he set up for me was not that good but I gave him a sarky smile when I opened my desk and a jack in the box figure jumped at me. Well, I suppose it wasn't so bad. It did make me smile.

Did I play one on Susan? No, you must be mad. It's taken a long time for me to get the courage to be with Susan. These April Fool jokes can go wrong. I've already upset her when I had that fight with Nigel so I'm not going to have a stupid April Fool joke backfire on me. Would you if it was someone you really liked?

But with Geoffrey it's different. I guessed that Geoffrey would expect something from me so I had to be sneaky. So you know what I did? Well you know Jack is leaving in a couple of weeks. Well I asked him to do me a favour. It took some persuading and I had to remind him a few times of things I'd helped him with in the past. Not schoolwork, of course!! Anyway, I borrowed my Dad's binoculars that he used to use in the war. The eye pieces are black so this helps my plan a lot. I put a thin layer of black shoe polish on both eye pieces. You know what's coming don't you. It's an old one but it's still very funny.

I got Jack to stand near the milk crate at break and to look up at the sky through the binoculars but not to touch his eyes with it. That was for someone else. I told all the lads except Geoffrey that Jack was working on a trick. Course as soon as Geoff saw Jack looking curiously though the binoculars he asked him what he was looking at. Now I gotta give Jack credit because he can sound like a scientist sometimes and he gives this chat to Geoffrey that he's looking at the weather balloon that was sent up from the Cardiff Observatory. Great colours on it, he says to Geoffrey.

He couldn't resist it could he. "Giss a look," he says to Jack grabbing the binoculars. Jack points in the direction where this weather balloon's supposed to be and up the binoculars go to Geoff's eyes and he's swiveling the thing left and right to find the balloon.

"I can't see it, Jack" he calls out. Jack moves Geoffrey a fraction and tells him to keep looking. It's very small, he says. Then a few seconds later tells Geoffrey he can see something falling.

"Blast" he says. You'll never get a "shit" out of Jack. "The atmospheric pressure up there can burst it sometimes. Shame, it looked really good."

Geoff took the binoculars away and handed them back to Jack. Jack couldn't help a smile as he looked at Geoff but he wasn't going to hang around. He shoved the binoculars and case in my hands said thanks and was gone. Geoff turned to look at him which gave us all a good view of the two black circles around his eyes. We started grinning of course and then the laughs just came and came. First, Geoff looked at us not knowing what was going on and then he realized. He put his finger to his eye and dragged it. It came back black. Seeing me with the binoculars he knew it was me that had done it. I was wondering what he would do next and he surprised me. His face looked hard and angry first and then he smiled, "Nice one boys, you really got me there. I fell for it." He clapped his hands at us.

We all still laughed and Geoff clowned about a bit winking and screwing his eyes up to make us laugh even more. It really surprised me. As I watched him I didn't know whether I felt jealous or happy for him. If he'd lost his temper I think everybody would have laughed at him more and called him a bad sport but he dealt with it in a really good way. Even when we got back to class he smacked Jack on the back and said "Great trick, Jack". I gotta say Jack looked relieved.

It's funny after this I felt bad about the things that had happened between us. I felt, well I felt a little sad and guilty. I couldn't forget the things he had done to me but then there were things about him that were OK. It made me feel guilty about what I'd done back to him. My trick to make him look foolish had not worked. In fact it made Geoff look good. It made him look a great sport. I'm getting mixed up about it all, you know. Does it happen that you can like and not like someone at the same time? You see, I know I don't like Geoffrey but I would never do anything to him unless he did something to me first. Like I told you before I didn't think I was doing anything to let him know how I felt. But he must have noticed something or he wouldn't have started on me. It can't be the Cardaog vs Glyndwr competition can it? Maybe there's something else that I've done that I can't remember.

At dinner time I talked to Susan about him. She'd seen us messing around with the binoculars but she didn't know what it was all about. I told it all to her and admitted that I did not really like Geoffrey but wouldn't do anything to him. He'd suddenly started to act badly to me and so I was doing it back.

Susan asked me if there was anything I'd done but like I told you before and said to her the only think I could think of was the Caradog v Glyndwr competition. Susan said that there must be something I don't know about and I should talk to him about it. Obviously, I didn't like this idea and she could see by my face. Do you know any boy that likes to try to find out what's wrong if another kid doesn't like him? Not if they are bigger than you, you run away and if you think you got a chance with one your own size you fight back. With Geoffrey I always think I got a chance to beat him. Susan's idea isn't what boys normally do. But she squeezed my hand and asked me to try it. What could I do?

So later in the dinner break I waited until I could see Geoff on his own. This can be difficult most times because usually Geoff is doing something with one of the boys or talking to Janet. But I got him when he was on the way to the bogs. I was hoping he was only going for a piss up against the bog wall. He was. I stood next to him and started pissing.

He glanced at me with a look that was wary like I was going to piss on his leg or something. Ever since Tom had given him a whack he'd been careful about showing what he felt to me but I knew it was still there, whatever it was.

I decided to start off saying something good so I laughed a bit and said he took the April Fool joke really well. He snorted but didn't look at me. We both finished pissing at the same time and shook the drops off putting our knobs away. It was all done in time and if you'd seen it you'd probably laugh. It was like we practised it.

He wanted to walk away but I tugged his arm to get him to stop. It was hard to get him to look at my face. "Why are you so angry, with me," I asked him. "It's not about the Caradog stuff, is it? Come on, it's only a game."

He snorted again and tried to go away again. I was about to let him put tugged his arm back again. He didn't like it and I think he had an idea to take a swing at me but he stopped. "Tell me," I asked him. "I know we are not the best of mates but we're in the same gang and we always got along until we got back to school. What did I do? I'd like to know."

He stood looking at me and I could really feel the anger coming out of him. At any second I could feel that he was going to spring at me and go for a real fight but he was trying hard to stop himself.

"It's not you, Gareth, you big-headed git or Caradog. You always think things are about you and no-one else matters. It's not you but you're the only one I can get back at." He was clenching his fists and unclenching them. I was ready for him to go for me.

I didn't really understand what he was on about. If it wasn't me he was angry with then who was it and why was I copping the blame? We just stood there for a minute or so while I was thinking about it. "So what did David do then if it wasn't me?"

He stood for a second squaring up to me then just laughed in a funny way, turned and left the bogs. "And Glyndwr are going to piss all over you" he called out as he left. I relaxed a bit and put my hands in my pockets. I just didn't understand it. If I'd done nothing then what had David done? As far as I knew David never saw Geoff that much unless he tried to tag along with us and I always stopped that pretty quickly. What did he do?

I left the bogs and looked for David in the playground. He was kicking a ball around with one of the boys from his class. I stood about ten yards away and gave him a shout. He looked up with surprise. I never spent much time with him at lunch break. His face changed a bit and he thought something was wrong. He left the ball and ran over to me. "What's wrong?" he asked looking all over my face for a clue. "Is Dad Ok?"

You know me enough now to know that I don't often hug my brother but I did then and of course he pushed me away quickly before his pals saw us. "Is Dad OK?" he asked me again. Geoffrey's right, I thought to myself. I don't think too much of other people but only what's happening to me. It's obvious I could see that my brother is so frightened of something happening to Dad and that we would be left on our own, sent to some relatives we've never seen or worse still be put in an orphanage. "No, it's not Dad," I said to him quickly. "It's something else".

I could see David relax once he knew Dad was OK but he was still nervous about what I was going to speak about. "I want to ask you about Geoffrey."

"Geoffrey?" he raised his voice in surprise. "What about him."

"Can you think of anything you might have done which has made him angry?" I asked him.

"Geoffrey?" He raised his voice in surprise again. "Why would I do something to him? Hay, has he said I've done something because I haven't. Nothing. Has he said something? Cos if he has he's lying."

I was confused. It was obvious that David knew nothing about this. Normally I wouldn't have bothered giving David an explanation but this time I felt I should. Of course he knows all about the feud between me and Geoff but I told him what happened in the bogs.

"Well if it's not you and me, then who's upset him?" David asked looking as puzzled as I was.

'David, I just don't know." I said to him looking around to see if I could catch sight of Susan. I needed to talk to her about this whole thing. When I found her and told her she was as confused as me but said that Janet might know something. Susan promised to talk to her and find out something. The bell sounded while we were talking and we walked slowly to the classroom but we were not speaking. I think we were both wondering what it was all about.

But as we reached the classroom I reminded Susan that Maundy Thursday was on 11 April. We needed to check with the other kids how they were doing. I wasn't in the mood but decided to forget about Geoff for now. Things are hotting up and now there's only two events to go - Easter and Sports day. Between Caradog and Glyndwr right now there are only six points.

Remember I told you before the things they judge us on for Easter:

Best Easter card
Best painted Easter Egg
Best reading from Bible
Best sung hymn

I'm beginning to wonder if it's worth it. We have a lot of work to do with the others and what does it matter really. So Geoffrey and Glyndwr win and Caradog and me, we don't. See what I mean. I said Caradog and me. Maybe Geoffrey is right. Maybe all I do is think about things and me. I don't often get to feel sad but while I was talking to Susan about what we would do I just felt this big feeling that nothing mattered. I never felt this before. Has it happened to you. I just felt I was falling into a big black hole in the ground. I think I stumbled a bit while I was walking with Susan. She grabbed me. She wanted to take me to the Headmaster's office but I told her it was nothing. I tripped. I could see she didn't believe me and she looked worried. I smiled and told her I thought this problem with Geoffrey was upsetting me. The canteen staff were still in the hall tidying up from school dinner and Susan made me go over to old Ma Brown to ask for some water. I got some and to be honest I did feel better after taking it. But I still was bothered about a few things. I'm writing it down in my book now:

1   Was I a bad person who only thought about himself?
2   Why is Geoffrey after me?
3   Why do I feel so sad? And why can't Susan, my Dad or anyone make me feel happy. Why?
4   Will this feeling go away or will it get worse.

I'm lucky though you know, most kids don't really have that much to do with their Dads. We watch these American shows sometimes on TV with American families. They hug and kiss a lot. You won't see that with us around here. No kid I know would want his mum or dad to hug and kiss them in front of anyone. You wanna be called a cissy? None of us do. A pat on the shoulder and messing up the hair is OK with us. Maybe sometimes when we're sick it's OK to be hugged and bothered with but no other time. OK you got to let grandmothers and old people hug you and make a fuss of you but that's it.

Most kids don't even talk that much to their Mum and Dad. Or their Mums and Dads are just too busy working or tired when they get home to talk to their kids – but my Dad is different. Well I think he's different. Hey, I just thought, what if every mum and dad is different but you don't really know because nobody wants to say how much they like them. It might be like a secret kept in the house. What do you think? Am I on to something with this one? Who knows, I'd have to drink the invisible man's potion and look in everyone's house without them seeing me. Now that would be something but I'd see things that I'm not supposed to see. Maybe it's a bit sneaky and not right to do that. Maybe.

But anyway, my Dad. I sat with him tonight before going to bed while David was watching something on TV. I told him about me and Geoffrey. He knew some of it anyway because of the fight with Nigel but I told him what he said anyway and I told him that I was feeling so sad and couldn't get rid of the sick, scared feeling in my stomach. I told him that I thought maybe I wasn't so good after all.

It all came out in a rush of course and I felt close to sobbing but I managed to hold it back. Dad sucked in his breath like he does sometimes and blew it out slowly. He placed his hands on either side of my face and kissed my forehead. He's never done that before but you know what.....it felt good. But I couldn't stop myself from taking a sneaky look over his shoulder to see if David might see. He was too busy watching the telly. See, none of us feel right with this affectionate stuff.

Dad took his hands away from my face and patted my hair with his right hand for a second or two. He sucked in the air and blew it out again. I'm going to try to remember what he said as much as I can. It went like this:

"It's a lot of things to be worried about, Gareth."

I nodded, waiting.

"Let's start with the big one, "he started to say. "Are you a good person? Have you done anything wrong? Are the police looking for you? "

"Well nothing like that" I said wondering what he was getting at.

"So what have you done?"

I thought about it. "I just don't feel that I'm being good to people and I feel bad about it."

He smiled. "This is nothing. Everyone feels like this. You're growing up Gareth and you need to know you can never be happy all the time or sad all the time. They both come and go."

He stopped for a bit and tapped his fingers on the kitchen table, thinking.

"You're reaching an age where you care about what you do and what others will think about it. Sometimes they will like what you do and like you and sometimes they won't. But you can't stay in the house all your life and not see people. It doesn't work."

He stopped waiting for me to think about it and take it in.

"Sometimes the things you do will be wrong and you have to say sorry and then forget about it. If you don't all the silly things you did in your life will pile up on your back like a dead weight and bend your back. You'll worry all your life if you do that."

I nodded again to Dad. I knew he had more to say.

"We are not angels, Gareth. Although I think you may be one of the lucky ones who has an angel to watch over you. I know you believe in God deeply and he puts us here to learn and to test us. If you don't make mistakes sometimes how can you learn? So if God can forgive you for these little mistakes you must learn to forgive yourself. You are a very good boy, I know. When I walk through Llandaff North I hear nothing but good about you and David. You both make me proud."

Dad really knows how to work on getting you to blub, you know. I'm sure he could see my bottom lip starting to move.

"Now on Geoffrey, let me think about it." I could see Dad turning his mind to it. "But remember you can't get everyone to like you. Sometimes they just don't and there's nothing you can do. Let me think about it. Are you OK now?"

I nodded again still a bit worried I might give myself away if I spoke. He told me to go and sit with David and let him think. He patted my shoulder again as I left. I sat with my face away from David to watch telly. He was absorbed in it so he didn't look at my face. If he did he might have seen something in my face but it was a good thing he didn't. I felt the black hole closing up the more I thought about Dad's words. It was nice too to hear that me and David made Dad proud. I'd find some way to do something good for David and Dad. This was a promise. I looked back in the kitchen to see Dad, the best Dad. He was sat looking out into space and just thinking.

\* \* \* \* \* \* \* \*

I didn't forget my promise. I went to see Aunt Nancy after school a few days ago and asked her to teach me to do bacon, egg and sausage. I told her I was old enough now and so she showed me. The good thing was I got to eat it after she showed me. So this Sunday morning before church I got up early while Dad and David were sleeping and made the breakfast. There is no way you can stop the smell of bacon and sausage going through the house and Dad and David came downstairs to see what was going on. But their breakfasts were on the kitchen table before they came down with a big pile of toast too.

They both looked so surprised, David especially. Dad was a bit worried but I told him that Aunt Nancy showed me and I wanted to help. The smiles I got from the two of them was worth it. But it's easy to get a smile when you serve up delicious bacon, sausage and eggs on a Sunday morning, isn't it.

\* \* \* \* \* \* \*

Dad was right of course. The sad feeling went away and I felt so much better. At school on Monday I even tried to chat about soccer with Geoffrey. He was not really interested and looking at me with suspicious eyes but I kept going and kept smiling at him. He probably thought I had something up my sleeve for the Easter competition now that the results were so close. But we didn't of course. Me and Susan were just planning in the same way. Just talking to the younger ones in Caradog and helping them with their work.

I think I figured out something by the way. I think there's some things you can't copy. Like Geoffrey could try what we are doing but it wouldn't work for him. He's never really had much time for the younger kids and they know it. He can do the things and he could help them but his heart would not be in it. If you don't believe in it or you're not interested it won't work. You know, I think it might be like that with everything. Sometimes, I dream I am walking down a path in a wood and it's winding in and out. It's beautiful in this wood and I want to walk all the way through. In the dream I know there is someone or something on the other side of the wood at the end of the path. I need to see this person or get whatever is at the end of the path. Then suddenly I come across this huge wall blocking my way. I know I can't go back so I start to climb over it to get where I need to go.

I think you must have a choice like this with everything but you have to believe you can do it. Guess what I'm thinking of right now. I'm not afraid of climbing this wall but I'm afraid of the rope over the river and walking across the black bridge along the ledge. I've talked myself into being afraid but if I believe I can do it, I can do it. In the summer I'm going to do it. I must get rid of the fear.

By the way, I mentioned this wall dream to Susan and how in the dream I climbed and climbed to get over it. You know what she said? She said well next time you have this dream walk along the edge to see if there's a door or gate and walk through or walk until the wall ends and walk around it. I felt dumb. What do you think? Are girls brainier than boys?

I think Susan is brainier than most but like I told you she's not loud and doesn't show off. She's so kind to the younger kids and she likes me so she must be pretty good, yeah?? We split the work like before with Susan helping the kids with egg decoration and easter card and me helping with the reading and singing. Well doing my best with the singing anyway. The parents will come in on Maundy Thursday next week and then we leave school at dinner time for the Easter Holidays. Two weeks off school. Yes!!

I haven't really told you what it's like on a parents day when they come in. OK, well you saw from the drawing I did for you that our School is big enough for us but when the Mums and Dads come we can't fit everyone in. Like you've seen our school hall outside my classroom is where we have dinner and also where we have our morning assemblies. There's not enough room for more benches or chairs for them so when we have a school concert most of the kids have to line up in the little building where Standard 1 and 2 are. Then the teachers call us over when we're needed. If you're in Standard 4 you get to be a helper so you get a chance to see what's going on unless you get called to the stage.

Everyone is excited at this concert because we know we have holidays to come. For me too it was a nervous time. We'd beaten Glyndwr once and they'd beaten us once but we were still in the lead. You see I know that Glyndwr are a bit stronger than us in sports so we have to do well in this one. Even the mums and dads in the hall are chatty and having fun. For them too there's a long weekend coming up with a break from work. You know everyone read well and sang well at this concert. Of course it hit upon me as usual that this was my last Easter at Hawthorn Road. I don't really think concerts will be as good whatever school I go to.

When the concert comes to an end Mr. Evans, the Headmaster calls all the kids in to pile on the stage and sit on the floors so they can see the final scores. Some of the little kids sneak off to sit with their Mum and Dad of course. Now with all the kids in the hall there's chattering and sniggering and laughing but Mr. Evans is great. He lets everybody have their fun and gets on with giving the final scores.

So how did we do. Ok, I know you're waiting so here it is:

|            | Standard 1 | Standard 2 | Standard 3 | Standard 4 |
|------------|------------|------------|------------|------------|
| Singing    | Glyndwr Caradog Llewellyn Hywel | Llewellyn Glyndwr Cradog Hywel | Glyndwr Hywel Caradog Llewellyn | Caradog Glyndwr Llewellyn Hywel |
| Reading    | Glyndwr Hywel Caradog Llewellyn | Caradog Glyndwr Hywel Llewellyn | Glyndwr Hywel Caradog Llewellyn | Caradog Llewellyn Glyndwr Hywel |
| Easter Egg | Llewellyn Hywel Glyndwr Caradog | Llewellyn Caradog Hywel Glyndwr | Llewellyn Caradog Glyndwr Hywel | Hywel Glyndwr Llewellyn Caradog |
| Easter Card| Caradog Llewellyn Glyndwr Hywel | Caradog Hywel Glyndwr Llewellyn | Llewellyn Caradog Hywel Glyndwr | Hywel Caradog Glyndwr Llewellyn |

Final Scores:

Caradog     45
Glyndwr     42

| | |
|---|---|
| Llewellyn | 38 |
| Hywel | 35 |

So how does the overall score look now? Like this:

| | | | |
|---|---|---|---|
| Caradog | 55 + 43 + 45 | = | 143 |
| Glyndwr | 42 + 50 + 42 | = | 134 |
| Llewellyn | 35 + 32 + 38 | = | 105 |
| Hywel | 28 + 35 + 35 | = | 98 |

It's close, isn't it but the Caradog blue ribbons are still flying. I just hope a lead of 9 is good enough because Geoff's Glyndwr are shit hot when it comes to sports. Just have to wait, plan – and hope!!

When the concert was over I asked Dad if I could spend the afternoon at Susan's house. I knew he'd say yes so I left with her and her Mum and Dad. Funny though, I still get a bit of sadness looking back to see Dad and David watching as we walk away. David looks a bit unhappy. It suddenly hits me that from next September we won't be going to school together. As long as I can remember we've done this and now we'll be apart. I wonder what he's thinking about it and of course I start thinking if he will pass the 11 plus and be with me. Hey, see I'm being sure that I will pass. No doubts now.

Susan's Mum gave us beans on toast and rice pudding. As you know these are two of my favourites. If she'd given us oxtail soup as well I'm sure I'd have felt like I was in heaven. We only just started the beans when Susan's sister, Jackie, got home from Canton High School. She has a dark blue uniform with a yellow shirt, navy and yellow tie, navy tights and a nice hat. I think she looks great in it but I'm a bit too shy to tell her. I think Susan will look great in this uniform too.

She comes to sit with us and her mum puts the beans on toast in front of her too. She doesn't tease us any more about being boyfriend and girlfriend which is good. It saves me from going deep red.

"So, you two ready to join me at Canton in September," she asks us with a grin and spooning up some beans with her fork.

"I'm ready," Susan says. "School is getting boring now. It's like it's really over and we're just waiting for the 11 plus results. It'll be good to start learning something new."

"Yeah," I said. "We tried to get Old Coxy to start giving us some algebra and geometry so we could get a head start but he told us to enjoy the free time."

Jackie laughed. "Well he might be right. Wait till you see the mounds of homework you're going to get. The only time you'll have is walking to and from school and maybe on Saturday. Sunday you'll just be doing homework."

"I'm looking forward to the homework," Susan shot back with a big grin.

"Me too. It's going to be fun." I said too.

"Oh yeah, you wait and see, kids. Like everything else the novelty wears off after a bit. Then you'll wish for the happy days of junior school," Jackie shot back at us.

Susan looked at her sister with a funny grin. "You never used to think this before. I remember when you used to fly through your homework but since Ralph……."

"Stop it, Susan," Jackie said pointing the fork at her. "You're still not so big that I can't beat you up like I used to."

They started going at each other like me and my brother but with words. I thought they were bound to be rolling on the floor fighting soon. But, suddenly they both burst out laughing and smiling. Family joking is hard to pick up on, right?

Later I found out that Ralph Williams is Jackie's boyfriend for about a month or so. Susan is in 2A and he's in 3S. I wondered if they knew each other from before or if they met outside school. From what we knew of Canton High, like I told you, it's two schools – girls and boys – separated by a big fence.

It wouldn't be like before where I could just look across at Susan and meet her at break and dinner time. It wasn't going to be as easy. When it was time to go home she walked with me to the front door and I asked her something that had been on my mind but I'd been a bit scared to ask. I stuttered a bit asking if she'd had a chance to talk to Janet about Geoffrey. She said she hadn't as Geoffrey was always around her but now the Easter holidays were here it would be easier. Geoffrey's family were taking a camping holiday in Minehead. She said this would give her more time to find out and with Geoffrey not around she might be more willing to speak.

\* \* \* \* \* \* \*

## Nobody Watching

The afternoon at Susan's must have done it. I woke up this morning thinking about the 11 plus results. They will let us know who's got through on the first Monday in May. They send the result by post. We don't get too much post so when the letter box goes I'll know what it is. The postman comes down our road at 7.30 in the morning so I'll have the result before going to school. I closed my eyes praying for my friends and me to pass.

I didn't want to keep thinking about it all the time so tried to clear my head of it. I could hear the tap of drizzle on the bedroom window and this was enough to get me thinking of the park and the river and we're on Easter holidays! Yes!! Ever since Christmas we've not really been able to play in the park other than make snowmen and have snow fights. We tried to get a sled going but we don't really have a big enough slope. It's great to see the green of the park again but after all that snow the ground is soggy in parts. We didn't try to get on it too much in March because of this but really we wanted to get across the park to the river. It seems like years ago since we played on the monkey rocks.

Course the river is out of bounds to us and we are not supposed to go anywhere near the river Taff or the monkey rocks. And if anyone caught us swinging on the rope out over the river God knows what would happen. But we do all of it any chance we get but we're pretty certain that parents and the parky have a deal. Every now and then a bloke turns up from the Council to repair the fence which runs along the path at the edge of Hailey Park and the Taff. There's concrete posts in the ground all along the edge of Hailey Park and they have this chain link fence in between the posts. We don't cut it or anything like that but you can pull it up from the bottom and squeeze under. We try to hide this from the parky by pushing it back down but after a while it curls up and then the links start to split away so it gets easier to get under. Hailey Park is huge so you only got to wait till the Parky goes towards the tennis courts and you're under the fence quickly. I marked where we go under on the map for you.

I got to tell you that going under the fence to the monkey rocks and the rope gets your heart going. This first Saturday of the holidays we all went under the fence. All of us except Geoffrey that is as his family are enjoying themselves in Minehead like I told you. We struggled a bit first to lift it because of the repairs but nothing was going to stop us. With six of us we all took turns at tugging it until we got it to lift.

We raced through the gap quickly getting a bit scared now that the Parky was working his way back from the Tennis courts, past the bowling green and playground to walk along the old canal path to the Old Oak tree. Wow, we were all excited. The ground on the other side of the fence was soggy and it was like a jungle again. The paths we'd trodden last year had covered up a bit with the spring growth but this was good. It let us know none of the bigger boys were using the rocks or the rope.

We stamped down a pathway to the monkey rocks. I got no idea why we call them the monkey rocks. Tom says that his Dad called them this when he was a boy as well. I think it's because they are close together and you can jump from one to the other like a monkey without falling in. Well, it's the best I can come up with. There's about twenty of the rocks covering about fifteen feet and one in the middle we call the bum rock. Why is obvious. It really does look like a bum with it looking like its split in two with the crack of a bum.

You have to slide down the dirt path towards the edge of the monkey rocks but already we could see the Taff was flowing fast and the water racing through the monkey rocks. Usually the rocks stick out way above the water but today they are half covered. This is good and bad. It means we can have a fast race with the ice lolly sticks we saved. What we do is save them up and write our names in biro on each stick. We block the gaps in the rocks on the one side that goes towards the Taff and leave open the one on the river bank. Once we done that we play one potato, two potato to pick the kid who drops all the sticks at the opening at one end of the rocks.

It's the first one that gets through the rocks to the other end that wins. One of the boys stays at the end of the rocks to whip out the winner when it goes through. Second and third means nothing. Sometimes of course they all end up on the river bank or get stuck cos you never know how the current is going to go. We have about ten goes and take it in turns to be the picker upper. This is the best fun because the other competition is to make sure you don't fall in when you're getting the stick. Someone always does though and it gets the best laugh of the day. I didn't laugh too much today though because it was me who slipped and fell in. It's not so bad by this section cos the water's only knee deep but you still get a good soaking. Course you know who laughs the most when I fall in. Thank God he's in Minehead!!

Usually you take your clothes off when this happens and squeeze them dry. Sometimes we light a fire to dry them too but today I didn't think it was so cold and we didn't have matches anyway. I just let it dry on me.

When all the sticks had gone and we cheered Dafydd as winner we unhooked the rope from the tree and took it in turns to swing out over the Taff. I hated this but could never tell the lads. You ever done this, swung out on a creaking rope over the river sat on the big knot at the end. First off you pull the rope up the bank as far as you can to sit on the knot and then let yourself swing out. You go down and then up high and you can't help looking down at the black water below, sometimes rushing and sometimes moving slowly. At least you think it's moving slowly but it's not. It's going faster than you think. Last summer Dafydd swung out over the Taff and the rope snapped at the branch and in he went. Thank God he's a good swimmer. Mervyn told me that out in the middle you could sink a bus there. The thought of it makes me sweat. I can only swim a bit, not like the other lads and when I saw Dafydd being taken by the current I didn't think of him, I was thinking of me. I was thinking I was glad it didn't happen the turn before when I was on it. You know what though, Dafydd was so lucky. Well he can swim good of course but also coming up the river in a canoe was Dudley our next door neighbour. He stuck out a paddle for Dafydd to grab and Mervyn his pal, paddled the canoe to the bank. I would have been shitting myself but Dafydd came out laughing and guess what? He didn't lose the rope. He held it up to show us he'd hung on to it. It almost made him a hero. If you lose a rope like that it takes weeks to find another. I'm not sure if I'd have been that bothered about the rope but that's Dafydd for you.

He's a quiet kid is Dafydd. He's closest mostly to Nigel. I think this is because Dafydd's mum and Nigel's mum are close friends. That day he fell in off the rope, of course he was soaking so we decided to get back through the fence and over to our house. It was getting late afternoon anyway so the boys went home. Dafydd had an hour or so before he would need to be back home. I got him a towel and a pair of my underpants - the clean ones that is - and we squeezed the water out of his clothes and hung them on the washing line in the garden. We should have washed them too to be honest because when they did dry off they smelt a bit from the river water and his mother sniffed it out. He didn't tell the whole story though. That would be stupid. He just said that he fell in by the monkey rocks. If she knew the true story they'd try to ban us from playing by the river for as long as they could. I've not known anyone from Llandaff North who drowned in the Taff from falling in but I think it might have happened to one of the kids when the mums and dads were our age. They don't really worry too much about the river to be honest but like I said we don't tell them everything.

What seems to be worrying them now is roads. Dennis, Gethin's brother, was the first to be killed in the roads in Llandaff North. For a long time I remember Dad was the only one with a car in Llandaff North but there's a lot more now. We used to be able to play in the streets of Hazelhurst Road and Hawthorn Road and it would be a couple of hours before you saw a car moving. But it's getting different now. We have to look out more often. If there's any more accidents I can see that they won't let us play on the street any more. It'll be the park, inside the house or nothing.

But anyway let's get back to Dafydd. He has the blondest hair you can imagine. He's a bit like Gethin because he listens more than he talks but then he likes to tell jokes. I think he gets them from his Dad – or used to anyway – and they're really funny. But he laughs at the joke the loudest, that's for sure. I told you he lives in Belle Vue Crescent so just around the corner from Nigel. You can see it on the map I did for you.

Dafydd might be quiet but he's tough also and clever. I know that when the results are out he's going to pass the 11 plus and I get the feeling he's going to do well at everything. Now you know me very well now so you're not going to be surprised when I tell you that I'm coming to think I'm going to do well too. I can picture it. I have these pictures too for not only Dafydd but also Philip and Geoffrey. I am not clear when I think about the others. I don't know why.

Dafydd's mother didn't work until recently. Now she works at the Tax office somewhere, wherever that is. His father you don't get to see much and you know I have never been inside Dafydd's house. His Dad is not like the usual Dads you see in Llandaff North. You know why? He wears a suit and carries a case with papers in it. Most of the Dads around here know each other and seem to get on ok. They meet up at the rugby club or the Station pub but Dafydd's dad doesn't go to any of these places. He's different. I asked Dad about him and he said he's a Civil Servant. Don't you think this is a stupid way of saying he works in an office. Civil Servant! It sounds like a polite butler in a big house.

I watched him once. I couldn't help it. He was walking from his house on a Saturday morning along Belle Vue Cresecent and then cut across to Ty Mawr Road to go to the station. I was at the top end of Hawthorn Road before the school. I know he saw me. His head was straight but his eyes flicked over to look at me and back again. There was no smile. It reminded me of a snake I'd seen at Bristol Zoo. Is this the father who tells Dafydd such good jokes, I thought to myself.

Like I said he's different. Not speaking to someone never happens in Llandaff North. You can't walk twenty yards without seeing some grown up who's going to ask how your Dad is, how you're getting on at school and mentioning Church or cubs or something. But Dafydd's dad doesn't do any of that. I wonder why – but I guess I'll never know. He doesn't come that much to Llandaff North now. Dafydd says he got a promotion to a job in London at the Home Office I think he said. Because they didn't want to move Dafydd just before the 11 plus Dafydd's father went on his own.

But you know what and I never said this to anyone before, I think me Dad and David we saw him last week at the Sandringham. You know I told you that Dad likes to take us there sometimes for toasted tea cakes and pop? Remember? Well we were there and I'm sure when I looked across at another table. I saw him and you know he looked in my eyes when I looked over and you can never forget his eyes. He looked at me for a bit and then looked away to talk to the lady that was with him.

I gave Dad a nudge and was about to ask him about it. But before I could say anything he said "I know. Don't look over again. Just get on with your teacakes. It's nothing to do with us."

To be honest, I was confused. If Dafydd's Dad was there where was Dafydd and his mum. Something was wrong and I think it made Dad act a bit funny too. He was quiet at the table and rushing us to finish. When we left and got outside he knelt down by me and David and said that we shouldn't tell Dafydd that we'd seen his father. I asked him why and he said that it might upset Dafydd that his father had come to Cardiff and might not have gone to Llandaff North first.

Dad's explanation did not sound right to me. You know what? I think it was really something to do with the lady Dafydd's Dad was with. Dafydd's mum looks like a mum. Ok, I know you're going to ask me what a mum looks like but I can't put it in words. You just know. This lady Dafydd's dad was with did not look like a mum. She was dressed like she was going out somewhere posh. But anyway, I never said anything to Dafydd. Just like I worship my Dad he worships his too. He's always looking forward to his Dad coming home for a weekend and always talking about him and his job in London. He talks too about moving to London with his mum after school is over so he can start in a London school. I will miss him but I hope it happens. I know I wouldn't want to be too far away from my Dad.

I think I understand how he feels. I try to imagine what it would be like if my Dad was working away and only coming home now and then. I know it wouldn't happen because we don't have a mum but still I try to think what it would be like. I'd hate it. Dads don't talk to you that much like a mum does but when they're around you feel safe and they can play football and cricket with you too, and give you sips of beer from their glass. See, Dads are not so bad, ay?

Dafydd sees his Dad every couple of weeks. He arrives late on Friday and leaves on Sunday afternoon. You can see how excited he gets as the time gets closer. He comes by train and arrives at the station around 8 o' clock. He meets the train with his mum. I'd like to be at the middle of the bridge looking down on the platform to see his Dad arriving and the look on Dafydd's face. In my mind I can see Dafydd and his mum on the platform. He is in his best shorts and shirt and his blonde hair is combed and brushed well. Dafydd's mum has on her best dress too and she's been to the hairdresser. She has black shoes with high heels. She has her hand on Dafydd's shoulder because like me he's too big to hold hands with mum or Dad. He's moving from one foot to the other as the train arrives at the platform. You can hear the long sound of the trains horn – beeeee-baaaaa – as it slows and the screech of the brakes as it slowly comes to a stop. You can hear the sound of doors clunking open all along the train and men mostly men coming through the doors. I can see Dafydd's Dad in his dark suit carrying a raincoat over his arm and holding an umbrella and briefcase as he gets out of the carriage door. He looks along the platform to see Dafydd and his mother waiting. I watch as Dafydd breaks away from the grasp his mother has on his shoulder and with Dafydd gone racing to his Dad she raises this hand to her lips as if she is shocked or surprised. She waits, she doesn't run like Dafydd. She is stood there in her best dress and shoes, her feet close together. In one hand she holds her bag hanging down at the side and the other is still at her lips but now I don't see surprise or shock but sadness.

My eyes go back to Dafydd's dad. I watch as he looks at Dafydd's mum and then at Dafydd rushing towards him. He walks towards the rushing Dafydd who rushes into his Dad throwing his arms around his dad's waist. It makes me smile as his Dad tries to hold him back but with raincoat, umbrella and briefcase it looks funny and clumsy. In my mind I see his dad lean over to kiss Dafydd on the top of his head. I'm surprised at myself for thinking this as this is not something our Dads will do. Dafydd seems to hold him for a long time and his Dad waits patiently but now he is looking across the distance between himself and Daydd's mum. She does not move and is in the same position as before but now she has moved her hand from her mouth and the two hands are held in front of her, the handbag hanging down almost to her shoes.

Dafydd eventually lets go of his Dad's waist and moves to hold his right hand which is holding the briefcase. As his Dad walks Dafydd skips in delight that he has his Dad back. They join Dafydd's mum and his Dad nods to her. She nods and smiles back but it's a smile you give when you are sad about something not really a happy one. They pause a bit to look at one another and then leave the station to walk home. I see Dafydd's mum move alongside Dafydd. She doesn't walk next to Dafydd's father. I wonder why. Mums always walk next to Dads. Always, don't they?

This is my imagination again. Don't you find too that you can look at a couple of people or a place and watch it for a while and then find that ideas or stories about them are growing fast like ivy up an oak tree. But let's see if I can explain this better. I think you can look at people and work something out from what you see. Sometimes it might be right but other times it's just telling a story but with David's mum and Dad I think something has happened. I hope it doesn't make David unhappy.

But like I told you before he's pretty tough and I hope he keeps on getting the jokes from his Dad and it all works out ok. While his clothes were drying in my house after he fell in the river David came back. I think I told you David really likes my friends. It's a pity we're not twins and then he could join in with us but like I told you he's too young to tag along with us.

Dafydd doesn't have any brothers or sisters and I think he misses this. Funny isn't it if you haven't got a brother or sister you want one and if you have them you think they're a pain in the bum. But you know I was watching the two of them talking and they get on really well. Dafydd loves books like me but he was showing a lot of interest when David run off to get his box of soldiers and the latest Airfix aeroplane he was working on. He showed interest in David's stuff and was asking questions that I would never think to ask because I can't be bothered. I felt guilty and still feel it now. I keep making promises that I'm going to play more with my brother and do more things with him but I don't. Am I a bad brother? I often wonder this. And it makes me wonder too if I'm a bad son. It's beginning to cross my mind that I'm just a selfish person. I been reading back through this diary, or whatever you want to call it, over the months and some of the stuff I don't like about myself. You know it's funny. It's like it comes out of you and you don't notice it and when you write it down and read it you find you don't really like the person you are. Anyway, enough of that. For me things are not so bad. I got Dad and David and Susan is my girlfriend and things are going well. But David doesn't have his Dad close now but he seems to be getting on OK. Remember that time when he didn't get picked for the football team. He just took it, like he takes things now.

Watching David made me make myself another promise to help other people more including my Dad. Not just to think of myself all the time and how things that happen affect me. I have to think more of what things mean to other people.

Sometimes I think God must send you messages about things like this. You know I been thinking about the way Dafydd is and then something happened which made me think more. During the week there was a lot of rain and we knew that the Taff would be high so we went over to look. There was no sign of the monkey rocks and the water was flowing fast and rising. When Dad found out we'd been over to look he told us to keep away as the Taff could overflow into Hailey Park.

On Saturday afternoon the river rose higher and part of the bank started to fall away close to Povey's field and Mr Bownes pig sheds. All the Dads and grown up boys made there way over to see if they could help. Me and David sneaked after them too to watch what was going on.

There were loads of blokes over there to help Mr Bownes but you could see it was dangerous as bits of the bank fell away into the river. They managed to get two pigs out of a stall and in a safe pen further into the field but then a big chunk of the bank slipped and the pig sheds moved like cardboard boxes in the wind and slipped down the bank. You never heard such squeals in your live as six pigs fell into the water. This water wasn't moving yet. The earth from the bank was holding off the current and the pigs were trying to scramble back up the bank before the water got to them but they couldn't. But you know what I saw something then I'll never forget. A couple of the other boys tied a rope around Dudley and he was down and in the water before any of the Dads could stop him. He was carrying another rope too. He grabbed one of the pigs before it got carried away by the current and tied a rope around it and held on. The Dads all rushed to help the boys heave on the ropes to pull Dudley and the pig up. It was a struggle you could see. Dudley is strong and stocky and the pig heavy. Me and David moved closer to watch what was happening. You could see Dudley twisting a bit with the rope and doing his best to dig his feet into the bank to push himself up. While he was doing this pieces of the sheds were being torn away by the river into the current. One of the pigs had scrambled on to a wide piece of the shed wall but the river pulled at it and the pig and wall floated away into the centre of the river. The pig could only try to balance in the centre. You know I swear to you that it looked up at us as the river took it away calling for us to help. The other pigs were still trying to scrabble up the bank but it was too steep and the water was now taking all the earth away.

With a big cry from the dads they heaved Dudley and the pig over the bank and Mr Bownes ran forward to grab the pig and lead it away to the pen with the help of some other dads. Dudley lay exhausted on the mud with the rope still around him. He looked up to see the last pigs being taken away by the current bobbing up and down like apples. He went to go back in again but his father and some of the other Dads held him back.

He strained to break from them but I think he knew there was nothing he could do and he let his Dad and the other Dads hold him back. But he still looked like a hero. Once he relaxed they patted him on the back and applauded him. Mr Bownes came over to thank him personally. I could see he was trying to press some money into Dudley's hands but Dudley put his hands in the air and shook his head. He didn't want the money. Dudley's Dad looked so proud of him. He shook him by the hand and patted him on the shoulder. I thought maybe he was going to hug him cos he learned forward like he was going to but he didn't. Dads never hug their kids out in the open only sometimes at home. Hugs are mostly from mums. But I wouldn't have blamed Dudley's Dad if he did. I'd always liked Dudley and it was great living next door to him but now we lived next door to a real hero. I knew this for sure when Dad brought the paper home a day or two later. His picture was in it along with the pig and Mr Bownes. I told you Dudley was a real hero. One day I hope I can do something like that. If Dad looked at me the way Dudley's father looked at Dudley I'd be so happy.

I forgot to tell you the day after the river came high we heard that the dead pigs had got trapped down by the monkey rocks against a tree that had fallen in. We went to look but not for long. I'd never seen anything dead before. The pigs were tumbled against each other, some heads out of the water and some under. They looked bigger. Tom said this was because of the water inside them. We got chased away when some blokes with equipment arrived and told us to bugger off out of it. Alun lobbed a chunk of mud down on them as we slipped through the fence back over the park. I see the pictures of those dead pigs in my mind now though as I'm writing this. Except for being bigger they looked the same but it was like their batteries had run down or something and they were frozen in one position like they were waiting for someone to put new batteries in. After seeing this I know one thing. I don't want to see a dead person especially somebody I know. It made me wonder if Gethin had seen Dennis when he got hit by the car. Did he see him lying in the street and try to shake him with his hands to get him moving. There's not much difference between sleep and death is there if you come to think about it. Sometimes David sleeps deeply and it looks like he isn't breathing and I call him and shove him until he jumps awake and lashes out at me. I don't mind that though. I don't want anyone close to me to be ….you know….gone. I can't imagine what life would be like without them around me. I just can't

\* \* \* \* \* \* \* \*

The rain went as quickly as it came and we had a spell of almost summer like weather for the rest of the Easter holidays. It's still muddy and wet in Povey's field and also in the Long Woods. I've been wanting to go on a long walk with Susan through the woods and up to Castell Coch. You ever been there. It's a great place but I think we'll have to go there when it's a bit drier. At least you know in the summer holidays it's going to be sunny mostly day after day.

On the Sunday afternoon before going back to school I went over to Tom's house. His mum and Dad were playing cards and his brother and sister were doing their homework on the kitchen table. Tom asked his Mum if we could use the front room to play monopoly. As she was OK with this Tom ran upstairs to get the box. I took the box off him and started to set it up. I like to organize the bank into 500, 100s, 50s and the rest of it and set out all the properties in colour order. Tom knows this and just lets me get on with it.

But the thing is we don't start to play monopoly. Tom starts to bring up memories from infants and how we sat next to each other from the first day and all the little things that happened while we were there. He talked about us going to the junior school and about our pals. All the fun we've had in Llandaff North with our friends. I'd stopped sorting out the monopoly a long time ago and was just joining in filling in what I remembered from some of the stories he was telling. It was funny and we started to laugh especially when he reminded me of the day that Simon left a whoopee cushion on old Coxy's chair and the time that Dafydd farted in assembly just when it all went quiet. We were laughing so much that Tom's mum came into check on us.

"I don't think I'm going to pass," Tom said suddenly. "You will I know. You're brainy."

"No I'm not," I said but starting to feel afraid. "Jack is brainy. I'm like you and Dafydd. Average."

"I didn't do that good, I know," he went on. "You'll be going to Canton or somewhere but it's Glantaf for me."

"You don't know that yet, Tom," I said to him. "I get afraid that I'm not going to pass too but we always do well in class. About the same."

"No," Tom was shaking his head. "You always do a little bit better. But anyway, I didn't do so good that day and it's just one chance to pass."

I just shook my head not believing him.

"Well, look, we might be in different schools but we'll still be friends, right?" he said to me but I was afraid. I couldn't think of a school without Tom in the class with me. It is April and in September we'll be in new schools. Do you ever think it would be good to keep things just as they are? Maybe not grow up. It's been great going through Standard 4 in Hawthorn Road Junior School and being 10, nearly 11 years old. Wouldn't it be great if it just kept going?

The laughter had gone now and Tom was thinking and so was I. Funny how things can go from laughs to sadness in a few seconds. I feel like I'm in one room where things are good and you have fun but whether we like it or not this room is pushing us towards another door across the way. We can't go back to the other side of the room and the door is getting closer. We don't know what's on the other side of that door but we know it's noisier with more people and it's scarier. We know as well that in that room there is another door on the other side and after that we know there might be more. The door in this room is going to open soon and take us through and there's nothing we can do. We might not want to look at it or think about it but it's there and it won't go away and none of the other doors will.

You know if I could lock this bloody door and stay here I would.

We didn't play monopoly that afternoon. We had some sandwiches and that nice mixed fruit out of a tin and then I went home to get ready to go to church for Evensong. While I was getting my stuff together I told Dad about Tom thinking he wouldn't pass and he said a funny thing. He said, "We've all got our different doors to go through. It's part of growing up."

But you know what I saw in my mind. I saw that the door I see in this room might be just the one I see. What if Tom's got a different door that I can't see and Susan too. If that happens then your friends just get further away from you. They won't be in the same room as you any more. But maybe some can see the same door as you and it's OK because they go through with you. They're with you when you get through to the next one but they might not be at the next door. I didn't want to think about the last door we go through. No, not that one, Not that one.

The 11 plus results are out next week. It's a door isn't it?

\* \* \* \* \* \* \*

When I got back home from Evensong I found a note from Susan on the mantel piece. Dad pointed it out. He said she'd called round hoping I'd missed Church that night. In her note she asked me if I would have time to go see her at home that night. Dad said it would be OK as long as I was only gone half an hour.

We talked outside her door because she didn't want to speak in the house. In the end Janet had told Susan the story of why Geoffrey had taken against me so much.

"He's scared that his mum will leave and go with your father," Susan said quietly. She dropped her eyes and then looked back at me to check my face.

"What!" I cried out and Susan made me hush. I whispered, "Why would he think that? Why?"

"Well, remember the August picnic last year?"

"Yes" I said. "I remember. Geoff's Dad had a bit too much and Dad helped him back from the Rugby Club. We all played cricket but Geoff's dad was sleeping. So? I don't see. Nothing happened."

Susan reached out for my arm. "Well not at the picnic, that's true but when Geoff's Dad woke up they went home and there was a big row."

"What happened," I asked.

"Geoff's Mum shouted at him because he got so drunk and made a fool of himself. They didn't argue while Geoff was around but when they were upstairs. Geoff heard his mother say that your Dad was a gentleman and would never act like that in public." Susan stopped and waited a bit looking to see how I was taking it.

"Yeah, go on," I urged. "What happened then?"

"Well, Geoff's Dad said he'd had a few good car sales that week and he was celebrating a bit." She went on. "Geoff's mum said that this was no way to celebrate and if it was your Dad he'd celebrate with you and David and not get stone drunk."

She paused again. I nodded for her to go on.

"Geoff's Dad said that your Dad must be a bloody saint then and perhaps she should go and live with a saint rather than a devil like him." Susan stopped again. She licked her lips a bit like she was nervous to go on.

'Geoff's Mum then said if your Dad would have her she'd go like a shot because he's twice the man that Geoff's Dad is."

For a second or two I wondered what it would be like to have her as a mother. I even thought that David would like it for sure. Geoff's Mum is prettier than Aunt Nancy, Aunty Margaret and a lot of other mums. She has a nice smile too and seems kind.

I only thought this for a second though. I know what it's like to be without a mother and I wouldn't want Dad to take anyone's mother away.

"You don't think it's going to happen, do you?" I asked Susan. I'd never ever seen Dad anywhere near Geoff's Mum unless there were street gatherings and things like that.

"I don't know but I don't think so," Susan said but she was looking awkward. "Gareth, I have something else to tell you."

Susan waited a bit again before going on. "I hope it doesn't get you upset but I had to talk to my mother about this. I made her promise not to say a word to anyone."

I nodded waiting. I wasn't sure what telling her mother would mean really.

"You know she laughed. She said that these things sometimes happen between man and wife. They get so angry they say things they don't mean just to annoy each other." Susan waited again. "Gareth, I was surprised. I've seen my mum and dad argue but they don't say things like this but maybe I didn't hear everything."

I thought a bit. In my mind I thought again how it would be good to spite Geoffrey if his Mum came to us but I shook this idea away. "He thinks it's true doesn't he. Geoffrey, I mean. He thinks his mum would leave to go with my Dad, doesn't he. He's got it stuck in his head."

"Yes," Susan said. "It looks like it."

"So what do we do?" I asked her.

"I don't know Gareth. Really, I don't know." She said to me. "Except….."

"Except…." I repeated asking her to go on.

"Maybe you should tell your Dad. He'd know what to do." Susan said quickly.

I thought about it. I didn't know if I could. I would feel so embarrassed and not really know what to say.

"Let's take it all in and think about it, Susan" I said. "It's a lot to think about first. Let me think about what we do."

"Ok", she said. "But we mustn't let anyone know that Janet told me."

I nodded, squeezed Susan's arm, said a quick goodbye and went home. When I got in I found it hard to look at Dad. I just went up to him, said I was tired and went up to bed. I couldn't face him properly yet. I needed to think. He was doing some jigsaw puzzle with David anyway so they both weren't paying much attention. If they'd really looked at my face they might have both asked questions. I thought I was going to bed to think but once I'd cleaned teeth, washed and got into bed I was asleep in no time. Sometimes, I think the brain decides you've heard enough or done enough for one day and puts the lights out whether you like it or not.

\* \* \* \* \* \* \*

Sunday 28 April was a great day for me. It was the day most of us from school – except Geoffrey of course - and other people too got confirmed at All Saints Church. Do you know what a confirmation service is? It's where you make your vows to God and Christianity. You've probably already been christened as a baby but at confirmation you have to do it for yourself. I already told you I believe in God so much and I know he's watching out for me. On this day I'm in my choirboy costume of cassock and surplice and Susan is wearing beautiful white dress and veil. I could see her so clearly from the choir stalls.

For this service the Bishop of Llandaff came to our Church. It was wonderful. Father Tebbit got us into a line in front of the Bishop – girls on one side and boys on the other. He asked us all if we were willing to affirm faith in Jesus Christ and then we had to repeat our renunciation of the devil and all that is evil.

The Bishop then went to each of us and put his hand on our head and said "Defend O Lord this thy child with thy heavenly grace, that he may continue thine forever and daily increase in thy Holy Spirit, more and more, until he come unto thy everlasting kingdom."

And then I said "Amen"

After he'd done this I'm sure I felt the Holy Spirit come within me. Something happened, I know.

When the Bishop had confirmed all of us we and the whole congregation sang the Apostles Creed. Do you know this one? I love it. Here it is:

I believe in God, the Father Almighty, Maker of Heaven and Earth;

And in Jesus Christ, his only begotten Son, our Lord

Who was conceived by the Holy Ghost, born of the Virgin Mary;

Suffered under Pontius Pilate, was crucified, dead and buried. He descended into Hell.

The third day He rose again from the dead.

He ascended into Heaven and sits at the right hand of God the Father Almighty.

From thence he shall come to judge the quick and the dead.

I believe in the Holy Ghost,

I believe in the Holy catholic church and the communion of Saints,

The forgiveness of sins,

The resurrection of the body,

And the life everlasting. Amen.

It's great isn't it. I say it as often as I can and always will.

The Bishop signed confirmation certificates for us and signed a blue prayer book which he gave us. He sprinkled both with Holy water. I hope God keeps me and my Dad and brother safe and Susan too and all the people I know. Even Geoffrey too and even though he doesn't believe in God maybe God is watching him too.

*PB: He's right about the doors but normally you don't realize this until you're older. I have one friend left from my school days. I have no idea where the others are but he's making me think to search on Facebook and Friends Reunited. Maybe, Gareth is right. These early friends might be very important to us – more important than we realize. Strong on religion, isn't he. Are kids the same way these days. Bishop of Llandaff? I wonder if…..Well, could be.*

# CHAPTER 10
## *May 1963*

It's Monday 6 May, The 11 plus results will be delivered to the house tomorrow. This morning I lay in bed thinking about two things. The first was what to do about the information from Susan and the second was had I done enough in the 11 plus exam to pass. I decided I would have to think about Susan's information later. The 11 plus was taking over everything. Tomorrow we will be waiting for the postman to deliver the result. Some kids will know before me because the postman delivers to their house first. Dad is not going to work tomorrow morning. He's going to stay home and wait with me. In school Mr Evans is going to get a big envelope with all the results. Maybe he's got it already. Maybe he knows already. I knew that today was going to be a funny day in school.

I was right about that too. Old Coxy kept us entertained with stuff that kept our mind off things. He got us to talk about Wind in the Willows. He talked about stories and how they were early man's telly. The man who could tell a good story would sit around the campfire with the others and tell tales. He said the stories were often memories of famous people in the tribe but not always the truth. Each story teller added new pieces to make it more interesting. Then he asked us to write our own story if we wanted to or do a painting if we didn't want to write. Me, I wrote a story because I like to do that.

It was quiet in class that day. There was none of the usual chatter and laughing. We all just got on quietly with the jobs. I looked around the class at my friends and Susan praying that we would all go through the same door together. Maybe something of the same thing was going through Geoffrey's mind. His eyes were closed and his hands together like he was praying. I'd never seen him do this before. I told you that he and his family don't go to Church but like Father Tebbit says everyone calls on God for help at some time, everyone.

The school day passed by but I couldn't stand the thought of going home just to sit down and read or watch telly. I asked Susan if she could check with her mum if it was ok for us to go over to Hailey Park for a walk before it got dark. If her mum said it was ok I asked her to meet me by the swings. I walked back home with Tom and David and as we reached Tom's house half way along Hawthorn Road I clapped him on the back.

"Well, tomorrow we'll know" I said to him. He just nodded and gave one of those smiles that doesn't really look as if you're happy. He didn't say anything but as me and David walked the short distance to Hazelhurst Road I looked back to see Tom watching us. I raised my hand to say goodbye and slowly Tom raised his to do the same. But you know as I turned and crossed the road to go home I wondered if our goodbye waves were not just goodbye for the day but GOODBYE for longer. I felt goose pimples on my arms.

Usually, I would reach into the letter box to get the key but seeing that I was miles away David did the job for me. He's a little sod like I told you but I think he understood that we were getting panicky about the 11 plus result and he was doing his best not to get on my nerves. When I slumped in a chair by the telly when we got in he even brought me a glass of Tizer. It was nice.

I asked him if he'd do me a favour. I told him that I wanted to go round the park for a walk with Susan and I'd be home before dark. I told him to tell Dad that I wouldn't be late. Now since me and Susan have been going out together David's really got to like her and I've caught him once or twice following us and then wanting to tag along.

"What about tea?" David asked. "Don't you want anything?"

I knew he really meant that he was hungry and would I make something.

"I'm not hungry," I said," But what if I make you a couple of cheese and onion sandwiches before I go?"

These are his favourites and a big smile came on his face. I made them quickly cos I didn't want to be late meeting Susan. Before I left I made sure the back door was locked and told him not to open the front door if someone knocked unless he knew who it was. I left him watching the telly.

I got to the swings before Susan. The play area was quiet. There were a couple of mums I knew with small kids on the baby swings. They called out to say hello and I waved back. Usually, I'd walk over and talk to them for a while but this time I wasn't in the mood. I got onto one of the swings and sat swinging slowly. The park was very quiet. I could hear the click of wood on wood from the old men and women playing bowls over the way and as I looked in that direction I saw Haydn Hughes sat on the park bench at the edge of the play area just looking out over Hailey Park. His legs were crossed and his shiny black cane was leaning against the bench.

I've told you about him, right? Remember, I was saying about old people and I didn't really have much to do with them. I said that I was going to make the effort to talk to them more. As I was thinking about this and watching him Susan came up and started pushing me from behind to get me moving faster. Once she had she got on the swing next to me and before long we were both flying on those swings. We got it so that we were both moving exactly in time – swinging back and reaching the same point then leaning back holding onto the chains and stretching our legs straight out. For a few minutes we glided side by side so that it was like there was nothing else in the world but me and Susan. There was just the swish of the air as we swung backwards and forwards and the creak of the chains keeping in time with us. It was like we were in a bubble, cut off from everyone turning to each now and again to smile at the perfect timing we'd managed but scared that one mistake would spoil the rhythm.

I didn't want us to fall out of step. A thought came in my mind that if we fell out of step one of us would pass and one of us would fail the 11 plus. It would be a sign. I thought if it happened it would be bad luck and I knew we would not be able to keep this timing for ever so I reached for her chain and brought us slowly to a stop.

"Why did you stop us" she asked me. "That was going really good".

I didn't want to say about the bad luck or what I was thinking so I pointed to Haydn.

"I'd like to talk to him if it's OK with you?" I asked Susan but I knew she wouldn't mind. She is great with the older people. It's me that's been useless at it. She looked surprised.

"Not like you, Gareth," she smiled and put her head to one side puzzled. I was a bit embarrassed about all this and could feel the red colour beginning to creep into my neck and face.

"Well Dad talks to him a lot and, you know, I think I should try a bit harder," I was all over the place. "Look, I've always been a bit scared of these older people and kept away from them. I want to try."

She jumped from the swing and pulled me up by the hand. "Come on then but don't expect to let me do the all the talking."

Hadyn Hughes looked up at us as we got nearer. I'd seen him sitting there many times before. The seat faces out towards the park but he likes to sit at one end and glance back over to see the kids playing. He always carries a bag of sweets and the kids know him and run over from time to time to get a few. He always has plenty. It's a bottomless bag, I'm sure. Hadyn is old, he must be way, way old. He has a thin grey face full of deep lines with white whiskers here and there where he didn't shave so well. There are white hairs sprouting from his ears and on the edge of his ears. He has very blue eyes which are always full of water. When it's cold they spill over into tears so you think he's been crying but he's not. He has thin lips and false teeth. If you are close to him and he's staring out into space across the park you can here him clacking the false teeth as they come away from his gums and back up again. You know, he looks like Albert Steptoe. He carries a black shiny stick with a silvery top and wears a trilby hat. I've never seen him in anything other than a dark navy suit with a white shirt and a blue and white striped tie. He wears black polished shoes which you can see your face in. I tried to shine mine like that with kiwi polish once but it wasn't like his. Mind you I suppose I should have washed the mud off first.

His look at us was like he was surprised that we were coming over to him. I can see why. I've walked past him with just a smile and a hello so many times and never stopped. He probably thinks Susan has pushed me into this, I thought.

He nodded to both of us but didn't say anything. Susan sat next to him on the bench and I sat next to her. I didn't think about it then but afterwards when I was writing this I wondered if I wanted Susan as like a fence between me and Mr Hughes. Susan protecting me from the old fogey, eh!!

"Hello, Mr Hughes, I'm….."I started to say.

"I know who you are Gareth Adams, son of Geraint" he said to me and I'm sure there was a twinkle of fun in his eye. "I thought you might stop ignoring me one of these days. Hello Susan, so you're walking out with young Gareth these days?"

She smiled back at him and spoke politely to Hadyn. "Yes, Mr Hughes. He's very nice when you get to know him. Oh! And Mum and Dad told me to give you regards if I saw you."

It felt a bit spooky. I didn't know that Susan had spoken to him before. I hadn't noticed. Funny, I thought to myself I noticed everything that Susan did. I took a good look at him. From what I'd seen so far old people were usually bad tempered and waved their stick at you to bugger off or spoke to you like you were three years old. Hadyn was different. I could feel that he was watching me closely.

Have you ever watched kids when they're talking to grown ups. If you watch closely you'll see most kids are not looking properly at the grown up. Their eyes flick to the grown ups face and away. Sometimes the kid can't stop moving, hopping from one foot to the other or jumping backwards and forwards. The grown up too is just saying things without thinking too much. You know, "how's your parents, where are you going for your holiday, how are you doing at school, haven't you grown, don't you look like your mother/father" and stuff like that". I mean about people that know your family but who are not family. Kids don't act like this when they are talking to their father or mother. It's different then. Dad talks to me like I'm more grown up than I am. And that's it! Mr Hughes talks to you like you're a person with something in your head like a mum and dad does. And you know what? The more you look at him the less old and weak he seems to be. It's something to do with his eyes, I think.

I was thinking all this while Mr Hughes was talking to Susan but even so I could feel that he was watching me even when he was talking to Susan. They were chatting like they were old friends and I started to feel left out a bit. Then I felt guilty. Like Geoffrey said not everything is about me. My mind wandered to the 11 plus results.

"You think a lot, don't you Gareth?" Mr Hughes had reached forward and nudged me and I grunted and mumbled a sorry. Susan laughed and I tried to stop the red colour creeping into my cheeks.

"Don't worry about it, son. It's good to think but don't forget what the poet said:

*"Act from thought should quickly follow, what is thinking for"*

I looked up at Mr Hughes but not so nervous about him now. I'd not heard anybody, unless they were a teacher, say poetry like this before.

"Mr Hughes knows a lot of poetry, Gareth" Susan said "And he must have read a million books."

He raised his eyes up and laughed like it was a cough. "Ah, Susan if only there was enough time."

Yeah, he did read a lot of books I was thinking. I could remember him sat on this bench in the summer time and he'd be looking down and I could remember seeing the edges of a book sticking up. Funny, normally I would have been wanting to know what someone was reading but mostly here you only saw people with newspapers or magazines. When I thought about why I had not really noticed Mr Hughes reading I blushed again. I had to admit to myself that I used to think that old people didn't matter. There, see! I've written it down now.

"Susan tells me that you read more than she does," he said his eyes twinkling at me. Something told me he already knew. I could see now that those eyes of his missed nothing. Huh, and I thought we were almost invisible to grown ups when we left the house. But not to Mr Haydn Hughes. He must have seen me many times lying on the grass reading some book or other. And goodness knows what else he'd seen.

I nodded to him.

"I think he'd rather be reading a book than coming to call for me at my house," Susan complained to Mr Hughes. She turned her head to look at me with a baby is upset picture on her face.

"That's boys for you when they get bitten by the reading bug, "he chuckled in that coughy way again.

They know how to play together, I thought. They're like good friends who are teasing someone else. I felt on the outside for a moment or two. You ever felt like that when someone you really like seems to know someone and like being with them more than you thought. I'd felt jealous of Geoffrey before now but never felt jealous of a grown up before especially an old one like Mr Hughes.

I think Susan saw some look on my face because she held my hand. "You don't like being teased, do you" she said to me and squeezed tightly on my fingers.

You know I was beginning to feel weaker in some way. I'd gone over to see Mr Hughes feeling confident but it was like I was beginning to melt or something. Something inside me was telling me it was a good idea to make an excuse and go home leaving Susan to talk to Mr Hughes.

I think she saw it in my face. She squeezed my hand more tightly. It's hard to go when someone is holding you, isn't it. If you pull your hand away it's like you're taking something away too. Something from the other person, that is. Am I talking rubbish or do you understand what I mean. I didn't want to take my hand away because inside me somewhere I knew that it would upset Susan and it might change things. I never wanted to upset Susan ever in my life.

"You read a lot, I think too, Mr Hughes," I said. I'd decided that I had to do something before I melted completely.

Those blue eyes in water looked at me and I looked back. I could see his face more clearly now. Yes, it was greyish with the white whiskers but there were little blue veins in his cheeks and thin lines at the side of his eyes. There was a two inch scar at the side of his head coming out from under the trilby. He was turned towards me on the seat with one hand on the back of the park bench and one resting on his knee. His hand was thin for a grown up but bigger than mine for sure. You could see veins standing out on the back of his hand and the bones underneath. The knuckles on his fingers looked bigger than usual on grown ups. Like Pop Rees in school his middle finger and the one next to it were stained with nicotine from smoking Capstan Full Strength yet I'd never seen Mr Hughes smoking in the park.

"He does. Haven't you seen him at the library, Gareth?" Susan said to me. "Mr Hughes is there every two or three days and he reads so fast."

I couldn't help myself from thinking 'And so do I'.

I had seen him there when I thought about it but while I stayed in the kids section, of course, you'd see him in the older sections. I remembered too that sometimes I saw him sat at one of the tables reading one of the books.

"I think Gareth can read pretty quickly, too. Can't you son?" I was beginning to think he had mind reading ability. He reached into his suit pocket and took out two bags of sweets that obviously came from Percy Evans shop. I'd know the bags anywhere. He put one bag in each hand and held them out to us. "This one's pear drops and this one's aniseed twist" he said. How did he know that I liked the aniseed twist and Susan liked the pear drops? We both dipped in and took a sweet.

"Can I ask you something, Mr Hughes" I said.

"All you like, Gareth. All you like."

"How old are you"? I enquired.

"I was 26 years old at the start of the Great War. So how old do you think I am"

I smiled at Susan and whispered in his ear. "He's testing our arithmetic," I said.

"Well go on Gareth. You can work it out quicker than me," she said. This wasn't true but I think she was pushing me to get to know Mr Hughes.

"That makes you around 75 Mr Hughes," I said back to him. "But of course it depends when your birthday is."

"Seventy five. That's right son. Seems your Dad was right about you, young Gareth. I already know Susan here is as sharp as a pin and I had a feeling you were too."

"So if you were 26 when the Great War started you were not in school and working." I said. "Where did you live? What was it like then?"

He laughed. "Son, you ignore me for years and then you want to know my life story."

Susan laughed too and I blushed red. "It's getting towards dusk now, son. Your dad will be home and wondering how long you will be. Same with Susan here. If you want my story I can tell you. You will find me here most days as you know."

He was right of course. Hailey Park was getting gloomy. The mums with their kids had gone home and the parky was doing a final check. "Yeah", I said. "I like stories and don't want you to rush it. He was getting to his feet and reached for his cane and so we did too. "You can walk with me to the edge of Belle Vue Crescent if you like" he said. He lived a few houses from the top end and so we fell into step with him. He walked slowly but firmly. I could see the stick was not to help him walk but maybe just like his suit, tie and trilby hat. He didn't speak to us on the way back and we walked with him as far as the edge of Belle Vue.

"I've lived here for so long." He said. "I've come and gone a couple of times but this is my home. It's a good place. A good place."

He said no more. Turned away from us, waved the cane in the air to say goodbye and went home. As we watched him walk away I said to Susan, "I don't know why I've never done it before"

"Better late than never." She said holding my hand. "Come on walk me home along Station Road and we can buy some Pear Drops from Percy Evans. I've got a taste for them now."

150

"And Aniseed twist," I said thankful I had a few pennies in my pocket. I wanted to keep as much as I could though. It's Susan's birthday in June. As we walked along Station road towards Percy Evans shop the thought of the 11 plus results came into my mind. I shuddered and Susan looked at me. "Getting cold," I said but she knew it wasn't. I'm sure this girl can read my mind.

\* \* \* \* \* \* \*

You know I told you once that when I was doing work to prepare for the 11 plus I used to sleepwalk and dream and things like that. It's the way I am. I didn't sleepwalk the night before the 11 plus result but I dreamed. And what a dream. Of course I'm sure you can guess what it was about!!

In this dream I was waiting for the postman but when he came he had no envelope for me. I asked him where it was and he didn't know. He told me he'd delivered a lot in Llandaff North but for some reason there was not one for me. He said I should ask the Head Master at school. I went inside to Dad and he told me not to worry. It had probably got lost and anyway Mr Evans would tell me. I raced out to school with David and on the way I saw Alun coming towards me waving his letter with a big smile on his face because he'd passed. When we got to Tom's house he was outside waiting for me and he'd passed. They were both looking at me but I couldn't say anything. David seemed to have forgotten what happened too and kept saying 'show them your envelope'.

We walked on to the school gates and everyone was there. Nigel, Geoffrey, Philip, Dafydd, Susan and Janet they all had passed and were waving their letters. Next thing we were sat in class and everyone was in their seats. Even Simon was there. They all had an envelope except me. Mr Evans came in and said that my entry had been disqualified because Mr Cox had seen me looking at Geoffrey's paper. I had been caught cheating and this meant it was an automatic fail. Geoffrey was looking at me and smiling and everyone else was looking at me like I should be ashamed. I kept saying I didn't. I did it fairly. I'm not a cheat. Then Mr Evans stood aside and I saw those boys who'd bullied us when we were playing cricket and they were with Ceri. Ceri said we've come for you and those bigger boys came running for me and started to drag me off. I started shouting and screaming………..

"Gareth, wake up, wake up," I heard. It was David and Dad was at the bedroom door too. David looked really worried and Dad was concerned too. I had a bad dream I told them.

I wouldn't want one like that," David said. "I thought they were killing you."

"Me too," I mumbled.

Dad said "Look it's six o'clock. We're all awake now so why don't I do bacon, egg, sausage, fried bread, mushrooms and grilled tomatoes as well."

"Your favourite, Gareth" David said to me. "Come on let's go"

"That's really great Dad," I said. "Thanks. I'll just wash and get dressed and be down in a minute. "

Dad looked at me and nodded. "Come on David, let's go."

I didn't really want it I bet you can guess. I was feeling all tight in the stomach and felt sick. The last thing I felt like was a fry up!! I washed and dressed slowly and after a while I could smell the food coming up the stairs. You know what? After five minutes my mouth was watering and I was rushing to get down to get at it.

Course breakfast was over and done with by 7 o clock and the postman comes at 7.30. Dad had the radio on for news and was listening to it in the kitchen and me and David were sat in the sitting room. He was reading the Victor and I was trying to read the Hotspur but it was no good. I just couldn't. I kept reading the same page over and over again with nothing going in. At quarter past seven I decided to go and wait outside the front door for the postman. David wanted to come too but I asked him please to wait inside. He did.

Outside the front door it was quiet. It was a bit chilly but the sky was very blue and it felt like it might be a great sunny day. I kept glancing up Hazelhurst road to watch for the postman. I could not stop moving and was pacing from the front door back to the edge of the pavement. I really needed to go to the toilet but put it out of my mind. I was scared the postman would come if I left. At just after 7.30 I saw him coming around the edge of Hazelhurst Road. He'd already delivered to Alun and was getting close to Geoffrey. I decided when he reached Janet's house I was going to rush down to him to see if he'd give me the letter a bit early.

When he was there I raced up to him. He was only 20 yards from our house but I couldn't wait any more.

He stopped when I reached him. "Please do you have any post for Adams house."

"Gareth, I'm not supposed to hand over mail in the street. It's against regulations. I have to put it through the letter box." He had a stern look on his face.

"But you've given letters to me before........"

"Gotcha, there Gareth," he laughed bringing his jolly face back. He held up a letter to read. "I got one yer for yer Dad. Looks a bit official too. I delivered a lot like this today. You know what it's all about?"

He winked and held the letter out. I grabbed it with a thanks and ran off. He called out a good luck while I was racing for the front door. I gave the letter to Dad in the kitchen. He turned the radio off and David threw the comic to the floor to come and watch with me. Dad read the address first and turned it over to look at the back. He picked up his pocket knife from the kitchen table opened it and slid the blade into the envelope and slowly cut it open. It seemed to take for ever. He put his hand inside the open envelope and pulled out the letter and unfolded it. He held the letter up and read it.

I couldn't wait. "Come on Dad. Please, is it yes or no. I have to know."

Dad continued to read and then looked down at me. He spoke softer than usual. "I think you'd better look for yourself, son," he said and handed me the paper.

"So did I pass," I whispered to him my throat drying up.

He pointed to the letter for me to read it. Have you ever tried to read something when you're in a panic. It's near impossible. The words are dancing all over the place and won't stay together and when they do it's like you're looking at a language you don't understand. I closed my eyes and willed myself to be calm and opened them to try to read.

It took me a while to focus but in the end I read it. There were only a few paragraphs. The answer I wanted was in the second one. I read it three times to make sure I got it right. It said that the Education Authority was pleased to inform that Gareth Adams had successfully passed the 11 plus examination and been allocated a place at Canton High School, Fairwater. It also asked Dad to confirm within 14 days that the place would be accepted.

I waited for a few seconds for it to sink in and then of course relief and silliness hit me. I jumped up and down waving the letter

*Nobody Watching*

and shouting out, "I did it, I did it, I did it" Dad was smiling and happy and David joined in with me to jump up and down.

You can't keep dancing around in a crazy way for that long so we stopped after a minute or so and I gave the letter back to Dad. You know what he did? He reached out his hand like I was a proper grown up for me to shake his hand. I took it and we shook hands. His felt big and rough but gentle and mine felt so small inside his. "Well done" he said with a smile. "Me and David, we are proud of you."

Then a reminder came of another room I needed to go to and I raced off to the toilet.

When I came back I was still so excited. I just wanted to go to school to be with my friends and to know that we were all together. The worry of my not passing had now gone but I was now worried for my friends. I needed to know.

Like I told you Dad was not working this morning so he came to the front door with me and David to wave us goodbye. I was in a rush to get to school. In school it was like some kind of party in the playground. Groups were rushing everywhere to check who had passed and who had failed. I stopped near the gates to watch it all with David. You know you could tell really just by looking. There were some with smiling faces where it was obvious that they'd passed and some sad and you knew they had not passed.

I went in to join the rushing and racing about and left David to find his friends. There was one person I was looking for and who do you think that was? Susan of course. She was with her friends in a corner of the playground. I waited until she saw me and when she did she came running over.

"Did you?" I asked.

"Did you?" she asked right back.

I didn't want to play the guessing game. "Yes, I got Canton. And you?"

"Oh!" she sighed and put her eyes down, "I thought we would both go to Cardiff High."

My face dropped. This was bad news.

"But we're both going to Canton instead!" It took a second or two for it to sink in that she'd been teasing me but then we hugged. The teachers don't allow this but today I didn't care. Then I held her hand and we rushed around everywhere to check with our friends. I tried to write about all the rushing round and loud voices and talking and relief and sadness and kids trying to show they didn't care but I couldn't. Just see in your mind kids running round like crazy. The big stuff for me to write down now is who passed and who failed, well anyway for the kids I've written about so far. I've done it alphabetically so I don't show favourites except me and Susan are at the top.

| | | |
|---|---|---|
| Susan | Passed | Canton High |
| Gareth | Passed | Canton High |
| Alun | Passed | Canton High |
| Dafydd | Passed | Cathays |
| Geoffrey | Passed | Cathays |
| Janet | Passed | Canton High |
| Nigel | Passed | Canton High |
| Philip | Passed | Cardiff High |
| Tom | Failed | Glantaf |

Mr Evans and all the teachers were really happy it was the best passing result they'd had in a long time. For a moment I wondered which school in Bridgend Jack would go to.

But you've worked it out, right. I got one result I wanted – me and Susan and passing to go to the same school and one I didn't want. I was losing my best friend Tom. Dafydd too for some reason was going to Cathays as well as Geoffrey. Janet was upset about this of course. Phil too had got Cardiff High which only the best go to or so they say.

So of all my close friends we'd all passed, except Tom. He'd known this would happen and how it happened I don't know. While Old Coxy was out of class I glanced on his desk at his papers. He had a list there of those he thought would pass and Tom's name was there. I wondered what was going through his mind. I thought about it a lot. It was a big exam for 10 to 11 year old kids like us. If you passed it meant one life and if you failed it meant another. Tom might still be with us. He gets a chance to take another test at 13. He must have been ill or nervous the day of the test. Tom is too clever to fail. How could it happen and why can't he do it again now to fix it so he can come with us. Some things I just don't understand. They just don't seem fair.

He was trying to put a brave face on it in school, I know. He was showing that he was so happy for us and laughing that he messed it up and would be with us in a couple of years. We all met as our band of seven and swore that we continue our gang forever. We would always be friends wherever were. Nigel wrote it up in school and we all signed it at morning break. It said

*We the undersigned boys of Llandaff North gang do hereby solemnly swear that now and forever more we will stay as friends for all our lives and this will apply whatever school we may go to. This has been said by all and what has been said let no man put asunder.*

I think when Nigel grows up he will be a vicar. That's for sure. He writes like one. We all signed it but not in blood this time. We did it at school and didn't want to risk being caught signing something in blood.

We all joined hands to say "I swear" and right then I believed it would be true. We would never be apart. Never.

But later I wondered. In the dinner break I chatted to Dafydd. "I'm really sorry you didn't get into Canton" I said.

"You shouldn't be, Gareth. I don't mind." He said.

"You don't mind."

"No. I put down Cathays as my first choice."

I was shocked. "Why would you do that?"

"I wanted to do something different. Like an adventure," he replied. "You'll be OK. You got the ones you want with you – except for Tom of course."

The look on my face must have been amazing to Dafydd. "Come on Gareth," he said to me. "Not all of us are like you and Tom wanting to keep things as they are. This is it. Things change."

I think something else was on his mind as well when he said this but at the time I didn't pick up on it. "But you only just swore that we would all stay friends." I said to him. It must have sounded like a whine.

He shrugged his shoulders. "Yeah, I know and maybe we will. But we can also make some more friends, right?" he said.

I thought about it later when I got home. I think maybe he's right. I like to keep things as they are but it doesn't happen. It's a dream isn't it? Things change whether you like it or not. Jack has gone. Tom is going to Glantaf. Dafydd is going to Cathays. We wanted our mum to be with us, didn't we, but she's not. But the truth is that nothing stays the same forever. It's always changing. There's nothing I can do to keep it the same.

Oh yeah, I forgot to say. It was the same with Geoffrey. That same lunch time I asked him about Cathays and he looked me right in the eye but making sure no-one else was around. "I picked Cathays, Gareth. I didn't want to be at the same place as you."

I didn't know what to say but because I've done nothing I just said "Your choice. But what about Janet?"

"Oh yeah, she would have picked Cathays if I'd told her but if I said anything it would be straight into Susan's ear and then yours."

I just walked away. There was nothing more to be said. It was time now for me to think about what I would say to Dad. He needed to know why Geoffrey was so angry with us and maybe he'd know what to do about it. But I am worried inside. I haven't got a clue how I will bring this up with Dad.

After school I walked with David and Tom towards home. Tom was telling a few jokes which was making David laugh. He likes Tom as you know so I said "Hey, Tom, why don't you tell your mum that you're coming with us today?" Straight away Tom said no. He said something about his Dad wanting Tom to help him with something. We said ok and see you tomorrow but as we walked away I looked back to see Tom's face changing. It was beginning to twitch the way it does when you're trying to stop yourself from crying. I think he really just wanted to be on his own. Tom has been really brave today. I think if I had not passed I could not have gone to school.

When I told Dad about the results he already knew. News travels very fast in Llandaff North. He was surprised that Tom hadn't passed as well. He said it was sad that one exam on one day in your life could mean so much. But he also said it was almost certain that Tom would be with the rest of us at thirteen when he retakes it. Dad said he's too clever. It will show in the end.

So the door opened and we got pushed through it and like I thought there was another door which others went through that I couldn't see. Me and Susan went through the same door and Tom a different one. I only hope it doesn't change things for us. Do you think this is a stupid hope?

\* \* \* \* \* \* \* \*

*Nobody Watching*

Is it always like this? Some big thing in your life which you've been waiting for comes like a big rock splashing in the water churning up everything and sending waves everywhere – and then it's gone. The water is smooth again as if the rock never was. Is it like that always? After a few days of nothing but talking about going to the new school it all fell away. We started to talk about Sports Day and the holidays. The grammar schools start two weeks later than junior schools so guess what?? We get eight weeks of instead of six this year. Yeah!!

But we have another eight weeks in school before the holidays come. They start at the end of the first week in July. It's such a long time to wait and school is getting boring. Still we have more time to sit and read any book we like and that's great for me.

At break it's a bit different. I know we swore the oath to stay friends - you know the one Nigel wrote but I'm beginning to wonder. Tom spends a bit more time with the kids who are going to Glantaf and Dafydd and Geoffrey spend a lot of time together. I suppose it was really going to happen like that. Maybe I do spend too much time wanting to keep things as they are. It doesn't work though does it?

I was happy when the school week was over. There were so many things to think about. I wrote myself a list on Friday night:

1   I have to talk to Dad about Geoffrey
2   I have to speak to Tom about what happens next
3   I have to get something for Susan's birthday
4   I have to meet up with Hadyn Hughes again with Susan
5   I have to work out with Susan our plan for Sports Day
6   I have to remind dad that we must go to the Whitsun Treat in Hailey Park in June

Most of these are easy but still I don't know what to say to Dad.

It must have been all that went on during the week and getting the exam result but you know on Saturday morning I overslept. And when I say overslept I mean it. Dad and David woke me up at 11. Dad laughed about it. Me and David have been waiting to have breakfast, he said, but it'll feel more like lunch now. David pulled at me to get me out of bed. So I didn't dress or wash but came straight down to see the pile of bacon and toast and sausages on the table. Me and David got stuck in while Dad fried fresh eggs for us. I was starving.

When we were done and I got washed and dressed and came back. I wanted to sit down and read a comic or two before deciding what to do in the afternoon but Dad wouldn't let me. He was fixing a cupboard in the kitchen and called me to get him another screwdriver from his toolbox in the garage. I think I must have puffed a bit with annoyance but after Dad had made such a great breakfast I didn't complain. I got up from the lounge and went out the kitchen door and down the path to the garage.

When I opened the door I got a shock. Someone had left a brand new Raleigh three speed bike still in the wrappers in the middle of our garage. Who left this here, I started to say to myself. What do they want to leave it here for? Stupid isn't it? It only really dawned on me that it was mine when I heard Dad and David chuckling behind me at my surprise. Who else could it be for, huh?

For a second or two I felt like crying with happiness. I'd wanted a Viking 5 speed derailleur but the Raleigh 3 speed with twist grip was great. It would be one of the best in Llandaff North. I wiped my eye with my sleeve and turned round to hug Dad. I think he was as happy as me. I said, come on David you can help me get the wrappers off and after my first ride up the lane and around the block you can have a go.

He couldn't believe it and was quicker getting the wrapping paper off than me. I thought I was just getting on to a brand new bike but once I was on it and Dad had opened the garage doors it was more. The bike is a smooth rider and glides out into the lane. It brought back memories of when Dad took the support wheels off my first two wheeler bike and we practised riding on the grass. Time after time I fell until suddenly the balance was there. I smiled as I remembered how I could only go straight and couldn't stop and Dad was chasing after me so I wouldn't go straight into the river fence.

But now I was on a smart brand new Raleigh with three speed and twist grip. Not 5 speed derailleur its true but a great bike. As I turned from the lane along Hailey Park into Hazelhurst Road I felt great. People looking at me would know that the bike really meant something else. It meant that I'd passed the 11 plus and was going to Canton High. A grammar school. And I'd escaped having my head shoved down the toilet at Glantaf. As I looked along Hazelhurst Road what did I see? Alun, Dafydd, Nigel, Tom and Geoffrey were riding along on their bikes. Of course Geoffrey had his for a long time and Tom had one too!

Tom pulled alongside me. "Hey, sleepy head we came for you at 10 but you're Dad said you were out for the count."

"Well, I'm here now," I said and looked at his bike. It was a Viking 5 speed derailleur racing bike just like the one I wanted and which me and Tom had talked about a lot. Tom saw me admiring it. "Nice bike," I said and feeling a spark of jealousy.

"Well who said you had to pass the 11 plus to get a new bike, ay?" Tom laughed and I joined in.

"Come on," he said. "Let's race down the road and see who's quickest." I grinned and started to get ready for the race but stopped. "Give me a few minutes," I said. "I promised David a ride once I'd gone around the block. I promised and he'll be waiting. Will you do me a favour? Will you ask him to race you?"

"Yeah," Tom said with a grin. "Send him round."

Turning the corner by the rugby club and back down the lane I could see David stood on the canal bank walk waiting for me. I was glad I didn't forget about him and kept my promise. He was excited as I stepped off the bike and helped him on. I gave him a push to get him going and stopped myself from saying "Don't scrape it." Dad watched me. "Your pals are out front waiting for you" he said.

"I know, Dad," I've just seen them. "They'll still be there when David gets back. "He can have some fun for a while and then I'll join them." Then I went on, "Thanks for the bike, Dad. It's just what I wanted."

"You earned it Gareth," He said to me. "I'm proud of you son." He turned and went back through the garage and on to the house. It's embarrassing when your Dad makes a fuss of you but it's still nice.

After five minutes waiting I wanted to ride the bike with my pals and was beginning to feel sorry that I'd let David have a go. I knew I might be nasty to him if I wasn't careful so I decided to think about Susan instead and what I would get for her birthday. Only a few weeks away. I was thinking about this so much that David was back before I expected him. "Sorry, I was so long," he said.

"You weren't that long," I heard myself say. "You could have had longer, but I'm glad you're back anyway."

I got on the bike and started to ride away but stopped to look back at David. "Why don't you get your bike out and come with me," I said to him. You should have seen his face!

"Can I?" he asked half thinking I was tricking him and would ride off as soon as he went into the garage for his bike.

"Come on. Get it quickly," I said to him, "Before I change my mind."

He was back out in a flash not really believing I'd be waiting. His bike is smaller. It's my old two wheeler that I got too big to use. It's getting too small for David as well. His knees are just about touching the handle bars. We rode alongside each other down the lane to join my friends. I could see that David was so happy to be with me and my friends. He is my brother but I don't really know how he spends his time when we're out of school. He's got a couple of friends I know who come to the door asking for him sometimes but there doesn't seem to be a gang like we have. I'd never given it that much thought before. I thought about Dad too. Who are his friends? I don't really know.

I forgot about it as we rounded the corner into Hazelhurst Road and joined my pals.

\* \* \* \* \* \* \*

That afternoon the boys had wanted to ride the new bikes over to Radyr. Tom's Dad is at the cricket club getting things ready for the new fixtures. I dropped out of it as I'd promised to meet Susan at 3 to take a walk round the park. And to tell the truth I had something else on my mind too. I think the boys were surprised that I dropped out specially Tom but even though I got teased about seeing my girlfriend they let it go after a while.

I waited outside the house for her. I was thinking of waiting for her on my bike but then thought it might look as if I was showing off. Susan wasn't getting a bike. She'd already told her parents not to get one. She said she'd rather have some money. When I asked her why, she said she wanted her sister to take her to town to help her buy new clothes. New clothes! What a waste, I thought. You know it was my first idea that girls might think a bit different to boys when it comes to things that really matter. Most of my pals are dragged into town by their mothers to get clothes. Dad has to take me of course but David's lucky he gets the stuff that I grow out of.

Susan was spot on time and we held hands walking towards the park. As usual we headed up towards the playground for the swings. I could see Mr Hughes too on the bench sat half looking out over the park and half watching the play area. This time we both waved and he raised his hand back. The swings were full so we got on to the roundabout. This can be crazy. You can get it spinning so fast that you can feel yourself being pulled off. Even then when you get off you're staggering round as giddy as someone who's had too much to drink. Hay, just like Geoff's Dad I thought and laughed out loud but quickly stopped thinking about it. It would lead to Dad and what I have to talk about soon.

After a while we gave up on the swings. The park playground was busy and kids were not giving the swings up easily so Susan said that we should go talk to Mr Hughes. "I hear you two did well," he said as we sat down next to him.

We both nodded. "Same school too so you'll be able to keep an eye on each other," he said and went on. "You'll be growing up now and start getting bad mannered and thinking old uns like me know nothing."

He said it with a smile but there was something else as well that wasn't a smile. "No we won't Mr Hughes," Susan said. "We'll still be good."

"You might be," he replied. "Sometimes girls keep being friendly and polite but boys. Well, we're a different animal aren't we son." He pointed to me. "We can be a bit nastier."

Was he saying this to me I was thinking? Have I done something that he knows about. Maybe he knows about me and Geoffrey. Nah! How could he? We're little kids and he's an old bloke.

He went on. "I was. When I got to be just a bit older than you. Nasty little bugger, I was. But then you get back to your real self when everything inside you has been jumbled up, knocked about and settles down again."

"So you're not a nasty old bugger now then," I asked with a straight face.

He laughed like a cough again. "No the medication keeps me on the right track, son."

"I think Gareth might like to borrow some of that medicine," Susan chipped in looking at me out of the corner of her eyes.

"Oh, yes," Mr Hughes said a little surprised. "Are you being nasty then Gareth?"

I didn't answer for a bit and both Susan and Mr Hughes stayed quiet waiting for me to speak. Something I'm beginning to learn is that when people go quiet and say nothing then it seems like it forces you to speak. The quiet just gets too much.

"Well not me exactly," I started but then I found I didn't want to talk about it. "It's nothing really and anyway I'd like to hear more about you. You said you were 26 when the Great War started.?"

I glanced at Susan. I think she was disappointed that I didn't say more about what she'd learned from Janet but I couldn't bring myself to talk about it. Not yet anyway.

"That's right son." Mr Hughes said. "I was 26 when it all happened and one of the lucky ones who made it through."

"But what happened before the war Mr Hughes," Susan asked. "You must have done a lot of things before that. You must have seen a lot of things here."

"Well I wasn't born here, you know," Mr Hughes replied. "I was born in Merthyr in 1888. Sounds a long time ago doesn't it but sometimes to me it doesn't seem that long ago. You'll know what I mean when you get older."

While Mr Hughes was pausing I was trying to think what it would have been like in 1888. I could see horses and carriages and people wearing strange clothes. Not like the stuff we wear today.

"We moved from Merthyr to Cardiff in 1902 when I was fourteen. My father was working in a coal mine but he had to leave. They were bad working days then and my father made a lot of fuss to the management about poor working conditions and better pay for the hard work the men did. It was a risky life down a pit in those days and if something went wrong you could be badly hurt or even killed. This would be disaster for a family if they lost their working man to an injury. My father said some of the men would prefer death to disability."

"So what happened? Did the pit owners stop him working? Ban him or something?"

"You'd think that wouldn't you. But no it wasn't them but they were very happy to see him go," Mr Hughes continued. "He was driven out by some of the miners. They thought he was a trouble maker and would cause problems for them. Little accidents would happen to him in the pit. Nothing that hurt him badly but enough to let him know that worse could come. So he left."

"Why would people do that?" Susan asked. "He was trying to help them."

"Mostly working men want a quiet life," Mr Hughes replied. "As long as they have enough to house and feed their family they're content. They'll turn a blind eye to the bad things and hope it doesn't happen to them. They don't really want to strike unless things get really bad."

"What happened to your father here," I asked.

"He didn't bother trying to organize workers that's for sure," Mr Hughes said and his voice sounded annoyed. "He got a job with the Council as a general labourer and stayed quiet for the rest of his life. He died in 1913 when he was 59. I didn't see him on his last days either and missed his funeral too."

"Where were you," I asked.

"I was in New Zealand then," he said and a smile came to his face. "When I was a kid at school and we learned about New Zealand at lessons the place fascinated me. I always had it on my mind and wanted to see it. I had this picture of green fields and trees as far as the eye could see with beautiful mountains, valleys and rivers. A big country but with not too many people living there."

"I've wanted to see it too," I said. "But it's so far away."

"It is and that's for sure," Mr Hughes replied. "But if you want to see or do something badly enough you'll find a way. When I was 16 I told my father what I wanted to do. He was fine about it but my mother wasn't too happy but in the end they let me go. I'd have liked to stay at school but there wasn't the money and New Zealand was pulling me. Back then we had some relatives in Liverpool and so I went to stay with them until I could get a job on a ship bound for Auckland."

He stopped and laughed. "I discovered I was no sailor though. Some people got sea legs and some can never get them. I was sick as a dog most of the way over."

"But you were only 16," Susan said to him. "Didn't you miss home, your mother and father and the other seaman must have been so much older."

"Yes, I missed home but the need to see New Zealand was stronger," he said. "A ship always has a few young crew who can get together. Some of the older seamen might be a bit rough and try to hurt you but there's always others that come to your aid. The work was hard but I was young and strong and could manage it. Mind you after the journey was over, I was in no rush for a long sea trip again. Once we reached Auckland and I got paid off I found some lodgings and started my search for a job. I wanted to work on a farm. I don't know why. I didn't know anything about it but I was willing to work hard just to get food and a place to sleep if necessary. I just wanted some time to walk through the fields and get to see some of that beautiful countryside."

"And did it happen?" Susan asked.

"Well I realized that Auckland was not the place to be to find a farm job. I used to go to the library to check through news papers and do some research on the best farm locations. Once I'd done that I headed to the Waikato region around Hamilton. I had to walk to a lot of farms but in the end a Welshman gave me a job. He used to farm near Brecon. That's the way it always works I think. I found people are always willing to help those who come from the same background and maybe speak in the same way.

"How long did you stay?" I asked.

"Well the farmer, Owen Rees, had a dairy farm so we produced milk, cream and butter. I found I really liked it once I'd learned a few things," Mr Hughes said. "As time went by I missed my mother and father and Wales less and less. I wrote to them of course and loved getting their letters back. I sent long and detailed letters describing everything and I was happy to get even just a few lines back from them. But my job and the beauty of the country kept me there and when I met Anne Ellis when I was 19 that was it."

I knew that there was no Mrs Hughes around so I thought that maybe she had passed away or maybe he never even married Anne Ellis but I didn't want to blurt out with an awkward question. Susan got in before me which was just as well. I'd probably have said the wrong thing.

"I think Mrs Hughes passed away some time ago if I remember rightly. Isn't that right Mr Hughes," Susan asked softly. I think she knew more about him from somewhere. Her parents, I guessed.

"Anne Ellis, who became Mrs Hughes later was a wonderful person," Mr Hughes said. I noticed his face was looking both sad and happy at the same time. "I was this rough farm boy of 19 years old and she was starting out as a teacher at the local school. Well somehow I won her over and we got married. Owen Rees helped us get a little place close to the farm and I thought maybe we would stay there for the rest of our lives. The years that followed were probably the happiest of my life but when my father died in 1913 I got a letter from my mother which didn't actually ask me to come home but the message was there. I discussed it with Anne and we decided that we should visit anyway and maybe persuade my mother to come to New Zealand."

Mr Hughes paused and laughed with that cough again. "I was just as sick on the way back as when I was a boy but Anne didn't even get a flutter in the stomach. Liverpool and Cardiff now seemed so big and noisy to me but surprisingly my country girl wife loved it and she hit it off with my mother instantly. It was easy to convince her to come with us to New Zealand."

"So….." Susan elbowed me to stop me asking.

But he knew what I was going to ask. "Anne died of pneumonia, son. A few weeks after she arrived she got caught in a downpour. It was almost freezing that day. She caught a cold of course and then the complications set in. That was it."

"She died so young," I said in amazement. It reminded me that my mother had died too early also. I sighed a bit. Awful things happen in life, that's for sure.

He nodded. "So I wrote to her parents and Owen Rees asking them to look after the house for me for a while. I couldn't face going back there to be reminded of Anne everywhere I went. The next thing I new the war with Germany started in 1914. They were recruiting in Cardiff for the 38th Infantry Division I got hurt fighting at Passiondale in October 1917. I was lucky to have lasted so long. I was in hospital for a while but got out at the end of 1917 and came back here. I got a job with the Council in the Parks Department and stayed there all my life. I think my father working for them in the past helped but also because I'd worked on a farm in New Zealand did too. The fact that it was a dairy farm didn't seem to matter to them. I've been retired now for God knows how many years. When the second war came along I was too old to get called up so stayed here and watched all the younger men leave but the second was a cleaner war. Too many men died for nothing in the Great War."

He paused and was thinking I could see. I waited for a while and then asked, "And you never went back to New Zealand,"

"Well, yes I did." Mr Hughes replied. "I went back in 1920 to see Anne's family and Owen Rees. In a way I was glad the war got in the way. I had been dreading the return to see Anne's family. I thought they might blame me for her death. As it turned out they were wonderful and so was Owen Rees. In the years gone by he'd rented out my place and gave me a good sum and a bit more. I was tempted to stay but there were too many memories of Anne. So like I said I saw out my time here mostly at Roath Park but we did a little work here in Hailey Park from time to time. That's it son. My life in a nutshell."

I wanted to ask him if he'd ever thought of getting married again. Would my Dad I wondered also. One thing I'm realizing is that it's very hard to know what is going on inside someone's head. It's so difficult to know what they're thinking or who they are really. How do you know if someone is a good person or a bad person if you don't know what they are thinking. But I think Mr Hughes is a good person and I realize we are lucky too. There has not been a war since I was born yet Mr Hughes here has seen two World Wars but there's something I've noticed. You know what it is? War is about death and killing but when you ask people about it who were there, they won't say so much. I think things happened that they want to forget. I think Mr Hughes must have killed enemy soldiers in the Great War and my Dad, Tom's Dad and Susan's Dad might have as well in the second world war. Can you imagine what it must be like If you'd been killing other soldiers and seen them die in front of you. Makes you shudder, doesn't it. A few times I've asked my Dad to tell me a bit about the Second World war. He won't say too much except that without it he wouldn't have met my mother. He said a good thing came out of a bad thing but wouldn't say any more about it.

I had been thinking too and must have been lost in these thoughts for a while. When I looked up I could see that both Mr Hughes and Susan were looking at me.

"Like I said son, you're a big thinker," he chuckled and went on. "So tell me what's this thing that's bothering you that young Susan here really wants you to talk about. And I don't mean your sports race against Geoffrey. Yes I know that's coming up and he's faster than you. So if you want a chance of beating him you've got to improve your training and your speed. Try carrying a couple of weights when you're running or a heavy bag on your back and then run again without them. See what happens."

This sounded like a good idea and I stored it away. But it had come for the time to talk about Geoffrey.

I wasn't sure about this to be honest, you know. I didn't want to say something that might cause a lot of problems but then doing nothing wasn't working either. So I gave a big sigh and started to talk to Mr Hughes. Me and Susan told him about what we'd learned from Janet.

You know what, when we finished, he sighed. "Kids are always thinking that one or other of their parents are going to run off at any minute. It happens for sure and Geoffrey has got himself in a mess over it."

"You know him?" I asked.

"Come on," Mr Hughes replied. 'I know all of you little buggers and knew most of your parents before that. Geoffrey is a bit like you, Gareth. He's stubborn with a streak of fire in him."

"Like me?" I thought. "You're wrong there Mr Hughes. Geoffrey is nothing like me.

Mr Hughes stroked his chin for a while thinking and looking out over the park. "You know what?" he said after he'd finished. "This is a job for a woman. You shouldn't say anything to your father, Gareth. Just leave it to me now."

"What are you going to do?" Susan asked.

"Well, this is between us," he said and waited for us to nod agreement. "I've known Nancy since she was a kid. I'll get her to speak with Geoffrey's mother about it. She obviously doesn't know what's going on with Geoffrey. Once she knows she'll put Geoffrey right but your father must know nothing about all this, Gareth, Absolutely nothing."

\* \* \* \* \* \* \* \*

After I'd walked Susan home I saw Dafydd by the school and on his way home. I could see straight away that something had happened. Dafydd was excited and angry at the same time. My face asked the question, I'm sure.

"Just as well you didn't come with us," Dafydd said with a smile. "We hadn't gone far when we ran into trouble. I think Tom's Dad's will want to give Tom a hard time when he gets back from Radyr cricket club. But we never got that far. And when his Dad gets the story he won't get angry."

I waited. "We'd only ridden a short way over the bridge and turned right into Radyr Court Road going along the bank of the river. So you know that flat piece of concrete that's a bit further down from the monkey rocks on the other side?"

I nodded.

Dafydd went on. "Well we decided we'd stop there and skim some stones across the river for a bit. Well of course once we got going we slipped up and stopped paying attention. No-one was looking out which was a big, big mistake."

I nodded again. I was picturing the scene. They'd all got tied up with the skimming and forgot to keep a look out. I wondered if I'd have kept watching if I was playing with them too. Would it have been different?

"Course when you're not looking something always happens," Dafydd said. "Do you remember that kid who tried to bully us last year and Ceri arrived in the nick of time?"

"I can't forget him," I said and I couldn't. I'd always been on the lookout for him. "It was him?"

"It was him - and his two pals were there as well," Dafydd said.

"Did they remember you all?" I asked.

"Not at first but let me tell you what happened, he said. "First the big kid calls out to us and we look around to see them. I remember thinking, shit this looks bad. He says to us we're breaking the law by polluting the river with stones. I could see they were spreading out a bit to stop us running away but we couldn't anyway. We'd left our bikes lined up together a bit away from us."

"There was no-one else around, No workmen or anyone" I asked.

"Nope, We were on our own. Then this kid who was with the big one he spots Geoffrey. Geoff had been trying to move behind Nigel to stop them from seeing his face but it didn't work."

He went on."So he calls out to the big kid. 'There's that kid that ran off last year. They're all those ones we ran into in Hailey Park playing cricket, remember?"

"Oh shit," I said. "I can imagine the look on his face after that."

"Oh, yeah," Dafydd said. "First he looked us over and then it all came back to him, didn't it. You could see it all working out on his face how he thought he was going to get us and then Ceri arrived to save the day. But most of all you could see for a second the shame he felt at his friends seeing him get beaten. I could tell we were going to cop it."

"Your big friend is not around to save you kids this time is he?" he said with a big smile. "You could see he was looking forward to giving us a bashing. The big git."

"Tom moved to one side a bit and towards him," Dafydd said, "He was trying to get some room between him and our bikes. Tom was thinking that maybe a few of the boys could get their bikes and scarper if they had the chance."

You know I could feel my own heart beating faster as Dafydd was telling me the story and I could picture the scene. I was glad I wasn't there and ashamed for thinking so at the same time.

He went on. "Tom says to him 'Yeah, we wish he was here too becos he kicked the shit out of you last time. You can't stand up to bigger boys so you come after smaller kids like us, right. Bullying us makes you feel good, does it'?"

My heart was pounding that's for sure.

"He froze a bit because now he was going to look bad if he took it out on us," Dafydd said, "But you could see he wanted to do it anyway. So he thought about it and came up with an idea that made him feel better."

"What was that?" I asked.

Dafydd laughed. "He told us we would be punished a bit for polluting the water and for being cheeky to our elders."

"Tom had moved around a bit more by now." Dafydd went on." The big kid hadn't noticed it but there was a branch about three feet long and as thick as my arm on the ground so Tom grabbed it and shouted for the rest of us to run and he made a lunge at the big kid to distract him. They all ran for the bikes except me. I don't know why I did it but I ran into two of the boys who wanted to chase after the lads and I slowed them down. One of them fell over." Dafydd laughed remembering this.

"Did they get away?" I asked.

"Yeah, once they ran for their bikes and jumped onto them they were gone." Dafydd said. "I glanced around and saw they were riding away. The two other boys were holding me tight now though. I couldn't do anything to help Tom."

I felt a little bit jealous. Tom was my best friend. It should have been me helping him not Dafydd. But you know what? I wasn't sure if I would have run away and left him. I just didn't know. I tried to picture myself staying and helping. I know that's what I would want to do.

I nodded my head for Dafydd to go on. "You better be quick then", Tom said to him." The boys will stop the first grown up or policeman they see and say a bunch of bullies are picking on little kids. With a bit of luck you'll only be in borstal for a couple of years."

And then he said to him, "You might have a few bruises too later. You see, then they'll go for my brother and Mervyn Pratt. They'll do for your sure. They'll find you wherever you live. Where? Fairwater. A few of them laughed. Ely? And there was nothing. So it's Ely he said. OK, well you all better be watching your backs now because I know your faces and I won't forget,"

"Tom was amazing," Dafydd said.

You know I could see the scene completely like I was there. Dafydd held by the two boys and struggling a bit to get free but watching Tom all the time. The big boy is glancing down the road thinking how much time he's got but also wondering if he'll get a whack from the branch Tom is holding. In my mind I can see Tom batting the branch on his left palm waiting for the big kid to move.

"He suddenly realised he had a load of other kids with him," Dafydd went on. "I don't think they really wanted to be in on this but they were probably scared of the big kid too. He realised that if they rushed Tom he wouldn't stand a chance even though he did have this hefty branch but the big kid didn't want to take a whack so stayed back. He told the other kids to move in closer and they were going to get Tom for sure. To make them think twice he started swinging the branch but he I could see he was getting scared now too because once they got right up behind him he was finished. And that's how they got him. They pinned his arms from the back and dragged the branch out of his hand. The big kid whacked him in the stomach but then I heard one of the others call out to leave the kid alone. He said just scare him a bit. He's only a little kid."

I was breathing faster now and could picture Tom's arms being held back and the big kid wanting to hurt him but not wanting to look bad in front of his pals.

"Then they heard it the same time as me," Dafydd said. "It was the sound of a car coming down the road with the horn beeping. I knew it was someone coming to stop them. They knew it too. They let me go and a couple of the kids started running straight away. Tom pushed the big kid back and told him to start running too but he was angry now and lashed out at Tom with his fist."

Dafydd pointed to the side of his head. That's where he caught Tom here but the scrapes on his face and legs are just where he fell and rolled away from the big kid. They all ran off when they saw the car coming but the big kid rushed forward and slammed his feet into the wheels of our bikes bending the spokes."

"Are they badly damaged?" I asked.

"Nah. A couple of quid and they'll both be good as new, but my Dad won't be that happy when he sees it," He said and then went on. "It was your Dad in the car, you know. When the boys got to the bridge they saw him coming from Llandaff and waved for him to stop. David was in the car too. Alun and Nigel jumped in and Phil and Geoff stayed to look after the bikes. Your Dad brought the car to a stop with squealing tyres and jumped out to get after them. I tell you I think if he'd got one or two of them he'd have killed them. You should have seen the look on his face. But they had a good start and were off like scared rabbits."

My Dad, I thought. I was so glad it was Dad who'd got there to stop it all.

"Is Tom ok?" I asked.

"Yeah, he's fine apart from a few cuts," Dafydd said. "We were really lucky your Dad was so close."

"And Tom's Dad doesn't know yet. About what happened, I mean," I asked.

"No, he's been working at the cricket club, remember, but he'll go nuts as well when he knows what's happened. Look, don't tell your Dad or anyone outside of the boys but Tom's brother is getting a gang together and they're going to find them tomorrow afternoon. That kid wanted to meet Mervyn and so he's going to but I don't think he's going to like it."

"No, I won't say anything. Not a word," I said. "Dafydd, I was really lucky I saw you but I think I'm going to call on Tom now. You were really brave, you know. I hope I would have done the same as you."

Dafydd grunted and I left for Tom's house. His mum led me into where Tom was sat on the sofa. I got a shock. He had a strip of plaster at the right side of his head by the temple and there were some cuts and scrapes on his hands and face. His mother said she'd get us both some pop and biscuits.

He was really pleased to see me and I was relieved he wasn't so bad as I thought. He repeated the same story that Dafydd had told me but he played down the parts where he'd been like a hero. As he was speaking I was thinking to myself, Tom, what's it going to be like when we're in different schools. Without you around to look out for us it won't be the same. He was talking excitedly even when his mum brought the pop and biscuits and she said to me that as soon as we'd finished I should go home so Tom could get some sleep. And so although we dragged out the pop and biscuits as long as we could I left him after a while. His Mum was waiting for me to get up and go and so a bit unwillingly I left.

Outside I didn't know what to do. I wanted to go home to talk to my Dad but also I wanted to tell Susan. I decided to run to her house and tell her. I felt that if she heard from anyone but me it wouldn't be right but word had got around. When she came to the door she already knew and was glad that I'd not gone along that afternoon.

Walking back home though I didn't feel that way. I felt I should have been with my friend. Oh yeah, another voice inside my head said, so that you could run away when the action started. I moaned in shame as I reached the house.

David sprang to the door even before I'd got it opened. "Gareth, Gareth you'll never guess what happened?"

I let him tell me. I didn't want to stop him as he poured the story out to me from the front door through to the sitting room. I glanced to see that Dad was in the kitchen reading the newspaper. The radio was on too. I listened closely to David and as he was speaking I realized it was the same story but with one or two little differences. I started thinking about this. You know what? I used to think that truth was just one story which everybody knew and that was it. But it's not, is it? Truth is whatever someone thinks the story is even though it might not be exactly what happened. So Tom, Dafydd and David believe slightly different things about the attack from the big kids. And what I've written down is the bits I liked best but in my head it has become the truth. There's something else I thought about too. If in a year's time I wrote down the story of the attack again would it be the same. Or another truth? You know I used to think that the history we get taught in school is what happened, but it's not you know. It's what someone thinks happened.

It struck me then that real truth is only there at the time something happens and is in the heads of those who are there at the time. Straight after the thing or event or whatever has happened the truth disappears and a story comes out which is close to the truth but not the truth. I'm not sure why this happens but it does, that's for sure.

All this went through my head as David was telling me the story, I thanked him. I told him that I'd heard in the street and gone straight to see Tom but he was too tired to tell the story. Hey, look, see I just made up another truth for David to believe. It's complicated, right?

When he'd finished we both went into the kitchen to see Dad. I put my hand on his shoulder so he would look up from the paper. 'I was listening," he said. "Tom is ok, thank God."

"It was lucky you were nearby," I said still holding my dad by the shoulder.

"It was but a pity I couldn't catch one of them. The police would have got all of them then. Anyway, the police will be looking for them now". Dad said and then went on. "It was lucky you weren't caught up in it too."

'Yeah," I said. "It was lucky."

I didn't tell him that the boys would be searching Ely tomorrow afternoon until they found them. Mervyn Pratt and our gang of Llandaff North boys would find them quicker than the police that's for sure. The parents would try to stop them going if anyone knew so none of us would breathe a word.

On Sunday evening I went over to see how Tom was doing. When I got there his mother answered the door and said "We've got a houseful here tonight, Gareth. Come in and join them." Inside I found Tom with his brother, Jack as well as Dafydd, Geoffrey, Mervyn and a few of Mervyn's friends. Everyone was in a happy mood and it was noisy. Jack got up to let me sit next to Tom on the sofa. He winked at me as he did. I looked around to see the happy, smiling faces. It was group of people celebrating a victory. I could see this. I noticed that Mervyn, Jack and the others had small bruises and marks on their hands and face. They had gathered a gang of boys the same age and size as the ones who had attacked Tom and got their revenge.

Mervyn saw me looking at them and grinned at me, "Gareth, "he said, "We had a tough game of rugby this afternoon in an away game but we gave the other side a beating they won't forget." He winked.

Everyone laughed including me, sharing in the joke and the victory. Mervyn and the bigger boys had punished the ones who had hurt Tom. As we were laughing and joking that evening it struck me that Llandaff North is a proper village which looks after the people who live in it. Old Coxy would say it's a community but I realised that it was made up of groups who connected when they needed to. There were the little kids who were watched over most of the time by their mums and dads and everyone in the village. Then there was our group from about 8-12 who were no longer watched over as long as we were in the area of our map and then there were the boys in their teenage years up to 17 or so who went anywhere and were not watched at all. The grown ups were the last group. It crossed my mind that we would be moving soon from the middle group to the teenage group when we started our new schools. It would be a different world.

At that moment in Tom's sitting room with all the laughing and joking and happiness it felt like belonging to something. I can't explain it so well. It was like we were sharing something that was important to us all. It was like we meant something to each other and even during that time the bad feelings between me and Geoffrey was put on hold. This was a time for us to be us. For us to be the boys of Llandaff North. I wish I could explain these things better. Do you know what I'm trying to say? I'm trying to say that we were not on our own, that there was a feeling of togetherness and something which brought us together when we needed to be together. Bugger it, I can't explain this. Maybe if I keep this book and look back at it ten years from now I'll know what I want to say in a better way. Hah, I hope so anyway.

We stayed for an hour or so like this until Tom's mother and father came to bring it to a close. Did they know what happened? Did they know where Jack and Mervyn had been? You know they said nothing but I think they did. I think all the grown ups did but it was a shared secret of which they were proud. I think they felt proud of the victory. Proud that their boys would not go into another area and hurt smaller kids but would take revenge if any of us were hurt by others. Is this a good thing or a bad thing, do you think?

On the way home I walked to the corner of Hawthorn Road with Geoffrey. We waved goodbyes with no bad feeling. As he walked away to his house I hoped in my heart that Mr Hughes had a solution. I hoped that we would fight no more.

\* \* \* \* \* \* \* \*

Dad came to my rescue with a brilliant idea for Susan's birthday. Her birthday is on 28 May The Beatles are in Cardiff at the Capital cinema on 27 May and dad got four tickets. He said to me that her mum and dad might not like it if we both went on our own but they might not mind if they went along as well. The cost of the tickets was a lot but Dad said it was OK and especially if Susan's Mum and Dad said yes. I'd bought Susan a heart shaped locket but it looked nothing next to the tickets. Anyway, she would get both if she could convince her mum and Dad to come with us.

\* \* \* \* \* \* \* \*

I don't think I'll ever see anything as fantastic as that again. I just hope my ears stop ringing soon. Susan did a great job in convincing her mum and dad to come with us but, to be honest, I don't think they needed that much persuading. Watching them at the concert they were just as crazy about the concert as me and Susan. I hope you get a chance to see the Beatles some day. It's not just the great music but the words of their songs and the way they sing it that makes them so different. You know there were girls there fainting in their seats they were so in love with the Beatles. I was really pleased that Susan didn't do that. They sang some great songs. Do you want to know what we heard. Ok we heard:

> Some other Guy
> Do you want to know a secret     (I really like this one)
> Love me Do
> From me to you
> Please, please me
> I saw here standing there
> Twist and Shout     (Everyone went nuts at this one)

You know the noise from the fans was deafening but me and Susan we loved it and I think it was the best birthday present I could have ever got her – thanks to Dad. There were two other acts I liked too. There was this bloke in dark glasses called Roy Orbison. He was good and a band a bit like the Beatles from Liverpool too called Gerry and the Pacemakers. It was just a great night that we'll never forget.

So if you get a chance please go see the Beatles. You will not forget it or regret it!!!!!!

Guess what? Susan was so happy with her birthday presents she kissed me right on the lips. Wow!! I don't think he Mum and Dad saw it. I don't think so.

\* \* \* \* \* \* \*

By the way, me and my brother we watched Leicester against Manchester United in the FA Cup Final on the TV on May 25$^{th}$. It was great Manchester won 3-1 and Dennis Law got a goal for Manchester. Last year we had to listen to it on the radio.

*PB's Note: Can you imagine an old guy in a park giving out sweets to kids these days. He'd be on the paedophile register right away!! And we've lost the community spirit of looking out for each other. It was almost tribal wasn't it – the way the community took revenge on the crime suffered by Gareth's friends.*

*Passiondale!! I love his spelling errors and grammatical lapses. It brings out the rush and excitement to get the thoughts down.*

*And who are the Beatles? Well, Gareth, wherever you are I guess you know now that they went on to be the most famous Band in the World.*

# CHAPTER 11
## *June 1963*

It was the Whitsun Treat today at Hailey Park on 2$^{nd}$ June. It's one of those things that just seems to happen and get planned and organized behind the scenes by the mothers. Anyway, I think that's what happens. And I can tell you that none of us are going to ask as we might get roped in to doing something. Ha, we're not stupid.

When you look out over the park on Whit Sunday morning you can see the mothers and a few fathers setting up tables and there's flags and streamers, ribbons and garlands and all kind of decorations hanging from poles that the Dads have put up. It marks out the area we use for the Treat. There's stalls too, like lucky dip and spin the wheel, find the treasure, lucky numbers, coconut shy, throwing hoops over a bottle and so many more. The dads mark out a place too for sprints, egg race, wheelbarrow races and obstacle races. And they put up a beer tent as well of course!! They set up a place to cook hot dogs and burgers, grilled chicken and to make bacon sandwiches. Some vans arrive too later on selling ice cream usually Mr Whipee and candy floss. It feels like Barry Island but in our own back yard of Hailey Park.

For most of the Dads there's no work on Monday and for us there's no school. It's half term and we get the week off. Yes!! It's always sunny at the Whitsun Treat and everyone has a lot of fun. Dad says we have it because Spring is turning into Summer and it's time to enjoy the weather and forget about the cold winter. But I said well why is it Midsummer's Day on 21 June when we've only just got Summer under way and then it starts to turn towards winter again. He laughed but he didn't have an answer to this.

Even people you don't usually see out and about from Llandaff North come to this and friends and relatives come along as well as people from neighbouring parts of Cardiff who know our Whitsun

Treat is the best one going. This year I noticed for the first time that some Dads and some of the bigger boys were at the edges of the Whitsun Treat area. I watched and when some people came that they didn't know or didn't like the look of they turned them away. I saw PC Wilson too on his bike riding up and then down the canal path next to Hailey Park a few times stopping to look at the event now and again. I realized he was there to put off anyone who wanted to cause trouble. Every now and then one of the kids ran over to him with a hot dog. They went down his cakehole in two bites.

Susan walked round with me and the boys. Janet was walking with Geoffrey too so we kept very close to them. We had a go at a few of the stalls. I like the coconut shy best. Dad's been given the job of running it this year so I wanted to show him and Susan as well of course how good I was. Because I'm good at cricket - yeah, who says - I like to think I can put a ball right on the spot. And you can but it doesn't mean you're going to get that coconut to jump off the hoop. The trick is to hit at the top first to get it to lean over and out of the hoop. Then with the next couple of balls you can topple it. Hey, I won one this year. I was hoping that Susan was watching me while I claimed the prize from Dad. She was in a way but she'd left the group to go and sit at one of the tables where most of the grandmas and grampies were. She'd taken a seat next to Mr Hughes and was talking to him. I guessed what the subject was but although Geoffrey is fine and there is no bad feeling between us I didn't like to leave. I waved instead hoping to get a chance to get away and sit with him later.

Next to the coconut shy Tom's brother and sister had set up a park discotheque. Well ok it was a record player on a table with a long cable running from the park to one of the houses for the electricity. Of course every now and then some little kid would stumble over the cable breaking the connection. So it was a smooth disco, ay?? Susan joined me there after a while but we didn't speak while they were playing the Beatles. We danced on the grass and every single one of us sang along with John Lennon and Paul McCartney and didn't miss one word or one "Oooh". Even some of the grown ups joined in and guess what they knew the words too. Then they did a twist competition and all the kids came to have a go. You ever tried twisting to Chubby Checker on grass? It's not easy but guess what Phil was brilliant and walked away with the prize. A giant size Galaxy bar so he was well pleased. I twisted with Susan and hoped that one of us would win the prize. OK, next year we'll be better. Next year. Next year.

We all then took part in the races – the egg and spoon, obstacle race and wheelbarrow race. I didn't go in for the sprint. Geoffrey won it but I didn't want to race against him yet. I didn't want him to know I'd been improving. I was getting better thanks to Mr Hughes idea.

As we all walked to the stall selling toffee apples Susan tugged my sleeve to hold me back. She told me what Mr Hughes had done. He'd been to see Aunt Nancy and told her the story. She understood straight away. She said a lot of the mothers point out to their husbands how good dad is bringing up two boys on his own. Yeah, he is good that's for sure. But she said that Geoff's mum needed to know what her son was thinking. Geoff's mum was embarrassed when Nancy spoke to her about what was happening. She said it was true that she'd said those things but it was just meant to hurt Geoff's Dad and get him to take it a bit easier on the beer. She didn't know that Geoff had taken it seriously and she felt bad that Geoff had caused problems with me. She asked Aunt Nancy if Dad knew all about it and was relieved that he didn't. She spoke to Geoffrey telling him how she'd been stupid to say those things to Geoff's Dad but he had to understand that it was said in anger. She would never leave Geoff's Dad for anyone. From what Mr Hughes said to Susan it had taken a weight off Geoffrey and he now felt very foolish for the way he had behaved. He told us to act like nothing's happened and not to make a fuss about any change in Geoff's behavior.

Two seconds after she'd said this to me a smiling Geoff and Janet brought us both a toffee apple each. It was over and thankfully nobody had to say anything. The record player started to blare out "She loves you, yeah, yeah, yeah" and we ran over to shake our heads, arms and legs in time to the Beatles. The music went on and on and I forgot to go to see Mr Hughes. When I remembered I looked for him but he'd gone. I made a promise to catch him in the park the following day before we started playing cricket.

Towards the end of the Treat when the sun was going down and it was starting to get dark Geoffrey found me on my own. Susan's mum and Dad had taken her home a little while before. "Ok," he said to me. I knew he was going to say something when he said OK. Geoff doesn't often say OK to me. "Yeah," I said, "You OK too."

"Yeah," he says back to me. It must have taken him a lot to say the next bit. "Hey look. Gareth, I've been a bit stupid about things between us for a long time," he said. He was looking down and then up into my eyes. "I got mixed up about something. It doesn't matter now but I won't do anything you know……." He trailed off.

I held out my little finger for him to take with his. "For real" I said this time. "No pretending."

"For real" he said and we shook little fingers. That was it. He nodded and ran off over to his parents and I looked for my Dad at the coconut shy and wondered where David was too. I saw them together and walked over. Well it was done. Geoffrey was straight but I'd never really like him. How could you really like someone who prefers Elvis to the Beatles. And he refused to dance when the Beatles were playing. Git!

\* \* \* \* \* \* \*

On Whit Monday the park was quiet. It was a Bank Holiday and so most people slept late. The park was a bit messy after the Whitsun Treat. There were a few people around cleaning and taking the poles down. Even the parky was helping out without grumbling at all the work but I think a few shillings must have changed hands to keep him sweet.

Like Whit Sunday it was a beautiful day and a great one for cricket. We played until noon time and stopped. There was no sign of Mr Hughes. It was one of those rare days when he went somewhere else or maybe was taking a lie in after a few beers. He didn't drink pints like the Dads but I noticed that his half pint glass was never empty for long. I smiled to myself. Why do grown ups get such a taste for that disgusting stuff. It's not even sweet.

We lay on the grass just chatting. We were waiting for time to go home for dinner. It would be like a Sunday dinner today as mums and Dads are home. Tom jumped to his feet though and said come on let's head over to Povey's field and mess around for a bit. I hoped he wasn't going to think of us being in the Army like we used to play when we were littler kids. I didn't fancy marching single file to Povey's field. We didn't thank God and on the way dumped the cricket bats and stumps in my back garden and then went on to Povey's field.

I told you about it before didn't I? You can check on my map if you've forgotten where it is. It's at the bottom of Hailey Park after the Old Oak tree and it's got long grass where you can hide and mess about.

Before we dived into the long grass we climbed the Old Oak tree for a bit. It's a play area on its own you know. As well as the carved initials that have been made on the tree over the years, kids have hammered big nails into the trunk for footholds to climb the tree and just like by the river there's a rope from one of the branches for swinging. We all had a go on this. When Tom was getting the rope to swing really fast one of the little kids from Standard 1, Philip Tell came along. He started to beg Tom to give him a swing. I thought Tom was just going to tell him to piss off but in the end he gave in and hoisted the kid onto his lap. We gave Tom a good push back and fore until he could get the speed up on his own. Phil loved it and was shouting out and laughing as they whizzed through the air. It was going good too until that sudden creak and crack came and the rope broke free from the branch sending Tom and Phil tumbling into the grass. Who was it said laughing turns to crying. Well Phil showed it. Tom had gone over and landed on the little bugger and there they were lying winded on the ground till we helped them up.

Tom got up laughing but Phil didn't. He was wheezing and blubbering and calling for his mum. He was limping a bit too. We told him to bugger off home to his mum and not to snitch on any of us. He limped off crying and whimpering while we did a repair job on the rope and got it back on the tree again.

Well I suppose the army bit had to come! Tom split us into two groups and we set up some stones with a stick in it on either side of the field. This was the flag for each side. Each group had to make their way through the grass to capture the enemy flag. The rules were that if you came across one of the enemy in the grass and you touched them before they got you they were out of the game. It's good fun and your heart races a bit as you're creeping through the grass because you want to catch someone rather than being caught. In this game your head is darting everywhere. This time though we weren't five minutes into the game when Dafydd stood up and called out, "Hey boys, forget the game. I found something here."

It must be a good find, I thought for Dafydd to stop the game as we like this one. We were often finding stuff in the field though. It was always a dumping ground for old junk people didn't want any more. Once I found about 10 years worth of Reader's Digest.

When we all got over to Dafydd he was next to a couple of brown boxes. Someone must have dumped them during the night because the boxes were still in good nick. "You're not going to believe what's in here" Dafydd said to us. We gathered round the boxes and Tom flipped open one and me the other. I think we both said "wow" at the same time. It wasn't Reader's Digest for sure and you know what I didn't know before then that you could get magazines like this. I took one off the top and Tom did the same. The rest of the boys dived in to get one too.

"I heard about these" Phil said. They're dirty books aren't they? Don't know why the call them dirty. She looks pretty clean to me."

We all laughed at that one.

On the front cover of mine was this woman who had knickers on but nothing on top showing these huge pair of tits. First of all there were gasps from all of us. We'd seen nothing like it. I had a look back in the box and there must have been about fifty in there. That meant we had about a hundred magazines to look at. I stood up to look around all the edges of Povey's field. There was no-one around. We all went quiet as we started to turn the pages of the magazines. There was page after page of different girls in different poses some with their tops off and some with it all off. If Alun had any doubts before what the shape of a girl was I knew he would have no doubt now. It was funny while looking at the magazines I felt a bit guilty and maybe a bit ashamed like it was wrong to look at them but I couldn't stop it. And while I was looking my heart was starting to beat and I could feel my knob getting really stiff.

We'd all gone really quiet except every now and then one of the boys would gasp with delight or amazement at what he was looking at. We were all in our own little world now turning page after page to see things we'd never seen or dreamt of before but I imagined I would dream of these over and over again now. For a second I let a thought of Susan come into my mind but pushed it away. There was no connection between Susan and the pictures of these girls here. Gradually, I think, we relaxed as we got used to what we were looking at. There weren't so many gasps now just chuckles and laughs and cries of "hey boys look at this one." I think at the beginning we were scared we were going to caught because we felt we were doing something wrong but no-one was there to catch us.

"Oh, I'm telling," I heard a voice say and for a second just froze. Then I recognized the voice. "It was David. "I'm telling. You're looking at dirty books."

He turned and ran off. Shit, I thought, dropping the magazine and ran after him. As I ran I thought how does he know they're dirty books. I caught him up by the Old Oak Tree and wrestled him to the ground. "Lemme go, Lemme go," he called out. "I'm telling, I'm telling". He hadn't been such a bad kid this last few months and I didn't want to whack him one so I thought I'd try to convince him not to blab on us. I held him tight on the ground though. I knew he could run like a whippet if I let him up. He's not as fast as me but if he's got a head start it takes a while to get the so and so!!

"What do you want to tell on us for", I asked him.

I said there's no point in it. If you got us into trouble, me and the boys will give you whacks for months. Then I had a brainwave. I said, "Why don't you come back with me, sit with the boys and have a look yourself."

"What" he said surprised. "You'll let me come and sit with you now and look at the books?"

"Yeah," I said. "I will. But you mustn't blab."

"And can I come with you when you meet the boys for the rest of this week," he asked.

Well I didn't fancy that one but right then I was more concerned about stopping him from blabbing on us. "Yeah, course," I said giving him a ruffle on the hair and pulling him to his feet. "Come on let's get back."

I was chuffed that I got us out of trouble and started to walk quickly back to the lads. I was keen to start turning those pages again. I glanced back to say something to David but he wasn't there. He'd turned and scarpered back towards our house. I turned and ran after him. He had a good start on me. I could see Aunt Nancy in our back garden. She was putting washing on the line. He was heading straight for her.

I caught up with him by the gate and he squealed as I got him. "Keep your mouth shut," I growled in his ear.

Aunt Nancy came to the gate to see what the fuss was about. "Aunt Nancy, Aunt Nancy," David panted out gasping after his sprint. It was too late. I just hung on to him squeezing hard. "Gareth and his pals are looking at dirty books they found in Povey's field."

There he'd said it and now we were in the shit for sure. I decided I was going to make him suffer for weeks to come and he could forget about me counting the days to Christmas for him. Aunt Nancy put her hands on her hips. She looked sternly down at us.

"Right," she said. "Well don't tell your father or any of the other fathers for that matter. Otherwise they'll be over there too. Your dinner will be ready in twenty minutes too so don't be late, either of you."

She went back to pegging stuff on the line. She had no more to say.

I was stunned. So was David too. He hadn't expected that and for sure I didn't. I was expecting her to go nuts. I was sure I was in the shit. "See," I said to David, "You little bugger. There was nothing wrong with it after all."

Well, he didn't know what to say now. He was sure he had me bang to rights and he went to sit on the old canal wall. I did too. I was wondering why the hell my Dad or any of the other dads would want to look at the books. I was sure they wouldn't be interested. But then I thought, who put them there. I didn't have time though. I needed to get back to the boys. And the boxes too, of course.

"I'm going back," I said to him. I stood up but he stayed where he was. He looked confused and I must admit I was too. You always think that it's clear what is right and what is wrong. It felt wrong to be looking at the magazines somehow but it was fun too. Maybe, I wondered, if right and wrong is different depending on who it is you talk to. I smiled to myself thinking if David had run all the way to Nigel's mother he'd have got the answer he wanted. I could see that this one was a deep one which needed a lot of thinking about but I didn't have time. The magazines were calling me. I left David and ran back over to Povey's field but the boys had gone and the boxes had gone.

I wondered where they'd put them because for sure no-one would take them home. They must have panicked when David ran off. I walked slowly back from Povey's field towards my house looking around for any sign of the boys or the boxes. Then I started thinking to myself again, who put the boxes there? It had to be a grown up because the magazines cost money and where did you buy them anyway? They must have been bought by a bloke. I couldn't see girls wanting to look at these pictures. They were obviously for blokes. I wondered who it was that bought them and put them there. Was it one of the Dads, I thought? Would they look at them? Maybe it was Geoffrey's Dad, I thought. Yeah, that's possible.

After dinner during which I got to tell you David never said more than three words. A record for him. So after dinner I went over to Tom's house and he asked me what happened. He couldn't understand why we hadn't got into trouble either. Anyway, he told me that when David ran off to blab the boys got the magazines back in the boxes and took them down the slope to the river. There was an argument then he said as to whether they should be lobbed in the river or hidden in that hole in the bank. What did you do, I asked. We hid them in the bank he laughed and punched me on the shoulder.

While I was at Tom's house Mrs Tell came to the door and asked for Tom. His mother called and I went with him too. Mrs Tell smiled at him. "I just wanted to come over to thank you, Tom," she said with a big smile on her face.

"What for, Mrs Tell," Tom asked. "What did I do?"

I guessed it was something to do with Phil and of course it was. "Philip told me how he was a silly boy and went on the rope swing on the Old oak," she said. "I must have told him a thousand times not to go on it but he doesn't listen. He told me that he got on it and was swinging and that the rope broke and he fell. Thank goodness you were passing and helped him home."

Tom nodded but didn't say anything. We could both see there was more to come.

"You should have come inside when you got him home," she went on. "We took him to the hospital straight away. He'll be ok in about six weeks the doctor says and they'll know when the plaster comes off."

"Plaster?" Tom asked beginning to realize what she was saying and I realised it too.

"Yes the silly boy fractured his leg when he fell but it will mend ok. He's very young." She said.

Well me and Tom were looking at her face trying to decide if she was taking the Micky out of us or if Phil had come up with the story to protect us. Looking at her face I decided that Phil had been a good sport and not dropped us and Tom specially in it. It made me feel ashamed that David would drop us in it very easily and I wondered if Tom was thinking the same thing too.

Tom smiled at Mrs Tell as she thanked him again and turned away to go but then she turned back saying "I almost forgot" and put a silver sixpence in his hand. Later Tom put in the children's box inside Percy Evans. He said he'd feel too guilty to spend it.

So Phil's story about what happened is true in Mrs Tell's mind. That's what she will always remember that happened. This is what I was thinking. If Phil had told the real truth then we all might have been in a lot more trouble. Truth is a funny thing isn't it?

And there's another funny thing too. We felt really guilty about what happened to Phil but only a little guilt about the magazines. See, I'm beginning to wonder if guilty and right and wrong is not just simply right and wrong. Maybe it has a score attached to it so you can have a 1 point wrong which is not so bad and a 10 point wrong which is terrible. Yeah, I thought this is a better system. Don't you think so? Well I do anyway.

And you know what? Later on we dived back over to Povey's field to get the magazines and they'd gone. The rest of the boys swore they never took them. God knows who did. But I tell you, it was a big upset for all of us.

\* \* \* \* \* \* \*

About six in the evening Susan arrived at my house. I was a bit surprised as we hadn't planned to meet up until Tuesday. I could see she had been crying and let her come in to sit down. David moved off the sofa to a chair on the other side of the room and didn't say anything. Dad came into the kitchen and could see she'd been crying too.

"I think you need a nice cup of tea with a lot of sugar, young lady," he said and went to put the kettle on.

"You didn't hear yet?" she asked me. I don't know why but my mind immediately thought of the magazines we'd been looking at. I thought she'd found out that we'd been looking at them. I had images of them being at Daffyd's house and his mother finding them in the shed and she going straight over to Nigel's mother. I could feel myself blushing red.

"Hear what?" I asked, not wanting to hear if it was the magazines.

"Mr Hughes, Gareth, it's Mr Hughes, "Susan started to weep again. "He died last night but nobody knew until this afternoon. He hadn't been seen. The lady next door has a key to go in and check if she doesn't see him for a while. She found him in the bed like he was asleep. But of course he wasn't".

The funny thing about it is when she told me I immediately felt relieved that it wasn't anything to do with me looking at pictures of naked women. Then I felt a surge of guilt, shame and sadness all connected with Mr Hughes. I should have gone to see him yesterday instead of playing and enjoying myself. That was twice now that I'd left someone and never seen them again. I felt like crying too. I looked at David first and wondered if he would blurt out in front of Susan what he'd seen us doing. I prayed not.

Susan was crying openly now and I was blinking back tears. Dad brought in a tray with tea for everyone and we gulped it down. It was hot and sweet and felt good. I tried to picture Mr Hughes sat on the bench in his pressed suit, wearing his hat and with his cane tucked in at the side of the bench. We'd never see that again and I'd never get a chance to thank him. Dad had overheard the news from Susan too while he was making the tea and he said a few words about him too. He said all Llandaff North would miss him. He'd been around here for a lifetime. Susan wanted to go home after she finished the tea and I walked with her. We made plans to meet the following day.

When I got back home I took David to one side. I decided it was time to have a chat about the magazines. Well it wasn't exactly about the magazines but about snitching. I said to him look there's gonna be times when you see your pals doing something that's......I didn't want to say wrong or bad so I said........that the grown ups wouldn't like. You can tell the grown ups for sure and be a snitch but I asked him what happens to snitches? Well he knew the answer to that one. He said they won't let me join in or tell me anything.

"There you go," I said." You got to stick with the boys."

"Right", he said, "you're right."

And then I said to him "Look if you snitch on me about anything (and he knew I meant the magazines) to anyone (and he knew I meant Susan) then I'll never play Subbuteo with you again. You got that."

"OK" he said. "I got it and I won't tell. But Gareth can I ask something?"

I nodded.

"Will you play Subbuteo with me now and I'll never tell, I promise," he said.

I looked at him. He was getting very clever, my brother. He wanted to blackmail me I could see, the little bugger. I wasn't having any of that. I said I wasn't ready yet but I'd play him later. The funny thing is in my mind I knew that I wasn't going to play as fiercely and I might even let him win. What is happening, ay??

\* \* \* \* \* \* \* \*

Hadyn Hughes funeral was at All Saints Church Llandaff North on 5 June. It was a working day for most people but the Church was almost full. Everyone was dressed in Sunday best and the organ was playing the solemn music that we always have when it's a funeral. A full choir was in place for Mr Hughes and nobody wanted to drop out for any reason. I looked out from the choir stalls at all the families who had turned out. I could see Susan and her family too. The church was quiet apart from the music. No talking and just a few coughs and shuffles here and there.

This funeral was different to most. There were a few people who wanted to talk about Hadyn Hughes, the man and his life. I got another surprise. They mostly told the same story. That after his father moved them from Merthyr to LLandaff North Hadyn had stayed there all his life. He had never married and never left the family home. He had been a great support to his father and mother throughout their lives and served the Cardiff Parks department well until he retired. He was a shy man but one who helped his neighbours whenever he could and was well respected in the Llandaff North community as a good and kind man. They all talked about the sad loss of his twin brother, Elwyn, who had died during the Great War. They said that Hadyn would have been by his side in that conflict if it had not been for a lung condition that prevented him from serving. They all said how Hadyn had grieved for his brother throughout the years and how he regretted not being able to serve along side his brother who he admired and respected. They were all old speakers close to Hadyn's age and they all mentioned in passing how Hadyn was the opposite of his twin brother. Hadyn was introvert, quiet and shy and loved only to be at home with the family.

Elwyn on the other hand was extrovert, sociable and a traveler. He had married they said and his wife had died during a visit to Cardiff before the Great War.

I just listened and wondered. Listened and wondered and pictured old Hadyn as my gaze turned to the coffin lying on the table before the altar. I was unsure what to think. Afterwards, when Dad got back from the wake in the hall behind the Church I was waiting for him at home. I could tell that Dad had drunk a few beers. It was like usual. His eyes were a bit glassy and he couldn't quite get the words out clearly like he usually did. But he wasn't too bad. I wondered what Geoff's dad was like if Dad was like this. Ten times worse, I thought.

"Dad, I want to ask you something," I said.

Dad flopped on the sofa and said, "Ask away son but be a good lad and make me a cup of tea first. You know the way I like it."

When it was done and I was sat next to Dad again he took as big gulp, nodded with pleasure and said, "OK, ask away."

"Did you know all this stuff about Mr Hughes, Dad?" I asked him. "You know he told me he'd gone to New Zealand, got married, Great War and all these things. But it wasn't true. It wasn't him. It was his brother. It was his twin brother that did all that."

"Yes, I knew about it," Dad replied holding the mug of tea and swigging it now and then.

"But it was a lie, Dad, all a lie," I said in a disappointed whisper.

"Well, I suppose I was a bit surprised at first when someone told me the truth," Dad said. "Everyone knows and he's been telling this story since his mother died. "Then I realized it didn't matter."

"Why?" I asked not understanding.

"Well it gave him a story and a reason to keep going is what I think," Dad said, "By all accounts he wasn't far short of being like Boo Radley for the early part of his life."

I looked confused. "It's from one of the books I have read, son, you know "To Kill a Mockingbird". Dad went on. 'Boo Radley is a bloke that lives at home with his parents and won't go out but he watches and knows everything. Seems to me that Hadyn became more like Elwyn as he told the story over and over and maybe in some way he became Elwyn. Maybe in his mind it was Hadyn who did all those things and Elwyn was the one who stayed at home. He didn't harm anyone did he and maybe if you do believe something enough it does become a kind of truth in your own mind."

Dad had put his finger on some of the things I'd been thinking myself. In some way I had felt that Mr Hughes had fallen in my thoughts in some way but when I thought about it I knew this was unfair. Like Dad said, he had not harmed any one and maybe it did him a lot of good. I was planning to speak to Susan about it but I guessed that she knew all about it anyway. For me it was best to think of Hadyn Hughes as the traveler who went to New Zealand, married and served in the Great War. And you know what, that is how I shall always remember him.

\* \* \* \* \* \* \*

I haven't felt like writing much since Hadyn Hughes passed away. It knocked me sideways more than I realised. I been spending the time with Susan a lot and working with the younger kids on things for the Sports Day coming up. It's in the first week in July. After Sports Day we have one more day in school and term ends. We'll have finished our life in Hawthorn. The new life gets closer and closer, ay?

There was a big event a few days ago though. There's a race going on between the USA and Russia to see who's best, well to see who's best at everything I think. But Russia got a first before America. They put a woman into space first on 16 June. Her name is Valentina Tereshkova and she orbited the earth about 50 times and spent three days up there in a capsule called Vostok 6. Can you imagine that? That thing must be so small that you can barely move. I think I'd go off my rocker to be honest.

The Sports day will be on Thursday 11 July. Dad's birthday is on Saturday 6 July. I'm going to have to talk to David about this and convince him that Dad will not want an Airfix kit or a Subbuteo team but something different. So I have two big things to think about.

I told you what we get points for on Sports Day didn't I?. This is the list again.

60 yards sprint

60 yards hurdles

Obstacle race

Bean Bag Race

Egg and Spoon

Wheelbarrow Race
Sack Race
Skipping Race
Three Legged Race
Final Relay Races

There's a lot of work to do and nothing has changed. Things are better now between me and Geoffrey but I still have to do my best to help Caradog win for a change. I know now though that it's not just down to me. It's going to be all of Caradog that will do it. I don't see it any more as a thing between me and Geoffrey. It's just Caradog versus Glyndwr.

*PB's Note: Everything was in paper print in those days. Now kids can stumble across all images on the internet and on satellite TV. And mostly nobody is watching what they are looking at or to whom they are chatting. They fend for themselves in cyber space. Gareth and his friends did so outside in the fresh air where ostensibly nobody was watching also but in a low level way they were.*

*Funny, too how it was the early days of space exploration. We don't pay any attention now unless there's a tragic incident or emergency.*

# CHAPTER 12
## *July 1963*

I've been talking to David about what we should do for Dad's birthday. You know what? He said to me that if we can't get Dad an Airfix kit then maybe we should find him a new wife. Actually, it's not a bad idea but there's no-one around in Llandaff North. All the ladies are married and the only ones not married are old grandmas or girls who are too young for Dad. He seems happy without a wife though. It's just me and David wouldn't mind having a mother like the other kids. Ah! Well if Dad does meet one we just have to hope she likes us too and isn't like the stepmother in Hansel and Gretel who makes the woodman send the kids into the forest. I said this to David and it made him stop and think. Yeah, I said, we might want Dad to have a wife but if she came she might not want us.

From what I can see living together as man and wife can be good or not so good. Most times you can tell by the look on the faces of the kids. If their mum and dad are arguing all the time it shows on their faces. You take Susan's Mum and Dad they get on really well and you go to their house and the mood in the house is good. You can feel it. OK, I've been there a couple of times now when they have an argument but it's over in a flash. It was the same at Jack's house. You remember me talking about him. The brainbox who's a bit on the fat side and liked the same girl as Simon? Both gone now, of course. But when Jack was living here and I went to his house it was the same kind of good mood.

The homes where it's not so good and the kids don't look too happy, well you don't get invited or go there anyway. I'm sure it's not so happy at Geoffrey's house. I don't mean it's very bad there but I think his Mum and Dad like to argue a lot. That's the feeling you get.

But you know what? One day when me and Susan get married I'm never going to be a sailor, soldier or in the airforce or in a job that gets you to travel away from home. From what I've seen you should always be together.

At the top end of Hawthorn Road opposite the school there's an old lady that rents out a room every now and then. Usually, it's a young couple who are starting out and saving or waiting to get a Council House but about two years ago a sailor and his wife came there. They had a little baby too in a pram. I was passing the school when they moved in and saw them. They were sat on the wall outside the house. The bloke was in a really good sailor's uniform and his wife was really pretty. So I went across to say hello, said my name was Gareth and asked them if they were moving to Llandaff North. They were both really nice and chatted back to me. He said that yes they were moving in but he only had a couple of weeks shore leave and then he was sailing to Africa and other places I'd never heard of.

I was only a little kid then so when he said Africa my eyes must have been out on stalks. I asked him if it wasn't any trouble if he could bring me back a coconut off one of the trees. He laughed and said yes he'd bring me back a coconut but it wasn't free. He said I must look after his wife, Mrs Marianne Skinner while he was away. She smiled too and said that means you must visit me every day until Able Seaman Mark Skinner comes home. She asked me if I could do that. I told them that they didn't need to worry. I would do the job.

Before he went off to sea I spent a lot of time with Able Seaman Mark Skinner and Mrs Marianne Skinner. I went on walks with them across Hailey Park and showed them around the area. They were always happy and smiling and lots of people came to talk to them. They liked Mrs Skinner specially. She had such a happy, smiling and lovely face and was friendly with everyone.

On one of the walks I asked Able Seaman Skinner if he would write me a letter from Africa. I said Dad is the only one that gets letters and it would be great to get one. OK. He said every time I write to Mrs Marianne Skinner there'll be one inside it for you. I was so pleased with this even though what I really wanted was for him to send me my own letter to my house.

I waited outside on the day Able Seaman Skinner had to board ship and walked with him and Mrs Marianne Skinner and the baby to the bus stop for him to start his journey to the ship. Mrs Marianne Skinner was crying a lot and black stuff was running on to her cheeks. It was all making me sad too. I think Able Seaman Mark

Skinner wanted to cry too. I could see him blinking a lot but then he was on the number 24 bus and gone. He called out to me "look after her" as we watched it chug along the road with Able Seaman Skinner and his kitbag holding on to the pole at the rear of the bus waving goodbye to me and Mrs Marianne Skinner. We waved till it rounded the bend along Station Road.

Mrs Marianne Skinner was still crying but she was dabbing her eyes with tissue now. "Is my face a mess?" she asked me. There's a little black here and there I said. She mixed up a bit of crying and laughing together. We were still at the bus stop but once she'd finished she crouched down by me. I could see her knees and the inside of her legs. She touched my chin with a finger so I was looking into her eyes. "You're a good boy, Gareth," she said. "A lucky girl will get you later but she'll have to wait because this girl needs you now."

You could have seen my smile from the moon.

"I need you to come to see me every day to see if I'm OK and when I go out for a walk in the early evening and weekends you need to come with me. Do you think your Dad will let you do that?" she asked me.

"Yeah, course", I replied. It wasn't my Dad that would be the problem it would be not meeting up with the boys so often that would be the trouble. But I reckoned I could get around that. I told Dad about it and he nodded. With the boys I told them that I'd been given a mission by Able Seaman Mark Skinner and that it was a secret that I couldn't tell them about right now but maybe later I would be allowed to.

So I did the job. Every day after school I would pass by. On hot days she would be sat on the wall pushing the pram to and fro and enjoying the sun. When she saw me now she called me "My Guardian." I liked that. Around 7 o' clock I'd leave the house and run up the road to knock on the door for her and she would answer to kiss my forehead and say that she was fine. On the weekends we walked in the park for a couple of hours and sometimes she was stopped by some men I didn't know who talked to her but I didn't leave her. I looked back fiercely saying nothing but staying to protect Mrs Marianne Skinner. I don't know why but I saw these men as the enemy.

Then one day she gave me a letter. "I forgot," she said. "It was inside my letter from Mark"

I looked at it. It was in an envelope. I'd never had a proper letter before. OK it didn't have a stamp on it but it was a letter. It had my name on it and the address. I opened it carefully and read the few lines from Able Seaman Mark Skinner. He wrote:

*Arrived Africa and in Cape Town. It is so hot and sunny. Got your coconut yesterday. Don't forget to look after Mrs Marianne Skinner. Yours Truly. Able Seaman Mark Skinner*

It was such a great letter and he got the coconut too. "He didn't forget the coconut" I said to Mrs Marianne Skinner. She smiled. "Able Seaman Mark Skinner is a good man, my Guardian. Just like you."

One day we were walking in the park towards the playground and she stopped the pram suddenly. "Let's turn round quickly, Gareth". I was surprised. It was always "my Guardian" now but we turned quickly. I looked back and saw a man get up from one of the park benches and call out "Hey, Marianne". She didn't look back and kept walking telling me not to look. Don't look. Well, we didn't look back but this bloke was quick and caught us up. He was puffing a bit as he went in front of Mrs Marianne Skinner and the pram making us stop.

"Marianne," he said to her and I could see his eyes were looking all over her. "It's been a long time. You look great. Got married too, I see."

He pointed at her ring, the pram and then at me. "And who's the bigger kid?"

"Hey, mister," I said to him. "My name's Gareth and Able Seaman Mark Skinner asked me to look after Mrs Marianne Skinner."

"Gareth is My Guardian," she said looking directly at this bloke. I didn't like him. He had a big smile, the whitest, straightest teeth I've ever seen and blonde hair which he flicked back now and then. Worst thing was he was wearing winkel-pickers.

He didn't answer me but laughed out loud. "So you married a jack tar," he laughed. "Away from home a lot too, I imagine. You need a bloke that's with you all the time, Marianne. You should know that?"

"Leave me alone, Des," she snapped at him and pushed past him with the pram. I followed quickly but looked back to poke my tongue out at the bloke. He hadn't moved and stood hand on hips watching Mrs Marianne Skinner as she pushed the pram away fast stumbling once or twice on her heels. I could see him grinning like a cat as he watched this.

Everything was fine for a couple of weeks but then one Saturday I turned up at the house and Mrs Marianne Skinner looked nervous. She was breathing fast and her face was a bit red. She had one arm to her chest. She smiled when she saw me and was glancing up and down the road. "Gareth," she said, "Will you walk the pram around the block for me. The baby needs some fresh air and I'm not ready for our walk yet. Keep walking round until you see me outside waiting for you."

"Ok," I said. I walked to the bottom of Hawthorn Road and turned left into Hazelhurst Road. I looked back. I was sure I saw someone who looked like that Des come out of Belle Vue Crescent and then look down Hawthorn Road. If it was him I must have scared him off because he turned upwards towards the school and Station Road. So I carried on walking round the block. I lost count how many times but Mrs Marianne Skinner did not come out.

Dad stopped me close to our house after a while to ask what I was doing. I told him the story and that I was waiting for Mrs Marianne Skinner. He told me I'd done my job and that it was getting late and I should go in. He said he'd take the baby back. I tried to argue but sometimes you can't argue with Dad. I went into the house.

He was gone for a while and didn't look too happy when he came back. He went to the kitchen to make some tea. "You should be in bed," he told me.

"I know Dad," I said but I wanted to know what happened to Mrs Marianne Skinner.

Dad waited while the kettle came to the boil and poured water into the teapot. He stirred it and sat down to wait for it to settle.

"She wasn't feeling too good, son" he said to me. "She was getting sick so we took her and the baby to stay with her mother. It's for the best."

I nodded. I knew it was best to be with Mum and Dad if you weren't feeling too good and she had looked funny like she was getting a fever or something. "Is she coming back, Dad," I asked him. "She's nice. I like her."

Dad smiled at me and ruffled my hair. "Yeah she's nice, son, and I know she really likes you too."

He paused. "I don't think she'll be back now. She'll stay with her mum until she gets better and then when Seaman Skinner gets back they'll move into a house of their own."

"Able Seaman Mark Skinner," I said to Dad. "You got to say Able Seaman Mark Skinner. Will they come to see me. He promised me a coconut, you know."

"Yeah, son, I know. He'll bring it I'm sure," Dad said to me.

A couple of weeks later I got a letter to my house. An Air Mail letter. It was from Able Seaman Mark Skinner. This is what he said:

*Dear Gareth. I am on my way back from South Africa. I will bring you the coconut when I get home. Thanks for taking care of Mrs Marianne Skinner. You are a good boy. Yours truly, Able Seaman Mark Skinner.*

I've always kept that letter you know. I got it now. A few weeks later he came to the house in his uniform. He looked great and I jumped up and down when I saw him. He gave me a parcel and said to open it later and winked at me. He came inside and I asked him where Mrs Marianne Skinner was. He said she was still a bit sick and was staying at her mother's. She would be better soon. We talked for a while but then I said I really wanted to open the parcel. He told me to go ahead and went into the kitchen to talk to Dad. They talked quietly so I couldn't really here what they were saying. Anyway, I just wanted to open the parcel.

It was great. There was the coconut, some aniseed twist that I forgot I told him I liked, a book of Grimm's fairy tales and a white envelope, I opened the envelope and found a pound note. I gasped. This was a fortune. I rushed into the kitchen with my presents to show Dad.

He looked and said to Able Seaman Mark Skinner, "You didn't have to do this Mark."

"Oh, yes I did, Mr Adams," he said. "Every job deserves a payment and this is Gareth's. We were lucky. He could have seen…..But anyway he didn't and I think it'll turn out OK."

'So when do you leave the Navy," Dad said to him and I saw Able Seaman Mark Skinner's face drop.

"In three months," he said. "It's for the best you know. I can't be away like I was. Have to forget about Petty Officer now, Mr Adams. It was close too. Very close. But this is for the best."

"Yes. For the best." Dad said back to him.

"You can't leave the Navy," I whined to him. "Who's going to bring me coconuts now?

"Don't worry, Gareth."he said to me. "I have a lot of friends in the Navy who'll bring them for us."

He left us shortly after that and me and Dad watched him walking down Hawthorn Road West to the bus stop. He waved all the way and I did too. I never saw him or Mrs Marianne Skinner again.

I thought about it a lot recently and you know what I discovered? You miss a lot when you're a little kid. You know there's something going on but you can't just put your finger on it. Now I'm getting older I think I got it. I think I know what happened but I dare not talk to Dad about it. I need to be much older to do that. I just hope that Mrs Marianne Skinner and Able Seaman Skinner are living together somewhere with their baby and that Des whatever his name is has gone to prison and is well and truly locked up.

So you see, this is why when I get married to Susan I'll never leave her. What you think I'm still worried about Geoffrey liking Susan? Well maybe he does and who could blame him. But as long as I'm here I'll keep the bugger, (even though he's a not so bad bugger now), away!!

\* \* \* \* \* \* \*

This Sunday evening me and David sat down to talk about what we will get Dad for his birthday. In the end we agreed on it. We decided that we should treat him to a meal in the Sandringham on Saturday and then take him into Evan Roberts so he can choose something and if he doesn't like anything there then we can go to Marks and if that fails into Woolies.

"We'll save money if he picks Woolies," David said and grinned at me.

"Shut up," I replied giving him a playful punch on the shoulder.

Once we agreed on it we went to find Dad in the kitchen. You probably worked out by now that this is his favourite place after work. He's got it all. The teapot, the larder and the radio. Although I don't like the stuff he listens to on there. It's all talk.

Anyway, we didn't give him a chance to argue. We stood in front of him and made him put the paper down.

"Dad, it's your birthday on Saturday," I said.

"Yes," he replied. "I'm afraid it is."

"We're taking you to the Sandringham for dinner?" David said.

Dad nodded.

"And then we go to Evan Roberts so you can pick your present," I said.

"Oh," Dad said raising his eyebrows. "That's a bit expensive."

"Well, we can go to Marks or Woollies if you don't like anything there," David replied.

"OK," Dad said. "Saturday it is then. Sandringham and shopping. All agreed."

And he picked the paper back up and left us too it. We'd already counted our money out in change and taken it all to the Post Office to change into notes. We had a lot now. Enough for his meal and a good present.

We took the bus in on Saturday and got to the Sandringham at half past twelve. This is a good time as it's not so busy. We let him pick what he wanted and we had our usual. Once we paid the bill but Dad did it for us we still had a pile of money for his present.

We walked all round Evan Roberts men's department and he looked at a lot. Everywhere we walked the floorboards squeaked and groaned and when they did a salesman in a suit arrived with his hands together and a big smile. "May I help you, sir?" they asked. Dad was in his Sunday best and me and David were in our party best too. If we weren't I knew this bloke wouldn't have given us a second look. I went there once before when Dad was in his work clothes and they didn't even bother coming over. They just looked at us thinking that we didn't have the money to spend. See, this is where blokes like that make their mistake.

Anyway, he decided after a bit that there was nothing he liked at Evan Roberts. Behind his back David looked at me and quietly said "Phew". So we walked down Queen Street to Marks. It's still posh but not as posh as Evan Roberts and they're a bit more friendly.

We went straight to the men's section for Dad to have a good look around. I think both me and David noticed the prices were a bit better here. Better for us that is. We watched him as he looked around. He was taking a big interest in ties. While he was looking through them a lady Sales Assistant came over.

"How can I help you, sir" she asked him.

"I'm just looking for tie," he said. "I'll find one, I'm sure."

"Ok," she said with a smile. "Well, let me just let you know that in this section we have the nylon ties and just the other side we have some silk ties if you'd prefer those. If you need any help just give me a shout."

Dad thanked her and went round to look at the silk ties. "She's nice that assistant," David said.

I grunted.

I had a look at the prices on the silk ties. I thought they were going to be way too expensive. I'd seen them at Evan Roberts too but the prices here were OK. If he picked one of these we could afford it and have change. This looked good.

We watched him carefully and it looked like he was trying to make his mind up between three of them. They all looked OK to me and I wondered why he just didn't pick one and have done with it.

She must have seen him thinking about it. The Sales Assistant that is. She came over. "Let me help you if you're deciding on colour," she said. Dad let her get on with it.

"Is this the usual colour suit you wear?" she asked.

Yeah I thought it's the only colour suit he wears becos it's the only one he's got. He nodded.

"I think this navy blue one is your best choice," she said. She held it against his suit and up to his chin. She stood aside to let us see as well

He looked over at us and we nodded with enthusiasm, I think.

"You have lovely boys," she said smiling at us.

"They have their good moments," Dad said.

She stopped for a second to look at Dad. "Pardon me," she said. "But aren't you Geraint Adams?"

Me and David shared a look. How does she know Dad?

"Yes" he said. "I am".

"I thought so. You were in the same class as my brother, Peter Tucker," she said. "But you were eleven years older than me. You used to come to our house a lot when you were about sixteen and I was around five years old. Peter is in London now."

Dad looked surprised. "Yes, I remember Peter. So he's in London." He went on, "You have a good memory for faces. I'm better at names. If I'm right you must be Linda?"

"Yes, you do remember", she said and went on. "You didn't come back after the War though."

"No, I went to the Midlands. Solihull," he said. "For a few years anyway. Been back a while now."

"That's good," she said and stopped. It looked like they were running out of things to say. But she went on, "Looking at the boys I think their mother must be very beautiful."

Nice one I thought. So you're saying my Dad is an ugly bugger.

"Yes she was," Dad said and dropped his head a bit.

"Was?"

"She died quite a while back," Dad said but he was getting uncomfortable now I could see. He hated talking about mum and her death.

"Yes, I lost my husband to illness a few years ago. A terrible time."

"Yes it can be a terrible time," Dad said to her. "But we made it through, didn't we. That's the thing." He changed the subject. "Well anyway. I'll take this one" he said holding up the navy blue tie. "Better pay for it or at least the boys will pay for it. It's been nice seeing you again"

"It was nice to see you too Geraint," she said as we left to pay at the desk.

"Dad would usually pay but it's his birthday," I said to her. I didn't want her to think Dad sponged off his kids. "We took him for a meal too."

"Happy Birthday, Geraint" she said to Dad.

He smiled back without saying anything. I'm sure he looked shy just the way I used to be. Have to give my Dad some lessons, don't you think??

We gave Dad the money to pay for the tie. He tried to stop us of course but we weren't having any of that. While he was at the desk David said, "You know that lady, Gareth. She likes Dad."

"Stop it" I said to him.

"Well she does and that's that."

There was no point my saying stop it again because David was off on a story all of his own.

\*\*\*\*\*\*\*

Well this is it. It was the Sports Day today. One day before the last day of Junior School. I'm writing this in the evening after it's all over. Well, I said I would write about the result whatever happened and so I have to do it.

You know the teachers and helpers do a great job of setting out the sports day area and the Parks people help too. It all takes place right outside my back door. Not all the parents come of course because it's a work day but you get a lot of mums there watching. I love it

See we have everything. The Parks bloke has marked out a track with white stuff. In the middle Mr Evans has a public address set up with microphone and speakers around the park. There's a results tent so when each race is over the winner, second and third take their number to the tent. Three teachers and helpers are at the finishing line and give out this number to the first three. It's great if you're picked out and given the number 1.

In the middle of the park each class has its own seating area with a helper or teacher to keep everyone in place. I don't know how they manage it but they seem to do it. The helper has to make sure that the right kids from the class they are watching gets to the starting point at the right time. That's not easy because there's usually two or three races going at the same time from different classes on three different areas of the park. When it gets going you can see loads of kids getting lined up for races, some at the winners tent and some rushing back to their class places.

Along the edge of the main running area there's loads of fold away seats for families to watch. You wouldn't think so many people would come to watch but they do. The really keen ones rush from side to side to watch their kids in races on one side of the park or another. There's some tables set up too selling sweets and pop, hot dogs and burgers and of course whenever there's a load of people together Mr Whippee turns up to sell ice cream and lets the tune sound off every now and then. I think he likes to remind people he hasn't left.

It was such a sunny day and I felt excited that this was it. But I also felt something different too going on inside me. Me and Susan gathered the Caradog sports captains together from each class before the Sports Day started and we told them to do their best. But I said something different this time too. I told them to enjoy it and have fun. If we won that would be great but if we didn't the best thing would be to come away knowing we'd given it our best shot and had fun trying.

When they'd gone back to their class places in the middle of the field Susan said, "You don't mind if we lose?"

"I want us to win," I said, "Really I do but most of all I just hope I can beat Geoffrey in a race. He's so fast. But if we don't win this year I think Caradog will next year. Let's do our best. I know you will Susan. No-one is going to beat you today."

"It doesn't matter if you don't beat him," she said. "We are going to win this year. You'll see."

Funny thing is at the beginning of this year it was all that mattered. I couldn't stand the thought of Geoffrey lifting the trophy with the red ribbons of Glyndwr on it rather than me lifting it with the blue ribbons of Caradog. Back then I really did not like Geoffrey and of course it got worse as we started to do bad things to each other. But when I thought about it, he was nothing to worry about. Look how scared he became that his mother was going to leave. He was terrified, I think. Now I feel it must have been awful for him. All that worry for nothing. He's the same as me really and just as scared that in the end I will come on top. All the brylcreem on the hair and the swanky walking is nothing. He's just like me and if we lose to him and Glyndwr it doesn't matter. What am I saying? It does but not as much.

There's seventy two races plus the final relay races at the end of the day so that makes seventy four in all. It's separate races for girls and boys of course This is the list:

60 yards sprint – that's just as it says

60 yards hurdles – they use these wooden blocks with a groove at the top and put a piece of can across it to jump over. The blocks are smaller for Standard 1 and get bigger for each year.

Obstacle race – you wriggle under a blanket, stop to pick up a hoop and go through it, put four blocks one on top of the other and then dash for the finishing line

Bean Bag Race – this is like a relay. The first runner runs the 60 yards to pass the bean bag to the next runner who runs back to where the third runner is and it's fourth one is the one who makes for the finish.

Egg and Spoon – this is just over 20 yards

Wheelbarrow Race – this one is over 20 yards too and is usually a big laugh. It's two in the race. One is lying on the ground. When the whistle goes to start the race the other one standing up picks up the other kid's legs and then using his hands on the ground they race the 20 yards to the finish.

Sack Race – this is over 20 yards too and a good laugh. You get inside the sack pull it up tight and then jump the towards the finish.

Skipping Race – You have to run while skipping over the sixty yards. The girls are always so much better than the boys at this,

Three Legged Race – two people race together. They stand side by side and usually put an arm around each other's shoulders. One of the teachers or helpers ties the right leg of one kid to the left leg of the other kid. This can be a good laugh too

Final Relay Races – the first leg is run by Standard 1 and the last by Standard 4.

I think Pop Willis organizes it and it's clever. He mixes it all up so that you don't get all the sprints together one after the other or all skipping races one after the other but he spreads them out through the afternoon. There's even a race programme so that after each race the winners are announced and the parents can write it in if they want. How they can know I have no idea. Have you heard one of these public address microphone things. After a race Old Mr Evans speaks into the microphone and it sounds like this. "The 2.15 fafafa whistle squeak was won by faffaa squeak whistle tap tap and second and third were fafafafafaf squeak whistle, whistle tap, @#@**@#!! thing".

No one cares though. It's all part of the fun.

I'm not going to go and tell you about each race. I'd be writing forever. I'll just tell you the bits you might want to know. I can tell you that me and Susan were not only racing fast for our events but rushing around to support Caradog in the lower classes wherever we could. So how did me and Susan do?

Susan she won the sprint, hurdles, skipping, obstacle and sack race. She was second in the others. She was just brilliant.

Me? I won the sack race, three legged race, egg and spoon, obstacle race (Ok the ones that don't involve speed but I practiced, right). Geoffrey beat me in the final run of the bean bag race and in the sprint. But guess what? We got a dead heat in the hurdles me and him.

The final relay races of the day is what we were waiting for. The way things were looking it was accepted that Susan would take Caradog to victory in the girls and they did. They boys were not so clear. Geoffrey was the fastest for sure and he had good runners in the lower classes. For Caradog I know that Geoffrey is half a yard faster than me and the Standard 1 and 2 Caradog boys are almost equal with the Glyndwr Boys but Billy Price in Caradog for Standard 3 is fast. He will be Standard 4 Caradog captain next year and for sure he and his team will win.

I got the boys together before the race and we talked about it. The kids in Standard 1 and 2 already thought we were going to come second. They knew they could not quite beat the Glyndwr boys and that Geoffrey would just beat me.

"That doesn't mean we will lose," I told them. "look at Billy. He'll win his section easily."

"Yeah but that's just Billy," they said.

"Ok," I said. "But look if you two can both stay close to the leader and hand over to Billy if it goes right it will give me a couple of yards on Geoffrey. Then I just have to stay in front. I don't want to give in now, boys."

"Yeah but it don't make any difference," the younger kid said. "they're still too fast."

"Well it does," Billy said back. "Everyone remembers this last race. Come on let's really run fast and see if we can upset them. If you stay close to them it's going to upset them and they might drop the baton. But whatever, we must not. Got it? We gotta give Gareth a chance to do it."

Billy was taking the lead. This was good. I looked at him remembering myself moving up from Standard 3 to Standard 4. He would be top Caradog boy next year and the rest of us we'll have gone on to our new schools. It hit me that this race was the last important thing I'd do at Hawthorn Road Junior School and then I was gone.

The younger boys nodded to Billy. They began to see it as more than a one on one race now.

"So are we going to fight like Billy said or shall we give in and I go tell Mr Evans now," I said. "We can do it if we push hard."

"OK, we'll do our best." They said but starting to believe it now. I made us all gather round to shake hands before we went to our positions around the course. Geoffrey was next to me on the fourth leg but neither of us spoke. We were watching the race start and too caught up in what was happening. Our first leg was not so good. There was a stumble at the changeover but the boy on the second leg ran like I never seen him run before. He was half a yard behind when he handed the baton to Billy. I'm sure Billy will be in the Olympic Games for Wales one day. He runs like the wind. When he came to me holding the baton and stretching out to me he had a three yard lead. I took it from him tightly dreading a fumble which might see the baton drop to the grass losing a yard or two and I needed that yard or two. But it stuck slapping into my hand and me grabbing it and making it stick like glue. I was off and out in front.

This was my only chance, I thought. I could not let Geoffrey catch me. For half a second I felt my legs turn to water and I couldn't get the speed to my legs and then the rhythm came and I started to run as fast as I'd ever run. I rounded the curve of the track and saw the finishing line forty yards away. It was still a long way to go.

I was dying to look back to see how much lead I had but this would be so bad. It would slow me and Geoffrey's speed would send him past me. I forced myself to keep looking at the finish and run, run, run. I've seen some things on TV where races go into slow motion and it felt like that to me now. I could hear my panting breath and the slap of my daps on the grass as I ran. I could hear the sound of the boys behind me straining to catch up and win the relay race for Glyndwr, Hywel or Llewellyn. But I was not going to let it go. This year it would be for Caradog.

In front I could see a crowd of parents, teachers, helpers and I saw Susan right in the middle of the finishing line with her white t-shirt and the blue sash of Caradog looped over her right shoulder and diagonally across to her left side. The blue seemed to grow large in my eyes.

I could see them cheering and urging the runners on but I could not hear them. I could only hear the sounds of the runners behind me. And the runner I could hear most was Geoffrey. I could feel him gaining on me inch by inch closing the three yard gap as we neared the line. My eyes now were only for Susan and the blue sash. This was what I was aiming for and strained to reach. She was screaming and urging but I still didn't hear it as the gap between us closed. Her fists were clenched and she was leaning over urging me on and I sensed too that she was warning me of the fast approach of Geoffrey.

Then ten yards from the line from the corner of my eye I saw the edge of a white dap. I could hear Geoffrey's rapid panting to try

## Nobody Watching

to draw alongside me. Something inside me exploded to force me to find more speed and to stop him from getting beyond me. I could not let him pass. Would not let him pass. The tape was stretched now across the line and in the last yard I felt myself dive towards it and out of the side of my eyes saw Geoffrey doing the same. To those watching it must have looked like we'd taken off both of us wanting to spring faster than the other and to feel the touch of the tape.

We landed almost together and you know I couldn't be sure if I'd touched the tape before Geoffrey or if in the last diving rush he'd beaten me to it. I sat up on the grass as did Geoffrey and we were both panting and wheezing and trying to get our breath back. For the relay races Mr Evans held all the place cards. He walked towards me and Geoffrey and you know I couldn't tell which one of us would get it.

He stopped in front of us – two wheezing and panting boys. I turned to Geoffrey swiveling on the grass a bit. Whatever the result now we'd had the best race of our lives and nothing would take away that feeling of racing towards the line. We'd both done our best. I held out my hand to him and he took it. We smiled at each other as never before. Maybe we would never smile at each other like this again but at that moment having finished the race and tested each other we were brothers. Whatever happened in the future to us and between us did not matter.

Mr Evans waited. He held up 1 and 2 and looked at us – and you know what? You know what? You think I'm going to say he gave the card to me, right? But he didn't. You know why? Because before he could give a card to anyone I stopped him and called my boys to join me – the relay team of Caradog. Seeing this the Glyndwr boys ran to Geoffrey as well.

Mr Evans smiled. You could see it. He stepped forward and held out the number 1 card to................................................
.............................................................................................
.............................................................................................
.............................................................................................
.............................. Can you guess?

Well you'll have to turn over this page to see!!!

Well are you ready?

Are you sure? You don't want to stop for a cup of tea or something and come back?

No? No need to start getting angry, you know!!

Well, he stepped forward and held out the number 1 to us. It wasn't mine to take. I had only crossed the line first. It was Billy and the two younger boys who won it. I pulled them in front of me and said, "Take it, it's yours. You lads won it."

They looked at me to see if I meant it and when they saw that I was, the two younger boys got Billy to take it. It was Billy and his group of pals who would take over now. Me and our gang of boys we'd fade away from the school. I remembered kids coming back to see teachers when they went on the to the grammar and secondary schools. Most of the time you didn't recognize or remember them properly. They'd grown and looked different. They looked out of place but I wondered if they looked back at Hawthorn Road junior school as a place that they loved and would never forget. A place where they were happy. I wondered too if these kids were happy in their new school. Did they really like being there or was it just like hell?

I don't know but when I gathered the boys around me for them to take the number 1 card I knew for sure that there's no going back and no staying where you are. You grow and when you grow you change or the world changes somehow and everything gets different. There's no way to stop it.

Later when me and Susan stepped forward to take the trophy for Caradog it was a great moment. I loved it. Me and Susan we were at the top. At that moment and now we are number 1. We are 11 years old and all the kids in our school look up to us. As I'm writing this though I feel a little shiver at the thought of it ending and the new life in the new school. In Form 1 we will be 12 and there are around twenty two classes right up to the Upper Sixth and around 700 pupils in all. In the Upper Sixth they are 18 years old in that group. We are going to be small and like gnats to them. What will it really be like, I wonder?

I was thinking all this while me and Susan took the trophy. Funny how something you dreamed of getting for so long doesn't seem as great when you've got it. My pals, the gang, were looking on at us as we held it. Tom gave me the thumbs up and there was a ripple of clapping from everyone, parents teachers and kids and then it was over.

We gave the trophy back to Mr Evans and almost immediately the noise disappeared and parents started to take their kids home. You could see them spreading out across the park going in different directions. Me and Susan watched it.

"We did it", I said. "Thanks".

"You got your wish," she said smiling.

"Yes, I got my wish," I did my best to smile back. I didn't want to say to her that now we'd got it, it didn't seem as exciting as I expected. I can't explain it properly but let's say getting the trophy is like a shining light and leaving Hawthorn Junior School and going to Canton is a dark light or shadow. It's like the shadow has made the light dim. Well for me anyway. I can see that Susan is just so happy we won. It makes me wonder if I'm the only one who thinks about what is going to happen from September and is scared as hell about it.

While I was thinking about this Dad, David and her parents came to us.

They were full of smiles and happiness for us and after the congratulations, hugs and kisses I watched Susan disappear with her parents. She was looking back and waving at me as they left. I smiled and waved back as we too made the shorter walk across the grass to our house.

Dad says I have an open face. I asked him what he meant by this once and he told me because every thought and feeling can be seen on it. He told me I would not be a good poker player. I think he was reading these things from my face as we walked home.

"You know, Gareth," he said to me. "You'll look back on this day when you are grown up and it will be bigger and brighter than it really was. And that's the good thing about being human."

"What do you mean," I asked.

"Well we remember the good things and exaggerate them. The bad things that happen to us we either forget or they become funny."

"Yeah?" I said thinking I'd have to wait years to see if it was true.

"The other thing is," he went on. "We get scared about the future. And you know what that fear of the future is usually worse than what happens. You wait and see."

I nodded. "Yeah, Dad," I thought to myself. "But what can you do about being scared. How do you make that go away."

\* \* \* \* \* \* \*

Let me show you the final tables too so you know how it all ended up. I'm not going to list all 70 or so of the races but just show you the final summary. Well here it is for the Sports Day:

Glyndwr        203

Caradog        199

Llewellyn      175

Hywel          163

At the time of the final relay race we'd already done enough to win overall but I didn't know. If I'd known I think Geoffrey would have beaten me. All I knew going into that race was that it was very close.

And for the final scores:

Caradog     55 + 43 + 45 + 199   =   342

Glyndwr     42 + 50 + 42 + 203   =   337

Llewellyn   35 + 32 + 38 + 175   =   280

Hywel       28 + 35 + 35 + 163   =   261

* * * * * * *

It was the last day at Hawthorn Road Junior school today. I made my mind up in the morning before going that I was going to enjoy it and remember it as a great day and you know it was.

Mr Evans asked me to do the reading at assembly in the morning and I read with the best use of my voice I could remember. I think it helped seeing the trophy with the blue ribbons of Caradog because I felt a surge of ....I don't know.... pride I think.

We played board games in class and kicked the ball around at playtime. During dinner break I spent the time with Susan. I wouldn't see her for a couple of weeks as Dad was talking us straight on holiday tomorrow. Most of the time we sat and talked about things we'd done and how we'd manage when we went to Canton. I will miss her while we are away.

At afternoon break we did what every kid has done for years on the last day. We played bomberino. You ever seen this. One team of boys line up with the first boy holding onto the wall. The others hold the waist of the person in front and then they lean over so there is a line of backs. The other team lines up and each one runs to jump on their backs and stay there springing off the last person bent over. The team that can take the most people on their backs is the winner. If you're clever you soon learn not to try and get a place in the middle cos that's where they usually land but no-one ever seems to get hurt. The teachers let it go on for a little while but break it up after a few goes. I think they're the ones who are worried about injuries.

This last day flies by. As I'm writing about it at home this evening it all seems a blur. It went so quick. Suddenly we were in the hall at the end of the day for Mr Evans and the teachers to say farewell to us and to wish the other kids a good summer holiday. Then it was done. He let us go early and there was a big cheer from all the kids. Some of us went round the classes to say goodbye to teachers we'd known for four years.

Last of all I went to see Mr Evans. I knew I would miss him and I hoped the Head Master in Canton was as good a person as him. We shook hands. He said some things about wishing me good luck and that I would do well at Canton and he told me not to be afraid.

How do you know, I thought.

I said that I would come back to visit and said something like it was a great school that I would really miss. But then I felt like I was going to cry and didn't want to do that so I wished Mr Evans a good holiday, said thank you and bolted for the door. It had been a good day for sure and as I walked out to find David waiting for me I blinked my eyes rapidly to make the tears go back. I didn't want David to laugh at me.

It was a good day. Not only that, it had been a good four years. This was like home and I felt I was leaving home. But it's not leaving home is it? It's growing up. I will be 12 years old soon and will have to grow up even though if I could I'd start this bit all over again in Standard 1 and maybe do things a bit differently and get it right. Hey, that would be something wouldn't it. To be able to go back and do things over if you didn't like the way it turned out.

Well on the way home I put my arm over David's shoulder and he didn't mind. I didn't look back either. There was no point. As we walked down Hawthorn Road to Hazelhurst Road I let my eyes go over the top of the houses to the direction of Fairwater and Canton High. I needed to look there now and not back at Hawthorn. Like it or not it was now lost for ever.

* * * * * * *

There was no time to think about anything after that. We finished school on Friday. Dad got us to bed early because we would be leaving on holiday for Cornwall at 5 in the morning. Dad didn't take us anywhere last year but now we're older he says we deserve two weeks holiday at a place called Looe in Cornwall. We went there a few years back when we were much smaller. We will be staying in a big caravan.

We left early today because Dad wanted to beat the queues at the car ferry to cross the River Severn. Dad struggled to get me and David out of bed but once were awake we were excited to go. It was chilly when we left the house and there was nothing on the road as we drove out of Cardiff towards Newport and on to the River Severn. There were a few cars before us in the queue for the ferry but Dad was pleased. It meant we would be on the next ferry out and not have to wait too long.

Me and David were a bit scared as we got on to the ferry. Dad drove down onto this ramp and you could see the water. It looked like it wouldn't take much to fall in. These blokes guided us on and we drove on to a turntable which they turned with ropes and pointed to the place where Dad should park. We stayed inside while the ferry made its way across. It wasn't too bad a ride and it didn't take too long once we got going. And then we were off at Aust on our way again down to Cornwall. I had the map on my lap to help Dad. He said I was the navigator.

When we started to get hungry Dad pulled us off the road just after Taunton and drove to a village café. We had such a great breakfast of bacon, egg and sausage with loads of toast. Dad was in a happy mood too but also he wanted us to eat up quickly so we could get back on the road. There was no problem about me and David eating quickly. Then we were off again and I folded the map like Dad had shown me to follow the route. We'd been though Bridgwater and Taunton and now we were headed for Exeter. I'd memorized the route and already knew we wanted Okehampton, Launceston, Liskeard and Looe.

We had a couple of piss breaks along the way. Me and David stood side by side behind some trees off the road. Once a couple of years ago David pissed at me when we were like this. I went nuts and drenched him with a full tank. Dad was mad with both of us and I felt really guilty afterwards. Whatever he does I'll never do that again.

We arrived in Looe just before 4 o' clock in the afternoon. We were tired but Dad wasn't. Once we were at the caravan site and Dad got the keys and let us in me and David wanted to sleep. I don't know why David wanted to. He'd spent half the time sleeping on the journey. Dad had a bed to himself and me and David had bunks. He wanted the top one and I was too tired to argue. I just flopped and slept.

There's not much to tell you about the holiday except it was just really great. We went to the harbour at Looe and fished with hand lines. Dad showed us the place where a few years before a big Blue Shark had been brought in which broke the British record.

On the first Monday away though Dad was angry and sad. He was reading a story in the paper about a girl who was kidnapped in Manchester. He told us to keep very close to him while we were out and always to keep him in sight. I tried to think what it would be like if me or David were taken by someone, away from Dad. It made me shudder. Why would they want to do that?

That week we drove to places like Polperro and Mevagissey nearby and one day we drove over to Newquay. But for me the time I liked best was when Dad drove us to Penzance. It was a really old place just like Looe but bigger. Dad let me look around the old bookshops and I bought a Penguin copy of Oliver Twist. I bought it from an old bookshop in one of the streets. It had a mixture of new and second hand books. It was a quiet shop and the boards creaked. The owner was a man about dad's age sat at the desk. He was reading a book and just glanced up to watch me when I came in and then went back to reading. This must be a good life I thought. When I chose Oliver Twist and went to pay for it, he smiled and told me to keep Our Mutual Friend for last. I nodded but didn't say anything and he went back to reading. You know I don't think he cared if he sold a book or not. I told Dad about it and he said that there you have aman and his work in harmony. Nice! I hope I get that.

We also went to a place called Mousehole. We were having such a great time Dad decided to book us into the Ship Inn for a couple of nights. He said that he'd take us around St Ives, Lands End, Porthcurno and Sennen before we went back to Looe. I would be writing for a week if I told you about all the things we saw. You know what, the best thing you could do is go see it yourself. For me I think I'd like to live there one day. The night before we went back to Looe the three of us walked up the path to the cliff top overlooking the sea. We looked out over a field next to a stile and watched the sun sparkling on the sea. Whenever I go to Mousehole I will come here. There's something about this place that I can't put into words. It just makes you feel peaceful and calm.

Oh and if you're wondering yes of course I sent a postcard to Susan. To be honest I sent two, one each week we were away and one to Tom too. I bought a really nice shell bracelet for Susan and for Tom I got him this pen which is incredible. You hold it up and its got a picture of a girl with a bikini. Then turn it upside down and the bikini's gone!! I had to buy it on the quiet when Dad and David weren't looking and I hid it safe too.

We drove back home on Saturday 28 July. I counted the weeks to starting at Canton. It was another six weeks and a couple of days to go as we started back to school on September 9th. As we drove out of Looe early on Saturday morning I asked dad to take his time. There was no rush if we got home a bit later than before.

You know what? I felt the holiday had been like dreaming and dreaming a good dream. Nothing bad had happened. Me and David even stuck close to Dad!! We'd enjoyed the fish and chips, Cornish pasties, Cornish ice cream, pop, crisps and kept away from carrots and peas as much as we could. It was like a dream you didn't want to end. It would have been better of course if Susan and Tom were there too but even without them it was something like magic. But guess what happened? During the last few days of the holiday what was coming up in September kept coming into my mind. I felt a sickness in my stomach and like I needed a crap a lot of the time. Have you ever felt like this? I wished I could find some way to stop September coming.

But of course I can't do that and even though Dad drove slowly and we had plenty of stops on the way I knew that some time we would be home and some time September 9th would be with us.

When we got back to the house there was a load of post all for Dad but also a letter for me. It didn't have a stamp on it and I recognized the writing. It was from Susan. She said this:

*Dear Gareth*

*I hope your holiday has been good. I liked the postcards. The pictures were so lovely. It made mum and Dad think of holiday too. So we are leaving on Saturday morning for Newquay. I wonder if we will see each other at the ferry or on the road.*

*Well, miss you and will see you when we get back on 12 August*

*Love Susan* xxx

*P.S. I'll send you cards too.*

I liked the love and the kisses but I didn't like it that she'd gone. A whole month without seeing her. At least, I thought I would be able to see Tom.

On Sunday morning I did not get up to go to join the choir and the Church service. I told myself I hadn't gone to choir practice so I wouldn't know the hymns properly. I was glad I did. Uncle Charles came over to talk to Dad around ten o'clock. They went into the kitchen and unusually Uncle Charles pushed the door closed. But the thing is you can't really close this door. I stood right next to it to listen.

Uncle Charles said that some foreign bloke had been around the village asking if there was a man living here who had a German wife.

"Did he have a scar on his face," Dad asked.

"Yeah," he did Uncle Charles said sounding surprised. "You know him?"

"No, I don't know him," my Dad said, "But I read about him. Greta used to keep diaries and after she died I read them. She talks about a Nazi who she hated but he wanted to marry her. He did bad things. He did bad things."

Dad's voice trailed off.

"Well don't worry, Geraint," Uncle Charles said. "You know nobody said anything and a lot of people anyway don't know you had a German wife. We'll keep a look out for him and most people won't tell him a thing. But there's always a chance. From what you said he doesn't sound like a good bloke".

"Far from it," Dad almost whispered.

"Maybe you should involve the police," Uncle Charles said.

"Maybe," Dad replied. "Let me think about it."

I rushed to the sofa and picked up the Eagle to read. Dad glanced over as they walked through to the front door. Dad's face was white as a sheet when he came back and you could see he was thinking. I didn't know what was bothering him but sometimes you just know it's not good to ask.

* * * * * * * *

On Monday the telly was full of pictures of some bloke, Kim Philby. He used to work for the British Government or something but then turned up in Moscow. He's been spying for the Russians. What a git!!

*JP's Note: We've got so used to the bridge over the Severn. Travel was so slow back then without motorways. The kidnap in Manchester was the start of the Moors Murders carried out by Peter Brady and Myra Hindley. They terrified parents for a long while. Nothing's changed: parents are terrified today.*

*That bookseller he saw on holiday could be my dream. Maybe the dream of every avid book reader.*

# CHAPTER 13
## *August 1963*

Dad's been a bit funny since we've been back. He's been thinking a lot and going through Mum's diaries. He's put off a few jobs he was supposed to be working on and one night a knock came to the door. He made me and David be quiet by putting his finger to his lips and he went to the door to listen.

He came back and pointed for me and David to go to the kitchen with him. We slipped out the back door and he sent us into the back seat of the car. Dad opened the garage gates and got into the car himself. We drove down the lane and came out by the rugby club. Dad turned the car into Hazelhurst Road and drove down it towards our house. He told us to sit absolutely still. As we drove towards our house two men were walking away. I looked and saw that one man had a scar on his face.

I didn't say anything. I didn't want Dad to know that I'd overheard him talking to Uncle Charles. We drove around for a couple of hours and David fell asleep. When we got back to the garage Dad closed the doors, picked David up easily and carried him to bed. He said good night to me too and told me to go to bed.

Dad woke us early the next day and gave us breakfast. I thought he'd let us go out so I could meet up with the boys. I hadn't seen much of them since getting back from holiday. But he wouldn't let us. He said that we needed to visit his brother.

"What, Uncle Dan?" I asked in surprise. I had vague memories we saw him once when Dad moved to Llandaff North from the Midlands but I couldn't remember where or what he looked like.

"Yes," Dad said. "There's some family business I need to sort out with him. It'll be good if you come to. Maybe you'll be able to see your cousin, Megan, unless he's sent her off on a holiday somewhere."

David seemed to go along with the plans easily but for me this was a big change in the way we'd got used to things in the summer holidays. I had no idea what dad was up to. We drove out to a place called St Nicholas outside Cardiff and on the way to Cowbridge. We stopped outside a big house in its own grounds with a five bar gate for the entrance. Dad opened the gate and got us to walk through on to the pathway to the front door.

Dad told us not to step on the grass on pain of death. I could see what he meant though. It wasn't like the rough grass we had on Hailey Park. It looked more like the grass you played bowls on like we had near the playground. There were flowers and bushes and trees everywhere. At the front of our house was a small wall, concrete and a privet hedge. If this was Uncle Dan's front garden God knows what the back is like, I thought.

Dad knocked the front door but he wasn't there. A cleaning lady came to the front door and told Dad that he would be back at 5.30. He'd taken a few weeks off to be with Megan. Today, they'd gone into Cardiff town she told dad.

Dad left a note with her for his brother to say that he had called with his sons and he'd be back later. Dad then got us into the car and drove us to Barry Island rather than going home. It was like being on holiday again. You ever been there? It's got really good shows, you know, merry go rounds, dodgems, a big wheel, jets, scenic railway, water splash, slot machines, rifles, roller derby and so on. You can spend the whole day there and never get bored. It's great fun. Dad must have spent a fortune on us because he didn't refuse anything and we went on ride after ride and from stall to stall. We only took a break for fish and chips and a load of pop.

Even dad joined in with some of the stuff especially the dodgems and the scenic railway and for a time he was laughing and smiling as he played with us. It was only now and again when whatever was worrying him came to his mind that he went thoughtful and stopped talking for a while.

Before we knew it the time had passed and dad was getting us spruced up in one of the toilets making us wash our hands and faces to get rid of the chip smell. He even got us a packet of polos each so our breath wouldn't pong when we met our uncle. Dads, ay!

When Dad rang the bell this time it was answered by Uncle Dan. I noticed he had a scar on his face too but he wasn't like the bloke we'd seen in Hazelhurst Road the day before. They didn't speak at first, just looked at each other. Somehow, I thought I was looking at a couple of boxers who were weighing each other up before a fight. It made me wonder about Dad and his life before we were around. What had happened in the years before we knew him as our Dad? I guess all kids wonder the same.

After a bit dad spoke to him. Me and David stood close to Dad looking up and not saying anything."

"Hullo, Dan. It's been a long time."

"Yes, Dan," Dad replied to him. "Maybe too long."

He put out his hand to Uncle Dan for him to shake it. Uncle Dan looked at the hand for a little while as if he was thinking about something and then took Dad's hand. I didn't know what was going on but it felt like something important had happened.

"Your boys look good, Geraint," Uncle Dan remarked. "Come on in. Let's see if Megan has left any Tizer, biscuits or a few pieces of cake. She's around the place somewhere too. Maybe in the garden."

Uncle Dan opened the door for us, stood aside and gestured for us to come in. He closed the door and led us through to the kitchen. It was bigger than our lounge. In a few seconds he put glasses, pop, biscuits, chocolate and slices of cake on the kitchen table.

"Take as much as you like," he said to me and David. "Your father and I will have a chat in my study."

Dad walked away with Uncle Dan but turned back to say. "Be good, boys and don't break anything."

Uncle Dan also called out too. 'When you've finished, you can go out into the garden if you like. I'm sure you'll find your cousin Megan there."

They left and me and David tucked into the stuff he'd put out for us. There was tons of it and it was great.

"He must be rich," David said. "This place is huge."

I nodded. Llandaff North and the terraced houses had always been home to me and places like this I'd seen but never imagined what it was like to live in one. We left enough stuff on all the plates to show we'd not been greedy.

"Let's go to the garden," David said. He was itching to get there.

'I'm going to find a bog," I said. "You go. I'll catch you up."

David laughed. "Don't mess up a bog here." He said. "Better to have a piss in the bushes out there. No-one will see you."

We both laughed at that. I shoved him in the back pushing him towards the door that led to the garden. He opened it and started to go through. "Don't be too long though, Gareth, OK?"

I nodded. "Won't be long."

I saw a small toilet just opposite the kitchen and used it. It was nothing like ours. It had several towels on a rail and different kinds of soap laid out. I used the soap that looked used and the towel in the middle. Before I left I made sure the place looked near enough as exactly as before.

I went to go back to the kitchen but stopped. I heard voices speaking further down the hallway. It was Dad and Uncle Dan. I was curious and went to look stepping on tiptoe to stay quiet. I came to a door which was open and heard their voices. I watched them though a gap in the door. They were sitting in leather armchairs. A small table was between them and on it was what looked like a bottle of whisky, I think. They were each holding a glass in their hand and sipping from it. I couldn't tell what they were talking about but they seemed friendly enough although the sound of Dad's voice was anxious.

I glanced around just to check if I was being watched and looked through another open door across from this one. It caught my attention. It was a room full of books. I walked over to it quietly and went in. It was incredible. I didn't realize one person could own so many books. There was never any need for Uncle Dan to go to the library. I didn't know where to start looking first and just went from bookshelf to bookshelf. There were no kids books here but there were stories I could tell as well as books about famous people, countries, history and stuff like that. It was paradise.

In a glass cabinet on one wall there was row after row of the Encyclopaedia Britannica. I gasped when I saw this. I wanted a set but I knew it cost a fortune to buy. In it there is everything you want to know. You can find the answer to anything. I got to my knees to look at the volumes behind the glass and felt what my feet had been telling me. This carpet was thick and my knees buried into it. I touched the glass disappointed that I could not reach inside and slide one of the volumes out to look up Patagonia or something like that. All the other books were open to touch but this was locked and there was no sign of the key. You know. I don't really understand why anyone would want to lock up books that tell you things. Everyone should be able to know, shouldn't they?

Anyway so I'm on my knees smearing the glass with my fingers and then I hear, "He'll not let you look at those, Gareth"

I was startled for sure and scrambled to my feet. I felt like I'd been caught doing something wrong. I started to feel my face going red as I turned in the direction of the voice.

There was a girl about my age standing next to David. "We came to look for you as you were taking so long." She said. "David thought you might have flushed yourself down the toilet."

David laughed out loud at this and the girl grinned. I could tell she was pleased that I was getting redder and redder. I knew I had to make myself sound a bit confident. "Sorry," I said. "I like books and couldn't help coming to look."

"You must be good at school then. Not like me and David, I think. You must be a swot," she said.

For a second I felt like I was being told off but her eyes were twinkling. I decided what to do. "Yeah, maybe I am a swot sometimes......but I also like to chase cheeky girls and boys." With that I made a monster face at the two of them and then walked like a zombie towards them growling "I'm gonna get you, I'm gonna get you."

OK, it sounds stupid but you know what it works most of the time. The two of them squealed and ran off back through the kitchen and into the garden. As I followed I quickly had to change my face and way of walking when I saw Dad and Uncle Dan looking at me from their doorway.

"You found the books then, Gareth" Uncle Dan said.

"Yes," I said feeling foolish and hoping he hadn't seen my zombie walk. "They're great. Really, they're great."

"Well maybe next time you visit you can pick out a few to borrow," he said with a smile on his face. I noticed that the scar almost disappeared when he gave a big smile.

My eyes popped out on stalks. "Yeah?" I questioned not believing my luck.

"So just play in the garden for five minutes or so and then we'll be on our way home," Dad said.

I went but not using the zombie walk until I got into the garden. Megan sounded posh but she was good fun and the three of us had a laugh in the garden. When we'd tired ourselves out we lay on the grass and talked about school next year. It didn't surprise me she was going to Howell's. She seemed to accept too that I was going to Canton.

"Me and my father will visit you next time, I think" she said to me and David.

"It's better if we come here," David said. "Your place is so big. Ours is tiny."

'It would be nice to visit anyway," she said. "Maybe my Father and yours are going to be friends now. Just like you two brothers are friends."

David aimed a punch at me just to show she was wrong and we all laughed. But the way she said it made me think. Something had happened so that they were not friends.

You know, Megan is nice. We had fun for an hour so and not five minutes and I was left wondering why Dad and Uncle Dan had not met up for so long and why we hadn't played with Megan before. I think grown ups are just like us. They have arguments and misunderstandings that don't matter so much really if they talked and put it right. Just like me and Geoffrey.

While I was thinking this Dad called to us. He was standing at the edge of the garden with Uncle Dan. I looked at them. They were so different. Just like me and David. The three of us got to our feet and joined them.

We'd had fun and we said goodbye to Uncle Dan and Megan with a bit of sadness, I think. It wasn't just that we were leaving them but that we hadn't had more time over the years to do this. Also it was sad to leave their house. It was incredible. To go home would be like going back to a garden shed.!!

On the drive home I could smell whisky fumes coming over from Dad. He was holding the wheel tight and concentrating very hard in driving. When we came to Ely roundabout we should have turned left to go towards Llandaff North but he missed it somehow and went round it to try again, but then he missed it again.

"Don't worry boys," he called out. "I'll get the bugger next time" and he did and we all laughed. But you know I couldn't tell if he'd done it on purpose or if he'd missed it accidentally. Whatever, it was funny and was just like when he speeds up to go over the hump back bridge to make me and David laugh. As I watched Dad the rest of the way home a smile was spreading across his face. Why? Well only he knows. And that's the same with all of us, isn't it. Only we really know what's going on inside our heads.

\* \* \* \* \* \* \*

Today the news on the radio is full of something incredible. They are calling it the Great Train Robbery because it looks like the robbers have stolen over two million pounds. Two million pounds! Can you imagine that?

They are so clever! There is a train that runs from Scotland to London and on it there's postmen who in one carriage are dealing with parcels and packets which are not normal post. It's the registered stuff with money and expensive stuff in it. They picked a place in the country to stop the train

You know how they did it? They stuck something over the green light so the train driver wouldn't see it and then used a battery to make the red light come on. So the train stopped. When the guard got out to see what the problem was and to try to call the signal station the robbers got him and because the door was open they got into the train and tied the postmen up. Then they got all the bags out into waiting cars and raced away. It took just 15 minutes to get all that money. The only thing that wasn't so good was that one of the robbers whacked the driver over the head.

But you know what? I know stealing is wrong and I would never do it myself. Ever! But I can't help wondering why I feel this one is exciting and I'm hoping that they get away with it. Why do I feel like that when I know they've done a bad thing??

\* \* \* \* \* \* \*

Next day Dad told us not to stay in the house for too long. He gave us money to get food at dinner time and said he would be back in the evening. For a while me and David sat on the wall outside the back gate and looked out over Hailey Park. We talked a bit about Uncle Dan and Megan. David had enjoyed himself there I could tell and he liked her. It was still a bit early and there were only a few people walking their dogs but later a few of the boys and some of the girls showed up. Tom was there, Nigel and Alun, Janet, Gaynor and

Rosalind. Rosalind had a cousin with her called Caroline who was from London. She was the same age as us and bragging that she didn't care about the 11 plus and a secondary modern was just as good as a grammar school. She was loud and confident and funny too. She told us a lot of jokes.

We took her round our territory and I let David stay with us too. We went to the playground and to the monkey rocks, the Old Oak Tree and Povey's field. We walked part way along the Long Woods too until we all started to feel hungry. We walked back to Hailey Park and split up arranging to meet after dinner. Me and David walked to Station Road and got pie and chips. We ate it on the park bench by the playground where Mr Hughes used to sit. It made me think about him for a while. It made me think too about what he must have been like when he was a little boy like me and what it was like back then. We finished and stuffed the papers in a bin and went to the water siphon to drink and clean our hands and face.

After we'd messed around on the swings and slide for a while we went back to the wall outside our house to meet the kids again. Caroline was talking a lot and she was saying she knew a way that two people could pick up someone with one finger each. She pointed at me and said you can go first. It was all to do with breathing and holding your breath, she said. She made me sit on the wall and breathe deeply a lot and then to hold it and she stood behind me and put her arms around me tightly and counted to five. I felt a bid giddy. She let go on this count of five and Tom and Janet put one finger each under me. I have no idea if they were able to lift me up. I didn't feel as if I'd moved a bit but she was going, "See, I told you. I told you."

She said it was her turn next and she told me to hold her when she was ready. She did a lot of deep breathing and then held her breath pointing for me to hold her. I did and counted to five just like she had done and let her go. Nigel and Rosalind went forward to lift her with one finger but I felt her falling back towards me and reached for her. I thought she was playing but she was not. She fell back of the wall and I fell back holding her. She scraped the back of her legs in the fall. She was not thin like Susan but chubby and heavy. I squirmed from under her to look at her face. I could see Alun running away down the path to the lane. She opened her eyes and stared ahead.

"You all right," I asked. I was scared.

"I can't see you. I can't see you," she said clearly. "I can't see anything."

"Can you get up?" I said. I had a feeling that if I could just get her on her feet everything would be fine and we could get things back to normal.

"No, I can't", she said, "I can't." and then her eyes closed and her head went to one side. They all ran off except me, David and Rosalind.

"She's dead," David wailed. "She's dead."

I prayed to God she was not. "I spoke to Rosalind. I was so scared. "Rosalind, I'm going to run to the end of the road to the phone box and dial 999 for an ambulance, OK. Will you stay with her while I do this?"

Rosalind nodded.

"You too, David?" I asked.

"No, I'm coming with you," he said. I didn't argue. I just wanted to run as fast as I could to the phone box and get help. I did and was dialling the number before David caught me up. He opened up the door to squeeze in beside me. There was a smell of old piss and stale farts in the box and loose dirty papers on the floor.

"999, what service do you require," the voice came.

"Ambulance, please" I said.

"Connecting you,"

It seemed an age before I heard, "Ambulance Service"

I told the woman what had happened and where Caroline was. She asked me if there were any grown ups present and I said no. So she told me to get one. She said the ambulance would be there quickly.

I raced back and on the way called into Aunt Nancy's through the back gate. She was in the garden and I saw Janet in the window upstairs. I told her that this girl Caroline had collapsed and she dropped the pegs on the floor and ran back with me.

Rosalind was still there and holding up Caroline's head a little of the ground. Her eyes were open again now and she was talking. Aunt Nancy took over from Rosalind and asked us what happened. We all went quiet. "It's my asthma," Caroline said. "I had an asthma attack. Left the ventilator in the bedroom."

"What happened, Gareth?" Aunt Nancy asked me and then I heard the ambulance coming with the sirens going. I started to say something but then just ran with David following me. I rushed through the back gate with him after me and slammed it shut sliding the bolt across as quietly as I could. I ran into the house and up the stairs to the bathroom. I pulled my shorts down, farted loudly and crapped diarrhea as fast as I could. When it was over I slumped my head over my knees and cried and shivered.

David sat on the floor outside the bathroom watching me. He was crying and wiping his nose with the back of his sleeve. "You don't think she's going to die, do you?" he asked.

"I got to leave," I said. 'The police will come for me, whatever happens. I got to go."

"Where you gonna go?" David asked.

"I'm gonna hide out in the Long Woods", I said. "They won't find me there. I know it too well."

"But it'll be dark, and there's no food and there's the old tramp." David wailed. "You can't go."

'I got no choice," I said back and I didn't see that I had. It was all over. I'd killed her and would go to prison. Nobody would want anything to do with me. I moaned when I thought of Susan.

I finished in the bathroom and washed my hands quickly. I found my sports bag under the bed and threw out my football boots and kit and then stuffed in some clothes. We heard a knocking on the front door and froze. It kept on knocking for maybe five minutes and then they went away. Me and David went downstairs quietly and I made two thick cheese sandwiches folded them in greaseproof paper and put them in a paper bag and inside the sports bag. I took two apples as well and half a bottle of Tizer.

"You won't blab on me?" I asked David. He wailed again and shook his head.

"Bring me some more food tomorrow," I said to him, "But be careful that they're not watching you."

"Where will you be in the Long Woods," David asked.

"Don't worry, I'll look out for you and when I see you I'll throw a stone in front of you, I said. "If you nod when you see it I'll come out but if you start looking from side to I'll stay put. I'll know they're following you. OK. You got it."

He nodded. "Ok Gareth," he whimpered. "But they'll see you when you leave."

"No, they won't if I'm careful," I said. "I'll look through the hole in the back gate and if it's clear slip out and run straight for the fence by the river. I'll get through the fence and make my way along the bank to the end of Povey's field and then slip out to get to the Long Woods. I thought it through. They won't get me."

David started to cry again and held on to me. I hugged him. It was terrible. I'd done a bad thing, the worst possible thing and my life was over.

"What's going on here?" Dad said and we both looked up to see him in the kitchen doorway.

"Gareth's running away, Dad", David said. "You have to stop him."

I couldn't look Dad in the face. "I know what's happened outside. Aunt Nancy told me. She's been waiting. She got the story out of Janet after that London girl was taken by the ambulance. Stupid girl should never have shown you lot that silly trick."

I looked up quickly. I was expecting Dad to blame me and be mad with me but it wasn't happening.

"You think I killed her, Dad?" I asked trying to blink back tears.

"Don't be so silly," Dad said. "It wasn't the cleverest thing for that stupid girl to teach you when she's got asthma herself. She'll be fine. A few cuts on the back of her legs but that's it. She walked into the ambulance in the end."

"She did?" I questioned.

"Yes and if you'd opened the door to Aunt Nancy she would have told you the same," Dad said. 'If you ask me she might even have been playing a game on you lot that went a bit wrong. So she got what she asked for."

'The police won't be after me?" I asked.

"No," Dad said with a snort. "Don't be silly. Anyway, where you off to anyway with that bag?"

I looked at it, my sports bag with a few jumbled clothes inside, cheese sandwiches, pop and apples and let it drop to the floor. I didn't want to say anything.

"Gareth was going to hide out in the Long Woods, Dad" David said. He'd cheered up now. There were dirty smudges where he'd been crying but his face looked like an angel again. It was like it was full of light. He's a lucky bugger, I thought.

Dad looked and made some faces and then said, "He…..what?....hide out…?" and then he just burst out laughing. But his laugh was so full of fun and not laughing at me if you know what I mean that me and David started laughing too until our sides ached.

When we stopped Dad said, "Well the packing was a good idea, son. But you did it for the wrong reason. We'll pack the suitcase and leave tonight."

"Why? Where are we going, Dad?" I asked.

"It's what I went to see Uncle Dan about." He said to us. 'We have a bungalow we both own in …… a place not far from here." He was going to say where but had changed his mind. "We used to rent it out and share the money. It's vacant now, so we can spend the rest of the summer holidays there."

"Where is it?" David asked.

"It will be a surprise," Dad said. "Just wait and see tomorrow. I'll pack for us. I think you boys have had enough excitement for one day."

Later, as we sat in front of the telly I could feel David close to me. His arm was resting against mine and his leg was resting against mine. He was close to me. We were watching Z cars which I like but him being close to made me think. When Caroline fainted they all ran off except David and Rosalind. Caroline is cousin to Rosalind and David is my brother. Relatives stayed with relatives. Tom is my best friend and Alun and Nigel are friends but they all ran off to leave me. I didn't think Tom would do that but he did. You remember me saying that when Tom was attacked by those boys I wanted to know if I would stay to help him. I still don't know but I know that Tom will run off now.

But you know what? I don't think he would have before, this time last year I mean. But now it's different because we are going separate ways. We are not connected now. He is going his way and I will be going mine. Take my Dad too. Something is going on with him. I don't know what it is but he's turning to his brother to help and not anyone else around here. I read in this book once that "blood is thicker than water" and I didn't really get it but I do know. In the end the ones that will stand by you are your family no matter what the feeling between you. That's what it means.

I put my arm around my brother's shoulder and he didn't resist. We are family and always will be.

\* \* \* \* \* \* \*

Dad woke us early for breakfast next day. There was the smell of bacon, eggs and sausage coming from the kitchen. Dad had pulled the stops out and made a full breakfast with a pile of toast.

"Get this down you," he said, "And we're ready to go."

"What about packing the car, Dad," I asked.

"Already done, son," he replied. "Just have a quick look around to see if there's anything you want that I might not have put in."

When we finished me and David had a good look round but Dad had done a great job. I took a couple of books I wanted and David a couple of toys but that was it. After we'd finished we squeezed into the back of the car because dad had packed it tight and we drove out of the garage. He stopped to get back out and close the gates and lock them. This was odd. He always left them open for when we drove back. I looked over a quiet Hailey Park as we drove away. This feeling came to me that we were leaving for good and the next time I came back would be to visit. I wondered if this feeling would turn out to be true. We glided quietly along the lane to the Rugby club and down Radyr Road and Evansfield Road to join up with Station Road and headed towards Llandaff.

I thought at first we might be going back to see Uncle Dan and Megan at St Nicholas but we turned away from that direction and then I thought maybe we were going to stay at Barry Island. That would have been fun!! But eventually he pulled the car off the road and onto a driveway at a place called Fontygary. We'd never been here before. It wasn't as grand as St Nicholas but all the houses and bungalows were separate with massive gardens at the front.

We got out of the car and Dad walked behind to close the gates. He walked the drive way to the garage next to the bungalow and opened the garage doors. It was clean and empty.. He made us wait by the front door while he parked the car in the garage.

"Whose place is this, Dad ?" I asked.

"You forgot already? It belongs to me and Uncle Dan," he said. "It was our parents place before they died years ago. Since then we rented it out, like I said. Every now and then we leave it vacant and do it up, replace some of the furniture but Dan looks after all that."

He opened it up and we went in. It didn't smell like a place that's been lived in. It smelled of new paint and disinfectant. It wasn't as big as Uncle Dan's place but it was big enough and the furniture was better than the stuff we had at home. It had two living rooms at the front. You could tell one was the best room for visitors because the other had the telly. In the middle was a dining room to one side and a kitchen to the other. And at the back there were two big bedrooms and a small one. Me and David could not believe it. It was just great. And when we walked out of the kitchen and round the back to the garden it was incredible. There were flagstones down and some garden furniture on it covered up with tarpaulin and then these steps up on to the garden. Honest, you could get lost in this garden. It was about twenty yards wide and I'm telling the truth it went down as far as eighty yards. It was lawn first then laid out for vegetables with a greenhouse at the side and then fruit bushes and after that fruit trees.

There was no park nearby but you didn't need it with a garden like this. There was everything here for me and David. After we helped Dad unpack the stuff we walked the road to find three little shops at the end. Two of them were for food but one was a newsagent selling comics and sweets so me and David were happy about that.

We walked down a lane a path at the side of the shops which led to the sea. It wasn't a sandy beach but a rocky one. David whooped in delight and headed for the rocks. The tide was in and he went straight for the small stones to skip them over the water.

On the walk I had been thinking about Caroline and what happened. I wasn't as terrified as before because Dad had not acted worried but I still had a sick feeling in my stomach. I was worried about her and what I'd done.

We sat on a large rock to watch David play. "Dad, can I ask you something," I said.

"Go on. Gareth," Dad replied.

"Did we come here because of the accident…..you know the accident with Caroline?" I asked.

Dad looked at me. "You know, you shouldn't worry about that." Dad said. "You did right to call the Ambulance but they only took her as a precaution. Stupid girl."

"So coming here is nothing to do with me?" I asked Dad.

"No, son, not really. Although maybe it's a good idea to get you away for a while," Dad replied. "I'm pretty sure she's the type of girl who'd want to make you feel guilty for the rest of the holiday. But no, coming here is nothing to do with you."

"So, we're staying a long time?" I asked.

"Till the end of the school holidays," Dad replied.

I realized this meant I would not see my pals for the rest of the holidays and wouldn't even see Susan. I had the shell bracelet for her.

I wouldn't know what happened to Caroline until we got back home either.

"There's something else too, son" Dad went on. "We won't be going back to Llandaff North either."

"Why? Where are we going?" I asked Dad not believing what I was hearing. I couldn't remember anything but living in Llandaff North. What about all my friends. What about all the people we knew. What about going to school.

"Well,"Dad replied. "I've been thinking about it for a while. We've lived in Llandaff North a long time and it's been OK but there's better. I've been doing some work near Roath Park. There's some houses which are only a few years old with a garden and semi-detached. It's walking distance to Roath Park. It's great there."

This was a bombshell. We'd been to Roath Park before and it is very nice but it's miles from Llandaff North and everything we know. "But what about schools for me and David?" I asked trying to find something that would keep us at our home.

"Well for David, it's easy. There's a junior school walking distance from the house," Dad replied. And for you it's a bit tougher. You get a bus from Roath Park into town and then another from Canton bridge to Fairwater."

I nodded but I couldn't see why we had to do this.

"You could change school if you wanted, later on," Dad said. "Go to one closer to home like Howardian or Cardiff High."

He's already calling the new place home, I thought. "No," I replied. "I won't want to change school. I'll stay at Canton," I said. I was already thinking that there would be no walk from Llandaff North to Fairwater with Susan and no walk with her back from school. There would be no meeting up with pals on Hailey Park like before. I couldn't really take it all in.

Dad must have guessed what I was thinking. "You'll see your pals at school," he said. "You wouldn't have much chance to see them after school, you know. You're going to be piled up with homework. But you'll be able to get over to Hailey Park on the weekend of course. If you want."

I nodded. He'd thought it all through but it didn't make it any less awful.

"I was thinking we might just stay here, you know," he continued. "But then I thought it's too far from Cardiff. You and

David would both have to go to new schools. You'd lose touch with your friends. It's nice here but I think you'll like Lakeside."

"Can we go back to Llandaff North for the day, Dad," I asked. "Before we go back to school, I mean. I'd like to see the boys and my friends just to tell them what's happening."

He nodded. 'Yeah, we can do that." He reached into his pocket and gave me a piece of paper. "You can write to them too if you like but use this Post Office Box number and just say you're on holiday by the sea."

David was still skimming stones into the sea but calling us now to come with him. "Let's join him then. I've got to tell David the news too," Dad said. He got up to go.

"I'll come in a minute, Dad," I said. "Better you tell him on his own."

Dad looked out at David and then back at me. He looks a bit older, I thought to myself. He didn't speak but stepped on the loose stones to make his way to David. I started thinking. Something wasn't right about the things Dad had told me. What he said made sense and Lakeside sounded really nice but Dad had never shown any sign of wanting to leave Llandaff North. I think he loves it as much as me and David do. There was something big that had made him decide to move us and it all started after Uncle Charles came to tell him about the foreign bloke.

Dad has a secret, I thought. I watched him as he was telling David and saw David drop the stone he was about to skim. He put his hands to his face to stop dad seeing the tears and Dad pulled him towards him to hold him tight. At the same time I saw him look up into the sky like he was making a prayer and there was a look of agony on his face. He suddenly remembered I must be watching and the look went. He turned his head to look at me and waved for me to come and join him and David.

I got up from the rock and walked towards them. "Dad has a secret," I thought again. "And I don't want to know what it is."

\* \* \* \* \* \* \* \*

That night I wrote to Susan:

*Dear Susan*

*You'll read this I know when you get back from holidays.*

*We came on holiday again to the seaside. It was a big surprise and we'll be here now until we go back to school. But I will come to see you for one day before we go back to school. I got news to tell you but I want to tell you when I see you. Write to me and tell me the best day. I don't want to come and find you are not there.*

*Let me know about your holiday. Was it great?*

*Something bad happened while you were on holiday. Rosalind brought her cousin Caroline (she's from London) around Hailey Park. She showed us this trick and got me to try it on her. She fainted and I thought she was dying. I was so scared. I guess you will hear about it. Let me know if she's OK.*

*Can't wait to see you.*

*Love*

*Garethxxx*

*P.S. Please write to the PO Box number I put at the top of the letter.*

    I had a picture in my mind of the letter lying on the mat waiting for Susan to come home at the end of next week. I thought about her in Newquay too with her sister and Mum and Dad. I tried to work out the earliest I would see her and guessed it would be the middle of the week after she got back. I decide to write to Tom too.

*Dear Tom*

*How are you doing? Dad took us for another holiday. Lucky us, ay? It was all a bit sudden.*

*Can you let me know what happened to Caroline afterwards. It scared the pants off me when she fainted.*

*I got something to tell you and the boys, Tom. Do you think you can see if they're all around on 15 August? I'll get to Hailey Park about 10 o'clock. Can you check if it's OK with Susan too. She doesn't get back though until Saturday of next week.*

*Thanks Pal. Please write back to the PO box address at the top.*

*All the best*

*Gareth*

As I was writing I had a picture in my mind of Tom running off. Something in my head whispered to me "You're on your own, now Gareth". I shook my head. "They're all running away," it said to me and I shook my head again closing my eyes to clear these thoughts.

A couple of days after we arrived we got a letter from Aunt Nancy. Dad had done a lot of planning I thought and had even thought to give the PO address to her. Her letter said:

*Dear Geraint, Gareth and David*

*First of all I'm sure you want to know what happened to Caroline. When they took her to the hospital she was fine. They could find nothing wrong with her but told her off for playing a stupid game. I think she was trying to scare the boys really. Janet told me that Rosalind had said that she might do something like this just to get the boys going. Although of course she is sticking to her story that she fainted. She's running round the park now with the girls laughing and shouting. Nothing wrong with her that's for sure.*

*Well Geraint, tell Gareth not to worry. It's all over now.*

*The house is fine. I'll pop in every couple of days to check on it for you.*

*Hope you are having a good time and write back to say when you will be coming back home*

*All the best*

*Nancy*

Dad showed me the letter. He said it was addressed to me too so I should read it. I was so happy to hear that Caroline was OK. I felt the sick feeling leave my stomach but I also felt ashamed about the way I behaved. I couldn't believe now that I was really thinking of hiding in the Long Woods. What happened to me to think that was even possible.

But also I thought, why would she do that? Why would she let me and the others believe something bad had happened to her. Why would she trick and frighten me like that. Can you explain it? Has anyone ever done anything like that to you? I don't think I ever would. Not something like that.

By the time Sunday came around me and David had done everything we possibly could in Fontygary. It was like a circuit. Play in the garden, go to the shops, go to the rocky beach, lie on the lawn and watch the aeroplanes fly in low to Rhoose Airport and play Crazy golf at the Mayflower pub at the other end of the road.

The crazy golf is not bad to be honest, especially if Dad joins in. But most of the time now he likes to sit outside the pub and watch us. Well watch us when he's not reading the paper and sipping beer that is. But he looks better and that's the good thing. He looks around though from time to time like he's expecting to see the man with the scar. I bet the answer to Dad's secret is in those journals. No way I'm going to find out what it is though, not until I've learned German anyway.

As the week went by I really missed Llandaff North and was just waiting to get letters from Susan and Tom. Funny thing was though that David loved it. He found a few kids his age who lived nearby and went off to play with them on the rocks by the beach. There were a few my age too around but I didn't want to make friends. If David was out playing I lay on the grass watching the aeroplanes or went with Dad to the pub. While he had his beer and the paper, I had pop and read a good book.

He came back once and said, 'Hey Dad, do we have to leave. I could go to school here."

I was shocked but before I could say anything Dad said, "Nice idea, David but the school is full. I checked. "

Dad winked at me. I didn't know what he meant. Did he mean he was saying that just to put David off or had he really tried to get him in the school. If he'd tried to get him in the school it meant that he'd thought about putting me in a school round here too. I sighed. I couldn't be bothered to ask.

On Monday two letters arrived for me, one from Susan and one from Tom. I read Susan's first.

*Dear Gareth*

*Hope you are ok? A lot happens to you when I'm not there. It was so good to see your letter on the mat when I got home but I was surprised you went away again. Do you think your Dad did it because of the trick that the London girl Caroline set up. Maybe your Dad thought it was a good idea to go away for a bit.*

*Don't worry about her, Gareth. She's awful. I saw her on Saturday evening after we got back. I called round to Janet's house and she was there with Rosalind. She's bragging how she scared you all. Anyway forget it.*

*Newquay was great. We spent a lot of time at the beach but it would be better if you were there with us.*

*What's this secret you want to tell me? You've got me guessing. Well, I'll know on Tuesday. Yes I'll be in Hailey Park at 10 by the swings on Mr Hughes bench.*

*Love*

*Susanxxx*

Her letter really made me feel good. If I'd been worried at all now about Caroline the fear had gone. I put it down to open the one from Tom.

*Dear Gareth*

*Hope all OK? You were away pretty quickly but you didn't have to be scared of Caroline. Why did you get the Ambulance? There was no need for that. Anyway, she's fine.*

*See you in Hailey Park on Tuesday. A few of the boys will be there and Susan for sure. So we'll know your big secret then.*

*See you.*

*Tom*

I read the letter a couple of times. It didn't sound like Tom. I felt he was laughing at me a bit. My best friend laughing at me!! Was he saying it was all a joke and knew about it? What do you think? I've written the letter out exactly as I got it. They were playing a big joke on me, I think and they were all in on it. Do you think so too?

Dad dropped me and David off at Hailey Park by the tennis courts just before 10. I felt in my pocket to make sure I'd brought the small package for Susan and wondered whether she'd like it. Dad gave us some money and told us to be back at the same spot at 5. He told us not to say where we're staying. Just say some house on the coast in the middle of nowhere.

David ran ahead of me as he wanted to call to see one of his friends opposite the school. I told him to meet me outside the school at 1 o clock so we could buy some food. I wanted to run too because it had been so long since I'd seen her. I was excited. As I came past the bowling green I saw her sat on the bench reading. I stopped for a moment to watch her. She looked older, bigger since I'd seen her last.

But also she was the same. It seems to me that everything and everyone around me is changing in some way and I'm standing there wondering what's happening. I felt some tears come and tutted at myself for being stupid. Do you think people feel that they are being watched cos Susan suddenly stopped reading looked ahead and then sideways towards the bowling green. She saw me standing there and smiled.

I was glad that there was none of the boys around when I got there so I could give her a kiss on the cheek and pass the gift to her. She gave me a small package too. We both agreed to open when we were home.

It was so good to see her. We sat and talked on the bench about our holidays for a while and then about Caroline. And after this was done Susan asked, "So what's the secret, Gareth?"

I swallowed first and told her the story. I said dad was keeping us on holiday until we go back to school and about moving to Roath Park. We can meet up before and after school for a while I said to Susan and I'll come over to Llandaff North on Saturday or Sunday. Maybe your parents will let you come to our house sometimes too.

I watched her face to see the reaction. She was thinking about it. "It won't be so bad, Gareth. There's the holidays too. At least you're still in Cardiff and not that far away."

She made it sound easy. "But there's something else, Gareth," she went on. "Dad's going for an interview for a job in Bristol at the end of the month. If he gets it we'll be moving to Bristol."

I didn't know what to say and while I was thinking about it Tom, Phil, Nigel and Alun arrived. They threw bags down by the park bench. We messed around for a bit while Susan was sitting watching us. "Where's Dafydd and Geoff?" I asked.

"Dafydd couldn't come. He's doing something with his Dad and Geoff. Well I guess…..oh yeah I forgot you don't know. They're emigrating. His Dad got some offer in Tasmania so they're all going. They'll be gone before Christmas."

This didn't really bother me but it made me realize that what I'd been thinking was true. You can't hold everything together. It's impossible. It all changes around you. I didn't want to think about what Susan had told me yet.

"Hey," I said to Tom. "Did you know what that crazy girl, Caroline was up to? It scared the life out of me."

"Yeah, she is crazy," Tom said. "Anyway she's gone back to London now. So when you coming back?"

"We're not," I said to Tom and the boys. Alun, Nigel and Phil were tossing a cricket ball between them. "Dad wants to move us near Roath Park."

"Hey, there's toffs houses round there," Alun said and then. "So how you gonna get to Canton. Or you changing schools." Funny, it didn't seem to bother them.

"It's not for toffs," I said. "I'm still going to Canton. I don't want to be away from my pals."

And once again it struck me that Tom would not be there. We talked a bit about me coming over to Llandaff North on the weekend and stuff like that and then Phil said, "Well you coming?"

"Where?" I asked.

"I told you in the letter," Tom said. "You know about going swimming at Llandaff baths. I told you to bring your stuff."

"Oh yeah, I forgot about that," I lied. There was nothing in the letter. "I'll stay with Susan and catch up with you after. See you at the Old Oak Tree round halfpast two?"

We agreed on it and they left walking towards Llandaff fields. I watched them for a while as they walked away lobbing the cricket ball between them. Tom hadn't answered the question about Caroline and if he knew about the trick. I felt a little sad as I watched them walking away.

"Hey, do you feel left out," Susan asked me with a laugh as if she were reading my mind. "I'm still here you know."

"Yeah," I said, "I know you are and thank God for that. But Susan if your Dad gets that job and you're in Bristol it's gonna be more than different. Geoffrey leaving for Tasmania doesn't bother me and me moving near Roath Park we can sort out but you going to Bristol.......I can't even think what it'll be like without you around."

"Well, let's wait," she said. "Dad says it would be a big move for him and a lot of people will be after it. Don't worry. Probably won't happen. Anyway, come on let's get on the swings for a while and then go for a walk."

And so we did. It was one of those times when we just laughed and chatted and enjoyed everything we did together. The time flew until I realized we needed to walk towards the school to meet David.

"Why don't you bring the food into the house," Susan said. "Mum will put it on plates for you and David. I'll get some to and join you both."

It was a great idea and so we did. We bought a couple of cod fish and a couple of pies and a huge pile of chips and peas and Susan's mum spread it out for us. She cut a load of bread and butter too as well pouring out pop. If Susan and her mum hadn't have been there me and David would have belched ourselves silly.

David's pal was going out to town for the afternoon so he asked if he could stay with me. I was Ok with this and as we had some time we started to play Ludo. We were having so much fun that when I looked at the clock I saw it was 3pm.

Susan looked too at the clock too. "You're late," she said. David looked at me too.

"It's too late now," I said. "They'll have left the Oak to go somewhere. No point in trying to find them. We don't have time. And anyway maybe they'll work it out and pass by here. Let's play some more."

Susan and David were OK with this and I was too. At the time I didn't think too much about it but later I realized that I'd broken with the old way we did things. But it had been going on for some time anyway. When we left I said to Susan I'd ask dad if we could meet up the following week and maybe go to Barry Island. Her face lit up and I knew it was a good idea.

On the way back to meet Dad me and David called at Nigel's place first, then Tom's and Alun's last of all. They weren't home and I said to their mums to say sorry I missed them this time. We got held up.

From Alun's we cut across through to the swings but they weren't there. I looked the whole length of the park and saw no sign of them. "They're probably on the monkey rocks," David said. I grunted agreeing. "You'll see them next time," he said and I grunted again.

Dad was already waiting for us when we got to the Park. Straight away I asked him if we could go to Barry Island next week with Susan. He said yes straight away. Things are getting good. I decided to write to her as soon as I got home.

When we got to Fontygary I opened the little package from Susan. It was the best thing I ever got from anyone. It was a bookmark but not just a strip of leather. I had loads of those. It was more than that. It was good leather and on it there were markings and patterns in gold and silver. Dad said it was runic or celtic from the ancient days. On the back she'd had written in silver "For Gareth the book lover. To remember always. Susanxxxxx"

Only a few words but it gave me a lot of things to think about.

\* \* \* \* \* \* \*

A couple of days later Dad brought home some post and there was one from the school which gave all the details for starting and the time we had to be there and a big list of school clothing we needed. Look at all the stuff they want Dad to get for me:

Long Grey Trousers
White Shirt x 3
Navy School jumper
Plain Black Socks x 3
Black Shoes
School tie
School Blazer
School Scarf
Navy raincoat
White 3 button T-shirt
Plain white shorts
Plain white short socks
White plimsolls
School Rugby Shirt – obtained from school
School Rugby shorts
Navy Track Suit
Rugby Boots
Cricket Trousers
Cricket Shirt
Cricket Sweater

It's going to cost a fortune!! In the letter it told us we could get all the stuff from shops in town and one of them was Evan Roberts. I like it there so asked Dad if it was OK for us to buy the clothes from there. He didn't mind. I asked him too why we couldn't buy the rugby shirt from Evan Roberts. He said it was probably because when I got to the school I'd be placed in a house team like Caradog with its own shirt and colours.

A house team! I'd never thought of that. It's going to be like the boys at Greyfriars school.

On Friday Dad took us into Cardiff town to get the uniform and clothes. When I tried the blazer on dad said it was like I was wearing Joseph's coat of many colours. We both laughed. He was right. I hope not too many people laugh. He made me try on the raincoat which has a secret pocket for hiding things and it went down to my ankles. He said that I would grow into it. As we sat in the school section I tried on more and more things to make sure they fitted me and as they did they piled up on the table next to us ready to be packed. David sat quietly on a seat next to us but watching me as I put on the stuff to show Dad so he could say smaller or larger to the assistant.

I said to him, "You'll be going through this next year. Then we'll be back at the same school together."

He nodded back and said "Yeah but I don't want to wear your Joseph's coat of many colours". I laughed. He was right. The Canton High School blazer is full of bright coloured stripes. I wondered what was going through David's mind. In a couple of weeks we'd be leaving Fontygary and going to Lakeside. He'd be going to the junior school there. Was he worried about it, I wondered. You could never tell with him. I didn't think so. I'd watched him since we'd been here and he was much better than me at making friends with the local kids his age. They came to call for him now. But with me and the kids my age nothing had happened. We just looked at each other and never spoke. David's going to be OK, I decided.

Dad got it all except for the cricket kit. He said we'd come back for that before the start of the season. When it came to time to pay and the bloke added it all up and gave the amount to Dad I must have gone white. The bloke looked and said that Evan Roberts has a club system so that you could pay the amount on a monthly basis with a small amount of interest. But you know what Dad just took out his wallet and paid it all in five pound notes. Five pound notes!! The bloke looked surprised too. But not as much as me. I'd had a peak inside Dad's wallet a few times when he left it on the bedside table but there was never five pound notes in it. Maybe just a couple of pound notes and a ten bob note. But you know what, it felt good inside that Dad paid it all in one go.

When we left to go to the car we all had a share of the stuff to carry. There was tons of it and our arms were aching when finally we shoved it all into the car boot. A step closer to the new school, I thought as Dad clicked the boot shut.

When we got home I started to think about my visit to Llandaff North and felt a wave of guilt that I'd not gone to the Old Oak tree to meet Tom. I decided to write to him to see about meeting up the day after going to Barry with Susan. I knew that if I posted the letter for the last post on Friday that Tom would get it in the morning.

He wrote back straight away and the letter was with me on Monday when Dad checked the box. He said:

*Dear Gareth*

*What happened? We missed you at the Old Oak last week. Waited for ages.*

*By the time you get this letter we'll be in Tenby. We are leaving today (Saturday afternoon). We'll get back a few days before school starts.*

*See you around.*

*Tom*

I'm disappointed about this. I should have gone over to the tree but I'd felt annoyed about the swimming. Ah, well. I'll see him when he gets back

\* \* \* \* \* \* \*

We went as two families to Barry Island. Dad gets on really well with Susan's mum and Dad which is great. And guess what? Susan's sister, Jackie, came with her boy friend from Canton High, Ralph. He's really good. While the grown ups sat drinking tea and coffee, well that's what they said, we all went round the shows. Ralph is a great kid and he told me all about life at Canton High. He said it wasn't so bad when you got used to it. The teachers were mostly OK but you had to watch out for a bit of bullying of the 1 swots (kids in the first year) and especially watch out for "the moth". He said this is the nickname they got for the Head Master at Canton. He said I would be lucky as my last name begins with A so I'd get a desk in each room close to the wall next to the door. If my last name was Williams I'd be in big trouble. He said 'the moth' roams the corridors looking in through the windows into classrooms. If he catches a kid misbehaving while the teacher has his back turned he throws open the door and throws a blackboard duster at the kid and never misses. Have you seen these blackboard dusters? It's wood one side and a soft pad on the other to clean the board. You're buggered which ever side hits you, he said. The wood hurts like hell and the pad covers you in white dust. I felt a little panic set in. The 'moth" sounded like a bully just as much as some of the older kids.

He told me that if there was any kid bothering me to let him know and he'd fix it.

Jackie said boys were always rougher than girls. She said there were some nasty ones in the girls school but mostly it was fine. Susan was lucky. She had her older sister to show her the way.

\* \* \* \* \* \* \*

Do you remember that time when Phil went on about being black? Remember those kids who bullied us as well? Phil said a bit about things in America. I thought it must be different there because the Americans used black people as slaves until President Lincoln sorted it out years ago.

So I always thought that it was OK in America. You know, black and white people living side by side just like we do here. But the more I see things on the news and see pictures in the paper I wonder if this is true.

I watched this bloke, Martin Luther King on the telly last night on the news. They showed his speech a few times now and Dad was reading it in the paper today. They've got the whole speech written out. When you hear this bloke speaking it sends shivers down your spine and gives you goose pimples. When you hear what he says, he makes you realize that in some parts of America white people still treat black people not so good and they still keep them apart. You know black people are not allowed to get on the same buses as white people or use the same swimming pools and they don't even go to the same schools. Well that's crazy isn't it? What do they want to do that for? Can you imagine if Phil was in a separate school to me and the boys. It just doesn't make sense, does it?

I copied down some of the speech from the newspaper for you to read. I had to take out loads but see what you think. I think it's some of the best stuff I ever read. Even better if you can get a chance watch him on TV saying it:

*"And so even though we face the difficulties of today and tomorrow, I still have a dream. It is a dream deeply rooted in the American dream.*

*I have a dream that one day the nation will rise up and live out the true meaning of its creed. 'We hold these truths to be self evident, that all men are created equal.'*

*I have a dream that one day on the red hills of Georgia, the sons of former slaves and the sons of former slave owners will be able to sit down together at the table of brotherhood.*

*I have a dream that one day even the state of Mississippi, a state sweltering with the heat of injustice, will be transformed into an oasis of freedom and justice.*

*I have a dream that my four little children will one day live in a nation where they will be judged not by the colour of their skin but by the content of their character.*

*I have a dream today!*

*I have a dream that one day in Alabama…..little black boys and little black girls will be able to join hands with little white boys and little white girls as sisters and brothers.*

*I have a dream today!*

*With this faith we will be able to hew out of the mountain of despair a stone of hope. With this faith we will be able to transform the jangling discords of our nation into a beautiful symphony of brotherhood. With this faith we will be able to work together, to pray together, to struggle together, to go to jail together, to stand up for freedom together knowing that we will be free one day.*

*And this will be the day when all of God's children will be able to sing with new meaning:*

*My country 'tis of thee, sweet land of liberty, of thee I sing*

*And if America is to be a great nation this must come true.*
*And so let freedom ring,……….. from every mountainside let freedom ring*
*And when this happens, when we allow freedom to ring, when we let it ring from every village and every hamlet, from every state and every city, we will be able to speed up that day when all of God's children, black men and white men, Jews and Gentiles, Protestants and Catholics will be able to join hands and sing in the words of the old Negro spiritual:*

*Free At last; free at last*
*Thank God Almighty, we are free at last*

It's fantastic isn't it? It makes you realize that it can't be so bad in Great Britain. We don't have things like this and I hope this Mr Martin Luther King is able to persuade all the good white Americans to live in a different way. When I see Phil next I'm going to talk about this, that's for sure.

*PB's Note: He's right. The MLK speech is as good now as it was back then. An amazing speech.*

*Gareth got me thinking about the 11 plus system too. It's true it's gone now but in a way it's back. There's more well off families who send their kids to private schools than was the place in the 60's. So maybe the private schools are the new grammar schools.*

# CHAPTER 14
## *September 1963*

One week to go and school will start on 9 September but this week we will move from Fontygary to Lakeside. Dad has spent a lot of time back and forth with people so we can get this place. We haven't seen it yet but he's shown us pictures. It's not like Llandaff North and Hazelhurst Road. It's not a terraced house. It's a new looking semi detached place with a small garden in front and a big one behind. Dad says there are three bedrooms so me and David will have our own rooms. That's going to be funny. We've always been together.

David doesn't seem to mind about it all. But he's more disappointed about leaving Fontygary than leaving Llandaff North. When I asked him why, he told me he never really had any friends there. Not proper ones. He said that most of the time he was following me and hoping that I would let him join in. He said he'd made a lot of friends in Fontygary and it made him feel better than Llandaff North. I was surprised but also disappointed with myself. I had not paid a lot of attention to my brother. Things would be different now. I was going to change on this. Hey, but maybe it will be me that needs to be with all his friends.

We are going to move in the middle of the week. I asked dad if we could do this because I wanted to go to Llandaff North on the last Saturday to spend some time with Susan and maybe Tom. I wanted to try out the walk too to see how long it would take. I would walk past the lake up Lake Road North and down Heathwood Road and into Whitchurch, cut across Whitchurch common into Gabalfa and then along Caldy Road into Llandaff North. My old home. Dad was OK with this but when I asked David if he wanted to come with me he said no. He said he'd stay with Dad. It looks like it was true then. He was never as happy in Llandaff North as me.

I wrote to Tom telling him I would be there on Saturday. Susan I planned to see on Wednesday while the removers were emptying the house. It would be the last Saturday before Grammar School and to me it seemed like it would be the day the door closed. I wanted to be in Llandaff North when that happened. It had not been the summer I'd expected. We'd had next to no cricket and I'd spent more time watching test matches on TV than I'd played real cricket with the boys.

It was meant to be a summer where I'd enjoy the last days of life after junior school and before Grammar School but it all went wrong for one reason or another. Saturday was my chance to put it all back and finish it as it was meant to be.

Dad was pretty good on the day we moved. He let us pack the stuff we wanted in boxes put aside for us. Me and David only bothered with the stuff we cared about and the rest we left to the three blokes who were packing. Once we'd done our bit dad said we could wander off for a couple of hours if we wanted to but we had to be back at the house by 2 o'clock as the blokes would be finished then and wanted to drive the truck to Lakeside. Of course I went to see Susan and I let David come with us. It was too nice a day to stay in so we decided to take a walk around Hailey Park and then past the black bridge up through the Long Woods. Susan's mum made sandwiches for us and outside we bought crisps and some pop.

The three of us were quiet as we walked like we didn't know what to say to each other or thinking about things that were on our minds. There was a good laugh when we bumped into Ceri Borthwick by the swings. Remember Ceri from a year ago who saved us from that boy? He made us laugh saying he was sorry he wasn't getting a chance to push my head down the toilet. We joked along with him for a while and gave him some of the crisps and pop. Then he shuffled off around the corner towards Gabalfa. Like I said it's a funny thing about Ceri. You never see him with anyone. I started wondering what goes on his head too before I realised we were all getting very fed up.

I challenged Susan and David to a run from the playground to the Old Oak. This cheered us up and David too, for sure. We laughed like mad when we reached the Oak, David just beating us too it. Stood there, I remembered how we formed our gang and how the Old Oak was so important to us. We sat down and opened the sandwich bag and tucked in. While we were eating I had an idea and asked David if he had his pocket knife with him. He did so I took it from him and climbed up the nails and to two branches above. I told you I never really liked climbing or heights but there was something I wanted to do.

I cut into a fresh part the initials SB and GA into a heart shape. They were calling out at me to be quick and asking me what was I doing. I said I was just putting my initials as a reminder. From this place I looked out and saw Dad coming out of the back gate. He had his hand to his forehead and was looking around for us. I called down to David to wave to Dad. It was obvious our time was up and he wanted us to go.

Me and Susan walked slowly holding hands while David ran ahead. I felt that everything was getting a bit rushed and I wanted more time in Llandaff North before we went. I felt suddenly disappointed that we didn't have time to walk down the Long Woods and promised myself that we would do it on Saturday. Maybe too I would cross the black bridge!!

Then all in a rush we were in the car. We dropped Susan at her house and we were gone driving towards Whitchurch and on to our new house which me and David would see for the first time. We needed to beat the van so Dad could open the house before they arrived.

The place was just like the photographs and David loved it. We sat in the garden in the sunshine eating more sandwiches that Dad had brought while he waited for the van. This house was so different from our house in Hazelhurst Road. There all the houses are terraced and there are walls both sides but you can still talk to the neighbours easily. The back gardens are not tidy though and there's the odd piece of junk here and there that I never noticed before until we came to this place. It's totally different. There is a netting fence separating us from the neighbours on both sides but because this house is semi-detached you feel the other neighbor is very far away. There is the driveway to the garage and the garage between us and them. Our garden at the back has a nice lawn and the grass isn't long. There are flowers at the borders and rose trees that look like somebody has cut them back here and there. At the end of the garden there is another net fence but also tall trees and bushes which separate us from the line of houses behind us. The trees are so tall you cannot see the house.

It makes me think that this is just not a different house but a different way of life. Me and David finished our sandwiches and walked onto the driveway when we heard the removal van coming. It pulled up outside our house and stopped. Dad was already outside the front door waiting to stop. I reminded David how long it took him to catch me if I went out the back door and he went out the front. I can't do that here, I said to him. We both laughed.

I took him past the van and down the road a little way while Dad was talking to the removal men.

"What do you see?" I asked David. He looked up and down the street.

"Houses," he said, "And a few cars."

"Anything else," I asked.

"No, there's nothing," he replied.

"Yeah," I said. "And now think of Llandaff North. If we were outside our house and looking up and down the street and up Hawthorn Road what would we see?"

David thought for a bit. "People and kids, dogs and cats, I suppose," he replied.

"You're right," I said. You're right. There's nobody out here. It's so quiet I think I should be walking on tip toe so not to disturb anyone. If we were back in Llandaff Norh now stood like this at least three people would have stopped to talk to us. You know that?"

David looked up and down the street again. "You know what, Gareth," he said to me. "I don't care. I like it here better. The house is nice. The garden is nice and I don't care there's nobody around. Come on let's go back to the garden and play."

He turned and started walking towards the drive and the garden and I followed. I thought about it. I could see that David was better at getting used to things than me. When I looked up and down this road I saw it as dead and no life here. Everybody lived behind their curtains though the funny thing is I felt more watched than ever I felt in Llandaff North with all the people around. I could feel their eyes on me here from behind the closed curtains. David, I thought, you may like it but give me Llandaff North any time.

On the way back David found a small plastic football tucked by the garage. "Come on," he shouted. Let's have a kick around while they're unloading."

I got rid of the bad thoughts about Lakeside and we got stuck into playing football. We made a couple of goalposts at each end of the garden with a few sticks they'd used for propping up flowers. We had a good laugh me and David and I suppose we must have been noisy. I heard the back door of the house next to us open up and two kids came to sit in garden chairs on their patio. I could see they were watching us although they were trying not to. I stopped kicking the ball to look at them. There was a girl. She was about my age and the boy looked a little younger than David.

"That's Richard's ball you're playing with," she said to us. She spoke like Megan but her way was a bit nastier. She reminded me a bit of Geoffrey. She tossed her hair and had that cocky look. She looked at us like we were urchins or something.

While I stared at her David replied, "Oh yeah! Who says? It was in our garden and that's finder's keepers, I think."

"He kicked it over there a few days ago and we couldn't find it," she said to David and glancing at me. I was still watching her.

"No, I didn't," the boy shouted at her. "You threw it over there when you got angry with me. It wasn't me who did it."

Me and David just laughed with that laugh that makes other people blush. You know the one.

She jumped to her feet when we laughed and scowled at us. "Richard!!" she snapped at him. "You are such an annoying boy." We laughed more and she got up and walked to the back door, opened it and went in. Richard watched her go.

"Hey! Rich," David called. "Wanna come over and play with us?"

Richard looked back at the house and then at us. "Come on," David said. "Your mum can see you from the window. Gareth will help you over."

Richard walked to the net fence and I lifted him over. He was light, lighter than David. I put him down next to David. "I'm David and this is my brother, Gareth" David said. "He's not so bad when you get to know him."

Richard smiled at us. He seems a nice kid, I thought, better than his stuck-up sister. "Let's play then," he said. "I thought we might get people moving in with no kids like the last people. I'm glad it's boys. Linda was hoping for girls."

So that's her name, I thought, Linda.

"She's angry with us, I think." I said to Richard.

"She doesn't like being laughed at," He said. "But you watch, she'll come back out in five minutes like nothing's happened."

We got on with playing football. Richard likes to be a goalie so he was having fun. He was right too, after about ten minutes or so his sister came back out and sat back on the garden chair and opened up a book to read. She didn't want to look at us I could see. I couldn't help comparing her to Susan. She was as pretty as Susan for sure but there was also something harder about her that put me off. But you know what I was so curious to know what she was reading. But I've noticed this thing about myself. If we are in the park or on the bus or anywhere and I see someone holding a book or magazine or reading it I want to find a way to read the title of the thing. Why is that? I don't know.

I was convinced with Linda that the book was going to be rubbish but I was still curious. Anyway, while I was thinking about it David gave me the opportunity. He sliced a ball over the garden and it ran close to Linda's chair. She could have got up to throw it back to us but she didn't. I jumped the fence and walked to get the ball. As I picked it up and stood up she stopped reading and rested the book title up on her chest. "You can't just jump over the fence any time you like, you know," she said to me. "You could at least ask permission."

She was reading Wuthering Heights. I was surprised. I'd not read this. I'd thought it was probably too hard.

"Next time, I will" I said and jumped back over the fence with the ball. I don't like this girl, I thought to myself. She makes Susan seem like an angel from heaven. It made me think of Saturday and back to Llandaff North where people walk the streets and talk to you. I laughed out loud to myself.

\* \* \* \* \* \* \*

For me Saturday couldn't come quickly enough. David seemed to settle into Lakeside really quickly. He had his own room and some new furniture and he'd found a friend next door. Richard had come to play with him in the garden a few times and was telling him a lot about the school at Lakeside. They were looking forward to going to school together the next week. My brother amazes, me I thought but I was pleased that he was settling in. Like I said he was better at this than me.

On Saturday morning I was keen to leave quickly. I really wanted to see Susan and Tom. Tom hadn't written back to me but I'd find him. I knew that. There was only one thing that disappointed me though. There was a steady downpour of rain. You know that rain which tells you that it is going to stay the whole of the day. This meant that there would be no walk and that Dad would take me. We left at 9.30 which was not early enough for me. David came in the car along for the ride. I was hoping I could persuade him to come with me but when we arrived outside Susan's house he shook his head. He didn't want to come. They waved their goodbyes and Dad said he'd be back outside Susan's house at 6.30pm to get me.

The rain was still drizzling away as I rang the bell at Susan' house. My plan for us to be out most of the morning didn't seem likely and they were not. We sat in the lounge first and listened to some music while we chatted about school and got stuck into chocolate biscuits dipped into mugs of sweet tea. I spoke to Susan about my worries. I'd never really got it off my chest before. I told her that I was a little bit afraid of going to Canton and leaving the junior school behind. I told her that I was worried that Tom was going to Glantaf and that I felt he was slipping away somehow. I told her that I was worried about Dad and the sudden changes with him and the things that had happened. I told her that I was worried about moving away and said that I felt Lakeside was a place without people. I said I was worried too that her Dad would get this job and she would be gone too. I told her that I was amazed at how David was taking it all so well and enjoying it. I told her about the kids next door to us and how David had slotted in so well with Richard.

"So many worries, Gareth," she said to me. "So many worries. But we can't stay as 11 years old forever, can we?"

She told me to wait and went out of the room for a while and came back with a Looby Loo doll. "Do you remember watching Andy Pandy?" she asked me.

I nodded.

"So this is a Looby Loo doll," she said shaking it so the yellow pig tails swung around.

I nodded.

"I used to be crazy about this doll a few years ago and wouldn't go anywhere without it, even school," she said.

I tried to think back if I remembered her carrying it but she went on. "I never thought I would be without Looby Loo. But you know what happened?"

I nodded for her to go on. "I rarely pick it up these days. It's there amongst the rest of my dolls as an ornament, I suppose. It didn't change one bit. It's the same old Looby Loo rag doll. But I changed. I grew up a bit and we – me and you – are going to grow up a lot more. We are going to be different."

In a way I suppose I froze. I think I wanted to scream out loud too. I wanted to go crazy and crash and bump things because I felt in a rage over something I could not stop. There was nothing I could to stop it. You know what I heard in her voice as well. I heard her saying that look we are boyfriend and girlfriend now but this is just for now. You and me we like each other that's for sure – but this is not for ever either. We are only kids of eleven years old and things are going to change, we are going to change. Well, I think you must know me by now and I can tell you that although she didn't say it, I heard it and I didn't want to hear it. I wanted everything in my 11 year old life to stay the same. If I had to lose things then I could accept in the end that it would be necessary to leave the junior school and go to the grammar school. I could accept leaving Llandaff North for Lakeside. I could accept seeing Alun and Nigel and Phil and Daffyd walking away from me. Reluctantly, I could accept seeing Tom disappear from me. But to see Susan go after dreaming about her for most of my junior school life this would be near impossible.

Is it crazy of me to think there is a possibility that me and Susan can get through grammar school years together. Is it crazy of me to think we can get through the teenage years and through our "O" and "A" levels and that we might even go to University together. Is this crazy? Is it crazy to think of something that goes beyond that too??

You don't have to answer. I know what you're thinking. But here's something I just thought. Right now I am writing this up to date. It is Saturday night 7 September 1963. I got more to tell you about this Saturday but let's stop a moment becos I thought of something. So far you got the things as they happened. Everything or most of it that happened to me since last year. I am afraid of what is going to happen next. I am afraid of losing everything. I am afraid of losing my best friend and my girlfriend. But……but what if I start another book along side this diary right now which writes about the future that I want not the one that might happen. If I write it out as I want it to be will it happen that way because I want it so much. Maybe writing it down makes it come true. Remember Hadyn Hughes and how he made his life different. What if I did the same if I had to. What if I did? It was real to him and the future I write down could be real to me. I'm going to start writing it as soon as I've finished this tonight. Maybe it will be like some kind of magic book which when you write the future it becomes the future. How great that would be.

For a moment or two while Susan was speaking I froze, as I said, while many things went through my mind. Mostly, I felt that it was all slipping away and I felt I did not have the power to stop it or change it.

So you know what? I'm going to do it. I'm not writing in this book any more. This diary is over. But you know what I'm going to do? I'm going to get myself two more notebooks. In one I'm going to write to the end on my wishes and dreams for the future and I'm going to pray that the way I write it is the way it turns out. In the other I will write what actually happens and I just hope that the real and the imaginary are so close.

So I'm closing this book now. This is the end. This is as far as I will take you and maybe there's a few things you're wondering about even now and you want to know what happens. Well you found this diary so I think you must be a curious person so now you have to find the other two journals. I've decided where they are going and as you have got this far whoever you are that's found my little diary, will you stop now? Can you stop now.

Well that's up to you. I think if you look hard enough you will find them. You've just got to think. Good luck!!

*PB's note:*

*And there Gareth shocked me. I hadn't seen this coming. It's true that as I was reading I noticed the growing change in his voice especially after the 11 plus result. But I didn't expect this.*

*I closed the cover of the book to think. I hadn't noticed the passage of time. It was late, too late to start thinking about where he'd placed the journals. But what struck me was this idea that you could create a future if you wrote it down. Interesting idea from an 11 year old boy! It was late and I needed to sleep but I* was also keen to discover the location of the two remaining journals. Ever since I was a boy I had always had a strong desire to know what happens next.

In the morning I re-read Gareth's journal searching for clues as to the location of the journals. His life was solely around Llandaff North, the place in Fontygary and the house at Lakeside. Therefore, I classified the search places as follows :

1  The Hazelhurst Road house or garage
2  Somewhere in Hailey Park
3  Povey's Field
4  Radyr Cricket Club pavilion
5  Hawthorn Road Junior School
6  The uncle's house at St Nicholas
7  The church hall
8  The house at Fontygary
9  The house and garage at Lakeside
10 A friend's house such as Tom or Susan

I decided to prioritise the most likely hiding places. I came to this conclusion:

The probable places were:

- The house at Hazelhurst Road
- Somewhere around Hailey Park or Povey's field
- The house at Lakeside
- The house at Fontygary

I thought the other locations were too risky of being discovered but I did not discount them. My reading of Gareth led to me believe that there could be some clever thinking in the way he had hidden the journals. I had some rerservations on Hailey Park and Povey's field but this was the area where so much of Gareth's early life had taken place. Instincts told me to leave it in. I decided to search these places first before I could consider his other homes. For one thing, I did not know their addresses. I only knew the general location. It would take me time to locate the exact places – and who would be there now. Forty six years had passed since Gareth had secreted the journal. Who was living in Fontygary, St Nicholas and Lakeside now. I doubted if I would find Gareth in these locations after all these years. I closed the thoughts on this. I did not want to start thinking of an adult Gareth. It seemed important for me to hold in *my mind his existence in time as an eleven year old boy. I needed to think of the time between 1963 and now as white space.*

*I started with the house first. I searched back again in the hole in the loft to be on the safe side but there was nothing there. There was no sign also of any other loose bricks on either side. Since the 60's the house had been lived in by several families and over the years it had been modernized and improved. I discounted any potential hiding places in any of the rooms now. Prior decoration would have led to the discovery of any secret hiding place. Gareth, probably would not have recognized the kitchen. All the fixtures are now modern and anything hidden there would have been discovered when the work was carried out. Bearing in mind the care he took to hide the main journal I anticipated that he would take as much care with the other journals.*

*The garage looked to be much more promising. When I bought this place I knew that the garage was the original structure built by Geraint Adams back in the late 50's when he acquired a vehicle. It was not a cheap pre-fabricated or wooden panel structure as many of them were in those days but built of brick with a sloping roof. Geraint had given it a slate roof to match the house. I had not looked inside it properly since I arrived mainly because I don't own a car yet. I use taxi or bus to get around.*

*The interior of the garage was clear and the cupboards empty. Nothing. No old boxes or rubbish; no toolboxes or crates. It was empty and swept clean. It is with out doubt the cleanest garage I have seen in my life. Yet my heart did not sink. Gareth was not so simple as to leave a prize in a place where it could be found easily. I looked up at the beams which held the roof in place. I knew it had to be checked.*

*I retrieved a step ladder from the house and commenced the overhead garage search. There was nothing obvious at the side edges and so I paid attention to the beams. Standing high on the steps it was easy for me to scan across the beams looking for something unusual. There was nothing: no packet or envelope but I knew anyway this was not Gareth's style. I was about to step down and take a rethink when something caught my eye. All the beams were clear but one beam – third from the garage entrance on the right hand side – had a slender nail tapped into it with half the nail protruding. The nail was half way along the beam and there was no reason for it to be there. We all know that sometimes when working we might tap in a last nail rather than throw it on the floor to be picked up by a tire but this is a house where Gareth lived. I was sure this meant something quite different. I moved the step ladder to the beam and climbed up. Sure enough, it was a simple nail tapped into the side of the beam. I looked up and down the length of the beam and then noticed a tin tack higher up close to the apex of this roof. To* reach it I needed to get back down and reposition the ladder closer to the tack. Climbing back up I stood on the top of the step ladder to reach the pin. I put my finger nails to it and pulled. In hindsight I should have used my other hand to steady myself on the beam but you always think of these things afterwards.

When I tugged upon the pin a section of wood came away with it more easily than I expected and whether out of surprise or being off balance I felt myself sway backwards. Clutching now for the beam was useless and in the centre of the garage there was nothing for me to hold on to. I tried to relax myself and it seemed an age before I crashed on to the floor. I lay there winded and bruised checking for injuries but nothing was broken although my right side would be bruised for a while. Rolling onto my back to wait for my breath to return my eyes surveyed the section revealed by my removing the pin. Remarkably the wood was still in my hand intact. It seemed most un-Gareth like. I had classed him as a thinker, cerebral; but here he had crafted a small door with the metal tack as a door opener. Even the shaft of the tack was bent over to be secure to the wood.

Gingerly, I reset the step ladder and slowly made my way back to the open section of the beam. I was deliberate and slow on this occasion as I had no wish to repeat the last fall. Inside the hollowed out section of the beam I saw a package which I eased out. It was a clear plastic bag of some kind which had been sealed with sellotape. I took it out from the hole and slowly returned to the safety of the garage floor. Over the years the sellotape had aged and withered and it peeled away easily from the plastic. Inside I took out a sheet of paper, the same type that Gareth was using for his journals. It read as follows:

You are curious! You found the first journal and now you've found this marker. You didn't really expect to find the remaining journals in the same location did you? That would have been too easy. But you have a chance now to get further. Have you worked out by now that I love reading? There's something about words isn't there? I'm getting used to how grown ups use words and sentences like it's a code or something. So if you want to find my journals let's see if you understand this:

*Come, cheer up my lads 'tis to glory we steer*

Good luck! Whoever you are.

I read it but I have to say that it meant nothing to me. I felt now, however, that there was a connection between me and this boy. I needed to know what happened to him. Of course he was born in an era where knowledge was difficult to acquire. Intelligence you are born with: no-one can add to this - it is a given. Knowledge in Gareth's day was acquired through books. I could only have understood his line of code if I had gained this knowledge through a specific book in his day or been involved in that activity or exceedingly patriotic. I'm not sure if so many know this line now. I know when I read it I did not. But I could do something that Gareth would not have anticipated. I went back into the house and opened my laptop and googled the line he had left me. Perhaps the more knowledgeable of you already knew this line.

It's the first line of the official march of the Royal Navy. That's what Google told me – and it's title: "The Heart of Oak".

Once it popped up on my laptop I could not help having an image of Able Seaman Mark Skinner. Had he taught Gareth this in those days? And where was he now and how had things worked out with him and his wife? Will we always be plagued by the Des's of this world who are like predators on the edge of our lives? I loath them also.

He was sending me to the Old Oak.

I left my laptop in haste and sprang from the room down the path and through the back gate on to Hailey Park. I looked to the right and to the line of trees running from the rugby club to the river path. In the centre still standing is the magnificent Old Oak. In my mind I saw the boys signing up to their gang in blood, Philip Tell falling with Tom to the ground and David running towards the house to tell Aunt Nancy about the boys looking at photos of nude women. It all flashed before me.

It was quiet in the park, a weekday. Here and there retired people were walking dogs but my eyes were only for the Old Oak Tree. I half walked and half ran towards it in that way that tries to say you are not in a rush but of course I was. This oak is wide and old peppered with sturdy six inch nails to help kids climb. I walked the base first but there was nothing of interest to be seen. I remembered the time when Gareth ran to the oak with his brother, David and Susan. He climbed the tree that day. He wrote about it.

I cannot say I am an athletic or adventurous person. To be quite honest with you, I had not climbed a tree until driven to do so by Gareth's message. Our generation does not climb trees or sport around on rocks by the river, do we? Well we do if it's a challenge in a computer game!!

I climbed the tree knowing that my search would not be easy. On the way up you can see many carved initials. I searched for GA and SB but could not find it here. I paused: there comes a point on this old oak where the distance between the trunk and the next higher branch is a challenge. I sat on the branch below looking down. Falling now I realized was not an option. I realized that it was here that Gareth had faced his fear of heights and won the battle. Like him I was no lover of heights. Looking out from the balcony of a 15 storey building was enough to send me dizzy. Yet here was this boy setting me a challenge to face my fear too and strangely knowing that an answer was above me my fear receded. I looked for Gareth's sign and found it on the branch above. It was the slender nail driven half in, the twin of that in the garage. Not looking down I reached up to grab the branch which would have been out of the range of an eleven year old and I wondered how Gareth had made the leap. For me it was a question of raising myself up onto the higher branch and searching. They were not tacks this time but screws. I cursed to be honest with you because I had left my Swiss Army knife behind and there was no way I could deal with the screws without it.

Funnily, the return to the same place seemed tougher once I had possession of a range of screwdrivers but I was determined not to be caught out. Gareth had been meticulous. He had removed a section of the branch to hollow out a cavity to place a similar plastic bag and then screwed back the bark and wood to cover the hole. However, nature has its way of reaffirming itself and once the screws were removed the "cover" did not come away easily. It needed to be prised away by a large screwdriver to reveal the similar plastic bag. And what also did I find when I removed the plastic bag? He had carved and stained in black the initials GA and SB. I wondered how he could have done all this and not been observed.

I was so delighted to find this item I wobbled on the branch and suddenly became aware of the distance between me and the ground. I wanted to get back down but by a slow route!! Somehow, it felt right to replace the wood cover and screw it back to the tree again even though the screwdriver had damaged the cover a little. Once done, I eased my way back to the ground, the plastic package safe in my pocket.

I raced back home and once again pictured myself as Gareth chasing his brother to the rear of the house. I even imagined Aunt Nancy there pegging out the washing. In the house I resisted the temptation to pull the bag from my pocket. Reading Gareth's words demanded time and attention with a reviving mug of strong coffee.

Once the coffee was ready I took it with me to my sitting room and took several sips before placing it on the table at the side of my easy chair reserved for reading. I took the packet from my jeans pocket and sat down to open it and take out the message from Gareth

Well done! I wonder how long it took you to find the answer. Hah, maybe you are in the Royal Navy anyway and so it would have been easy. Well as you have found this it seems that you need to know the answer. So I won't hold you up. The clue is at the bottom of this paper and the password is "Truth or fiction".

At the bottom I found a 1960's postage stamp stuck to the paper. It crossed my mind how cheap it was to post a letter in those days and then I put my mind to the clue. Either Gareth had posted it somewhere which would lead me to further analysis or he had placed it at the Post Office by the railway station.

It was now lunchtime. Time had flown in pursuing the clues and so after lunch I walked to the Post office. It was not that busy and I waited until the last customer had gone.

"Do you hold packages?" I asked the Postmaster.

"What, you mean items that can't be delivered or post restante items?" he replied.

"Well it's not a usual one," I said back to him. "I think about forty five years or more ago a package was left for me."

He looked at me as if I was crazy. "You don't look anywhere near your 40's," he said back. I'm sure he was narrowing his eyes.

I decided to be a bit creative. "No, I wasn't around then," I laughed. "My grandfather left me a note to say he'd left a package here years ago and that he wanted me to collect it."

"There's nothing," The Postmaster responded looking at some pigeon holes behind him. I went silent, my mind working to think what else that postage stamp could have meant. I saw a look of remembrance come across the Postmaster's face.

"Wait a minute," he said and he disappeared into a room behind. I saw him reaching for keys. He came back a few minutes later. He was carrying a large envelope.

"If it's yours," he said to me. "You must know what happens next."

I was tempted to say that I was at the Post Office because I really did want to know what happens next next – but I didn't. In this place there could only be one thing that happened next.

"Truth or fiction?" I questioned my voice rising perhaps in disbelief, unsure if this would trigger the release of the package.

His face broke into a smile and held the large envelope out to me holding it in his two hands. I took it and tucked it under my arm. It felt comfortably pleasant resting there.

"You know I'd forgotten about it," he said. "There have been four Postmasters since 1963 and I've been here for 20 years. When I took this place over the outgoing Postmaster went through the safe items with me and showed me this package. He told me the story that had been handed down to him. The story was that in 1963 a young boy called Gareth Adams came in here and asked how much it would cost to store a package in the safe for a long time. The Postmaster then didn't really want to do it so he quoted a price of £10 for twenty years. The story is that the Postmaster didn't think the kid would have the money but the kid puts his hand in his pocket and comes out with two fivers. Apparently this boy Gareth Adams was really anxious for the package to be stored. He gave the boy a receipt and told him that the person coming to collect would need to give the Postmaster this receipt to claim it. The boy asked the Postmaster if it was possible to use a password instead and showed the Postmaster that he had sellotaped a smaller sealed envelope to it."

The Postmaster held out a very small envelope to show me. It said "to be opened when this package is claimed." He handed me a slip of paper which had come from the envelope. It read: "Only to be given to the person if this person says the words "Truth or fiction". I smiled as I read the boy's handwriting; handwriting that I had come to know so well.

"Can I keep these as well," I asked the Postmaster.

He shrugged. "No reason why you shouldn't. I'm only going to throw them away now."

I thanked him, put them in my pocket and turned to go. "Just a minute," he said. "Would you mind letting me know what's inside. I'd forgotten about this envelope for years but I used to be very curious about the contents."

I hesitated. I really wanted to take the envelope home and open it alone. "I know what it is," I said to him. "It's the final section of my grandfather's diary from 1963. I have most of it at home."

At least I thought it was the journals. I had a moment of doubt and looked at the envelope. This one he had stapled. I broke through the staples gently to open it and looked inside. I concealed my surprise to the Postmaster. I could see only one book and envelope which I knew would be a message to me from Gareth. I withdrew the familiar looking journal to show the Postmaster.

"My grandfather's memories," I said to him and returned the journal to the envelope. I thanked him and started to leave.

"He must have married young," the Postmaster said.

Why didn't I say Uncle, I thought. Why did I say anything at all.

"Yes," I replied. "To his childhood sweetheart, Susan." Then I turned and left deciding enough conversation was enough.

At home I returned to my easy chair in the sitting room and removed the journal and small envelope from the packet. The envelope was addressed like this – "To the curious reader". I opened it.

So you have made it this far! But the last one was easy, right? It didn't take too much for you to work out that you had to go to the Post Office. But now it's not so easy. You only have one journal here. So which one is it – Truth or Fiction. You won't know until you find the other one and you will need to be very good to find it. Good luck!!

*And that was it. He'd given me just one. I couldn't wait to read it. For now I would not think of the missing journal or if I was reading truth or fiction. I opened the journal and started to read.*

I knew that I needed to stop thinking. It was still raining and we could not go out so I asked her to get the tiddlywinks so we could have a laugh doing something very different that would take my mind off thinking about all these things. It worked. For an hour or so we had fun and then Susan noticed the sun was coming out around 11.30.

"Come on, let's go" she said, "Before it decides to come back.

Outside it was wet but the clouds had broken up to show strips of blue. It looked like we could get at least a couple of hours sunshine if not the whole afternoon. We walked down Hawthorn Road and past our old school.

"Stop it, Gareth", Susan said to me and gave me a playful punch on the arm. I think I must have sighed without noticing it. I turned to tickle her under the arms. It sets her into squeals of laughter. I'd made a decision. What's going to happen will happen. Most of the things going on I can't change so I decided I had to accept and think of a way to make it better. On our way to Hailey Park we passed by Tom's house. I'd said in the letter I'd meet him around 2.30 so I decided to check if it was all OK. Aunt Margaret answered the door. She smiled when she saw us and wanted us to come in but we said we were out for a walk.

"Tom said you might drop by," Aunty Margaret said. "He wanted me to tell you that his Dad has taken him into town and this afternoon they're going to watch a football game at Ninian Park. He said to say sorry and he'll see you next time."

We thanked her and she closed the door. There was a choice here and I could see it. I could really get fed up by Tom pissing off to town with his Dad or I could be pleased that I had more time with Susan. I made the choice.

"Well, we got the whole day together then, "I said to Susan and tickled her again as we turned from Hawthorn Road into Hazelhurst Road and crossed towards the lane.

"But what If I'm going to see Janet?" she asked.

"Are you?" I replied as I hadn't thought of that.

"Well no. But I was going to get my things ready for school on Monday." She replied back.

"OK, well I'll help you," I replied.

We didn't walk for long in Hailey Park. It was empty. The rain had kept people away and we kept to the path. The grass was soaking. But once the rain started its slow drizzle we made our way back to Susan's house. Even though it was raining we took it slowly. I looked everywhere taking into my mind the pictures of places and roads but also bringing up memories of things that had happened here all through my childhood. What a place, I thought to myself. I've been lucky.

It didn't take long for Susan to sort her things out for school. She dressed up in her school uniform for me too. She looked great and the navy blue hat that looks like a bowler hat looks good on her. Then her mum had a great idea. She said she wanted to see a friend in Whitchurch and what if we went on the bus there. She said me and Susan could go to the Plaza cinema and watch "In Search of the Castaways" and she gave us the ticket money.

I don't remember too much about the film but I remember the woman taking us to our back seat with a torch and she smiled when she saw me and Susan holding hands. When we sat in our seats I put my arm around her and held her and left it there. But guess what after a while the bloody arm went to sleep but I didn't like to move it then. I thought she might think I was annoyed about something or that I didn't like her any more. It was only when she asked if we should get a drink and some crisps that I could move it. Maybe she knew how I was feeling!!

When it went dark in the cinema I kissed her on the cheek and she turned to kiss me quickly on the lips. I love that you know. I don't know about for you but when it happens to me with Susan it make my insides flip up and over.

Susan's mum was waiting outside when the film finished and we got the bus back to Llandaff North. Again I looked at all the places as we went over the railway bridge and down into Station Road to the bus stop. My home, I thought, and always will be.

Before I knew it Dad was tooting the horn of the car outside and I left saying my goodbyes to Susan and her family and promising to meet Susan outside school on Monday morning. Then me, Dad and David were gone and travelling up towards Whitchurch and back to our new home in quiet Lakeside.

At home I heard the football results later. Cardiff drew with Sunderland 3-3. I thought about my friend Tom for a while. We had gone separate ways.

\* \* \* \* \* \* \*

Monday morning Dad dropped me off at Llandaff. He insisted on taking me but I didn't want to be dropped right outside school. Anyway, I thought if I walked from Llandaff I might see Susan along the way. David came with us. He was allowed to start school a bit later and Dad would take him in. He was looking forward to it. I can't say I was. I had butterflies in my stomach and a sick feeling.

I was a bit early so walked slowly down the road from Llandaff to Canton High School. I waited for a while at the lane which I knew Susan should come from but I could not see her. Nigel and Alun arrived though and they shouted out when they saw me. I had no choice but to walk with them the rest of the way to Canton High School. Outside there weren't as many as I was expecting. There were about thirty of us. We were all wearing navy gabardines and they were all too long and too big.

Me, Nigel and Alun stood together looking at the other kids who like us were in small groups from their junior schools. They seemed OK to us and what I mean is they looked as lost and as nervous as us.

I saw Susan with Janet coming along the road to the girls' school and was about to dash over to talk to them but I couldn't. Just as I was about to dash over to them the doors to the school opened and a lady stood there and called us in. I turned to wave to the two girls and they waved back before Nigel and Alun tugged me to go with them.

The lady held the door open for us. "Come on in boys," she said, "And remember this is the last time you come through this door unless you're with your parents. It's the back entrance from now on."

She pointed to a door across the way where loads of boys dressed like us were walking through. We followed. When we got through the door I saw it was a huge hall with a stage and steps leading up to it on both sides. Teachers in black gowns sat there and one teacher was old with a white face and white hair stood at the front of the stage urging us all to hurry up.

I looked around and saw row after row of seats. It looked to me like it could fit a thousand people. Most of the boys had already taken seats in the first few rows and we must have been about a hundred but barely seemed to make a difference to this hall.

We were shoved towards seats in the third row and sat down. No-one was speaking and the faces of the teachers were without smiles. So different from the chatter and smiles at Hawthorn I thought. There is no warmth here, was the thought going through my mind.

The teacher with the white face in the black gown shuffled to a wooden stand and put papers on it. He looked around at all of us and told us he was the Headmaster. He gave us an endless list of rules and forbidden things. Who could remember it? I have no idea. This was a terrible place that only spoke of things you couldn't do.

I looked around at my friends next to me and the boys along the rows. They all looked the same as me, nervous and maybe even a bit scared. He kept on talking and talking and then he stopped and called forward three teachers. They were our form teachers.

One of them went to the wooden stand and told us his name was Mr Waters and he said was form teacher of 1A. He said that he would read out the names of the boys in his form followed by the house they were in. He said if our name was called we were to follow him. Mine was called and after it he said James House. He didn't call Nigel and Alun's names. I left the row with the others boys to follow Mr Waters out of the hall and along the ground floor corridor to an empty classroom. He put us in the seats alphabetically so because I am Adams I got the first seat in the first row against the wall and near the door.

The first day at school was just one teacher after another coming in to give us exercise books and text books and telling us we had to cover them in brown paper. Each teacher went round to ask us where we came from and which was our last school. At Hawthorn I never felt scared of speaking up in class or speaking from the front at assembly but this first day something happened to me. I felt scared to speak for the first time. My voice shook as I spoke and I went red. I was glad I was at the front so not many could see me. One scared me a lot because when I said I lived in Lakeside he said this was too far away and I should really go to Howardian. I didn't like it here but at least there were boys I knew. In Howardian I would know nobody.

At break time I looked for Nigel and Alun in the playground but the place is huge and I couldn't find them but I did see Ralph, Jackie's boyfriend. He remembered me straight away and we chatted for a while. He said to watch out for bullies and not be scared. He said the same as my Dad did and to get in the first punch even if you got a lot more on you afterwards.

I found Alun and Nigel at lunch time and we went to the hall where they gave school dinners. When we got there an older boy was sat at the head of each long table taking about 12 boys including the older one. Once we sat down a teacher called for quiet and told us these were our seats for the rest of the year. I didn't each much and left before Nigel and Alun. I thought I might see Susan at the fence and went to the other side of the play ground where the fence looked on to the girls school. There were many girls in their playground and I waited and waited but didn't see Susan. A bell rang and took my view away from the girls playground to the boys school. I looked across at hundreds of boys in striped blazers and outside against the fence was me.

As the day wore on I began to notice some boys were more outspoken than others. Some boys like Peter Ballantyne right behind me cracked jokes and got the class laughing. Fast remarks came into my mind and I wanted to join in but I didn't have the courage. I smiled and laughed with the rest and sometimes turned round to say something to Peter but I could not talk out to the whole class. Peter seems Ok. I like him. Most of the kids in this class seem OK.

When the class ended and it was time to go home I rushed to get out and to the front of the girls school. They were coming out too. I saw Susan and Janet with a group of other girls I didn't know as well as Jackie, her sister. They were laughing and smiling together. You know what? I felt a stab of jealousy. Susan had made friends with other girls and I had not really tried. I felt outside of it all in a way and not belonging to this school. Alun and Nigel seemed to have melted in to the school life like pieces of ice that disappear into warm water. Yet I felt like a piece of ice that was not melting just floating along the top of the water and partly in the water but not really fully melted into the water.

Susan came up to me with a smile and introduced me to her new friends. I can't remember their names. They walked with us part of the way until we took the gully that leads down towards Llandaff North. After they'd gone Susan chatted with me and Janet about the school day and they were all excited about it. I listened and said things back with fake enthusiasm. In a way I was glad when the turning point came for me to walk up to Whitchurch common and along Heathwood Road to home. I said to Susan I'd see her tomorrow unless it was raining and then I'd take the bus. If it was dry I'd see her. You know, it was just nice to be on my own after all the talk and so many people and so many new things to do and learn. It is so much to learn I reckon that they will kick me out after a year because I will have failed all the exams.

At home David talked and talked about school and that he was going to some kid's house the next day. Dad asked questions about Canton and I answered smiling as much as I could. Where I longed to be was back in Standard 4 with the gang listening to Old Coxy, doing the milk duty and chatting with the little kids. I'm the little kid now, you know, and I really feel it. After tea I said to Dad and David that I was tired and would put brown paper on the books and sleep early.

The next day was raining and for the rest of the week I got the bus from the lake and then a 32a or b bus to Fairwater from the stop by the Angel hotel. Sometimes I saw Susan at the fence and we chatted for a couple of minutes but often her friends were calling her away.

Wednesday is sports day for all Form 1. After Assembly Mr Waters did the registration and we took our sports bags and went straight to the gym. The sports teacher is called "Killer" and you can see why. He shouts a lot and carries a black dap which he whacks you with if you speak out of turn. He made us change into our kit and told us to line up and get issued our rugby shirts. I got a James shirt of course.

On the rugby field at the back of the school Killer and a couple of the other teachers started us doing laps and sprints. He then sorted us out into forwards and backs. I ran fast that day so I got put onto the wing. The rest of the morning we got taught the rules and practiced scrums, passing and lineouts. For much of the time the ball didn't come my way but I realized that I liked it on the wing. I like rugby a lot.

On the weekend I wrote letters to Susan and Tom and tried not to talk too much about the old days but I felt they were the old days. Alun and Nigel now had a new group of friends. They waved when they saw me but we only met up at dinner time at the table.

On the second week of school on Monday it was dry and I waited for Susan at the gully but she did not come. Janet told me she and her sister weren't coming today. In the playground Ralph came up to me. I've decided I like him a lot not only because he's the boyfriend of Jackie. It's just that he's decent and friendly

"Hey," Gareth he said as he came up to me. "I was at Jackie's house on the weekend. Susan gave me a letter for you. I know what it says, well most of it, but I'll let you read it on your own."

Do you ever get that feeling in your stomach where everything drops away and you feel like falling? That's how I felt. I didn't speak but took the letter from him. I went to the corner of the fence at the furthest part of the playground. Not too many people come here and here I opened the letter. It said:

*Dear Gareth*

*Dad got the job. You'll be reading this on Monday and I won't be in school. Dad doesn't want to work in Bristol for too long on his own so we are going to look at schools today. Once we've got the right school we can look for a rented house nearby until we find our own.*

*So we'll be gone a couple of days and back on Wednesday. I'll see you then and at the end of the week come to our house and I'll tell you what's happening.*

*I'm sad about it all because you'll be so far away and I was just getting used to new kids at school. Jackie is really mad about it all but she'll come round.*

*Don't worry. We will still meet up. Bristol is far but not that far and maybe we will meet up by bus or train later. Anyway, we'll talk when I get back.*

*See you*

*Susanxxx*

There's a picture isn't there. I don't know what it's called. It's a face with a bald head and all swirls behind and he's got his hands to his face and his mouth is a round "O" and it's called the "scream". I think it's a silent scream that no-one hears but goes on and on. That's what I did when I read this letter.

It was all over. They were all gone. I was left behind like that piece of ice floating on the water; on it but not melting into it.

I don't remember much about that Monday and Tuesday. I was gathering homework and I could feel that after the first week things were beginning to get tough. Looking round my class I could see that groups had formed and friends made. I wasn't in any group with anyone. I said few words all day unless a teacher or another kid spoke to me. Peter Ballantyne wanted to try and every chance when there was a break he asked me questions and got me to talk. He is really OK.

On Wednesday it rained but I didn't care. I let dad think I was getting the bus but walked from Lakeside down Heathwood Road and waited for Susan by the river bridge at Llandaff North under some trees. I was cold and shivering but felt warm when I saw Susan coming with Janet. They were sensible. They had on plastic macs over their gabardines and were carrying umbrellas.

Susan saw me shivering although I tried not to let it show and she sheltered me with the umbrella putting her arm through mine. As we walked she told me about the school at Bristol they found which was a girls grammar school like Canton. They also found a really nice flat nearby with three bedrooms and her Dad had put a deposit on it. It meant she would be leaving Llandaff North sooner than I thought. She told me the date and I tried to do the calculations for how long she was going to be around but my head wouldn't work.

When we reached our schools she asked me if I was OK. I'd tried to stop shivering and not to show her I was feeling cold. She looked at me long and then kissed me on the cheek and rushed after her friends into school. I stood there watching her go. You know I think as long as I live I will never forgot this moment. It was a small kiss that felt like care and affection mixed in together. Ah, I guess you'll think I'm am expert on kisses now but it was what I felt right then. It was a moment I could have asked God to last for ever with nothing afterwards. You ever felt like that.

Instead as I saw her walking away into school I dragged my feet heavily towards the boys school and Assembly.

\* \* \* \* \* \* \*

Well, I need to tell you that I'm writing this after it all happened and I wrote the stuff above the dots too just now. I think I will be famous when I get back to school on Monday. I have been away since that Monday. Monday 16 September. After I dragged my feet into school I don't remember much. I got through the assembly in a half dream and when we left I never made it to our classroom. I remember falling down the three steps to the corridor for 1a and then waking up briefly in a room with white walls and white sheets and going back to sleep.

I stayed three days at the hospital and my arm was stiff taped to this board so they could drip antibiotics and stuff into me. I remember Susan came with her parents and sister to see me on the second day there but I didn't say too much. I kept falling in and out of sleep. After a few days Dad took me home in the car as he told them he was taking time off to look after me.

Before we left I heard him talking to the doctor. I was just coming out of sleep but kept my eyes closed. They were talking about me. The doctor was telling Dad that I had pneumonia but it was made worse because I was run down. He asked Dad if anything had been worrying or bothering me lately. Dad surprised me that he knew. My Dad can always take you by surprise. He had worked out that I was upset about going to Lakeside, leaving Llandaff North and starting at Canton, Tom going to a different school and Susan leaving the area.

"Gareth likes stability," Dad said. "He is struggling to adapt and it's affected him but he'll come through. He's bright and strong."

The Doctor said, "Yes he is strong but I advise that he stays here a few more days, Mr Adams. He will improve more quickly."

"I think the other way," Dad said. "The danger is over and he needs to be with his father and brother in his own home. I'll get a nurse to come in periodically to check on him every day for a few hours as well as regular visits from our GP. That should do it don't you think?"

I heard the Doctor sigh and say, "OK, well there's forms to sign." Then they left me alone again and I fell back to sleep.

It was much like that at home too for a while. The amazing thing was that I didn't feel like reading when I was awake. Well, to be honest, I did but when I picked the book up I couldn't manage more than a page. Dad was just great and even David was fine although most of the time I could just hear him downstairs playing with his new friends. But not being able to read gave me plenty of time to think and I had a lot to think about. By the time Susan came to visit with her family on Sunday afternoon I was beginning to feel better even though I was still falling asleep more than I was awake.

She stayed with me for an hour while Dad chatted with her parents downstairs. She loved it at Canton it was obvious but she'd accepted that her Dad was moving to Bristol and she had to go. She said they were moving on Sunday 29 September but she was coming to be with me on the Saturday afternoon before. I need to learn how to accept things like her. So far I'd been unable to. It was a great hour with her but in the end tiredness came and my eyes started to flicker. Dad knows my routine in this illness and a couple of minutes after I was struggling to stay awake he arrived in my bedroom and said to Susan that I needed my medicine now and more sleep.

She kissed me again before she left and in seconds I was asleep again.

During the week I grew stronger. The weakness gradually left me and I wasn't sleeping for long parts of the day like before. I was starting to read again too. The Doctor said that I would be able to go back to school the next Monday. I can't say I was looking forward to that - in fact I was dreading it but there was no way out of it. I got surprised on Saturday morning when Peter Ballantyne arrived with his father. Somehow he'd got the address from the School Secretary and persuaded his dad to bring him over.

I was downstairs in pyamas and dressing gown but it was good to see him. He brought me up to date with what was going on and said he's made a special effort to write clearly so I could copy what I'd missed from his books. He left a few with me. He said that I'd given everybody a fright when I fell down that day and the boys were looking forward to me coming back.

The boys, I thought. None of the boys from Llandaff North had come to see me or write and I'd forgotten to ask Susan about them. They must have known but the funny thing was that I only thought of it when Peter said 'the boys". It didn't seem to matter any more.

There's not much I really want to write about Susan's visit. Before she arrived I had this feeling in my mind it would be the last time I would see her. She would be in Bristol and me in Cardiff and there was a chance we might have one or two visits during the year but that would be it. I knew this in my heart. She is a lovely girl and some Bristol boy near her school or home would charm her until I would be nothing but a boy she would remember as her first boyfriend. I knew now too the same would be true of me. What I've learned most this last year is that nothing lasts for ever. It's not supposed to. But it didn't stop me feeling a pain as well as a happiness to be with her that last afternoon although this time I did not fall asleep. Her Mum and Dad brought it to a close and what I knew was her last kiss brushed across my cheek and tingled there for a while. I came to the door with my Dad and David and we waved them goodbye and I watched as she sat on the back seat of her Dad's car turning to wave and wave until the car turned around the corner and was gone.

On Sunday Dad suddenly asked in the morning if I was OK for a visit to Uncle Dan's. I said yes straightaway. I liked Uncle Dan and Megan was fun too – and there are his books of course. Megan wasn't there when we arrived. Uncle Dan said that she'd gone to spend the afternoon with one of her friends from Howells school. David wanted to go into the garden as the sun was shining and there was no rain but I asked Uncle Dan if I could spend time looking at his books. He nodded that he was OK with this and I spent a nice half hour looking at books. I was sat reading Robinson Crusoe when Uncle Dan appeared by me and sat on a chair opposite me. He asked how I was and stuff like that and then pointed to the scar on his face.

"It used to be a lot worse than this." he said. "I hated it. Your Dad can tell you all about it."

I nodded not really knowing what to say back.

"It's a terrible thing sometimes being a kid. It was terrible me being kid with this," he said. "I thought everyone was looking at it and it would make me angry. Then one day I hit on a solution."

He stopped. "Yes," I said urging him to continue.

"I realized I was a caterpillar," he said with a smile.

"A what?" I questioned in surprise.

"A caterpillar," he laughed. "I decided to go into my chrysalis for a bit and hope that I would come out like I should. Like a butterfly everyone would gasp at in admiration rather than tut at when I was the caterpillar with the cut."

"Did it work?" I asked.

"Things only work if you want them to work, Gareth" he replied getting to his feet. "It always depends on you."

He passed by me, tapped me on the shoulder with his hand and said "You can take any book this time and bring it back next visit." Then he went back to Dad. I went to the shelves and picked out "Tom Brown's Schooldays".

Well, of course what Uncle Dan said got me thinking and I kept on thinking about it in the car on the way home. I hadn't been in our garden properly for a while. It was getting gloomy but I decided a short walk to the end of the garden was a good idea. The air was cold now but I'd put a jacket on and it was good to be in the quiet of the garden. I could hear traffic though maybe going along the Lake Road or somewhere. It was a quiet drone. I stopped half way back to the house and looked up into the sky. I couldn't see any stars. It was full of cloud now. I said out loud, "A caterpillar."

"You won't find any up there," a voice called out startling me. I looked into the gloom at the house next door. Peering, I saw the outline of the girl Linda sat on a chair outside her house."

"I didn't see you," I said.

"You've been sick then. So David says," she said and I smiled thinking David knows everyone these days.

"Yeah," I replied "But I'm over it now. Back to school tomorrow."

"Lucky you then," she laughed.

"Yeah, lucky me." I repeated back to her.

"You're not a fan of school then?" she asked.

"I don't know," I said back. "It's not what I thought I suppose and now when I go back it'll be harder."

"It's always hard if you ask me," she said. "I'll have to try getting sick too."

I wondered if she thought I'd been faking it. The silence from me must have asked the question.

"Not that I mean you weren't sick, you know. David told me about all the stuff at the hospital and …..you know," she said sounding a bit embarrassed.

"I don't remember much about the first week," I said. "I must have been crazy to walk in the rain. Anyway……"

"Sometime it would be nice to be invisible, right? Or like your caterpillar sitting quietly and waiting…..waiting."

She was getting close to what I was thinking myself and had decided. Maybe she's a bit like me I thought but if I spoke back to her it would open up something that I had decided not to do for a while.

"Yeah, I think so too," I said. "Well it's getting a bit cold for me. I'd better get back inside. See you around."

"If I can," she called out as I walked towards the back door. Had she understood my plan I thought as I walked in. I realized that there was a lot more to Linda than I first thought.

*******

Dad took me to school. I came late and missed assembly but went straight into class. You know they gave me a welcome applause when I got in. I said thanks and took my seat. Peter reached forward and gave me a few more of his books.

"But you'll have to work quickly on the copying tonight," he said. "I'm going to start needing books back from tomorrow." I reached into my bag and gave him back the other ones. I'd worked all Sunday evening to catch up.

At English Literature that day "Clint" Eastwood mentioned that it was a good idea to keep a record of every book you read and he gave us an exercise book each to start recording them. To me this was a great idea and I wished I'd started a long time before. He'd brought a stack of forty books or so in a box and told us to come up and pick one. I was first up being close to the table and swiftly sorted the books till I found one that got me. It was King Solomon's Mines by H. Rider Haggard. It would be the first on my list.

A few days later I was in the playground early one morning leaning against the wall of the Dutch Barn waiting for the bell to ring and reading. I looked up every now and then of course to see what was happening. I noticed a boy called Lee Stephens arrive. He was getting known as a bully and liked to pick on some of the smaller kids in Form 1. Usually he had two other kids with him but they hadn't arrived yet. I could see he was looking around for someone to bully. His eyes settled on me reading. I wasn't small for sure but I think he thought I was chicken. I felt my heart beating as he got closer.

He stopped by me and I looked at him. Up close we were about the same size. "Adams put that book down and run twice round the barn."

I laughed out loud and hit him with the book straight in the belly. He had his hands in his pocket so it was obvious he wasn't expecting a response from me. He was winded and leaning over. I got close and pulled him up. "Let's race together," I said to him. "I'll give you a start seeing as though I got you with a quick one in the guts. Do you want another one to make you go faster."

I was so scared as I was saying this and wondered if he'd call my bluff. He looked around but none of his mates were there. I pushed him to get going and he started running. I ran alongside him.

"I thought you were sick, Adams," he said.

"I was but I'm better now and wait till I get really fit," I said back to him.

At this he laughed. "Hey, Adams. I thought you were just another one of those stupid swots in 1a but I can see you're OK." He gave me a shove as we ran.

I didn't think Lee would bother me again but you could never be sure. If something about me upset him he might try again but he wouldn't do it without his mates with him. In this first encounter I'd come off lucky.

I waited another week for the novelty of my being back to wear off and then hoping no-one would notice quietly I slipped into the chrysalis and tried to become invisible. You'd think it would be hard to become invisible at school but it's not. I found it was easy. I stopped talking to kids except Peter Ballantyne. I avoided answering questions in classes unless I was directly asked. I said no more than was needed in answering. At break time I didn't play football or chat with any group but took my book and found a quiet place by the bike sheds where I could read without being bothered. I stopped going to school dinners and made sandwiches the night before going to school. I told Dad a few of my mates did this and it was better than the school dinners. I didn't join any clubs at school although I was tempted by chess and drama. On Wednesdays at sport I started to fumble the ball when it came to me on the wing. I watched the eyes of "Killer" pass over me to someone who was nearly as fast but with a safer pair of hands. The hardest part was disappearing from Ralph. I kept a look out for him and dodged away from him at every opportunity. I think he forgot about me once he had a replacement for Jackie. After a while he didn't look out for me. And for a moment too I wondered if God had left me also. He'd allowed everything to be taken away. My school, my friends, Susan were all gone. Then I wondered if it was some kind of challenge He'd given me. In any event He made it easy for me to fade away into the background.

For that was it. I disappeared into my chrysalis to think about things and I had a lot to think about. This is my list. It's not in any order but just as it came to my mind in looking back through these words. But who knows, maybe you will see something on the way I've listed it which I've missed. Here you are then:

Susan
Writing
Cricket
Ceri Borthwick alone
Disliking Geoffrey
My Dad and the man with the scar
My brother and everything about him
Friendship and how it disappears
Bullies
Crossing the black bridge
Dad and our mother
Dad and Linda Tucker
My life in Cantonian
God
Tom before and after 11 plus
The Facts of Life
Welsh Rugby
Not being believed
Truth – what is it?
Martin Luther King
JFK
War
Old People
Death
"Doing the little things well"
The Beatles
What is love
Fear
Swimming
Bravery and being a hero
Reading
Understanding people
Jealousy
Cornwall

Dad and Uncle Dan
Megan
Belonging
Revenge
Linda next door in Lakeside
Growing up to leave behind Looby Loo
Standing still
Belief
Truth or Fiction
Invisibility
Coming out of the chrysalis
The future
Susan

Later, I will come out when I've sorted these things in my mind. You know, I feel that this time is not my time. It won't be this Gareth Adams then though. It will be another. Who knows what this Gareth Adams will be like. I thought I was OK but if you look back over the mistakes and stupidities I made this last year when you go over this journal you'll see different.

See, it's pathetic. Will the Gareth Adams to emerge be kinder, more clever, have more courage, be better with friends, better with adults? Or is he going to be worse? Well I don't know. We'll have to wait but he will have to emerge whatever. One thing I've realized this last year is that you cannot go it alone. Without people on your side and with you there is no chance. If you can't talk to people and speak up you're finished. If you can't do this work at school there's no progress to a better education. I have to remember St David and "do the little things well". I know I can do this for me but can I do it for others as well and in a way that is unseen. I should, shouldn't I – because I am unseen!!

For now, I'll focus on school work and when the chrysalis pops it'll be time to be with people again. So for now I'll fade into the background and work. It's easier when there's nobody watching.

*I finished it quickly and read it again. It felt like the true version to me but how could I know. I needed to find the final journal and make a comparison. But mostly I needed to think about what Gareth had written and also I wondered what happened to Gareth, the man. Was he also able to maintain his period of invisibility – his chrysalis time as he called it. I thought back to my own time at school. I was more like Peter Ballantyne but I was aware of kids like Gareth who* tried to fade into the background. At best we ignored them and at worst they were the butt of classroom taunts. But maybe we all have periods of "chrysalis" time. I feel I am in mine now. It has just arrived later than it did for Gareth. Maybe this is triggered for all of us by a particular set of circumstances. Wherever Gareth is I hope he emerged from the chrysalis in the way he wanted.

In the weeks that followed I needed to carry out a lot of research. Gareth was right he had set me a task that was not easy. Although I searched in many places in Llandaff North it was purely to confirm what I knew. The last journal was not there.

But my research did uncover the following:

1. In June 1965 Geraint Adams married Linda Williams (nee Tucker). She was the M&S assistant. She died in April 2002 and Geraint passed away in December 2003

2. Gareth left Cantonian High School on completing his A levels – three straight A's. There was no record of which University he attended.

3. I discovered the addresses in Fontygary Road, Lakeside Drive where they lived and the address in St Nicholas where his Uncle Dan lived. At the St Nicholas and Fontygary Road addresses no-one of an Adams name had lived there or owned the properties for over 25 years. At Lakeside Drive it was a little easier. The estate of Geraint Adams sold the property in early 2004 after Geraint Adams death. It was sold by Elisabeth Adams. Yes, Geraint and his wife produced one child.

4. Neither Gareth, David or Elisabeth Adams are now living in the Cardiff area.

I won't bore you with all the details of the research I needed to do or discoveries not related to Gareth with the exception of one. I was in the Station pub getting a beer and asking the barman if there were still people leaving in Llandaff North from the 50s. The barman pointed out Dick Wilson to me. Do you remember PC Wilson that Gareth mentioned. This was him. I bought him a pint and sat next to him. He's in his 80s now and told me that he'd been retired from the force on a Sergeant's pay for twenty five years. I mentioned to him all of the names that Gareth mentioned and he knew all of them. He told me that most had left Llandaff North years ago. Only one was still around mentioned by Gareth and that was Philip Tell. He told me I'd find him in the bar. I asked the barman to point him out to me and went over to him. He was in his mid 50s and he knew all the names too. Without me asking he told the story of swinging on the rope with Tom and breaking his leg. He laughed about it. He said that he'd last seen Tom about 10 years ago and thought he was in Manchester now. He dimly remembered Gareth and his brother but his eyes widened when I mentioned Dudley Potts who lived next door to them. It came back to him. He confirmed that they left Llandaff North when he was a small boy. He said too that he knew Dudley very well. He'd only died recently and had been battling against alcoholism for years. Dafydd, Alun, Nigel, Phil and Geoffrey he remembered them all but they had all gone at some stage and their families. There were only a few left now. I was disappointed that he did not remember Gareth too clearly but it was a long time ago.

The most important thing is that, a day or two after this conversation with Phillip, I discovered the location of the other journal.

I found it in Fontygary. The place was sold out of the Adams' possession in 1965. Since that time there were three owners. I visited the last to talk to the most recent owners – Mr and Mrs Ian Reid - who had lived there for five years.

Of course they wondered who I was and what I wanted. I had already decided that the best solution was to tell them what I'd found and all the clues. They smiled when they saw the journals and the envelopes with Gareth's writing. They relaxed a bit and their smile was a smile of knowing.

"Yes, I understand what you mean," Mr Reid said to me. "I've seen a book like that."

"You have?" I was surprised. "You found it?"

"Well not me exactly. Our boy, Simon." He answered. "When we first came to live here he was about thirteen. He's the youngest. Our other two are seven and nine years older but Simon was always the explorer."

"Where did he find it?" I asked him, now beginning to feel anxious.

"Well, Simon was looking through cupboards in the garage when we first arrived. He was always expecting to find some hidden treasure. He pulled out one of the drawers - you know the sort that holds nails or screws – and found an envelope taped underneath it."

"It gave the location," I said, my heart sinking.

"Yes, Simon came to show it to me. I can't remember now exactly what it said. It told us to stand at a point at the edge of the back garden and take so many paces forward and then some to the right. First off we didn't find anything but then I got Simon to pace it out. We found it then and of course as you know it would have been paced out by a boy."

"So you read it," I queried, sad that I was not the first to get to it.

"Well bits of it about his school and so on," He paused a while thinking. "In fact if I remember right he said a relative or friend might come to get it. Yes, he said if we hadn't found the first two then someone would come who would have them asking for it. And sure enough you've got them."

*"Do you think it would be OK if I could see it?" I asked.*

*"I'll go and look in Simon's bedroom. He used to keep it on a bookshelf there. He's not here now. He's at York University," Mrs Reid said to me.*

*When she returned I could see she did not have the journal but she was carrying an old small envelope. I could see it was the same style as used by Gareth.*

*"it's not there," she said. "He must have taken it with him to York but the envelope he found with it is here."*

*She held it out to me and I took it. "I'll give him a call on his mobile to ask him where it is. She went out of the room. I opened the envelope and slipped out Gareth's message:*

*I have left a package in the garden. Stand at the edge of the pathway and count sixty paces forward and then ten to the right. Dig down two feet and you will find it. Maybe you have not found the other two items I left in other places. If you only have this item please keep it. One day a relative or friend will come and ask you about it. I hope you will do this for me.*

*I couldn't help but smile. He was right. He was making it difficult. He knew this would be found by someone else. He'd hidden it in a place where it could be found. I knew now that there was another message for me somewhere. A message for me? I smiled to myself. Has such a strong connection been established between me and Gareth?*

*I hadn't notice Mrs Reid return. Maybe I was musing longer than I thought. When I looked at her she said, "Yes, he's got it with him in York. He sounded excited that you'd come to ask about it. He wants to know about the previous journals. He said he'll bring it with him when he comes home for a weekend visit – that'll be in two weeks."*

*"Would he – and you of course – mind if I went up to see him and to look at the journal? I asked.*

*"It means that much to you?" Mr Reid questioned.*

*"Yes, it does Mr Reid. The last journal gives some answers. Answers that I need to know," I replied.*

*"No, he won't mind at all," Mrs Reid said. "I'll write down his mobile for you and you can get in touch with him."*

*I thanked her and paused to think.*

*"Mr and Mrs Reid, Could I ask a favour? I said returning the slip of paper to the envelope and handing it back to Mrs Reid. This one was not for me.*

*"What do you need?" Mr Reid asked.*

*"Do you mind if I look in the garage?"*

*"Why, do you think there is something else? Mr Reid questioned.*

"There might be actually and it would help piece together the final story," I said.

"Yes, go on Ian. Show him the garage," Mrs Reid said.

"Come on then," Mr Reid said, getting to his feet. I think he felt all this was a complete waste of time to be honest and I wasn't sure he liked the idea of me going to visit his son in York. It's the way we've become – suspicious of everyone.

Mr Reid's car was on the drive and he opened the garage doors to reveal a spacious garage.

"Where did your son Simon find the envelope?" I asked him.

He walked to a line of cupboards at the back of the garage and showed me. I was right it was an easy find. He'd meant for this to be discovered easily.

I cast my eyes around the garage looking for Gareth's marker. This garage is brick built and the roof has metal beams. After seeking Mr Reid's permission I looked in the cupboards but I knew this was a false hope. Gareth wouldn't put something there and if he had Simon would have found it.

But I knew there would be something here. I just knew it. My eyes roved every nook, cranny and beam and then I saw his marker – the nail. This time it was protruding from the middle of a brick in the second row below roof level on the right hand side six bricks in from the garage doors. I asked Mr Reid if I could use the step ladder placed at the back of the garage. He nodded his assent and I climbed to look at the nail. It was one of Gareth's for sure. I looked around for a tin tack or other marker but could see nothing. I put my fingers to the nail and tested it. I felt the brick move. I took out my knife and scraped the mortar a little. When I'd done this and tugged again the face of the brick – about half an inch – came away from the rest.

Mr Reid was watching and I heard him say, "Well I'll be damned."

It was the usual setting. The message was inside a strong plastic bag. I removed it from the brick cavity, thinking again at how detailed Gareth was in these things, and stepped down the ladder to join Mr Reid.

I handed the packet to him. He looked at it and then at me. "I think you should open it," he said. "I think it's for you anyway."

To be honest I had hoped that Mr Reid would say this. I opened the sealed bag to withdraw the envelope. It was addressed to "The VERY curious reader". I slipped out the paper and read:

So you found this! I wonder did you find the paper I hid under the drawer or was it found by someone else. And does that someone else now have the journal you long to finish. If you have the journal you will know that it gives you the choice of truth or fiction. But also if you are curious – and I know you are curious – it may provide you with more searches and more investigations.

*If you don't have the journal then you need to hope that people share the same curiosity as you. Maybe they want to know if someone will come or maybe they do not have this curious spirit and will throw the journal into the bin.*

*By the way, my curious friend, I'm eighteen now and just leaving Cantonian. Now that's something else for you to ponder.*

*Good luck again!!*

Why would he do that, I thought. Why leave this message at eighteen. I thought the voice sounded older and now I knew. He was confusing me with so many things.

I held it out for Mr Reid to see but he waved it away. "It's yours," he said.

Back inside the house Mrs Reid gave me the mobile number for Simon, their son. I said that I would be in touch with Simon quickly and visit York. As an after thought I gave them my card with my details and wrote my house address and mobile number on the back. I wanted them to know that I was safe. I thanked them both and left to walk to the bus stop. At the bus stop I took out my mobile phone, checked the number given to me by Mrs Reid and called Simon.

Tomorrow I will take the train to York and will get the answers and maybe more.

*End*

Printed in Great Britain
by Amazon